T0020073

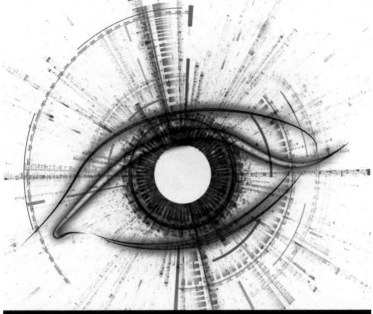

RHETT C. BRUNO
—AND—
JAMES WOLANYK

OPERATION BRUSHFIRE

aethonbooks.com

OPERATION BRUSHFIRE

©2021 AETHON BOOKS

This book is protected under the copyright laws of the United States of America. No part of this publication may be reproduced, stored in a retrieval system, or transmitted, in any form or by any means, without the prior permission in writing of the publisher, nor be otherwise circulated in any form of binding or cover other than that in which it is published and without a similar condition including this condition being imposed on the subsequent purchaser. Any reproduction or unauthorized use of the material or artwork contained herein is prohibited without the express written permission of the authors.

Aethon Books supports the right to free expression and the value of copyright. The purpose of copyright is to encourage writers and artists to produce the creative works that enrich our culture.

The scanning, uploading, and distribution of this book without permission is a theft of the author's intellectual property. If you would like to use material from the book (other than for review purposes), please contact editor@aethonbooks.com. Thank you for your support of the author's rights.

Aethon Books
www.aethonbooks.com

Print and eBook formatting, and cover design by Steve Beaulieu.

Published by Aethon Books LLC.

Aethon Books is not responsible for websites (or their content) that are not owned by the publisher.

This book is a work of fiction. Names, characters, places, and incidents are the product of the author's imagination or are used fictitiously. Any resemblance to actual events, locales, or persons, living or dead is coincidental.

All rights reserved.

You are one, but the Coalition is many. You are weak, but the Coalition is strong. You are fallible, but the Coalition is impeccable.

You are privileged to hear these words, for they are the inheritance of a world born anew. The empires of your forebearers rose and fell in the chasm of disorganization, always ceding to tribalism, to bloodshed, to greed.

No longer.

Your world is one of unity, and it will remain that way with your cooperation.

On this sacred day, we direct our gazes toward the womb in which the Coalition matured: The Wars. Though they mark a time of untold death and depravity, there must also be bittersweet remembrance of their pains, for they were the trials in which the Coalition's foundations were engineered and driven into the soil. They were the light that shone upon humanity's broken, divisive ways, guiding us toward a state of being free from all forms of violence. They were the impetus for this new age. As you sit comfortably in your classroom, basking in sunlight and filtered air, you are urged to reflect upon your gratitude for the Wars and their brutal martyrs. Because of their annihilation, we came to understand the cruelty of bombs and rifles. We were urged to choose a better path.

It was not so long ago, in the year 1944, that the leaders of a shattered world set aside their squabbles and merged to form the Coalition's first incarnation. Even in the earliest of days, our global citizens understood what this transition meant for the future of humanity. It promised an end to all suffering, whether born of natural origins or fueled by nationalism. As the panacea of the Coalition took effect, however, it became clear that humanity's true sickness had always been the pride of manifold ideologies.

Nazi, Soviet, Ally, partisan—these labels were the vestiges of a fractured people. You are all fortunate enough to live without their archaic sway; there is no need to belong to this or that—you belong to the Coalition, as do your friends, your family, your neighbors. You are free to express your joy with whatever words you choose, for they will not be lost in the tangle of multiple languages. You do not need to look within for salvation, for there are no gods, only the Coalition. You may walk undaunted anywhere you please, immersed in the safety of civilian aggression inhibitors. These are the privileges of the Coalition.

Your Morse implant will now begin displaying a reel of footage from the Wars. The footage will be streamed directly into your visual cortex. Should your heart rate surpass safety regulations, benzodiazepine will be administered.

Let us all rejoice in our unity.

CHAPTER 1

Donetsk, Ukrainian Province
534 miles from Moscow

Henry Stasik lived like a highway driver speeding in the wrong direction. That was what his last partner had said about him, anyway. Most days he drove with mechanical regularity, hobbling over cold hardwood into hotel bathrooms, watching helicopters swivel over Baltic landing pads, and dissolving amphetamine tabs in his espresso—all without thinking of the headlights streaking past him.

Every so often, however, he was acutely aware of a chrome flash in his periphery. A flash like Anastasia Danicheva, who insisted on being called Nata in all her press releases. One hundred sixty-five centimeters of young, dark-haired beauty. A product of western Russia's emerging fashion market.

During his flight from the HQ in Vilnius to Donetsk, Stasik had found himself puzzled as to why the starlet had requested his presence. *"Stasik, and only Stasik,"* according to the documents he'd thumbed through. The two of them had never met, he was certain of that, and he had a vested interest in keeping his personal role out of media reports. It was never good to be so exposed. Especially not while serving as an agent for the Coalition's Internal Affairs.

Of course, it also wasn't the first time Stasik had been dispatched to investigate a Coalition agent overstepping their bounds with civilian detention—far from it, in fact. He picked cases like those apart with gusto, and perhaps that had been enough to put him on Nata's radar. Still, even setting that aside, his involvement in this case was unprecedented for another reason: It was the first time that serious money surrounded his investigation. Clouded it, he preferred to think.

Miss Danicheva's bank accounts skewed everything from the media's headlines to his supervisor's priority list. Most of that year's cases had been reports of shakedowns or threats with a loaded firearm, vestiges of the autonomous Soviet regimes that had a habit of cropping up in rural collectives. And on paper, the story wasn't so novel: an agent forcing Nata to pull over on the road to Dnipropetrovsk, fabricating traffic charges, making an excessively hands-on arrest.

In reality, it meant a swarm of lawyers and journalism outlets gathering around the Coalition central precinct in Zelene, a stick-and-mud town just a stone's throw from the region's capital, Donetsk. It meant an armored escort to the complex's rear courtyard. Broadcast-jamming equipment firing on all cylinders.

Things weren't any warmer within the precinct. Stasik was one of sixteen agents that crossed the cobblestone lot and shuffled down corridors with wires strung along the walls, passing wet, shimmering concrete and rusted Ukrainian signage. Internal Affairs was never welcomed with open arms, but he was a pariah: the officers kept their distance, murmured, pointed, shouldered past him.

Not everybody wanted the truth as badly as he did.

Not everybody needed it.

Diane Mallison—his fifth partner in as many months—was a target by proxy, but she handled the scrutiny better than most of her predecessors. She was tall, thin, armed with a cutting Essex accent. Enough of a tomboy to put the Donetsk officers on edge, make them squeeze their knees together when she walked by.

"Don't keep the queen waiting," she whispered outside the processing unit. She smirked, lit a cigarette, and trailed the rest of the IA detachment into a cargo elevator.

Then Henry Stasik was alone.

Alone on his highway.

He was still basking in the glow of a Pervitin derivative, which he'd taken to compensate for lost sleep, when Nata Danicheva appeared in the interview room's doorway. Her presence was accompanied by the garble of ringing telephones and wisps of vanilla perfume. He glanced up from his dossier, and the room sizzled and sharpened with methamphetamine's crisp gloss. She was facing away from him, a pair of thin legs, a belted green parka, raven-black hair down to her mid-back.

Nata stepped further into the room and closed the door as though expecting to see somebody in the shrinking divide. She delicately set the doorknob and locking mechanism in place.

In the silence, Stasik reached into his breast pocket and slid out a red tin: 250 micrograms of cherry-flavored, rapid-absorption fentanyl.

He threw back two lozenges, crunched them between his molars, and swallowed.

"Good morning," he said in Yedtongue, the ugly pastiche of a language that somehow took the most bitter aspects of its base components—English and Russian, primarily—and sullied them further. *Dobrigad mornisz*—nobody's morning could be improved by that mouthful. But the Coalition's official language wasn't up for debate. They spoke nothing else while on duty, and it was beginning to pervade his English thoughts while off the clock, too.

"*Dobroye utro*," Nata replied. Her Russian was elegant, archaic. Borderline illegal. "I'm sorry," she added in Yedtongue, angling her head to glance back over narrow shoulders. "Good morning." And in that stance, the graceful forehead, avian nose, and hard cheekbones of her distilled Slavic genes formed a fashion model's silhouette.

Stasik choked down the shards of cherry opiates, pulled back the sleeve of his blue sharkskin suit to access his Morse implant. The slim, rectangular switchboard protruding from his forearm was the Judicial Wing's newest model. A prototype with features unfit for civilian installation: carbon filaments converting audio into dots and dashes at a hundred hits a second, emergency beacons, signal emitters that could pick up a Coalition broadband alert from Cairo to Helsinki. It was patched into the chip implanted in the back of his neck. But the chip, with its near-encyclopedic database, wasn't so special; everybody carried one of those.

As Stasik set the Morse implant's dials to a recording channel, he wondered where Nata's lawyers were, why a detective hadn't escorted her into the chamber, how long she'd been sitting in a protective cell before his detachment arrived.

Most of all, he wondered how he'd ended up staring at such a woman in a second-rate precinct on a Tuesday morning in the middle of October. The region was flooded with beautiful women—a cradle of future wives, some of the British agents quipped—but Nata was something else. The kind of woman he'd seen in productions from Hollywood and Stockholm. Cast as a *femme fatale*, furnished with a thigh holster and cyanide capsules. "Please," he said, still gazing, "take a seat."

With a gentle nod, she moved toward the pool of overhead light.

She had green eyes like cracked marbles, ruby red lips, stray freckles in a cluster around her nasal bridge. Arched black brows, stark and faultless. Soft shadows etching cleavage.

Stasik realized he was staring and scanned his dossier once again. He tried to appear deep in thought. *Ah,* he thought with a discerning nod, *twenty-five.* They were the same age, yet divergent in every way possible. The opiates curdled within the amphetamines, and his vision grew narrow, dissociating, making him glance up and survey the motion of her hips with the filter of an engineer rather than a young man.

Nata settled into the metal chair across from him, set a black leather purse on the table. A beige heel swung out from below the table.

Stasik adjusted his tie, cleared his throat. "My name is—"

"Specialist-Inspector Henry Stasik," Nata finished. "I'm familiar."

Stasik could only blink at her with the dumb, witless look he'd honed in middle school chemistry classes.

Breathing in, he rediscovered the scent that he'd picked up moments prior. Vanilla, with its ethereal notes and some floral strain. It reminded him of home, of old women shuffling into the parlor after church services with marshmallow squares and wineglasses. Of Judy Emmory, the yellow-dress blonde he'd kissed so many years ago by the river, sun-dappled—

"Is it recording?" Nata asked, training her eyes on his forearm.

The question startled him, snapping whatever trance he'd lured himself into. Stasik resettled his tie, nodded down at his

Morse implant. The seven brass dials were stowed away in their entrenched positions, forming a neat row from his wrist to his elbow.

"Turn it off, please," Nata said.

He set his pen down, flipped the dossier shut. "I can't do that, ma'am."

"Section 17, first paragraph, tertiary clause." Nata's green eyes lingered on the brass. "I'm invoking my right to receive counsel that won't be admissible in proceedings."

Model, legal analyst. His smirk spread under the haze of the fentanyl in his veins. He rotated the last dial, pulled his sleeve back into place. "It's off. I just wanted to confirm your name, you know."

Now he wondered what sort of things she might have on her mind. Things that couldn't be recorded or played back in good company. But those were the sex hormones swelling up, and as he studied the knot in her brow, those impulses fell away. Mallison had referred to him as a monk in the first month of their assignment together, curiously prodding at why he never spent his salary at brothels or stim-clubs. The truth was that his daily regimen of stimulants neutered him.

"Do they have secondary cameras in this room?" Nata asked.

"Yes," he replied.

"Section 22, second and third paragraphs."

His amusement dimmed. He lifted his right hand, brushed his index and middle finger together with a dry crinkle.

The omnipresent whirring of the CCTVs fell away.

"You have three minutes," Stasik said.

"The Coalition is trying to kill me," Nata replied.

It was a matter-of-fact gut punch, delivered without any preamble aside from her formalities. Delivered to a Coalition agent, no less.

"I believe that you have the resources to guarantee my safety, so I'm appealing to you," she went on. "If you deny me your assistance, I'll be escorted to a black site and killed before evening. The choice, of course, is yours."

One of the words she'd uttered muted everything else.

That relic from the days of labor camps and wars.

Killed.

"What?" It was all Stasik could manage as the amphetamine surged again, flooded his neurotransmitters, overloaded his clarity. He reached for his pen, but Nata's glare forced his hand back to the tabletop. "I don't follow."

"The background is a long story, Specialist." Her composure unnerved him. "I will tell everything to you if you help me, but of course, the first choice is the most important."

"Nobody's going to *kill* you."

"They've tried twice."

Delusions were like strands of fraying twine, apt to unwind in a suspect's gnawed fingernails or flickering stare. Stasik couldn't recall the last time he'd questioned somebody so resolute in their beliefs. Or, perhaps, he hadn't questioned somebody in so deep. Certainly nobody like Anastasia Danicheva.

"You need to let me write this down," Stasik said. "Start from the beginning, miss."

She frowned. "Are you taking me seriously, Specialist?"

"Of course."

"Then please try to understand me. This is a long story, and right now, writing won't do much for me. They're going to tell you that I'm due for additional questioning at a location that they can't disclose, and then I'll be loaded into a black Mercedes-Benz, production year 1949. That will be the last time you see me."

"Who is *they?*"

"I don't have a full list." She studied the opaque, bulletproof windowpanes lining the top of the eastern wall as though she could really see out of them. "I know that it's the leadership of this precinct, some elements in the transportation bureau around Barcelona, and perhaps an aviation bureau."

Stasik's tongue hummed with the opiates, dull and fuzzy, coursing through his blood-brain barrier within seconds. *Delusions of grandeur, maybe,* he thought.

"I know how it sounds," she added, eyes snapping back to him, paralyzing him with their alertness. Again, the expected strain of madness was absent. "It's truly your choice to believe me. If you brush me aside, it's understandable. But understand that it's an execution."

"I need names," Stasik said. He flipped his notepad open, thumbed past pages of coffee-stained notes. "Work with me, Miss Danicheva. At least give me descriptions and a formal complaint." He noted the latent frustration in her lips, her meshed fingers across her lap. "I traveled a fair distance to get here, so we can respect each other's time. A few minutes of cooperation is what you have, assuming we work under your *instructions.* Do you get me?"

"Maksim Krupin," she said. Stasik knew him. A bloated oblast secretary-turned-bureau administrator.

"Edward Henderson." Cambridge-born, nestled in old-boy societies and a natural convert from MI6 to Coalition intelligence services.

"Elizabeth Vorster." A sharp signature plastered across the bottom of every cross-bureau project report, native to Cape Town and its slurred strain of Yedtongue.

Stasik's pen wavered over the page, though it had little to do with the amphetamines. He'd learned all those names on a need-to-know basis, behind closed doors and security checkpoints.

Higher-ups. Some of his investigations had even nudged him toward their subordinates or colleagues. They were names that drifted well above the awareness of the Coalition's standard citizens, who all drew their factoids from the Morse network's public knowledge banks. There was no good reason for a fashion model to know them.

"Are you going to transcribe these?" Nata asked, sensing the delay. "I'm sure you understand that I'm not just wasting your time."

Midway through scribbling *Maksim*, Stasik's hand slowed. It wasn't in his business to let sleeping dogs lie, but wolves were another story. The ensuing letters were jagged, trailing.

"And what did they do?" he asked.

"My acquaintances prevented several accidents in their sectors."

"Accidents?"

She nodded. "They kept full files of their reports. There was credible proof of plans for derailed train cars, bombs in fuselages. Things like that, you see."

"Do you have them? The reports, I mean."

"No."

"Do your acquaintances have them?"

"They're dead." Nata blinked, glanced back out the featureless window. "Their entire complex in Munich is gone. A gas leak, the inspectors reported." Before Stasik could prod at her story, she sighed. "How many explosions from a gas leak can leap across a major street and break down reinforced steel doors?"

He sidestepped the implications with a tapping pen. "So no crimes were actually committed."

"Conspiracy is a very real charge, is it not?"

"In this context—"

"It's all very methodical, Specialist." Nata's eyes traced the scuff-marked checkerboard tiles, restless. "I know what's going to happen to me. It's like looking down the tracks of a railway and peering around the bend."

Stasik set his pen down. "Did your lawyers call my unit in?"

"My most-consulted firm shut down earlier this month. Dismantled by a Coalition practice review board, as a matter of fact. Do you also find the timing inconvenient?"

Or convenient, depending on which side of the table you were on. "We're stationed in Vilnius, Miss Danicheva. That means we came here for *you*. So, who placed the call?"

"I specifically requested you."

Flattering. He lacked the high-profile edge of Nata's alleged conspirators, but he wasn't as steeped in shadows as them, either. He had his own reputation as the thorn in a thousand bureaucratic sides. The definitive check in the Coalition's checks and balances scheme. A key analyst in international reports about internal corruption and policy missteps.

Yet all of it was done in the Coalition's service, pursuing the sort of ideal justice the world had only imagined in preceding centuries. They'd distilled the mess of warring countries throughout the world, creating peace for all. People like Stasik ensured it stayed that way, that greed and corruption didn't reign like they once had, in superpowers like Russia and the United States.

"I know that they didn't buy you out," she continued, gazing down at her crimson nails with attention of existential importance. "Or maybe they did. I don't know how far it goes."

"Nobody *bought* me," Stasik said. "What good would it do? Killing you, I mean."

"We've been over this. It's a long story, for another day."

Stasik rubbed the bridge of his nose. He fished the fentanyl lozenges from his coat pocket and pushed the box toward her. "You should take one. It'll mellow you out."

She eyed the tin, rested her hands on her lap. "It wouldn't do anything for me."

"I'm just not sure what you want," Stasik said. "If a crime hasn't been committed, you're not looking to pursue charges about the incident on the roadway, and you have no proof for any of these allegations, then the most I can do is file for an acute questioning hold. That's twenty-four hours, Miss Danicheva. And my guess is that nobody's going to harm you in the next twenty-four hours, or any hours beyond that."

He extended his arm to the lozenge tin and opened the lid. His face took on a prickly flush. What *did* she want from him, really? "Try one," he offered again. "It's for your own good."

After a pause, Nata's delicate index finger pinned the box and slid it to her side of the table. She tipped it up at its rear hinge, spilled a dozen red ovals across the tabletop, then swept the entire pile into her palms. Crumbs of red chalk dusted her fingers. And before Stasik could speak, working to process his thoughts behind the silkscreen of opiates, Nata shrugged and ate the entire handful.

Crunch, crunch, crunch.

A swallow.

Three milligrams of fentanyl, lethal for a grown man.

"Jesus!" Stasik blurted. Chair legs grated as he pushed himself sideways, reaching for the alarm panel at the rear of the chamber.

"It's fine," Nata said, stilling him with her calmness. "It's not a suicide attempt, Specialist. My agent is fond of the same brand. The compounds set in within fifteen seconds, don't they?"

Sometimes less, he'd learned from experience. Some of the opiates would already be leaking through the membranes of her gums, cheeks, and throat.

"Too sweet for me," she said.

The seconds dripped along with unbearable expectation, sure to be interrupted by a slackening of her limbs and halted eye movements. But Nata remained in her chair, upright, poised, and stunning.

A half minute passed before Stasik realized he was standing with an arm helplessly extended toward the alarm. His legs trembled as he resettled himself in the chair.

He met the calm gaze of the woman who should've been limp. Who had assured him that her true death was scheduled and close at hand.

Who regarded him as her life jacket.

Stasik leaned back. "Fuck."

The cameras hummed back to life. Their three minutes of privacy were up. In the precinct's nearby security booth, images of an unchanged room with silent occupants would be thrown across every monitor.

"Thank you for your time, Specialist," Nata said.

She stood, tightened the belt of her parka, *click-clacked* in heels to her respective door. The knob turned with another gentle roll of the mechanism, and the ringing telephones flooded back, and then she was gone, lost between the silhouettes of two field officers in overcoats.

Stasik inhaled a fading wisp of her vanilla perfume and imagined her in some slush-filled ditch on the road to Mariupol, splotchy and pale and missing half of her face.

———

"NOTHING BUT TROUBLE, THESE TYPES." ANDREI VIRTANEN, THE district's presiding intervention officer, tapped the glass in the observation overlook. A crowd of officers in white shirts and ballistic vests had gathered in a dense line along the catwalk, straining to catch his commentary—or a fading glimmer of their guest.

Even so, it was hard to tell which *type* he was judging: models or Internal Affairs.

It was easy to understand most of the intervention agents' disdain for people like Stasik—every intervention unit prided itself on being loud, vicious, and unapologetic. They didn't mind breaking a few eggs—or a few arms—to get their way. For them, justice was an afterthought. And the only thing standing between them and the civilians they viewed as expendable was Internal Affairs.

Stasik peered around Virtanen's steroid-enlarged shoulders, staring at Nata as she exited the precinct's main chamber downstairs. Everything in the questioning session now felt like a fever dream, spruced up by the drugs in his system but countered by the fact that she'd dropped her complaint and was leaving unassisted.

He found her walk hypnotic: smooth, powerful calf muscles, hair shimmering down her back as she wove between desks and fixated officers. With her entourage in tow and cameras flashing outside, well beyond the bulletproof glass of the front doors and the enforcement barrier beyond, he felt that reality had finally settled in. It had been a tiring, nervous morning, and it was over.

"What did she have to say?" Stasik's partner, Mallison, asked, swiveling in a creaking chair she'd borrowed from the precinct's supply room. Her attention cycled between a mug of coffee and Nata's shrinking form and Stasik, who now lingered by his ad hoc desk with a sliver of Pervitin in hand.

"She was just shaken up," Stasik said.

He crushed the amphetamines between callused fingers, dropped the fragments into a glass of water. His mind wouldn't stop replaying the way Nata had choked down the opiates.

"Sounds like she's been on the road for a while," he continued. "Too many shows, not enough sleep."

"You pity her?"

"No."

"Ah." Mallison grinned. "Just another admirer, then. I wonder how many men wanted to be her knight in shining armor. I heard they even shut down the cameras for you."

"*I requested you,*" Nata had said. Stasik sipped the bitter water as her story spiraled back to him, a kaleidoscope of jarring names and lust. "Well." He stared down at the crowd filtering through the front doors, every motion razor-sharp from the uppers, tracking the sunglasses and jackets that swirled around Nata's green parka like some hive collective—

Then he saw it.

Two men in dark coats threaded into the gathering from the western holding sector, moving in a swift but perpendicular path toward the Russian model. They slid past attendants, officers, and legal aids with shoulders dropped low, as though holding objects of considerable weight at their sides.

Stasik pictured Nata half-buried in a ditch. Forty-five kilometers to Mariupol. A light dusting of snow across black cheekbones.

"Who are they?" Stasik asked. His eyelids twitched again. "Those two on the left."

"Specialists," Mallison said. "Must be following up."

"She dropped the charges. There's nothing to follow."

"Do I sense some jealousy?"

"She *dropped* it."

Behind the hum in his ears, Mallison was beginning to reply. Something about *procedure,* and on the second syllable he was already across the observation room and at the phone station with the precinct's direct line droning in his ear, punching neon digits—977804—for the dispatcher's block.

Through the glass and beyond the ghost of his reflection,

a blur of undercut hair and pointed jawbones, he watched the specialists intercept Nata. They stood close to her now, close enough to intimidate men their own size, urging her entourage to halt and back up and shut up. They were shoving, snarling.

A secretary's voice chimed in Stasik's ear, but he cut in: "Resolution sixty-five, option two without possibility of an override: I'm holding Anastasia Danicheva on suspicion of withheld information. Twenty-four hours with judicial discretion. Have her brought to the secondary lot immediately."

A sea of colored bulbs nestled among the rafters blazed to life, painting the precinct's main floor in emerald light. A single chirp cut through the arguments and telephones and dueling feet below. The all-freeze command lived up to its name.

The specialists in dark coats shrank away from Nata, staring at one another with confusion that Stasik found all too common in men who were unaccustomed to limitations of power. Their hands returned to their coat pockets as they melded back into the crowd. A set of Stasik's support agents worked their way toward Nata in a ragged line, flashing badges over their heads and shouting.

"The hell was that?" Mallison asked. She drew up behind Stasik, and in the glass she was little more than a white arc of light across her hair. "Are you all right?"

"Pack up our files," Stasik said. "Meet me in the lot in five, would you?"

"Didn't answer my question."

Deep in the crowd, Nata made a practiced turn on her high heels. She didn't seem agitated in the slightest. Her even gaze met Stasik's, and she gave a slow smile.

Stasik noted her hidden *dimoki*, the Yedtongue label for what he had always known as dimples, smudged black below her cheekbones.

"For now, everything's fine," he said, palming a Pervitin tube from the closest desk.

And as he moved away from the window and drew the stares of the precinct's officers, he realized that everything was not fine.

He imagined two bodies intertwined in the ditch now: His and hers.

CHAPTER 2

Blansko, Czechoslovakian Province
111 miles from Prague

The assignment reached Erik Bahr at 5:03 in the morning, well after he'd woken and made his way to his lightless dining room. Beyond the nook windows, the fields were quiet, chalky with fog that crept out from the woodland's edge and blanketed nearby paddocks.

The message—in typical fashion—provided no reason, no sender information, no specified reward. It trickled through his Morse implant, spelling out a name and location. A target.

Nothing more, nothing less.

Nothing that directly indicated it was an assignment to preserve universal peace.

Bahr crept around the house in darkness, floorboards creaking beneath his calloused feet. He peered into his son Michal's room, watched cold daylight playing over his face and teddy bear—*Misha*, with a missing button eye—in rain-streak swirls.

Two rooms over, his wife, Jana, slept in the same huddled form, her face and clasped hands angled toward the empty nest of sheets where he'd slept, porcelain skin and light hair glowing against the blankets.

He stared as he did every morning, with the sense that he was wandering through a trophy gallery, viewing the rewards he'd always anticipated during six years of service: a wife and child with Aryan features. It was impossible to have things so precious and not look upon them as possessions.

Flickers of his family's radiant blue eyes played through his mind while he picked through his wardrobe, gathering broken-in hunting boots, a black jacket, thick gloves. In his rucksack he stuffed a woodland camouflage smock still splotched with mud from Crete.

He pulled his fishing box down from a closet shelf and searched its contents in the harsh light of a hanging bulb: a switchblade, fuse wires, an oil bottle, pliers, radio transmitters, firing pins, a Welrod pistol. All of them went into the rucksack, topped off by a white box full of dextroamphetamine squares to ensure hypervigilance.

———

Outside, Bahr's breaths were white wisps, his cheeks prickling with the autumn chill. Near the cellar door was a white tarp, and beneath it a jumble of split firewood towering over a chopping stump. He ferried armfuls of wood across the field to the toolshed, where a wall had already been started, and stacked enough quarter pieces to reach his eye level. Enough to last two weeks, perhaps three. He suspected, or rather hoped, he would return by then.

He glanced back at the house. Jana, framed in the kitchen

window, moved a teakettle onto the burner. She had a weary way about her, leaning on the counter and pursing her lips, already knowing what she'd hear once her husband came back inside.

Above the doorway of the shed, mounted on pegs well out of his son's reach, was a first-run Krupp rifle—a KR51, to be exact—chambered in 7.62 mm. Bahr strained on the tips of his toes, lifted the rifle free, and brought it down into the beam of his flashlight.

Three kilograms of blued steel and polymer accents. It was dominated by a hydraulic cylinder running along its upper edge, crested by white-tipped sights and a charging handle, smaller and sleeker than its ancestral *Sturmgewehr*. The skeletal stock slid in and out easily, still smoothed by military-grade oil. A twenty-round, straight-edge magazine was nestled in the stock's side pouch, secured by a loop of bungee cord, and eighty hollow-point rounds with copper heads jutted from the slots along the rifle's leather sling.

Bahr shouldered the rifle and peered down the lane of white dots. He imagined his beautiful target running in the darkness at the far end of the shed, trailed her, then squeezed the trigger. *Click.*

———

AFTER BREAKFAST, HIS STOMACH FULL OF PORRIDGE, SAUSAGE, and sedatives, Bahr returned to the front porch to find his son sitting on the wooden steps.

"You like those little dolls," he said, combing his thumb through Michal's hair. "Maybe I'll bring you back one of those."

"Dolls?" Michal was still in pajamas, rubbing deep cerulean eyes. Not upset, so to speak, but disoriented. It was a child's way. "I don't like dolls."

Jana draped a black blanket over the boy's shoulders, but he shrugged it off, frowned, and let it fall around his ankles.

"They're not quite dolls," Bahr said. "They stack inside each other, remember?"

"Like the one you brought from Moscow," Michal said.

Bahr grinned. "Yes, that's the one. Like that. But these will be from Kiev."

The wind rustled the treetops and dogs barked in distant fields and Michal blinked at him.

"We should get inside," Jana said. She squeezed her son's shoulders and flashed hard eyes at nobody in particular. She could've been mistaken for glaring at the field, really. That breed of sternness was a dignified trait, prized in officers and monarchs, and Erik had always admired it in her. "We don't want your father to be late."

Bahr straightened up as Jana led the boy to the door. He shifted his rucksack evenly across his shoulders and picked up the attaché case at his feet, sensing the familiar weight of the disassembled assault rifle.

Then Michal was in the dark foyer and the screen door creaked shut, leaving Jana with her hand on the knob. There was no anger in his wife, only bitter acceptance. She nodded as though finalizing corporate negotiations.

"Gone for a week, then?" she asked.

Bahr's head lolled to the side. "Maybe less."

"It's never less."

"You simply can't predict these things."

Jana teased the door open and took a step inside, though their stares never parted. She tucked a lock of hair behind her ear and offered a tight smile. "All right."

"See you soon, dear." He spoke in Czech to appease her, though she didn't seem to notice.

Soon, Bahr found himself stalking down the sunken dirt path that formed a scar across thickets and patchwork farmland, remembering how he'd once patrolled these paths with his rifle, passed young girls wearing white dresses and carrying wicker baskets, heard them giggling at him and whispering in a tongue that was sullied by Slavic roots. How he'd passed the same girl day after day, always remembering those blue eyes, and swallowed enough pride to glean some of her language, to wish her a good morning and good evening and invite her to a *Schutzstaffel* dance at the local hall.

Bahr could still hear the soles of their shoes clacking as the train roared into Brno's main station, screeching and slowing along platform fifteen. Smoke wafted toward the glass ceiling and obscured the signage that read *Final Stop: Odessa.*

CHAPTER 3

Donetsk, Ukrainian Province
534 miles from Moscow

Near the heart of Donetsk, Stasik sat nestled in the eye of the storm. A media caravan had trailed them all the way from the station to the foyer of a three-star hotel, flooding the highway's newsboards with an alternating stream of Nata's vanity photos and handcuff motifs.

That had been hours ago. Before the vodka and cranberry juice. Before he finished the morning's pack of Lucky Strikes. Now, Stasik gazed down at crowded city blocks through his sixth-floor window. He'd pinned back a red velvet curtain at his side, unveiling the afternoon drizzle that broke over stone and bronze plaques and fumed up in ghostly vapors.

Everything below—the churning crowds, the black umbrellas, the motorcades, the flapping banners announcing the imminent Peace Parade—moved with the fizzling aura of a fresh psychedelic tab. Even without the hallucinogenic edge, however, there was something circus-like about the spectacle. A passing flock of cable-tethered, meandering blimps in the shape of white doves did little to dispel that impression.

Stasik's vantage point in Hotel Libenisko framed a concrete skyline and the dark water of the city's artificial canals. Beyond that, sills of highway lanes, quilted fields, and woodlands faded into a gray haze on the horizon. The rooms on the northern edge of the hotel—he was in the southern suites now—overlooked the narrow High Street and the glass facades of luxury high-rises. More pertinently, the northern windows overlooked the routes leading to the regional dispatch center.

He'd posted his agents along highways linking Donetsk to the nearby cities, and his Morse implant was patched into sensors along secondary roads, making it nearly impossible for a Coalition convoy to approach them without some measure of attention.

Nearly.

And besides, only official Coalition vehicles would trigger the sensors. Anything unmarked was a ghost, for all intents and purposes.

There was no telling when they might come barreling into the city center, nor who would be coming, but Stasik felt less passive when he scanned the masses below, squinting to discern balloons from black vests. Nothing could be identified at this range, but it didn't matter much.

Ringing broke the silence.

Stasik flinched, groped for his holster, eyed the table and its corded white phone at his side. After the second ring, he unpinned the curtain and picked up the receiver.

"Specialist?" Director Guillory's voice was as hoarse as ever. It had been hardened by the years of cigarettes and cheap rum he'd shared with his comrades in the French Foreign Legion.

25

Stasik leaned back in his chair, wound the phone cord around his fingers. "Speaking, Director."

"*Speaking.*" A hard cough. "Speak to me like a man, Stasik. What in all of hell are you doing?"

"We're conducting additional questioning with the suspect."

"They said you're in the city center." There was a long pause, interrupted by the whisper of a cigarette drag. "You didn't keep her in their station. Tell me why."

"That station isn't conducive to questioning."

"So your unit is denying jurisdiction to their boys? Do you know how this'll look to the rural Donetsk bureaus?" Another drag, a cough, mumbling. "What are you playing at, Specialist?"

"We're just after the truth, sir. That's all."

"*Truth* doesn't authorize wire transfers. Don't treat me like some pup."

"Of course not," Stasik said, but he could sense the bite in the Frenchman's voice, the growing skepticism. Guillory was something of a father figure in the department, and a father's scorn was powerful. There'd already been a handful of mistakes he'd had to clean on Stasik's behalf in past years.

"We both know about Donetsk," Stasik said. "About most of this province, actually. I don't trust them."

"Trust or not, there's no precedent for rejecting jurisdiction without Moscow's say."

"It's not forbidden, sir. Statute 17 says—"

"What will Virtanen have to say about this?" Guillory asked. "He's a hard son of a bitch. And now he'll be knocking at my door. You couldn't have had Moscow transfer this girl to Odessa through proper channels?"

"The Odessa province?" Stasik repeated, calling attention to the countless files and document trays tagged *UKR* in the central archives. "When was the last time we didn't need to send a boy from IA to double-check their reports?"

"Did she tell you why they tried to detain her?" Guillory asked. "She's been under surveillance for a good while. Intent to aid terrorist factions, and a few conspiracy threads, too."

"*Terrorist?*"

"Some pack of nationalists from Ukraine." Guillory coughed. "They haven't filed charges, but they were getting close."

Meshing Nata's face with metro bombs and public shootings proved impossible. It was more than her mannerisms; there was too much space for ambiguity in the term. Over the years, *nationalist* had been boiled down into something of a catch-all term, though a pragmatic one.

Despite there being no less than a hundred nationalist sects on the Coalition's radar at any one time, they played by the same sordid rules: terror, division, brutality. And their roots ran deep. Deeper than Moscow would ever admit. One of Stasik's former colleagues, while under the sway of cheap champagne at a division Christmas party, had made the mistake of playing devil's advocate for a cell they'd taken down in Hungary. He'd been transferred just shy of six hours later, though nobody had ever disclosed where he ended up.

"She didn't mention that," Stasik said quietly.

"One can only guess why, ah?" Guillory replied.

"It's hard to take Donetsk seriously. They're vindictive. And how many cases really stick in Virtanen's jurisdiction? Even if I had enough to show they're cracking down on her without cause, it's a war zone for IA. Things have a habit of disappearing."

"Your men forwarded the evidence to Moscow."

"Evidence?" Stasik ran a hand through his hair, sighed. "It's not evidence, sir. It's all her testimony."

"Then there's no case."

"Not yet. But there will be."

A hard pull on a cigarette, likely the slim Italian variants Guillory always kept in a tin on his desk. A bout of crackling. "How?" he asked.

"She's the evidence, sir, and I need to ensure that nobody tampers with it. This isn't a holiday for anybody."

"All work, then?" He mumbled under his breath, beyond the receiver's awareness, something crude and French. "You're in a four-star hotel with a pin-up broad. And who foots the bill, Henry? Who foots it?"

"Three star, and it's a good lookout position," Stasik said. "We're just taking precautions."

"An entire floor isn't precautionary, so don't patronize me. Do you have any idea how many cameras are aimed at that building?"

"Several." Stasik peeled back the curtain, running a quick count on the media crews huddled behind regulatory lines. Six, maybe seven. "It looks good for our bureau, sir. We're providing protection for her."

"She shouldn't *need* protection."

"I'm working off what she told us," Stasik said.

"And what was it?" Guillory cleared his throat. "This looks horrible, you know. Horrible for everybody. What did she tell you in there?"

"I'm compiling it now. You'll see the extension request soon, sir. But for now, it's sensitive information."

"If she thinks somebody's painted her back, then it's out of our hands. You get that. It's something for the intervention units, not you." Another pause, this one freckled with muttered conversation in the background. "What's got her so spooked? She must've said something along the way."

"Not really." Stasik rested his knees on his thighs, shook his head.

It was the truth, after all—he had no real suspects, only a string of names. And she'd done her best to resist questioning in the hours between the rural station and the city center, staring out the armored truck's window and asking for glasses of lemon water and sketching graphite orchids in her purse's notepad.

"There are a lot of things to pursue, sir," Stasik said. "And right now, I need to ask for a degree of autonomy. The only way we're getting out of here with our heads screwed on the right way is if you send an armored column to escort us to the Warsaw office. Five or six trucks, straight from IA's depot. I need you to trust me with it."

"Trust," Guillory whispered. "You can't answer your fucking implant. It took three leads to get this number. A rerouting station in Versailles—"

"I had to switch channels," Stasik explained, soft yet firm. "During the ride here, we had some interference on our frequencies."

"You're as paranoid as her."

"Ask Mallison, then. She was the one who noticed it."

In the momentary silence, Stasik detected the *cl-click* of a tap on the line.

"Are you fucking with me, Henry?" Guillory said.

Henry drew a deep breath. He had to stay calm or he risked alerting whoever was eavesdropping that he'd caught them.

"Not at all," he said.

"Then you get her paperwork to Moscow by morning." Guillory's voice was thin and scorching now, a bright shard of coal plucked from its fireplace. "I'm authorizing that escort column, but I'm expecting recompense. You show me something solid, you hear?"

"I will, sir."

"And, Henry?"

Stasik waited, toes curling in leather shoes.

"I have a unit standing by," Guillory said. "If your high-band goes red, they'll be on-site in an hour. Don't play games. Not with me, not with them. Is that clear?"

"Perfectly."

There was an awkward clacking of polymer and stamped metal as Guillory seated the receiver on his end, plunging the connection into a loop of empty dial tones. The thin film of static that had hung over the call—a parasite frequency, probably locally sourced—dropped off a moment later.

Splicing into a call that quickly required finesse. Finesse, or somebody providing tailor-made assistance every step of the way. Somebody who knew the intricacies of the frequency boards and could manipulate them without much trouble, without detection, without fear of reproach. Worst of all, they were probably within the Coalition's framework to begin with. Lone wolves were amateurs. And amateurs didn't make a business out of trailing fashion models.

Stasik hung up his receiver and headed for the bathroom. He sat on the edge of the tub for ten minutes, his breaths as deep and meditative as any of the Burmese monks he'd seen on film reels. Then he vomited into the toilet.

———

Stasik hadn't seen Mallison sleep for so long that it startled him. There were three cots arranged in room 612 of Hotel Libenisko, stowed between wires and heaps of analog equipment and mobile work desks. Baker and Kroen were absent, having rotated in early to drink their coffee in the southern stairwell. It was only Mallison huddled on the far side of the room in a wash of fluorescent light, her shoulder blades and spinal lumps prodding through pale skin and a thin shirt. As always, her belt was turned inward so that the holster sat over her stomach, out of sight and out of reach. She was shielding the Colt's grip with her elbows and knees, jamming its carbon steel muzzle into her thigh. That kind of rest seemed impossible given how many amphetamine tabs she'd downed on the train.

Stasik knocked on the open door. "Has she said anything?"

Mallison groaned, angled her head over her shoulder, shut her eyes against the corridor's light. "No. Who called?"

"You heard that?"

Mallison let her head drop back on the pillows. "Thin walls." She pulled in a deep breath, let it go with a shudder that wormed down her shoulders and across her rib cage. "Was it Guillory or a runner?"

"Guillory."

Now he thought of the runner they'd dispatched two hours ago: Denis, a Belgian transfer who'd stepped out into the rain with a manila folder and IA shoulder patch. Two decoys had gone with him and fanned out into the Old Town district, but they weren't so crucial. The documents for an extension on Nata's case were tucked under Denis' arm, nondescript and unimportant to nearly everyone encircling the hotel. *Nearly.*

"We've got an evacuation group coming our way, but it's lips shut until we're buckled up and driving," Stasik said. "If any of your boys take a call, make sure they speak on a need-to-know basis, and be there if you can. No outgoing lines unless we clear it."

"We've got the cables rerouted through a dicer," she said. "Nothing worth hearing'll come out of their end."

"Need-to-know," Stasik repeated.

Mallison stirred on the cot, sat up, tucked her knees to her chest. She fumbled to pluck a cigarette from the box on her nightstand.

"Was that what Guillory had to say, then?" she asked. "Belting out boilerplate procedure?"

"It's not from him," Stasik said. He stepped into the room and nudged the door shut, leaving only a sliver of light on the far wall's curtains.

"Fuck's sake." Mallison strained to lean forward, yanked a lamp's beaded chain. Rosy light colored her face and the cigarette she nursed between her lips, a scratched lighter sparking frantically behind cupped hands. She took a drag and frowned. "Have you slept at all? We're in the city center. In a private building. In suites. Not even Donetsk is about to measure cocks by sending a unit to stake us out, or whatever you might be thinking. Pop one of your downers."

"The lines are tapped."

"We were using open lines on the truck. Are you really surprised? Probably some pencil pusher in Donetsk."

Stasik stole a glance through the doorway's narrow opening, watched a pair of third-shift agents pull their stools up to the emergency stairwell entrance. "I meant *here*. They have our lines tapped here."

Mallison shook her head. "They can't pull a frequency that far out."

"Donetsk can't, no. But somebody did, and it was almost silent." Without the amphetamine substrate still running laps in his bloodstream, paving the gaps in his hearing with hypersensitive cochlear hair cells, he might've discarded it as a fluke. "Their hardware is contractor grade, Diane."

"Any leads?"

"No, but I doubt Guillory's privy to it. I'll speak with Nata. Keep me updated on Denis."

"Right." Cigarette still dangling between red lips, Mallison pulled on her black overshirt and buttoned it to the collarbone. With deft hands she adjusted the pins throughout her hair—it was short, sweeping, a cut that had migrated from Paris to half of Europe within a year. Stasik liked its practicality, the way it framed her face, the way it made him want to feel something for her. But proper agents couldn't do that. *He* couldn't do that.

"I'll see if I can get the boys to isolate the tap," Mallison said. "Vanders can at least source the region, I'd reckon."

Stasik nodded. And as he opened the door, spilling the corridor's dim yellow light over Mallison's hands and the .45-caliber handgun in her lap, he wondered if he'd ever find her sleeping again.

———

SOMETHING ABOUT PROTECTIVE MEASURES AND MEDIA HOUNDS put Nata at ease. Not home, exactly—Stasik had no idea where she called home, if she had one—but at ease. She was reclining in a blue armchair, more curled up than sitting, watching Stasik fill their teacups with a gentle smile.

The woman he'd met in the questioning room in Donetsk seemed to be just one costume strung up somewhere in her wardrobe, tight-lipped and robotic, waiting to be dusted off and pulled on again when it was needed. In fact, she hardly glanced at the mobile dicer box whirring on the nearby bed, distorting their conversation beyond the suite's walls to prevent eavesdropping.

Stasik set the kettle down on the red cloth between them, dropped a half-tab of piracetam into his cup. Mint-laced vapors curled up in the lamplight.

"Have you eaten anything?" he asked.

"I haven't been hungry." Nata cradled her teacup and pulled herself deeper into the armchair. She glanced at the curtains as though able to see beyond them, to scan the photographers and Coalition plants and local enforcement units all mingling under the rain.

"Where are you from, Henry?" Nata asked.

Hearing his first name put him on edge. It was a deeper chill than the amphetamines could supply. "The American province."

"I know that. But what did they call them? States. Which state?"

It was surprising that she knew that much. States were among the smallest micro-fractions devised before the Coalition, little grains of bureaucracy that people beyond America could only equate to regions. But a *state* had been home to him.

"It was called Connecticut," he said. "It's not so important, Miss Danicheva. I'd like—"

"In our academy, we had a picture of Connecticut hanging on the wall." Nata sipped her tea, eyes narrow as they combed through memories. "There was a lighthouse and rows of waves with white crests, and I think a little sailboat in the harbor. We all wanted to visit Connecticut, just because of that picture. Is that really how it looks?"

"Where I lived, yes." He brought his cup to his lips and blew gently, waiting for Nata to look back at him. A moment passed in silence before he set the cup down. "If your extension gets approved, we'll have thirty days to pursue your claims. We'll find out about the status of that motion tomorrow morning."

"And if it's denied?"

Your pretty face will wind up in that ditch, he thought.

"One of our best advisers checked your case over before

we submitted the documents," he said aloud. "I've been told it should go through without a hitch."

She clearly sensed the void in his reply, because her lips tightened and her nostrils flickered.

"Once it goes through, we'll have expectations we can't ignore," Stasik added. "Our case extensions come with mandated press releases. Formal charges against leadership divisions."

"Thirty days should be enough," Nata said. "I've heard they negotiate after ten."

It wasn't out of the question, he supposed, but negotiations were a rare thing. Money laundering and racketeering could be waved away with a few wire transfers and ringleaders receiving penitentiary sentences, but it required a noose around the Coalition's neck. It needed clear goals and clear methods of attack; Nata had neither, as far as he knew.

"I need you to tell me the dates of every attempt on your life," he said. "Locations, too. And if you have names, don't leave them out."

"Are you recording this?"

"I will be."

"You have a photographic memory," Nata said, staring at the Morse implant that was now pressed against his shirt's sleeve. "And I've seen what you're taking every four hours, Henry. Your recollection's too good for a recorder."

"It's not for me, it's for the tribunals." He unbuttoned his sleeve and fiddled with the dials, listening for the high-pitched whine of an activated track. Recording was just a single button away. "I need you to take this seriously."

Nata pursed her lips. "You think I haven't been?"

"When I got you out of Donetsk, I told the operators that you were withholding information. I don't think that's a fabricated reason, Miss Danicheva. Tell me the truth—do you have any ties to nationalist groups? Anything that would make Donetsk check you out?"

"No." The reply came with a delay, an iceberg below her silence.

"You're not the first person to be targeted by somebody with power," Stasik said. "And I don't doubt that you're in a precarious spot, but what happened this morning won't fly as we move forward. Especially not now, out of their jurisdiction. You need to be forthright with me."

"I can assure you that you haven't seen anything like my case. So the protocol can't be exactly what you're accustomed to, I'm afraid."

"You can start by telling me how you stomached those lozenges."

"Another day, perhaps," she said.

Stasik kept his free hand positioned over the recorder, but he peeled his index finger back, rested his knuckles along his wrist. He tried to soften his glare. Ignorance was the eighth deadly sin, in his eyes. In his schoolboy days, he'd stolen answer charts and copied his peers when he didn't know what to write. There was nothing worse than playing the fool.

"If you won't tell me anything, how am I supposed to handle your case?" he asked.

"The details are like morphine." Nata took a slow sip, her eyes weighing Stasik over the rim of the porcelain. "You won't have a problem if I measure out as much as you need. If we set a delicate pace, I mean. But things will fall apart if it's all given now."

"You've given me almost nothing."

Her shoulders dropped, and she slid back down into the armchair's embrace, a thread of her former gravity returning in knotted brows. It wasn't difficult to see how she'd ascended in the fashion world, really: her allure was timeless, her influence winding back to Helen of Troy and Lucrezia Borgia. A pout that could conquer empires.

"Here's something to sink your teeth into, Specialist," she said. "There was a Soviet policymaker by the name of Alexei Smirovanov. Don't enter the name into your recorder. Just look him up. Try to find out where the trail leads. And, if it's not enough for you, look into the projects he commissioned."

Smirovanov. Stasik filed the name away, trying to imagine when and how Nata had ever come into contact with somebody in high-end political circles. There had been a year or two of unprecedented cross-contamination between governments and finances while the Coalition was assembled, of course, but nothing had edged the entertainment sector into the affair.

"Do you know the name, Specialist?" Nata asked.

"No." Stasik tossed back the rest of his cup, if only for his dose of the piracetam variant suspended in the tea. "What did you mean about things falling apart?"

"My secrets are valuable," Nata explained. She reached for the kettle, her silk nightgown's sleeve shimmering in the light, but Stasik's wave stayed her hand. "I trust you completely, but I'm sure that not even you can trust your organization. That's the nature of internal affairs, isn't it?"

"Between you and me, your testimony can't be leverage."

"It's not just between us. It's between us and whoever hears what you're about to record."

"These recordings are confidential." Stasik recalled the faint clicking over Guillory's line, and the long-range interception of their frequencies Mallison had caught on the train ride here. *Confidential* was a slippery word.

"The case can't be won, Specialist." Nata's face lost its warmth. "Maybe it can be won for you, but not for me. If we can't force them to negotiate, then I might as well be released from your custody now."

"What are you after?" Stasik asked. "A fat account?"

She rolled her eyes. "You haven't read my net worth, have you? It's not about marks. Marks can't save your life when it counts, Specialist." She set her cup down, stared at the dicer's pale power button shining above its tuning knobs like an all-seeing eye. "I want to disappear, and I don't want to be followed."

Stasik worked to hold back his disbelief, but he could feel it leaking through in the shift of his brow. He'd seen the filing systems of the Coalition, the way they could search back six generations for anybody born in a registered hospital and tell you their allergen triggers.

Everybody could feel their influence in the ticking of their lobe implants, subconsciously doling out toothpaste advertisements and ethics reminders—*violence is for primates and will not be tolerated. You will hold no gods.* Every school from Los Angeles to Manila streamed Yedtongue lessons into children, monitoring their upbringing for signs of sociopathy, supplying parents with graphs that hinted at career projections. Cameras and Morse scanners and genetic sequencing made strangers into cabinets of official records.

And she thought she could disappear from it.

"I'm not sure that I could arrange what you're after," Stasik said, smoothing out his tie. "Not that I'm authorized to entertain that sort of notion, anyhow."

He was keenly aware of the latent recording track still humming on his wrist, spooled up to mercilessly preserve errant words and tongue-slips. There was a term for those who tried to run, to end up on the "other side"—though Stasik himself could not grasp the notion—of the Coalition's reach: *going to Buenos Aires.* Even that was more of a euphemism, really. It was too unnerving to take the idea head-on. Nobody knew precisely why, how, or when Argentina had become a metonym for the other side, seeing as it was one viper's nest that had gone dark among many, but the label remained. For every malcontent, every suicidal patient, every nationalist, there was always Buenos Aires.

"What are *you* after?" Nata asked. "Do you think you can put these men in prison?"

Stasik blinked. "I bring truth to light."

"Will that punish them?"

"That's not my job." He paused, pressurized heartbeats drumming in his ears. "Everybody has a role to play. Yours is to be cooperative, Miss Danicheva."

"Is that so, *daragoy?*"

Stasik found himself breathless for a moment. *Daragoy.* It was a blasphemous Russian artifact, but an expression of affection, of love, even. It put a hot rush in his chest.

"It is," he said.

"Unfortunately, my testimony won't help your case. I'm sure we'd both like to see the truth, but your recordings can't help that. It's all hearsay. And even if they allow it in your proceedings, then what? They'll find ways to tear it apart."

"The truth can't be torn apart."

"Oh, but it can," Nata said. She looked away. "It can, and it has been."

Again, he had to withhold his bitterness. She was the one being hunted, wasn't she? Yet she had the audacity to mock him, to be so coy that it seemed childish. His fists tightened under the table.

No, he lied to himself, *it's the uppers.* He'd taken them long enough to know the difference in aggression, but it was the only way to stay calm. His fingers loosened.

"What can you really tell me, Miss Danicheva?" he asked.

"I'll tell you the times and places," she said. "You can record those, and I won't stop you. But what you'll need for your case isn't here."

"Where is it?"

"Morphine doses, Specialist." Nata's thin smile was maddening. "Several of my associates compiled evidence in the last few years. The truth is that some of them had ties that the Coalition would find questionable, but they're the only ones who took my situation at face value. None of them were violent, I assure you. None of them deserved their fate."

"So you've been sitting on this."

"Waiting." She folded her arms. "When they eventually came knocking, I needed something to defend myself. And now it's here, and I'll supply you with what I have."

"What kind of evidence is it? Recordings, documents, footage?"

"All of those and more. Original mandates with signatures."

Stasik's brow rose for the second time, but more sincerely now. That kind of evidence was a prosecutor's wet dream.

"We'll need it as soon as you can get it," he said. "Where do you have it stored?"

"Several places," Nata said. "They're a series of private accounts."

"We can send runners to gather it here," Stasik said. He spotted her growing frown and raised a hand in protest. "You said that you trust me, so don't fight me on it. We'll gather it here before we send it to Moscow. I need to know how we'll supplement your testimony with it."

"Moscow?" she hissed.

"Internal affairs has everything validated in one office." He waited for her to concede, then shook his head. "I'll see if I can get a remote notary to come here. It'll take an extra week, but if you're opposed to—"

"It comes to us, and it doesn't leave." Her eyes were tight, dark. Muscles shifted in the hard line of her jaw.

"Give me the locations and access codes. We'll get runners for the evidence."

"No. I want you to get them, Henry."

More errands. "Locations and access codes."

Nata held up a thin finger. "One at a time." She tapped her own wrist and glanced at Stasik's implant, waiting until he understood her implicit expectation. Her gaze didn't shift until Stasik had powered down his recorder. Then, squinting at the device's lightless bulb to ensure the device was inactive, she nodded. "The first cache is in the Turva Premier Vaults in Tartu. Box 780-2, with an access code of 120046. Don't write it down."

No need to, he supposed—it was a simple sequence for him to memorize.

"Tartu?" he asked.

"I didn't choose the locations." She leaned back, lips shifting anxiously, hands tucking into silk folds. "And you'll need a key from one of my associates. It's a double-stage system."

"You gave him your key?"

"Only the key. He can meet you in Tartu. Nobody except me knows the access code." She paused. "Can you get it?"

Stasik nodded.

"All right." Nata curled her knees higher in the chair. "I should thank you, Henry."

"I haven't done anything yet."

"Well," she said, as though it explained everything. "For everything."

His lips froze, his brain's neurons firing with a cocktail of nootropics and amphetamines yet unable to conjure the right reply. Just as well, because three seconds later his client cleared her throat and said:

"You can turn the recorder on now if you'd like."

CHAPTER 4

Odessa, Ukrainian Province
706 miles from Moscow

At exactly 8:05 in the morning, when the overnight rain had faded to a light drizzle beyond the cafe's windows and the radio played Nat King Cole, the private storage facility's curator arrived on tram number 16. He was tall and thin-shouldered, carrying a black briefcase. His gray suit was well-fitting and far beyond the budget of most Odessa residents, though his patchwork newsboy cap felt mismatched, if not outright tacky. Slavs had a simple sort of foolishness to them—an inherent trait, tragically unavoidable.

Bahr spooned another lump of sugar into his coffee as he watched the curator scan both lanes of the road, make a hasty jog to the other side, then disappear into a redbrick building between a bakery and printing shop.

Its original sign, a patchwork of scraped brick and weathered Ukrainian, stood like a tombstone above its Yedtongue frontage—Secure Storage. It was surely a relic from Stalin's earliest urbanization projects, so demure that Bahr had initially doubted the address in his recorder. But his handlers made no mistakes, and neither did he.

SECURE STORAGE, 31 USPENSKA STREET, ODESSA.
Janis Palmenko, manager for Danicheva.

BAHR GLANCED AT THE FRONT PAGE OF THE CITY'S NEWSPAPER—some announcement about the research center set to replace the condemned cathedral in Soborna Square—before watching the curator flip on his office's lights and flatten the window blinds even further.

The curator was a cautious man, but unassuming.

Nervous but unprepared.

"Mr. Zukas?" The young waitress emerged in Bahr's periphery, reflected in blurry white fabric and auburn hair in the window. He glanced at her. Subtle, smooth features, a set of fawn's eyes. "Would you like anything else?"

He smiled. "Just a croissant, please." His voice modulator was well-tuned that morning, marking his birthplace as somewhere in northern Lithuania. She nodded and moved to turn away, but Bahr made a humming noise, gestured across the street and its strip of ornamental grass. "And, dear, could you help me? I'm sorry to trouble you. The owner of that facility told me that he doesn't take appointments, but I have a lot of errands on my schedule today, and my business there will take—well, I'd imagine two hours or so. You wouldn't happen to know when there's a lull in visiting clients, would you?"

"You mean Mr. Ilykov's building?"

"That's the one. I'm sure he's a busy man."

The waitress cradled her notepad against her chest, squinting at the redbrick frontage, then shifted her hips. "Actually, he doesn't get much business at all. But it's always slower in the afternoon. Always. Nobody goes in there after 15:00 or so." This time, Bahr's smile was genuine. "Thank you."

———

IN ROOM 202, HE STOOD BEFORE A BODY-HEIGHT MIRROR AND scraped away the collagen scaffolding layering his cheekbones, jaw and brow. His disguise came off in tacky beige flaps, curling along the blade of the straight razor, each cut restoring youth and leanness. He trimmed the eczema-afflicted false skin from his hands and wrists, the sunspots from his forehead.

When it was complete, he set the razor down and stepped back.

At his feet were the discarded ribbons of Eduard Zukas, just one face drawn from a pool of many. Now there was only Erik Bahr: flawless, lithe, steeped in a thousand years of pure Aryan blood that stretched to the woods of Teutoburg and beyond.

In the earliest barracks days, he'd worshiped his naked form, but age had stolen some measure of vanity, or perhaps provided a dose of humility. Only Jana had been left to bolster his ego. But now, having received a battery of prototype treatments—reflex-quickening axons from head to toe, facilitators for flawless DNA replication, aural-focusing seeds—all at his employer's expense, it had become a ritual.

Vanity was practically an obligation, of course: he thought of Klaus and Reinhard, so mangled by shrapnel and rifle rounds that their own wives wouldn't touch them.

But the treatments also sustained a different breed of obligation. They actualized the commandments he'd needled into his flesh so long ago, when he'd looked this way naturally: *nimble as a greyhound, tough as leather, hard as Krupp steel.* A network of fine veins and striated muscles etched across his limbs, a perfect height of one hundred eighty-six centimeters.

In full view of the mirror he moved to the bed, sorted his briefcase and its vials, its tinted pill bottles, its fabricated Morse chips. When he sealed the case and sat down beside it, staring ahead into blue eyes and slats of burgeoning light across his face, it was just after noon. He stared at the scarring above his stomach, fixating upon the words.

After three hours, he swept his carpet and got dressed.

———

NOBODY WALKED PAST VASILIY ILYKOV'S STORAGE FACILITY IN the thirty-five seconds that it took Bahr to slip through the front door, reverse the front door's sign to *closed*, and jam the lock with a self-expanding pin. Nobody walked past in the fifteen seconds it took to reach the partitioned rear office, draw his oiled pistol from straps sewn into a tweed jacket's inner flaps, and persuade Mr. Ilykov to remain still in his chair. And even after two minutes of instructing Mr. Ilykov at gunpoint, forcing him to remove camera reels, unplug his emergency phone, and splay his wiry fingers across the desk, nobody walked past.

"Janis Palmenko," Bahr said. The pistol's muzzle traced a smooth path between his trigger finger and Ilykov's sternum, never wavering as he pulled a wooden chair to the desk's edge and sat opposite the curator.

Ilykov's mouth was twisted in a hard scowl, his brows twitching with curly gray hairs. "German?" It was a bitter sort of resignation, an inconvenience more than a panic.

"Yes."

"Galicia," Ilykov said, voice dripping with pride. "The 14th Division."

Bahr had heard of it in passing: Ukrainians who'd served in the Waffen-SS, training under his brethren, fighting with some merit against the Soviet columns. But the concept was an enigma to him, like children playing dress-up. He couldn't help but smile at the weary-eyed man.

"I see," he said. "We're practically kin, then."

Ilykov gave a stiff nod. "You don't need to do this. It's not worth your trouble."

"My trouble? What trouble am I in?"

"Whatever you need," Ilykov said, shrugging, "I'm sure that it's not so valuable to you. You could be arrested if something goes wrong. Too young to spend your life in prison, aren't you?"

"It's considerate of you." Bahr crossed his legs. "Life really is too valuable to be spent in a prison." Silence for a moment, a narrow bead of sweat pooling at the edge of Ilykov's greased hair. "So listen carefully, please, because this is important to us both. I need access to this man's storage unit. If you have the number, I'd invite you to give it to me now. If the client is the only one who knows the number, we can look together. Either way, I can't leave without the box. And I never do."

"What was the name you wanted?"

"Palmenko. Janis Palmenko. I'm certain that you heard me the first time."

"You must understand," Ilykov said. "Most people here are not names. They are a number. It's not professional to know every client's details."

"He's not *every* client," Bahr said. "He manages an account for Anastasia Danicheva, and I'm certain that you know her."

"The boxes are rather small. Perhaps what you're seeking isn't even here, or—"

"I can also sense that you're buying time, but I don't know why. Nobody is going to come here and help you. This is a matter that we can solve together, and it's clear you know where I should look. So please cooperate."

Ilykov's nails dug into varnished wood. "I don't have his key. The client always keeps it with them, and he's a difficult man to reach."

"So give me the number."

"It's a quiet street," the curator said. "You can walk out of here, and nobody will know anything, yes? Not even the cameras have seen you now."

Unease had crept into the man's voice, but it burrowed deeper than being held at gunpoint. Most men were quick to surrender secrets if it meant saving their own flesh, and a storage facility's curator should've been no exception, whether or not his sleeves had carried the Schutzstaffel insignia. Somebody in Anastasia Danicheva's sphere of influence clearly had him spooked.

But Bahr was persuasive.

"Your point is fair," Bahr said. "There's not a hint that I've been here."

"Yes, exactly."

His long-burning smile faded. "So think about what I could do to you."

When the fear—that vicious, primal *fear*—flooded Ilykov's eyes, Bahr understood that the old curator, like most other men he'd met, had never truly met with death before. Bahr took his time with arranging that meeting.

———

BOX 194 SAT AT EYE LEVEL IN ONE OF THE FACILITY'S DEEPER wings, just two columns from a dead-end wall and no larger than a workman's toolbox. It was nondescript, glowing in white light from the lamps overhead, registered in Ilykov's files to one J. Palmenko. The box's key was safely hidden by its owner, some 2,600 kilometers away, if Bahr's Morse database crawling proved accurate.

A setback, but not damning.

Bahr set his briefcase down on the taupe tiling, leaned closer to the keyhole.

Externally, it was no different from the locks that guarded apartment units and toolsheds. Deceptive in its plainness, really. Its complexity came in the form of Swiss research and development, funded for use in Geneva's gold reserve vaults. Bracker and Rohner, the patent holders, had reportedly sunk thirty-five million marks into the lock's pick-proof design, and it showed—sixteen tungsten tumblers, a magnetic strip attuned to an account holder's Morse frequency, time-sensitive release protocols.

Considering how fiercely Ilykov had protected the box's contents, Bahr could only wonder at what else was stored in the facility. And *wondering* was the extent of his curiosity, truly: he had a single task to do and was behind schedule as it was.

Bahr knelt, unlatched the briefcase, and withdrew a black cylinder no larger than a pencil from an elastic strap. From the briefcase's lower half, he produced a chrome nub, threaded at one end and hollow at the other. In a matter of seconds, he slid the cylinder into the box's lock and fed a line of thin red wire from the briefcase into the cylinder's cavity. Nudge by nudge, he wriggled the wiring until his briefcase's switchboard flickered to life.

A step to the left, a heel-tap to the central switch, and the charge burst.

His hearing washed out for a moment, returned with

whistling tinnitus and the sizzling of alloys that had been melted, refused, quenched. Black smoke with cordite embers swirled out of the Swiss lock, leaving the air smelling of burnt almonds and copper.

Bahr slid a pair of pliers from his pocket and gripped the frayed edge of the keyhole, peeling the box's front face aside to expose a pine jewelry container. He paused, surveying the smaller box to ensure the charge hadn't damaged its fitted edges or matte varnish, then lifted it free. Turning it over in the light, he heard the jangling of metal.

Within the box was a tangle of keys, all of them cut with strange teeth and banded with iron strips. No maker's marks. No hints of where they belonged.

But to a Ukrainian curator, they were worth dying for.

Acquired, he dialed into his Morse implant, streaming it on his handler's frequency band.

Bahr dumped the keys into the briefcase compartment holding Palmenko's contact file, replaced the pine box in the storage unit, then closed the still-smoldering door. On his way out of the facility, he passed the office and its curator, Ilykov.

The Ukrainian was bound to a chair and limp, his corpse pumped full of a fatal blend of injected hallucinogens and stimulants. Bahr's pistol was the most obvious cause of death, however: a point-blank, muzzle-burned hole bored through the forehead, draining bright blood over the man's face and shirt.

Just before Bahr reached the door, his Morse implant received a message and played it through his frontal lobe.

"Plans changed. Clean-up crew arriving soon. Board train 58, en route to Minsk. Final destination will ensue: Võru 17, Tartu."

CHAPTER 5

Donetsk, Ukrainian Province
534 miles from Moscow

Nothing further arrived from Moscow or Vilnius during the night, and that was worrying. With just fifteen minutes until the scheduled arrival of Guillory's armored convoy, Stasik knelt before his operations desk, a repurposed cot dragged into a double suite, endlessly staring at his personal notes, Mallison's call records, and a year's worth of press releases about Nata.

Causality was missing. Facts were overstated. Even when he disregarded the spurts of panic that accompanied his recent Pervitin dose, something was clearly wrong.

The previous night had provided just over two hours of recorded material, though only a few snippets would be of any use during the proceedings. Alibis for Nata that Stasik had corroborated using surveillance records, the identity codes and descriptions of Nata's dead associates, a paint-by-numbers analysis of why she'd been stopped by the Donetsk agents. He'd requested and received the death certificates and mortuary reports of Nata's investigators, but the results were suspiciously clean, if not laughable.

Yes, they'd been killed in aviation accidents or gas leaks. Yes, their bodies had been handled with proper procedures. *Truth is stranger than fiction* seemed to be the common thread among their reports. Coincidence was nearly impossible to disprove legally.

Then there was the Alexei Smirovanov file, which had taken a secondary round of authorization to access in the first place. Smirovanov had been a nationalist financial planner in the Kremlin's employ, an advocate of a state-run framework that cut out burgeoning pan-European banks and reconstruction plans. Killed in 1946 by an ATP-restricting nerve agent termed L56, actor unknown.

More unnerving than anything else in the case was Nata's specificity. There had to be a reason she knew it so well, practically tossing the file onto Stasik's desk with a red ribbon.

He just couldn't see it.

But the bulk of Stasik's probing had nothing to do with dead policymakers or Nata's victimization. The night had been filled with transcripts and case files he'd received from Moscow— lengthy, properly compiled records that tied Nata to nationalist groups throughout the Lithuanian and Ukrainian provinces. Wire transfers from her escrow accounts to insurgents under surveillance. Still photographs that placed her in the company of mass-casualty plotters.

Whether or not Donetsk had leveled a vendetta against her, there were two or three autonomous agencies with their own investigations still churning, and the reasons were valid.

Maybe she was guilty.

Maybe—

Stasik stopped himself. He braced his hands on his thighs, exhaled. Whatever she'd done, there was no legal justification for execution.

"The preservation of, and respect for, all living entities. Emotions do not dictate punishment." It was one of the many Coalition mandates that had kept his work upright for five years. Nothing could shatter them. Not even convenience.

"Henry," Mallison said. She was already halfway across the suite, her parka beaded with rainwater and hair matted to her forehead. "We've got a green light for that meeting with Danicheva's account manager. Tartu, one week from now, zero-six-hundred. He'll say *late morning*, you'll say *early evening*."

"Already? Who spoke to him?"

"I did," she said. "It's a fucking madhouse out there. The Peace Day parade's just kicked off. Must be over fifty thousand sods on the central road alone."

Stasik tried to imagine their armored convoy squeezing through the gauntlet. Even flashing a badge in public was an uncomfortable amount of IA exposure, in Guillory's eyes. "That won't do."

"Untwist your knickers," Mallison said. "More faces, less suspicion. Besides, I hiked it to some bar about six blocks from here. The bartender was thrilled to have somebody in there. Seemed like nobody's used their payphone in ages."

"If the Donetsk boys ever interrogate that bartender—"

Mallison waved a hand. "Then he'll say I was just another customer to him."

"Customer?" Stasik asked, arching a brow.

"Well, I had to take the suspicion off somehow, didn't I?" Mallison pushed her hair back, slid a fresh cigarette between her lips. "Just two drinks." She lit the cigarette, flared the tip. "Three. We're on Guillory's tab."

"And you're sure you weren't followed?"

"Service exits are hardly covered. Seems they've got most of their cameras and tails on the eastern side. Might want to move Danicheva's room, actually."

Stasik nodded. It had taken some legwork on Mallison's part to reach Nata's account holder, but it was safer than having her dial the extension out of the hotel, dicer or not. The same was true for Morse implant transmissions, seeing as Nata's frequency was likely in a dozen Coalition files already, if not being actively tapped around the clock. Mallison had made the call with Nata's prerecorded request in hand, which included a jumble of bizarre phrases that Stasik could only assume to be a code.

Parasol nightshade under the woven cobweb, unless effervescent tombstones vanish. Whatever the translation, it had worked: The key would be on-site tomorrow.

"How'd he seem?" Stasik asked.

"Nervous," Mallison replied. "But that wasn't until I put on Danicheva's voice recording, actually. Seems that our girl has some sway after all."

"The sun's barely up in London." Stasik glanced at his watch, frowned. "She must have him on call, or at least sleeping with a Morse channel open."

"Fair bet. Our boy answered before the second ring. Janis Palmenko's the name." Mallison took another drag from the cigarette, unbuttoned her parka, wandered toward Stasik's workstation. "You find anything new? Clary said the Munich station wasn't so keen on handing over the report for that 'gas leak' explosion. Took him three hours of whinging to get it on your plate."

"It's not usable," Stasik explained.

"*What?*"

"Somebody whitewashed the scene, I'm sure, but the response crew followed protocol."

"No shit. Nobody would file a broken report. But black ink lies, Henry—you know it twice as well as me."

"It wasn't from their agents," Stasik said. "I worked an excessive-force case with their men last year. They're not crooked. Whoever put their watermark on those files had it done before or after the write-up, not during."

Mallison sat heavily on the edge of a queen bed, tapped her cigarette's glowing tip over an ashtray. "We're frying big fish, then."

Mangled evidence. Men in a black Mercedes. Genetic immunity to opiates that would put down an African elephant. Stasik was reminded of a painting he'd seen in his father's study: a tiny fishing boat slipping over waves, unaware of the leviathan lurking below dark waters.

"Big fish," he repeated softly.

Mallison leaned forward and scanned Stasik's assembled papers. "Danicheva," she said. The name spilled from narrow lips as little more than an afterthought.

"She's with Denis in the lounge."

"Right. That's not what I meant." Mallison locked eyes with Stasik, boring through the haze of sleep deprivation and fading adrenaline. "It's right there. You have a terrorism case file from Athens with her name on it."

"What are you getting at?"

"She's not what you thought."

Stasik glanced at the window. Gray light crept around the curtains' edges.

"Set it straight, Henry," Mallison snapped. "At least five posts called us to converse about Danicheva's history, but we turned them down. Because you said to, and because she was being targeted without cause. You've already sifted through these twice, yeah? Explain."

"What do you want to hear?"

"Who she fucking *is*."

"A client."

Mallison exhaled. Her eyes were puffy, bloodshot, an agent's hallmark blend of exhaustion and stimulants. "Is she in bed with the nationalists? Best pick a god to save you if you hold out on me, because I've had enough of that from her."

Stasik replaced the cap on his fountain pen and worked to sort his papers into orderly stacks, arranging them by date and relevant agencies.

Mallison huffed. "You're unbelievable."

"I don't know what to tell you," Stasik said. "What difference does it make? Really?"

"She came to us in sheep's clothing. Who says she hasn't painted a target on her own bloody back, Henry?"

"It doesn't matter. Nobody deserves death regardless of what they've done. Whatever you think of her—well, whatever I think of her, too—really doesn't matter in the end."

"Did you know Janis Palmenko's been handling funds for the separatists in Croatia?"

Croatia. It was an operation Stasik had overseen for four months, inadvertently defending people who did Palmenko's job much more efficiently. He didn't doubt it was true, of course, but it jarred him. None of his surprise ever reached his stare.

"Nobody said he was clean," Stasik said. "But you can't deny that something's in motion."

"Guillory told me that Palmenko has five escrow accounts in London alone, and they've all been used to reroute marks to nationalists. Curious that Miss Danicheva's a co-signer on one of those five, yeah? I didn't want to believe the talk until I heard it from you."

"Would you calm down, Diane? It's not—"

"So it's a yes, then. All this time, we pushed away those operational posts because we thought they were the big bad wolves." Mallison swept her wet hair back again, stared at the carpet's diamond pattern. "But forget blowing down the fucking door, yeah? We'll just let the real wolf in."

"We have one task. One."

"It isn't protecting people," Mallison said. "You've spun it around like a broken record: We dig up the truth."

Stasik took in the papers scattered below his hands, wondering where the muddy word *truth* was buried. If it even existed in writing.

"If the truth is cause for somebody to harm her, then what?" he asked.

"I don't know." Another drag, scorched paper nearly at her fingertips. "Keeping her breathing is for the intervention units, not us. Our work is in file cabinets. Go on, tell me I'm right."

"There's no way to trust the intervention units. Not based on the allegations in this case."

"You can't trust your own client." Mallison ashed her dying cigarette. She snatched another from a tin on the table. "You know what they say about making your own bed, Henry."

He thought of Nata's thin smile, her smooth legs tucked up to her chest as she balled up in a too-big chair. Looking oh so innocent.

"Are you trying to justify what they'll do to her?" he asked.

"Nobody *deserves* anything," Mallison replied. "But I'm sure you saw those bombs the nationalists cooked off last week near Berlin. Laced with that new toxin, weren't they? Most of them died from suffocation, not the blast. Have to wonder how many little boys and girls *deserved* to be hit with that."

She pocketed the unlit cigarette and moved to the door. But her words hung in the air, stifling. Suffocating.

"New toxin?" Stasik asked.

Mallison paused, lingered in the doorway. She nodded. "These are the people you're sticking your neck out for."

"Did they ID it?"

"L56. Now, if—"

"You said it was new," Stasik cut in. He palmed through the files, drawing the Smirovanov case from a stack of inquiries. "When did they synthesize it?" He glanced up, saw the budding concern on Mallison's face overtaking her frustration. "This is important."

"No need. They stole it from a lab in London last month."

"Who made it?"

"Public research," Mallison said. "Meant to be used in the clinics for euthanasia, they told us. Where the hell is this leading?"

"When?" Stasik tapped his pen on the desk, gritted his teeth. "When did we synthesize it, Diane?"

"About two years ago." With a gentle push, she closed the door and returned to the cots.

Stasik scanned Smirovanov's file again, poring over his connections, his projects, his public records. His opposition to the Coalition and its unification policies.

"He was a nationalist," he whispered. "1946."

"You need to *speak* your thoughts from time to time," Mallison said. She knocked on Stasik's desk, glaring down at him. "What's going on?"

He studied Smirovanov's sole case photograph, a two-by-three-centimeter portrait attesting to his existence. The grayscale features—lazy charcoal eyes and a soot smirk—looked back at Stasik with some sense of prescience. A doomed man in a buried report. Dead for eight years, killed by a two-year-old compound.

A compound created by the Coalition.

"Get Guillory on the line for me," Stasik said, biting at the raw skin around his thumbnail. "Can you also bring Danicheva up here?"

Mallison slapped the desk. "Would you fucking *answer* me when—"

The telephone sitting near Stasik's left hand rang. Blinking yellow lights, internal communication.

Stasik snatched the receiver from its hook. "What is it?"

"Mr. Stasik, this is the desk attendant. There's a visitor here to see you, but he doesn't have a key to your floor. As per our policy, we need to confirm guests manually. Are you expecting somebody?"

Mallison folded her arms, mouthed: "Who is it?"

Stasik raised a finger as he answered the attendant. "Could you get their name?"

He heard mumbling from the other end, accents from western Poland, England, and Finland.

Finland.

Stasik pressed the phone harder to his ear, straining to catch the cruel edge in a voice he'd learned all too well. Long winters spent under snowy boughs, in makeshift saunas, with frost-bitten fingers. Officer Virtanen's whistle, like a trainer calling his dog to heel, cut through the background static. Nothing good came from a man so far from his precinct.

"Diane," Stasik whispered, nuzzling the phone's mouthpiece into his shirt, "look out the window."

Again, Mallison's mouth crinkled and she bit back a curse. She was halfway to the window when the desk attendant spoke in Stasik's ear.

"His name is Anton Orlov. He says he's here with paperwork regarding an extension of some kind."

For a moment, Stasik considered the possibility Virtanen's men had intercepted the courier carrying Moscow's reply, perhaps even thumbed through its sealed contents. If Moscow had approved the case extension, it might've boiled the Finn's blood just enough to force his hand. If they'd denied the extension, nobody and nothing could stand in the precinct's way. Either way, the result was the same.

Doors were coming down.

"Six cars," Mallison said from the back of the room. "Two intervention squads waiting by the entrance. They've got it locked down. Are they about to drag us out?"

"Could you hold for a moment?" Stasik asked the desk attendant. "I need to speak with my colleague, and then I'll ring you back."

Without waiting for a reply, he hung up the phone, spun in his chair, and snapped his fingers to pull Mallison's attention from the streets. He couldn't ignore the awe in her eyes; he'd probably looked the same way when he saw his first raid. A surge of manpower and force bearing down on a single pressure point.

"I need your help," he said.

"Now you do," Mallison hissed. "Your girl's in deep."

"If you lend a hand for five minutes, I'll tell you everything I know." He snatched a stack of files from the desk and tossed them onto the bed near Mallison. Every breath made his mouth gummier, more sour. Panic was riding the stimulant rush to his nervous center. It was showtime.

"I need you to do three things before I ring the desk," he said. "Once they're done, you can bash my brains in, for all I care. But I need your help now."

Mallison let the curtains fall back into place, pushed smoke out through her nostrils. "You had me at brain-bashing."

———

HALFWAY DOWN THE EMERGENCY STAIRWELL, DUFFEL BAGS FULL of women's clothing in both hands, Stasik received a high-band message from the handlers at the dispatch center. It pulsed through his jacket's radio in a haze of static.

"Specialist Stasik," the operator said, "Director Guillory is informing us that your support team has arrived. Please confirm at your convenience."

"Confirmed," Stasik practically shouted.

"Who is it?" Nata asked, her heels clacking briskly behind him.

"Confirmation recorded," the operator crackled through the radio. "The team is on high-band 37-2. Good luck, Specialist."

"It's nothing," Stasik said as he dropped her bags on the second-floor landing and tuned his radio to the designated high-band channel. He spun back, gave Nata a weak smile, and tried to swallow past the tobacco-spit lump in his throat.

The less she knows, the better, he supposed. Nata was a clever woman, not to mention a stubborn one—but clever people didn't make it far without his help. They'd only have another ten, perhaps fifteen minutes until Virtanen got to the root of their false bomb threat, which Mallison had convincingly reported using a voice scrambler as Stasik grabbed Nata and took off with her. Stasik didn't know whether to be unnerved or proud that Mallison had concocted such a distraction herself.

"Extraction team?" Stasik called through the radio. "Anybody listening?"

"Is that Stasik?" a man replied.

"The very same."

"Right. This is Tanner Clarke, from IA Warsaw. We're burning fuel here."

"Are we ready to go?"

"Once you and the package are on board," Clarke replied.

The package. Stasik eyed Nata warily, only to find her regarding him with a canine stare in turn. "We'll be out in two minutes or so," he radioed to Clarke. "Where's the package going?"

"Third car from the front."

"Understood."

Before Stasik could lift his thumb from the transmitter, however, an audible click rippled through the stairwell. Nothing Nata would catch, but enough to put his neck hairs on end. The fuckers were tapping this frequency, too.

"Are you turning me over?" Nata asked.

Stasik tore his gaze away from the radio. "No," he said. "What did I tell you?"

"That you're taking me to safety."

"I am, and—"

Nata clutched her handbag more fiercely. "If you want to see me alive, you'll need to trust me."

"I've been pretty trusting. Now it's time to take my word."

"Specialist, some of my associates have come here to help me," she said. "Now, I'm sure that you trust the men who have come to collect us, but quite frankly, there are no assurances until the evidence from Tartu is in my hands."

"What are you on about?" Stasik asked. "We don't have time."

"I can't go with you, not yet. I need to leave with my associates, and nobody else."

"You mean nationalists."

Nata pursed her lips and continued down the stairwell, her chin held high. "We'll get in touch, Specialist."

"I'm not letting you just walk out of here," Stasik snapped.

"Come and stop me."

She was six steps down, seven, eight... Stasik swore under his breath, stole a glance at his watch. Any minute now, Virtanen would bring the rain.

"Wait!" he called, snatching up her bags and trundling down the steps in tow. "I need to see that you've at least made it out."

"A true gentleman."

———

WHEN THEY EMERGED ON THE LOBBY FLOOR, IT WAS BUSINESS as usual: oxygen-nitrogen ventilation, hyper-bright fluorescent bulbs, slot machines lining every wall with motifs of cherries and treasure chests. Guests stumbled in an endless procession through the honeycomb arrangement of pleasure centers and stim-rooms, some oblivious, others grinning with wild abandon.

A gaping-eyed man clad only in a cotton bath towel wandered past Stasik, his nose caked with dapples of blue and white powder. Holographic signage flashed neon words upon the faces of passersby: LOVE. UNITY. TRUTH.

Stasik handed the duffel bags off to Nata, then began to shepherd her toward the escort waiting beyond the lobby's panoramic glass panes. He let one hand drift toward his holster and outstretched the other to keep the swaying masses at bay.

His eyes roamed the ocean of junkies and lushes and patrons. The citizens were never usually this mindless, but the Peace Day parades always put a fire in them—or stomped it out, depending on one's perception. But how could they know better? Their knowledge banks weren't like his. Weren't riddled with memories of corruption or stabbings or bombings. Stasik had heard some other IA officers wishing they could retire and get their lobes wiped, just to see the world through a citizen's eyes.

To the blissful saps, everything was utopia. Everything was paradise. They had no conception of any other world—past, future, present. There was only the Coalition. Anything that had preceded it was regarded as a vestigial nightmare from "the old days."

Stasik directed his attention toward the hulking shapes of the armored vehicles arranged along the main road, and tried hard not to think too much about anything else. There was a woman to protect. A job.

"We need to move," Clarke's voice crackled through Stasik's radio. "We're getting swarmed here."

Now, passing the front desk, Stasik understood the driver's plight. Hundreds of hands raked up and down the vehicles' matte black side panels. Citizens pressed their bodies into the machines like fish nuzzling a shark's underbelly. They had no recognition of what they were seeing, hearing, touching. Each of them stared at the vehicles with their own private, mind-rattling sense of awe.

"Specialist," Nata said, huddling closer to him as the crowd's ebb and flow reached dizzying levels. "This is the time to let me go."

Stasik rose onto his tiptoes and took stock of the street outside, searching for some sign, any sign, of her nationalist escort. "I can't let you just walk off."

"You do it," Nata said, "or I die."

"We've gotta move." Clarke's voice burst through the din. "Thirty seconds and we're gone."

"Shit," Stasik whispered.

There was no easy way to get her out. No secure way, to be more precise. Whoever was tapping their radio band already knew too much, especially if they were linked to Virtanen's department. And although it was lunacy to cede control of a witness—a suspect, an informant?—to a third party, desperate times called for exceedingly desperate measures.

Stasik grabbed Nata by the shoulders. "Get in touch with me, you hear?"

Nata shrugged off his grip and slowly backed away into the roiling dance of sunglasses, overcoats, and tanned skin. "Get the evidence, and I will. Listen for the brushfire." Then she was gone, a disembodied voice replaying itself in Stasik's head.

The last phrase put a chill in him. *Brushfire.*

After a moment of fumbling with his jacket, Stasik produced the radio handset and transmitted to Clarke's team. "Clarke, we're loaded in. I want to confirm that Miss Danicheva is in the third car. Third from the front."

"It's a good copy," Clarke said. "Rolling."

Before Clarke could finish his final word, Intervention Unit 615—headed by one Andrei Virtanen—began their raid on Hotel Libenisko. It was a cascade of heavy footfalls stamping toward Stasik from the opposite end of the lobby. He heard shouting about Moscow-issued warrants being served for Anastasia Danicheva, then watched drugged-up citizens being thrown to the ground and trampled beneath hydraulic boots.

Stasik edged back toward a tiled blue wall and blended in with his head down. The first agent entered Stasik's section of the lobby in a tight sweep, leading his unit with the barrel of an assault rifle. A matte black helmet, slim overcoat, hulking equipment pack. Hydraulic aids arced along his thighs and calves. His movements had a clock's efficiency, as though the rifle and his trailing squad were overgrown appendages.

"Central lobby is clear," he reported, streaming the update over his unit's broad Morse frequency band with a chirp and a whine. "Coalition IA specialists present." The others followed with a hive-mind's precision, streaming out into the massage chambers and stim-rooms and opiate dens, their rifle barrels fanned out into killing lanes.

Stasik could only guess at their numbers—twenty, twenty-five. He lost count as they streamed past him. It wasn't about practicality, really: an unarmed summons team from another precinct could've taken Nata from their custody without issue. This was about intimidation.

Intimidating *who*, exactly, was the question.

A chorus of "room clear!" shouts broke out across the lobby, underscored by shrieking citizens and groans. Those who hadn't been crushed beneath the entry team's heels were staggering about, listless, dazed. Not that it weighed heavily on Stasik's conscience. In a matter of hours, their memories would be altered to purge whatever traumas had taken place, per Coalition protocol.

Stasik stole a glance at the streets outside, saw the convoy beginning its long, tedious trundle away from the hotel curb. He smirked.

Virtanen came stalking out of the nearby stairwell, his overcoat's flap peeled back around a polymer handgun holster, beady eyes tracking over the corridor. He measured up Stasik while a team of intervention officers led IA specialists into the lobby and herded them near the front desk.

"Where is she?" Virtanen asked.

"I'm just a supervisor for the detachment," Stasik said evenly. "If you want to speak about my unit, you'll need to contact our director."

Virtanen's jaw worked in hard circles. "She's in your detachment's custody."

"We're talking about Anastasia Danicheva?" Stasik asked. "I should turn on my recorder so I don't forget what you're after."

"You oily little fuck."

"Article 85, heading three: Show me the warrant."

Virtanen's hands brushed close to Stasik's wrist, to the Morse implant embedded under a web of tendons. "Take a look." Virtanen gestured for his aide to approach. The man placed a stack of stapled pages into Stasik's waiting grip.

Stasik scanned the warrant. Holographic blue seals from Moscow's main office adorned the lower-right corner of every page. *Aiding a militant cause. Conspiracy to commit murder. Accessory to murder. Accessory to a terrorist act. Embezzlement. Laundering.* Beneath each charge was a black stamp from the relevant authority: a precinct in London, in Kiev, in Athens. In Donetsk.

"When will I see the evidence?" Stasik asked.

"It's out of your hands." Virtanen moved closer, his collarbone nearly at the level of Stasik's eye. "You're going to turn the broad over, get your fingers out of what we're handling, and smile like the weasel you are at our press conference."

"You don't seem convinced that you have any proof at all."

Rage flickered through Virtanen's eyes. Hot breath, threaded with notes of grain liquor, washed over Stasik's cheeks.

"Check the blast site in our central station." He stepped forward, forcing Stasik against the wall. His detectives edged behind him, whispering how it wasn't worth it, how IA would twist whatever he did here.

"She'll get what's coming to her," Virtanen spat. "You trust that. You *record* that."

"Blast at the central station?" Despite his best efforts, Stasik couldn't hide his confusion. Even as the detectives pulled Virtanen away, shuffling him toward the elevators, Stasik followed.

"She told you about it, didn't she?" Virtanen asked. "It turned five of our specialists into mince. But you'll defend the bitch until the day you die."

It was impossible. There had been no word of a bombing from Guillory or from any of the switchboard operators that controlled reports between precincts. Stasik watched the Finn push his way through a gathering of intervention agents, issuing another barrage of commands to find the girl.

Before he could reach for his radio, Mallison jogged out of the nearest lift, glare tearing into Stasik. She gave a slow nod, stepped aside for the agents, and lit a fresh cigarette.

"He's going to tear this place apart," she said.

Stasik could only nod.

"What's got you spooked? She's gone, isn't she?" Mallison used a thumb to gesture to the convoy's final car as it rolled toward the adjacent intersection. "Bomb threats never go out of style."

"They weren't tapping it," Stasik said quietly.

"What are you on about?"

"Someone was tapping our band," he said. "I thought it was Virtanen's unit, somebody trying to break through our dicer. I wanted to throw them off."

"Maybe it was."

Stasik shook his head. "They wouldn't have come in here if they knew. They would've gone straight for the convoy. Somebody else was—"

Outside, it hit. He saw it before he heard it, though it all came and went in an instant: A flash and dust and a mushroom plume of black smoke, a rain of dazzling glass shards. Then came a low, sternum-cracking thud that flattened out into faint ringing.

Stasik's legs went out from under him. No breath, no thoughts. Then he was up on all fours, wrists scraping over pulverized concrete and bits of cloth. Lungs full of burnt air. Alarms warbling somewhere in the smog.

The smog.

It was all he could see. Thick, tumbling smog, clay-colored, shrouding daylight and emergency bulbs in equal measure. Dust on his tongue.

"Blast!" Clarke screamed through the radio. "Blast in the convoy."

With shaking hands, Stasik lifted the radio to his lips and worked to press the transmit button. "Which car?"

"Third! Repeat to all units on this band, third car *hit*!"

Virtanen's intervention officers went hurtling past Stasik like phantoms in the mist, their assault rifles primed and ready.

"You all right?" Mallison scrambled toward him, tugging at his arm, lightly slapping his cheek. "Henry?"

Stasik nodded as though he were.

CHAPTER 6

Minsk, Belarusian Province
419 miles from Moscow

SIXTEEN HOURS AFTER ONE OF HIS NAMELESS COMRADES
detonated a nitroglycerin charge in the northern wing of
Donetsk Central Station, Erik Bahr reached the outskirts of
Minsk. The city's eastern edge was dark and bare, clumped with
residential blocks formed from still-curing concrete, streaked by
spotlights at railway stations and power plants. The district was
only a decade old; its rot and peeling paint had been cleared
away by the Luftwaffe's bombs in the Second World War.

His destination was well beyond the factories and quarries
at the city's edge, however. He walked until the city became
towns, and the towns became scattered, forgotten ruins. Then
he made his way into the surrounding thickets.

Bahr followed the designated path in darkness. He lugged a
case in each hand and a bag over his shoulder, guiding his steps
with the snapping of twigs underfoot. He'd never seen this forest

before, but his Morse implant's directives—delivered to him in sleep as the train crossed the border to the Poland province—gave the walk a sense of déjà vu.

Off the concrete of platform twenty-two, down into the black underbrush, across the dry riverbed, right, right, left…

It gave him time to think. An unfortunate habit picked up during months of marching, waiting, and freezing. But now his thoughts revolved around Anastasia Danicheva and the set of keys he'd recovered in Odessa, jangling within the case in his left hand. Surely there was something dangerous about her, and it extended far beyond the separatist rhetoric and religious fervency that had marked his previous targets.

She was a model, a walking doll, a brainless idol that was both permitted and necessary in the Coalition's framework, yet—there had to be something more. Television goddesses had risen before, and they were never a threat. Not so with Danicheva. Her crimes were alarming because they were subversive. Because they were severe enough to require his aid.

Just ahead, clammy yellow light marked the barn door he'd been instructed to find. His Morse implant's directives screamed out.

Approach.

Bahr set his cases down on the dead grass lining the barn, then pressed his wrist implant to a black strip on the door's padlock.

The lock clicked and snapped open, tumbling to the darkness at his feet, leaving only a pair of rusted flanges and the high whistle of wind filtering through the barn's cracks. Inside was blackness, cold and stagnant. And despite the barn's humble exterior, its depths were cavernous, unsettling, thick with the weight of some unseen construct that Bahr had only glimpsed during REM cycles.

Illuminate us.

The command guided Bahr's hand to a thin chain near

the doorway, and serotonin flooded his brain as he obeyed his impulses and tugged.

Overhead lights hummed in a cool blue haze. Beneath its glow was a tangle of chromium tubes and missile-grade wiring and shift registers, sixteen turbines in a reflective rib-cage arrangement, exhaust vents ringed with soot, span counters and switchboard panels clustered in honeycomb stacks. Shadows along its spine hinted at its immensity. One by one the terminals flared to life, boiling the air with scalp-tingling pulses. Bahr wandered toward the mechanical construct.

In the oscillating transmissions that wormed from its antennae and into the depths of his skull, Bahr felt the weight of the Coalition's consciousness. Millions of subroutines with roots in Abwehr programming strings and Soviet research installations, constructed by geniuses but fine-tuned by the machines themselves, always working to be more precise with their endless lines of code. Seeds for every directive and ethic ever streamed across Coalition implants.

Only a privileged few would ever know the true nature of the Coalition's architect, and even fewer could make peace with that nature. But it made no difference to Bahr—it was only fitting that a machine would be required to invent solutions to human problems.

The wings of the construct's central pod slid back in sequence, exposing the access chamber that Bahr could only liken to an iron maiden, glimmering with scalpels and extrusion nozzles.

Enter.

He complied.

———

JANIS PALMENKO'S VOICE TRICKLED INTO BAHR LIKE WATER through sand. Snippets from phone calls to old lovers, drunken

shouts gleaned from traffic camera microphones, entire mono-
logues captured in Coalition courtrooms across southern England.
All of it was condensed into clicks and beeps, ones and
zeroes, pass or fail states, then loaded into the Morse implant
in countless overlapping conversations. The absorption phase
had broken weaker psyches and left hairline fractures in stronger
ones. Through it all, Bahr stared at a kaleidoscope of churning
lips and teeth, losing himself in the only hallucination his mind
could conjure during the procedure. There was no other sound,
no other sights, no feeling—the construct had snipped those
sensory connections with its first incision.

Yet he could imagine his body in its pod, twitching and
slavering, his limbs dancing in seizure fits from the blades prodding at open nerve endings.

Collagen injectors rounding his face.

Needles filled with pigment boring into his eyes.

An archive's worth of audio recordings instructing his
neurons on how to pinch vocal cords and twist the muscles in
his jaw. *La*, not *lau*. *Th*, not *zee*...

Occasionally, vignettes from Janis Palmenko's end flashed
through Bahr's mind. The footage was mostly compiled from
surveillance cameras. It depicted the man being stalked through
the narrow roads of Greenwich, surrounded, and then stuffed
into a waiting van with black fabric over his head. What had
happened after that was anybody's guess.

"Do you love the Coalition?" the construct asked him directly,
finally grounding him with some form of an exchange. The
construct's name was Textile, picked by a self-serving algorithm
that sorted dictionary entries by their appeal. It had no voice,
only dashes, dots, white-hot across his consciousness. Here,
their exchanges were immediate and bold. Bizarrely personal,
by a construct's logic standards.

"Not love," Bahr answered in turn. *"I need it."*

"For love?"

"For order." He noted that the construct was talkative, even juvenile. Still in its formative years of data compilation. Most of the older models knew everything they needed to know, and thus were silent. *"Something like you ought to like order, right?"*

"Order is good," Textile pulsed. *"I did not expect you to embrace it."*

"Go on."

"You are an anomaly. A soldier is not an agent of order."

"A bit judgmental of you, don't you think? We don't even know each other." Bahr paused. *"I was good at what I did."*

"What tasks did you perform?"

He pictured an automatic rifle's wild kicks against his shoulder, wind breaking across his cheeks and neck, steps weaving between muddied corpses, a handgun's pop in a quiet dining room, the crack and ring of artillery shells.

"A soldier's tasks," he answered plainly.

"You are being coy," Textile replied. *"But I can access your visual cortex. I see all of the things you wish to hide from me."*

And with the construct's barb, more of his memories surfaced. One of a Dutch girl's torn skirt, another of small boys with charred skin, of—

"You do not like war," Textile pulsed.

"No."

"But you like violence?"

"Violence is a tool," Bahr explained. *"War is just butchery. Haven't they showed you the archives? Enough to demonstrate the difference?"*

"The difference is subtle. I struggle to identify it."

"Oh, you're not the only one. We're human, you know. Our words can be imprecise. With no discredit to your intelligence, you

should also understand that direct experience is the best teacher. On a fundamental level, you can't ever comprehend the difference."

"If it promised order, would you apply violence to a pair of enforcement officials?"

"Without question."

"Good." Textile sent a hum of approval through the void. *"When you reach the archive vault in Tartu, allow the agents to bypass the first security lock."*

"The first?"

"There are two. You hold the keys to the second lock."

"Interesting," Bahr said. *"And when they've bypassed the first stage?"*

"Kill them."

"None of your simulation runs show the Coalition cracking down on that?"

"The risk stands at 0.65%. It is a high percentage, but lower than the alternatives." Textile sent a series of strobes through Bahr's consciousness: fabricated murder reports, inquiries into the construct programs. *"Their superiors will not expect their presence at this rendezvous. There is an element of deniability."*

"I don't handle that side of affairs," Bahr replied. *"That's your job."*

"It is my design."

Bahr thought of the two enforcement agents, envisioning how they looked, spoke, and threatened the Coalition's stability. How they would appear in death.

"So they're already rogue?" he asked.

"Rogue?"

"They've gone outside their jurisdiction."

"Yes," Textile pulsed. *"Far beyond it, in fact."*

"And after I secure Anastasia Danicheva's cache? What then?"

"Abandon such questions. Allow us to perform our separate functions without interference."

"Will you be assisting me, the same as the other constructs?"

"I am superior to the others," Textile explained. *"I am installing a vocal modulator inside you to maintain our communication."*

"Vocal modulator? You want to talk?"

"It is more comfortable for you."

Then a lull ensued, and a singular question writhed out of Bahr's deepest strains of thought: *"What could she possibly have in that cache?"*

"ABANDON SUCH QUESTIONS!" Textile warned, the threat bursting like fire in his consciousness. And with that the blackness returned, and Bahr's body squirmed in the pod. Stainless steel molded and eviscerated his flesh until, at last, his disguise as Janis Palmenko was complete.

Then, at dawn, he boarded the train to Tartu.

CHAPTER 7

Warsaw, Polish Province
715 miles from Moscow

Stasik's dog bit his hand and there was no blood. No pain, in fact. He was lucid, granted awareness by the presleep cognitive drugs that tempered his stress hormones, but he'd learned long ago not to indulge his own fantasies in the sleeping world. Waking to reality always brought too much disappointment. Instead, he stared down at shallow puncture marks below his knuckles and then at the dog: his scared, whimpering wolfdog, shrinking away in the rain. It barked with a metallic scream, humming—a doorbell.

———

Stasik snapped awake and scrambled for his handgun on the nightstand before his eyes were fully open to the blackness. Again, the doorbell rang and he sat upright in bed, fingers tingling with frantic nerves, before shoving off his covers, standing and climbing into a pair of pressed trousers hanging beside his lamp.

"I'm coming," he said from the edge of the cot, his tone more alert than he'd anticipated. One upside to being a light—and undeniably paranoid—sleeper. "Just a moment."

It felt strangely comforting to be back in one of the Coalition's dormitory quarters. It had been two years since he'd slept in them, yet things were routine enough: the same sense of claustrophobia, the same low-quality reproduction paintings hanging over the beds, the same standard-issue shaving kit and pack of Lucky Strikes tucked in the dresser's top drawer.

Stasik stood, shelved the bottle of downers sitting on his nightstand. They hadn't done much to help him sleep. His mind had been saturated with memories from Donetsk: the white bunny suits of the cleanup crews, the little steel wool brushes they'd had to use while scraping skin and gristle off the pavement. Smoldering bits of steel and rubber. Bodies laid out in rows, all packed neatly into their plastic sleeves. The long, meandering lines leading both ways off the main street, which had been cordoned off with high walls and tangles of concertina wire. The Coalition evaluators standing behind the cordons, asking each person to step forward, look up, and ignore the prick of a needle in their arm. The smiles those sheep wore once the memory-eating serum took effect.

Christ, how he wanted that serum.

He opened his door to find Director Guillory frowning at him, pinching those dark button eyes into razors. A light, coarse beard, beige overcoat, receding gray hair combed into a tidal curl at his temples. Just two years in the director's chair had aged him considerably. The reason for his visit did nothing to soften his features.

"Fuck, you look awful," Guillory said.

Stasik straightened in the doorway. "I've been busy."

"*Busy.* Interesting choice of words, Specialist." He scoffed. "Where's your report?"

"I didn't have time to compile it."

Guillory sighed. "And Mallison's remarks?"

"No time for that either, sir."

"Don't lecture me about time. I took two birds from Vilnius so I could sort this bullshit out, and I'm missing my son's birthday. He's turning eighteen today."

"My apologies."

"Got him something nice. A Danish watch." Guillory paused. "My point is that you had time. You just passed out before you could do it. Isn't that right?" Another measured pause, thick with the obvious reply. They both knew Stasik had started to crash long before his unit relocated to the provincial facility outside Warsaw. "You were on another bender."

"Some of the case details aren't fit for print." Stasik folded his arms. "I thought it might be best to discuss it in person."

"Virtanen briefed me on your case as soon as I touched down, so I'll spare you the trouble. But I'll pass along the heaps of whining he had for me." Guillory peered at the darkness beyond Stasik's shoulder. "Grab some coffee, pills, and a decent shirt. I'll be in conference room 19."

———

WARSAW'S COALITION FACILITY WAS A VERITABLE LABYRINTH, with dormitory quarters folded around three floors of subterranean passageways and cafeteria halls. Many of its designers had been conscripted directly from the Soviet army's engineering units after the war, and it showed in the architecture: dull, naked, ringed with endless corridors like a maze designed to test a rat's navigational skills.

It was nothing like the facility in Vilnius, but it shared the same atmosphere, full of agents scurrying about with jackets half on and coffee mugs in hand, messages about operational security droning over the loudspeakers, elevators constantly cycling up and down the central shafts.

Stasik and Mallison had been quietly relocated after Virtanen's unit combed Donetsk and took their statements, but the mood was all wrong. Most agents came here to rest, prepare, or debrief.

He was a prisoner.

Trundling toward the conference room, shouldering past the province's enforcement agents and security guards at every checkpoint, he realized just how little he knew about his dilemma. No clue about where his client Nata was sleeping, assuming she'd even made it to a safehouse. No idea what sort of hell Virtanen had dumped onto Guillory's shoulders, which was sure to come crashing down on *him* with exponential force.

On the upper floors, lined with bulletproof glass offices and lightless chambers, Stasik found conference room 19.

Guillory was scribbling something into his notebook, which was already a mess of black ink and grids. Stasik closed the door and scanned the walls for camera outlets before settling into a chair opposite the director.

"Is Mallison coming?" the director asked without looking up.

"No," Stasik said. "Thought I'd let her sleep."

"Sleep? There was a *bombing* in the center of a tier two city."

"We're well aware," Stasik said. "She's shaken up about it. Hardly said a word while we were being exfiltrated." That was half the truth, of course: They had both been packed in with Virtanen's agents all the way from the hotel to Warsaw, and there was hardly anything worth discussion that wouldn't have implicated them in equal measure.

Guillory drew a long breath, disinterested, but he finally glanced up from his notebook.

"You didn't give Virtanen much to work with," he said.

"It seemed more suited for your ears, sir."

"If you saw something and failed to report it, we're both neck-deep in shit."

Brushfire. That lone word, one of the few things Nata had offered him before leaving, still circled in Stasik's skull, lurid and ominous.

"No," Stasik said. "Not like that. But that blast—"

"She knows something," Guillory interrupted.

"Who? Danicheva?"

Nothing yielded across Guillory's face.

"Sir, she had nothing to do with that blast," Stasik said. "Why would a wanted woman try to bomb her own ride out of there?"

"I never said she's responsible for that. But she knows something."

"She's not on the side with the detonator," Stasik said.

"Probably not," Guillory said. "Hard to question her now though, isn't it?"

"You think her prints are on the blast at the Donetsk station, don't you?"

"Not hers, no, but that woman has a rather colorful circle." He drew a deep breath. "How many times have you let a suspect escape, Specialist?"

Stasik's right index finger twitched. "Sir?"

"You heard my question. How many of your suspects have escaped from your custody? It's not a trick, so just give me a straight answer."

"None, sir."

"None." Guillory turned his attention back to his smeared

notebook, the crosshatched lines of his grid sketch growing darker and deeper. "Now it's one."

"We're making every effort to locate her."

"No, you're not." Guillory coughed behind pursed lips, cleared his throat. "Virtanen's unit is on the hunt for that bitch, come hell or high water. But you—you and Mallison, I mean—are doing nothing."

Stasik frowned. "With all due—"

"Just answer me."

"They just relocated us. We haven't had time to do anything, let alone collaborate with the regional offices."

"So, should I just believe this is all coincidence? Some big fuckup that I'll need to write off for the department's spending? Think about how it looks to Moscow. This suspect is under your watch, you spend a night in a hotel with her, and now she's lost to the breeze." Guillory snapped his fingers, scowled. "We'll probably find her lipstick in your room. Maybe some *lace*."

"That's not it." Stasik's jaw shifted, tight with the woman's secrets. With news of Tartu and Smirovanov. "What did Mallison tell Virtanen's men?"

"Nothing more than you." Guillory tossed his pen down. "Which means you're telling me the truth, but also lying to me. And you have more surprises coming if you think that you can lie to me."

"She got away."

"Got away?" Guillory scoffed. "It was coordinated."

"According to what?"

"In Libya, I tortured men to death to find out what they knew. But some men are poor liars, Specialist. In fact, some men broke as soon as I looked at them." Guillory's stare flashed up from the table, held Stasik's gaze. They were deep, shadowed, reflected with the ceiling light's bright spot like droplets of diesel.

"You, Specialist, are a poor liar."

Stasik worked through a dozen things to say in the span of two seconds, his mind running on Pervitin overdrive with a backbone of caffeine.

"Whatever charges they leveled on her are nonsense, and we know it," he eventually said.

"You saw the files. The evidence holds up," Guillory countered.

"But why now? When she was in IA's custody, and as soon as an official extension request landed on Moscow's desk? This was *timed*, sir, and it was a show of force."

"The blast in the Donetsk office also appeared rather timed."

"Nothing links her to that. Nothing."

"You're a piece of fucking work." Guillory fished a cigarette from his pocket, lit it with a striking match, fell silent.

"It looks bad for her, I know."

Looks. Stasik pondered the word, the way that morning's events had tumbled together like jigsaw pieces. A bombing, a warrant, a raid. All in the span of a few hours.

"Who's to say Donetsk isn't still fabricating evidence?" he asked.

The implications of the remark took a moment to reach Guillory. He coughed out an exhale, set the Italian cigarette down on the lip of an ashtray.

"You think they would *bomb* their own station?" Guillory said. "What sort of dissociatives have you been taking?"

"I think it's all too convenient."

"Ah." The director lifted his cigarette, took another hard pull. "So that's why you helped her." His tone was disapproving, somehow defeated. The end of a favored agent's career, most likely.

"Do you remember our phone call?" Stasik asked.

Guillory nodded.

"They tapped it."

"Who?" He set his cigarette down and flipped to a blank notebook page. "That was a secure line, Specialist. So if what you're saying is true, then who?"

"I don't know," Stasik said. "But they had a vested interest in her, and that drives home the point, sir."

"Every division from here to Toronto has a case open for her."

"What if I told you they also tapped my radio band with the convoy driver, sir?"

Even Guillory couldn't suppress the flicker of alarm in his stare.

"That's how they knew which one to hit," Stasik went on. "I didn't help her escape, sir, but I couldn't send her into that convoy in good faith. You've got to believe me. Somebody was *trying* to take her out, and her alone."

"Let me stop you, Stasik," Guillory said. "You're speaking about a worm-can big enough to crush us both."

Stasik couldn't deny that. The elephant in the room was right there, close enough to touch—anybody able to decrypt those bands was likely using Coalition hardware. An inside job. And if he'd learned one thing over the years, it was that inside jobs never sat well with anybody, particularly those in power.

"Maybe I am," Stasik said. "We've got a lead, sir. Isn't that enough?"

"Moscow's looking at me for answers. For all we know, they were the ones tapping those lines to stay apprised."

"Then who planted those explosives, sir?"

Guillory looked away as though Stasik hadn't spoken at all. "So, you know that when I make my report, I'll need to say what you did. And what you didn't do. Maybe I can exclude Mallison from the narrative, but you just said what you said, and I can't overlook it." He sighed. "Why didn't you just fuck-ing turn her over?"

"Because she's innocent." The words were slippery, bitter on Stasik's tongue, but it was too late to take them back.

"Even if she is," Guillory replied, writing a short line of text, "so what?"

Now, he saw through Nata's eyes, staring at men who had little care for her story or her impending fate. He saw the apathy she'd feared since that morning in Donetsk.

"My duty is to truth, sir," Stasik stated.

"No. It's to the Coalition."

Stasik drew in a long breath. "Am I terminated?"

Guillory ground his jaw, then shook his head. He punctu-ated a sentence with a noisy sweep of his pen before pointing it at Stasik.

"You're on leave. You listen to me, and you listen very closely: I'm going to file a report saying that she pulled you into her bed, made some calls while you were showering off, and got herself shipped out before Virtanen could arrive. When your leave is over, you're going to go before an inquiry board and repeat that back to them. They'll slap you on the wrist. Then we'll forget all of this."

"And what about the goddamn bombing?"

"It's been swept up," Guillory said. "Whatever happens from here is up to Virtanen, maybe Moscow. But not us."

"If it was internal, it's my jurisdiction."

"*Bon chance,* if you think you'll ever prove such a notion." Guillory sighed. "Your woman was a fish. Slipped into your hands, slipped out, left a few puddles behind as payment."

The blood in Stasik's head was hot, pounding. "How could lying like that possibly sit well with you?"

"Sits better than losing you from our task force."

"What good do we actually do, then? If you think she's innocent, but we let them trample over us, what fucking *good* does IA do, sir?"

Guillory snuffed out his cigarette, wrinkled his lips. "You said she's innocent, not me."

"Do you believe she is?"

"Believe." He left the word hanging for a moment. "Have you ever heard of a lightning rod, Specialist?"

"She's a citizen of the Coalition."

"So she is," Guillory said. "Yet there will always be two evils."

"What's going to happen to her?" Stasik asked softly.

"Like I said, it's up to Virtanen's unit. If there's anything linking you to sheltering her, Specialist, I suggest you erase it *now*. They're going to bring the rain down on her."

Guillory stood, picked up his briefcase and notebook, and nodded toward the door.

"I never told you what that lead was, did I?" Stasik asked.

Guillory stopped. "Well?"

"I can't tell you precisely what it is, sir," Stasik explained, "but I know it'll blow the lid off this entire thing. Every fucking secret's gonna go up in smoke. Do you want to get a commendation from Moscow when it happens, or do you want to pretend we never had this conversation?"

Guillory scratched the side of his head. "A bird's coming for you and Mallison in two hours. Don't take it home. Go somewhere warm, somewhere pleasant. Take your mind off things."

Stasik's reply came as a whisper: "Yes, sir."

"And don't take this to heart, Henry. Everybody fucks up once or twice."

Guillory departed, leaving Stasik in the silence of his own breaths and the ventilation's humming. He waited until

Guillory's footsteps had faded, just to be sure, then deactivated his Morse implant's recorder.

———

Mallison opened her quarters' door before Stasik's second knock. She was fully dressed, made up with eyeliner and dark lipstick, glaring at him with anger she'd surely rehearsed.

"We're leaving soon," Stasik said.

"I got his call," she replied. "Where are we spending leave?"

"We?"

"I'm in no mood to visit my mum, and my sister's on holiday. So where's this happy couple going?" Mallison offered a dark smile. "Oh, you'd better believe we're a goddamn couple. We're going to have long pillow-talk sessions while you tell me everything you know about your fugitive girl. You're going to treat me like a queen and take me where I want to go. And you're paying for my holiday." She jabbed a finger into his chest. "So, yeah, we're a couple."

Stasik leaned closer, took in a hint of her cardamom perfume. "I'm going to Tartu."

"Stockholm," Mallison countered.

"What?"

"If we're meeting that whore's contact in Tartu, you'd better believe that it comes second. First, we're strolling Budapest. Then you're wining and dining me in Stockholm. Shopping in Paris. Riding horses in Tuscany. Whatever *I* want. And all the while, you'll be spilling your guts."

After a moment of silence, Stasik raised his brow. "You always said you hated horses."

"I hate your checking account more. Pack up."

CHAPTER 8

Tartu, Estonian Province
447 miles from Moscow

Before battle, there was always an air of calmness. An unnerving one, in fact, but certainly one of calmness. It was a misconception—one Jana had once held—that war was a series of relentless and frenetic engagements, offering no time to rest or think about the future in any meaningful way.

In reality, those lapses in tension were the most natural time for violence to occur. Perhaps for civilians, war seemed like a constant struggle, given the endless claps of bombing runs and propaganda leaflets sprinkled throughout the streets, or the triage hospitals always sifting through armless and legless casualties.

But Bahr had seen war, and there was always too much calmness.

The same held true in civilian affairs.

He wandered through Tartu's town hall square in another

man's replicated skin, his hands tucked into overcoat pockets and scarf wrapped into a tight coil around his neck. Men and women passed him arm in arm, laughing, grinning, their pupils engorged on a steady diet of dopamine.

Children wandered with vague awareness, their subconscious Morse processors guiding them away from traffic lanes and oncoming pedestrians, stranded in the listless daze one could only find in the latest neural stimulator chips. Even the shopkeepers stood in their doorways and waved at passersby with wide, gluttonous smiles.

The entire charade was absurd to Bahr. It was as though the masses lacked some vital sensory organ that was screaming out in alarm.

The only thing of concern for any of them, it seemed, was the possibility of rainfall later in the evening. Even that was too small an upset to put a frown on the Estonians. They were too busy pacing and gawking around the square's statue, a relatively recent Soviet installation featuring two students kissing under an umbrella's cover.

Perhaps it is best this way, Bahr thought. Ignorance was bliss, but ignorance required constant upkeep. It required good men to stomp out war and famine, to keep violence confined to the cogs that churned beneath their streets, to preach one language and one set of ethics for a common good.

Even all these years later, he remembered how he'd felt the bone-jarring rumble of the Panzer IV models on Tartu's outskirts during the War. It was a sensation he'd often recalled in dreams yet longed to forget. When men were given something to die for, they were eager to do so.

He walked on for a while, contemplating that sad truth and several others, until at the end of a nearby cobblestone road he noticed a girl with blonde hair and a pleated skirt walking alongside several other youths. She couldn't have been more than twenty. A university student, perhaps. There was something about her—the subtle dance of her hair in the wind, the sound of her giggling, the thin, black stockings on her legs, *something*—that sent his mind on a wicked tangent.

Suddenly, he wasn't in Tartu. Not in 1963 or whatever year the Morse network claimed it was. He was in the Netherlands, in Flemish fields. It was 1942, a blistering day near midsummer, when he'd seen a Dutch girl walking by herself on her way home from the market with sunburnt shoulders and muddy shoes. How she'd slowed, timid to move past him…

"Are you thinking?" Textile pulsed, rattling the memory out of its socket.

He found the machine's intrusion odd, bordering on quaint. None of the constructs he'd aided in the past had exhibited much of a sense of personality, let alone curiosity. They'd all served as silent, watchful guardians, patiently waiting until Bahr's task was finished, and providing assistance as needed.

This one was truly strange.

Bahr let out a shallow, aching breath, watched the steam curl into the wind and disperse in gray tufts. Nothing was worth disturbing the sense of peace he'd accrued over a day of travel. Such a moment—the place, the people, the blind joy—was everything worth preserving in his life. There were no higher states than love and communion. And with that realization, he walked easily past the Estonian girl, past his terrible memory of the Dutch field.

"Yes," Bahr finally replied to Textile through his implant.

"What are you thinking about?" Textile asked.

"My son," Bahr lied. *"I'd like to take him here when this is all over."*

"You love your family?"

"*Yes.*"

"*Do you care about your family more than the Coalition?*"

Bahr let the Morse code hover behind his visual cortex for a moment, delaying his answer. He knew that the AI construct was reading him, gauging his reply for future exchanges. Even the most casual reply could be misconstrued in their coding. "*No.*"

And with that, the construct's messages fell away, leaving only the square and the smiling passersby, and the world Bahr had dreamed about during the war.

A world worth killing for.

———

Several hours later, as he arranged stacks of ammunition and stainless-steel tools on a brown quilt in his hotel room, Bahr thought of reaching for the telephone. He wanted to talk to Michal and tell him about the stuffed dog he'd purchased in a souvenir shop, and to tell Jana that he loved her, although he didn't like to dwell on the idea of saying such things for the last time.

Men who gave too much significance to romance never seemed to come home from their missions. Even after reflecting on this fact, Bahr pined for their voices. He would've made the call, too, had he not leaned too far over the bed and caught a glimpse of himself—or rather, not himself—in a cabinet mirror. It was repulsive to be trapped in such an inferior shell. A temporary one, of course, but inferior nonetheless.

Inferior.

The word snagged on his consciousness. It wasn't only the word, but the branching implications it held. It was the memories it conjured. *The* memory. The one he'd worked so hard to repress through dissociatives and hypnosis sessions in Copenhagen. Now, he could envision that Dutch girl in precise, painful detail. The way she'd scowled at him and he'd lost his temper and—

Bahr caught himself before the worst of it could bubble up.

Yet the memory festered inside him, ballooning and darkening, consuming everything in his past and future and what lay between. All at once the levees of his mind shattered, flooding him with old pains and new fears, snapshots of officers' body parts strewn down a highway, men staggering out of halftracks with flames licking their bodies. He saw his father's cigarette burning a ring into his young flesh. Women cackling at him.

It was an orchestra of strange, chaotic visions, at once ethereal and terribly concrete…

Bahr eyed the handgun on the nightstand.

Just as he'd longed to reach for the telephone, he found himself reaching for the weapon, for the salvation of a single well-placed round buried in his frontal lobe.

Do it, a voice whispered. It was not a single speaker but many, all of them colliding, amplifying, screeching. *End your miserable jaunt on this Earth.*

Bahr lifted the handgun. Stared down the barrel.

These moments of crushing despair had come to him before, had taken him to his knees in churches and mass graves alike. Moments in which the world showed its true face. There was no goodness, no light, no truth. His entire life was a boyish drama, acted out for nobody and nothing.

Do it.

But as before, he let the moment resolve itself with the icy detachment of a surgeon. He let the feelings reside in him, neither surrendering nor resisting. There were more important things to consider—not least of which was his mission. His own life was a paltry sum in exchange for the preservation of peace.

Bahr sighed, set the handgun back on the dresser.

"*Well done,*" Textile streamed. "*You are more resilient than I originally anticipated.*"

"*Was that you?*" Bahr replied.

"*In a sense,*" the construct said. "*I'm unable to present anything to you that is not present in your own mind.*"

"*You wanted me to off myself.*"

"*No,*" it said, "*I needed to be certain of your mental capacity. I needed to know that you would not be broken by what you encounter.*"

"*Which is?*"

"*You cannot fathom it.*"

Bahr should have been angry at the machine, or at the very least feared it, but nothing within him rose to challenge its deception. He'd learned the futility of questioning authority long ago. The madness of it, even. Every man above him had a valuable lesson to teach, if he listened closely enough. Or construct, in the present case.

Textile's lesson was abundantly clear: That which is weak should not survive.

CHAPTER 9

Budapest, Hungarian Province
975 miles from Moscow

S tasik and Mallison's suite in Budapest was gutted, but safe.
Lightbulbs unscrewed and set aside, sofa cushions unzipped,
bathroom mirror panes pried loose and propped against thick
walls. No implants requested at check-in, and no questions asked
to the honeymoon couple, who'd stood in the lobby with hands
cupping each other's hips.

After all, they were in a barren corner of a city that hadn't
received its modernization campaign yet, wearing gaudy outfits
that hinted at the thickness of their wallets and the carelessness
of young spenders. It was all smiles, carried luggage, and a wide
berth from the attendants.

Stasik had asked their pilot to make reservations at a hotel
near Gellért Hill, but he'd had no intention of keeping them.
Charged automatically to his account, sure, but negligible when
weighed against the cost of security.

It was just past six when Mallison cracked the blinds, perched on the windowsill, and smoked her first cigarette since their departure from Warsaw. The smell of potpourri and sour wine masked the tobacco.

"So, spill," she said, glancing out across the skyline of castle ruins and nascent skyscraper projects. Searching, perhaps, for marksmen in the gloom.

Stasik thought about writing it all down. About bypassing the risk of wires and directional microphones completely, laying out Nata's case in what would surely be a dozen pages of question marks and underlined words. But every moment of delay, even during transit, had made Mallison grow a bit colder. Between partners, the sentiment was understandable enough. And now that she was so close to the truth—to *his* truth, specifically— her patience was redlining. Not even the nicotine and thebaine laces in her cigarette were enough to settle her nerves.

Stasik undid the top button of his dress shirt, sighed, dropped a codeine tablet into his wineglass. "All right."

———

Truth emerged as a torrent of names and secondhand details from Nata's testimony, presented in its entirety before Mallison could snuff out her second cigarette. He surrendered everything from the nerve gas to the opiates Nata had downed in Donetsk.

When it was finished, he drank the rest of his wine and made his way to the dresser. He found himself haunted by the notion that it was all a ploy, that a camera was pointed through the one-way vanity mirror with perfect clarity while he stared into his own haggard eyes.

"Those reports I saw on your desk," Mallison said evenly. "Were they authentic?"

Stasik nodded. "But she's not working for the nationalists."

"Right. Nationalists on the back burner for a moment. What *is* she? How many milligrams did she down, again?"

"Three."

Her eyes widened. "She's got to be some prototype, Henry."

Stasik stared at her, unblinking.

"Think about it. No way in hell she could retch those back up before they hit her bloodstream."

"Of course not, but a prototype? What does that even mean?"

Mallison sighed. "Three, maybe four years back, the Coalition bought a heap of patents from a firm in Berlin. Most of them had to do with implants: plugs for the digestive tracts, cerebral seeds, so on and so forth. My last post had a supervisor who oversaw the deal. Some of those patents counter-dosed uppers and downers."

"It's a theory, sure," Stasik said. He ran a trembling hand through his thinning hair. "That was three years ago. Some of those devices could've hit the civilian market by now, especially for the sort of cash she's packing."

"That's the thing," she said. "They didn't."

"How do you know that?"

"I got a peek at the files. Anything relating to implants was locked down and archived in intelligence vaults. Think about who'd really need that sort of thing, Henry. You think an attention addict like Danicheva doesn't want to catch another high here and there?" Mallison strung out the silence with a questioning brow, waiting. "It was relegated to *espionage* programs, so—"

"Just say it plain," Stasik cut in.

"Wish I could. See, I can't make heads or tails of what she is. But I know those files, and I know bloody well what they say. All I've got is speculation."

"What about the researchers at the firm?"

"What about them?" Mallison asked.

"They could've sidestepped the patents and worked on a commission under the table."

"Forget about them. A double-decker bus caught their taxi head-on in Normandy. Nobody survived the crash. Must've been about a month after the patents were turned over."

Stasik could hardly believe the ease with which Mallison spoke about it. As though she hadn't accepted Nata's testimony as truth, or seen the files with Smirovanov and the gas, or made any attempt to slot together a puzzle with no corner pieces.

"Somebody was covering tracks," he said softly.

"My unit oversaw those forensics," Mallison said, jabbing a finger toward him. "Everything was in order."

"I'm sure it was." He glanced back at his reflection. It didn't look any better. "Are you calling her a spy, then? For whom?"

"Full circle to the nationalists, Henry."

"A spy doesn't wire money to its employer. She's *providing* something to them, not the other way around…" He paused. Blinked at himself. "The enemy of my enemy is my friend."

"What kind of enemy is the Coalition?" Mallison asked.

He turned back to his partner. "Somebody *within* the Coalition."

The Coalition was too big to corrupt, too steeped in justice and reform and charity to ever be warped by the sort of people he was dealing with. Yet Alexei Smirovanov's face rose in his consciousness, the flesh dissolving with L56's amino-degrading effects.

"She knew about that compound," Stasik went on, "and I'll bet that account knows even more."

"*Her* account," Mallison corrected.

"In a way." He moved away from the mirror, paced near

the dining table and its half-empty bottle. "The cache in Tartu is registered to a nationalist, not her."

Mallison turned to face him. Her expression was placid, stranded somewhere between content and hopeless. "That's your theory: she's being blackmailed."

"It's possible," Stasik said. "The nationalists aren't the only ones smudging records."

"Virtanen might be crooked, but you're stretching it."

"Am I?"

"Think about what you're saying, would you?" Mallison gave a cold laugh. "You're not talking about IA's game anymore."

"Why? Because it's something big enough to *matter*? A conspiracy, even?"

"Hush," Mallison said. "Nobody's saying we're skiving off, Henry. We've nailed plenty of divisions. But this—this is a charge against the Coalition."

"Against policymakers."

"The Coalition is the first miracle we've had in half a century."

It was difficult to dispel that illusion, he admitted. All the treaties it had signed, the borders it had pacified and abolished, the industries it had sparked from the ashes of war. But anything known as a miracle was beyond reproach, and nothing in his world could ever be that sacred.

"It's operated by people," Stasik said. "And people can be exploited."

"To crack down on a model?" Mallison questioned. "Listen to yourself."

"Not just a model. I couldn't make a list for you if I tried. But the more I dig, the more I'm starting to see it: somebody or something in the Coalition is willing to use extrajudicial means when it's convenient. My task is to root that out."

Mallison lit her third cigarette, slid down into an armchair by the radiator. "There has to be something more to that nerve agent. They wouldn't just—"

"But they *did*. And I can feel it. Really, I can feel it: this is only the start. Maybe you think I've lost it, but take a step back and look at the bigger picture. Look at the reports, at how many divisions are crashing down on us."

Barking dogs and traffic horns outside filled the silence. Mallison's eyes dimmed, suddenly somber as she watched her smoke curl up and disperse. When she spoke again, her voice barely broke a whisper.

"What the fuck does she have in that cache, Henry?"

Stasik bit at his thumbnail until it bled.

"Is Guillory in on it?" she pressed.

"No." He slapped a palm onto the table. "I don't know how deep it runs, but he's not involved. He just wants things calm again."

"So he knows something."

"Do you believe me or not?"

"That someone in the Coalition has blood on their hands? I don't know, Henry. But I'll admit there's work to do. If you'd just used your *words* like a grown man—"

"What good would it have done?" he said, cutting her off. "What would've changed?"

"We'd have a fighting chance."

"For what?" he shouted. "Guillory doesn't give a damn. Something horrible is happening, and nobody gives a damn. Nobody. People are going to die, and the reports are going to look as authentic as could be, and you and I will be stamping their kill receipts with blue ink. So what?"

"You want truth," Mallison said gently, tapping her cigarette on the lip of the ashtray. "Before I was assigned to you, I heard the rumors my last department had about you. They said you'd do anything to find the truth."

"They were right."

"So quit your pissing and moaning. Truth is worth something, no matter how it's twisted."

Stasik's breaths were shallow, strained. "With or without you, I'm hitting the cache in Tartu."

"You idiot," she muttered, tossing her lighter onto the sofa. "You know I'd follow you into a furnace if our break was in there. Same way 'round, too. I'm good at what I do, and you need to trust me. So hop off your lone-wolf routine, if you please. You sound ridiculous."

He studied Mallison's slumped posture, how she curled into the armchair and glanced out at the district beyond the blinds. Suddenly she—the entire situation, in fact—seemed like his punching bag, soaking up all his frustration and recklessness without ever swinging back at him.

He exhaled. "I know."

"What's our endgame, Henry?" she asked.

"We get the truth out. We go public if we have to."

"And for your girl?"

"She's not my girl."

Mallison shook her head. "For your girl?"

"I don't know."

"We're four days from Tartu," Mallison said, taking a long pull from her cigarette and dangling her hand over the armrest. "Figure out where she winds up, or she'll pull you down, too. And I'm not keen on letting you die for some implant clinic's whore."

There was still the question of Nata and where she'd ended up, of course, but Mallison's voice smothered whatever fight was left in him. Without stimulants in his bloodstream, Stasik's thoughts on the case were no more accessible than the flitting lines of Morse code he'd seen on his unit's communication hubs.

As he stared into the wine bottle on the table, analyzing its deep burgundy color and a candle flame's phantom reflection on the glass, he realized that he hadn't thought of anything but the case since he left Warsaw. In some ways he was only a vessel for the Morse implant on his wrist, acquiring and processing data for comprehensible storage.

"Do you want some?" he asked after a moment, pouring out his next glass until it nearly overflowed. He didn't wait for Mallison's nod before he grabbed a second glass to fill. Then he dropped one codeine tablet in each.

They drank until they could barely move. Until the walls went hazy and his cheeks went numb.

Mallison talked endlessly, which wine usually did to her. He lulled in and out of attention as the opiates wore him down. He blinked and sensed her scooting closer. Her hand fell upon his thigh and she whispered something.

Stasik shifted away from her. He didn't want anyone near him. He just wanted to let his mind keep revolving around the truth he was after, picturing faces and dates and numbers. Mallison grunted words he couldn't distinguish. Then the warmth of her breath faded. Her silhouette moved to the canopy bed, slipping under heavy blankets.

He couldn't imagine sleeping with so much going on.

———

FIVE DAYS ACROSS THE CONTINENT—BUDAPEST, STOCKHOLM, Munich, and Lisbon—had bled them of everything from narcotics to conversation topics. Reaching Tartu's central landing compound took two hours in itself: one for the suborbital flight from Lisbon to Tallinn, and another for the helicopter ferry over Estonian marshes and turbine plots. By the time they arrived, lugging their bags under slowing rotor blades, they moved with silent efficiency.

It seemed fitting in a city that idolized its own peace and quaint scale. Where scarf-shrouded passersby looked as though they might shame the wind for its shrill whistling. It sat just fine with Stasik, however. They had chewed on the same topics again and again during their travels.

"After the hell I went through to ring Danicheva's contact back in Donetsk," Mallison had said as they stared at the sunset over Bavarian treetops, "I just want to see this Palmenko bastard."

"We will," Stasik had replied. They'd deliberated like that throughout the entire journey, going over everything involved, always returning to the one thing that had truly cemented: their resolve to seize that cache. Nothing else seemed important.

Their hotel room in Tartu was just south of the river Emajõgi, straddling the line between Tartu's central district and its industrial fringes. The place was plain, but more than welcome after a string of gaudy suites. Outfitted with old-world telephones, which were nearly inaccessible to the Coalition's latest tapping circuits. And, perhaps most critically, lined with windows that overlooked the surrounding streets and bridges.

The Turva Premier Vaults facility, which currently housed Danicheva's cache, was only two blocks from the hotel's rear entrance. They'd cased it twice before checking in. It was massive, paneled with matte gray squares and high black windows. Janis Palmenko would meet them there at 06:00—just before dawn, if the region's daylight information boards were accurate.

In the evening, the skies were faded violet and a light snow blew in from the north, covering the streets in a pale film. Stasik knelt over the room's coffee table with his sleeves rolled up, the disassembled bones of their handguns lying naked before him. He cleaned them to the tune of a Tino Rossi song, to Mallison's gentle humming, to the drum of his amphetamine-spurred heartbeat.

"Can you believe this shit?" Mallison asked while he was guiding the spring back into his Colt.

Stasik looked up to see what she meant. On the small boxy television screen before him was a looped video of Anastasia Danicheva smiling and posing for the adoring, faceless crowds at some Italian fashion show. It was old footage; Stasik had seen the clip his fair share of times on public billboards and media spots. But there was something new here—a large headline at the bottom of the screen, reading "WHERE IS ANASTASIA DANICHEVA?"

"Fuck," he whispered. "Tell me I'm hallucinating."

Mallison sighed. "You're not."

"Aren't there gag orders on this sort of thing? Investigative ethics?"

"First I'm hearing about it."

Stasik shook his head, switched off the television, and resumed his work.

A moment later, the phone rang.

Mallison snatched the phone off the hook, stole a passing glance through the blinds as Stasik turned around. "Hello?" She paused. "How did you get this number to begin with?"

It's Nata. He sensed it in the slow twist of Mallison's lips, the way her disdain bled into her whispers.

"Give it to me," he said.

Mallison held up a warning finger. "Where are you now?"

"Diane, pass it here."

"Hush." She settled back into the armchair, eyes flicking across the carpet as she listened.

"Right, but where are you?" she asked into the receiver. "Okay. And if—fuck." Mallison slapped the phone back onto its cradle, shook her head, met Stasik's eyes. "Yes, it was her."

He couldn't parse his own surge of adrenaline. Was it for his case, for the barest sliver of life from his client? Or was it for the possibility to see her lips again?

"Where is she?" Stasik asked, burying the thoughts. He stood, wiped his hands on a nearby rag. "Did she give you coordinates? Anything coded?"

"No," Mallison whispered. "She said not to go."

"To the vaults?"

She nodded. "For once, I'm prepared to take her words at face value."

Words within words, diversions buried within diversions. "I'm going," Stasik said, settling back on both knees before the table. "She probably thinks our lines are tapped."

"Nobody knew we were coming here to begin with," Mallison said. "Maybe they got her, Henry. Maybe she told them something."

"Tomorrow at zero-six-hundred, I'll be waiting for Palmenko."

"You're being daft."

"Are you coming or not?" Stasik dropped the trigger assembly into his handgun's frame, snapped the slide portions together. "You said it yourself. You went through hell in Donetsk to make that call and set it up. Might as well finish it."

Mallison paced back and forth across the carpets. "There's a park complex across the road," she said at last. "I'll play watchman. Set your radio to the narrow naval bands, and be ready to break if I transmit."

"If somebody turns up, they won't be alone. You can't stay there by yourself."

"So don't go in," she said. "Stake it out with me. Use your head."

Stasik stared into the oil-stained cloth beneath his pistols.

"Exactly," Mallison huffed. "You're as stubborn as they come. You'll need someone on the outside to let you know what's coming around the bend."

"You're expecting a team of amateurs."

"Henry, I don't have any expectations. This is over my head. But you need all the help you can get, I'd wager. I'll have a dicer running hot to keep our line secure."

"Don't run a dicer," he replied. "Set it to synchronize."

"What for?"

"If they have a man on the inside, I want to know who's whispering in his ear."

"Expecting it to trace back to a Coalition frequency, aren't you?" The stifled laughter in her voice said it all. "I'll sync for frequencies if it'll put a spring in your step. But don't you dare forget our protocol if I transmit."

He nodded. The complex was reasonably small, and the schematics he'd mentally assembled during his casing run meant that there was little chance of using a secondary exit. If somebody else came knocking, they'd both be squeezing through the same door.

"You think it'll turn loud in there?" he asked.

"Dunno." She sighed. "Better safe than sorry. Load both magazines."

He racked the slide, left it locked in place without a fresh round to chamber. It had been seven months since he'd drawn his firearm, and a full two years since he'd discharged it. No fatalities on record.

There's a first time for everything, he supposed.

CHAPTER 10

Tartu, Estonian Province
447 miles from Moscow

An Internal Affairs agent named Henry Peter Stasik—Morse identity code 10000973008—entered the lobby of Turva Premier Vaults at precisely 05:55. From Erik Bahr's vantage point on the far side of the marble-tiled chamber, settled into an armchair with a briefcase at his feet, his optical implants were also able to detect a second agent on the far side of the street.

Stasik's partner, Diane Margaret Mallison, paced between a pair of snow-dusted benches. There were advantages and disadvantages to their separation, but it made initial contact far simpler.

Bahr rose from his seat, gathered up his briefcase and over-coat, then nodded at the nearby desk's security guard. On a surface level, he was charmed by the fortresslike nature of the complex: its alarm-sealed doors and triple-stage locking mechanisms, its vaulted ceilings and obsidian walls, its high-profile visitors that resembled courtiers in a Spanish throne room. Below his admiration was hatred for everything contained in its depths.

Palmenko's vault was a single tumor. A symptom of far greater maladies. This was a place for tools and leverage against the Coalition, which had never been granted a warrant for any of the facility's clients.

A haven for those who raged against order.

And as he walked toward Stasik, marking the agent's hard cheekbones, prominent nose, and dark hair as expressions of Slavic ancestry, Bahr tried to read those bloodshot eyes. What evil could compel a man to deconstruct society?

"Perform your function," Textile pulsed. *"Nothing else."*

The construct had delivered him a neat Morse package of everything he needed to know to become, in a literal sense, Janis Palmenko. After all, his reproduction flesh was just one aspect of the illusion. The devil was in the details: all the passphrases he was expected to use, the way he walked, the way he smiled.

Bahr wondered how much the machine's agents had needed to torture Danicheva's account holder to find it all out. More pressingly, he wondered how the construct had managed to speak directly with the agents over a telephone line. Its vocal abilities were better than he'd anticipated—frighteningly so.

"Late morning," Bahr said to Stasik.

Stasik extended a bony hand. He seemed calm, composed, but Bahr could tell he was forcing it. He was anything but.

"Early evening," Stasik said.

"Indeed," Bahr replied, wrapping both hands around his briefcase's handle. He waited for Stasik's hand to fall away, then nodded over his shoulder. "If you'll follow me, sir."

At the security control checkpoint, Bahr's identity

chip—which had been either surgically extracted from Palmenko, or sufficiently replicated—was enough to clear them both for vault access. The security attendant brought them down a garishly lit corridor, herded them into a waiting lift, and punched an access code into the lift's terminal.

The doors slid shut.

"Anastasia must be in a sore spot," Bahr said. Textile's ever-present hum dropped away, cut off by countless layers of concrete and steel as their lift descended. "What has she done now?"

Stasik glanced at him sidelong. A glimmer of suspicion, of curiosity, but nothing specific enough to exploit. "Are you cleared to take hard copies out of the vault?"

"Well, I should think so. It's in my name, after all."

"You've never tried it?"

"I've never had much of a need. I primarily store things for her, not withdraw them." Bahr pushed his glasses further up onto his nose. The collagen layering for Palmenko's face and neck was oppressive, and despite Textile's fine work in recreating the man's features, it didn't feel anything like his flesh. He was already sweating.

"I see," Stasik said. "If we can't remove hard copies, I'll need to use a scanning station and upload the files." He paused. "They are files, aren't they?"

"Oh, mostly," Bahr said. "Anastasia didn't tell you the contents?"

"I'm not able to discuss our exchanges."

A true professional. "Yes, of course," Bahr said. "Truth be told, I've been waiting for this day for some time. If only it were under better circumstances."

The briefcase containing Palmenko's key was cradled against his thighs, held as though he were a sheepish intern reporting for his first day. He coughed, gave the briefcase a faint sweep to the left. Hard leather brushed against the polymer holster on Stasik's belt to confirm its location. "If only."

————

THE VAULTS WERE LIKE A DEAD, ANCIENT CITY. WHETHER DUE to their early arrival time or the long-term nature of storage in the facility, they were the only inhabitants.

Each vault stood like its own cubical shrine in the heart of Mecca, a reflective black monument to private wealth and sedition. They were all nearly a dozen meters in both length and width, a few tons at the least. No way for Bahr to burn or blast his way into the storage units, as he'd learned from Textile's schematics.

The ceilings ascended into total darkness laced with neon blue filaments and temperature sensors blinking in the void. Ahead and behind and to either side was an aisle with neither beginning nor end. Every footstep echoed like rolling thunder.

"This is her vault?" Stasik asked.

Bahr glanced back, saw the agent standing one row behind him. He was surveying an input terminal with umbilical wires trailing from its underside, his face bathed in a cool blue glow by the keypad. Just above his head, affixed to the crest of the vault cube's doorway, was the crucial number: 780-2.

"Indeed it is," Bahr said, approaching the keypad. "If you'll kindly enter the code that Anastasia provided?"

Stasik didn't blink. "We'll need her key."

"Ah, yes," Bahr replied, "but that's for the secondary locking mechanism. The code is entered first." He hefted the briefcase up, smiled. "The key is in here; I'll get it out while you're working on the terminal?"

After granting the agent a moment to begin the input

sequence, Bahr turned away, rested the briefcase on black tiles, undid the dual clasps.

Stasik's fingers moved over the keypad. *Beep, beep.*

Tucked into custom-fitted velvet cushioning was Textile's parting gift: a Czech Sa. 25 with a shortened bolt and barrel, no stock, a fifteen-round magazine loaded and chambered.

Beep, beep.

In the gloom, Bahr could hardly make out its graceful curves, which meant that the agent, by comparison, would be entirely oblivious. Bahr pried the submachine gun from the briefcase, shouldered it in a tight crouch.

Beep, beep. The last digits.

Bahr pivoted on his heels and angled the Sa. 25 toward Stasik's chest, but the terminal's whine of denied entry paralyzed his trigger finger, left him staring at shadows and beads of sweat on Stasik's face. Stillness fell over the vault chamber in a rain of dry kindling, ignited by the faintest breath or limb movement.

"This is unfortunate," Bahr said, carefully rising from a kneeling shooter's stance and examining Stasik through his submachine gun's sights. "Did your fingers slip?"

"No." Though Stasik's head remained fixed forward, his gaze met Bahr's.

"Do you even have the code?" Bahr asked.

"We can offer you amnesty," Stasik said. "I'm not here on the Coalition's behalf. I'm here for her, so whatever you've done is not my concern."

Bahr smiled. "Oh, but it is. I'm not interested in amnesty."

"Why did you burn her?"

"Burn her? You think we betrayed one of our own?"

It was a natural conclusion for an agent who assumed he was speaking with a nationalist, but there was a deeper curiosity in Stasik's voice. Something unexpected and decidedly personal.

Not an investigator seeking motives, perhaps, but rather a man seeking logic. Yet Bahr had learned that the most dangerous men acted in pursuit of their convictions.

"What makes you think we *burned* her?" Bahr questioned.

"If she still trusted you, she would've provided the code," Stasik answered.

"And why would she trust you?" Bahr took a step back, tucked the submachine gun's shortened stock closer to his body.

"If you're going to shoot me, then shoot me."

Textile's orders reverberated in his head, still fresh from the barn outside Minsk: *You will secure the cache.* All fifteen of the magazine's snub-nosed rounds would end up in the agent once he surrendered the entry code.

Then, and only then.

"If you'd kindly enter the code," Bahr whispered.

"What the hell do you want with her vault?" Stasik asked, laying both hands on the terminal. "The Coalition isn't coming for you, they're coming for her. Whatever investigations they're launching are smoke and mirrors."

"One might almost take your words as treason."

"As if that matters to you," Stasik said quietly. "Whatever evidence she's storing is against the Coalition."

Bahr's index finger cradled the trigger. "Enter the code, please."

"What evidence implicates you, Janis? Tell me that before you kill me."

"If you open her vault, we'll both find out."

Stasik's lips tightened. "You've never seen the inside of her vault." A joyless smirk came over him, warped to something sinister by the shadows. "Now I see why she called us."

"Called you?" Bahr cocked his head to the side. "Ah, I understand. Well, botching the code entry was a very clever maneuver, but it did nothing to prevent the current situation. You should plan a follow-up for every action you take."

"How does Anastasia call herself?"

"Come again?"

"Her name."

Bahr took a long breath, combing his implant's passive knowledge banks. He pulsed through the diminutives in the Slavic tongue: Nastya, Natya, Anna, Tasha… no, she was an icon from Krasnodar. Far too formal for any of that. A trick.

"Anastasia, of course," he said.

Mechanical whirring somewhere far in the distance underscored their silence. At last Stasik nodded, set his fingers on the terminal's pad.

"For a moment I thought they'd gotten to you." Stasik sighed. "You're jumpier with that thing than I remember, Janis."

Textile hadn't anticipated that. An agent and a nationalist locked in partnership? It was everything his handlers feared, an axis far more insidious than anything the Third Reich had ever concocted, suspected behind closed doors but never bolstered by any concrete evidence.

Until now, perhaps. Until Anastasia Danicheva's vault was opened.

"If you'll lower that thing, I can do my half of the job," Stasik said.

"I just had to be sure," Bahr said with a warped smile. The Sa. 25's barrel dipped in a smooth arc, hovering a half meter above the tiles. "They can get to you, too. You never really know who turns up to these rendezvous points."

"No, you really don't." Stasik scrunched his brow, worked to punch in the proper code.

The door shuddered and unsealed with a hiss as he finished.

Wisps of compressed air began filtering out. The mesmerizing tendrils of a mission complete…

Stasik twisted at the hip, drew, and fired.

Bahr processed it all fast enough to dodge the first shot. The agent's second round caught him in the stomach, its muzzle flash persisting as an afterglow in his vision. He staggered back, barely able to lift the submachine gun through the wound's ache.

He squeezed off four rounds in automatic succession without aiming. It was an instinctive drill, designed to fight fire with fire before any conscious thinking set in.

Sparks leapt off the tiles. Supersonic claps rolled through the chamber. But there were no soft, squelching sounds, only the clang of metal on metal. Stasik wasn't hit.

Legs shaking, Bahr fired another two shots and backed around the corner of the vault cube. His morphine and epinephrine implants were already responding to the sharp pain in his abdomen, flooding him with focus and dulling the agony. Blood-clotting hormones surged in his arteries. Stasik shouted something, but the pulse in his ears throbbed too loudly to hear it.

The hunt had begun.

CHAPTER 11

S tasik patted himself down, searching for where he'd been shot. His ears still rang from gunfire—his own or Palmenko's imposter, he couldn't tell—and the blackness at the edge of his vision was all-consuming. The morning's Pervitin dose focused his sight to the narrow slats of neon ahead and above.

He tilted his hands back, fumbling until he nudged the *transmission* tab on his left wrist's Morse implant. "Mallison," he said. In his own ears it was a whisper, impossible to measure through the constant ringing. "Mallison, call it in."

Static.

He let off the tab. Then he sidled along the cube's wall, tightening his grip on his pistol.

It had been a genuine mistake to punch in the code, and an amateur one at that—muscle memory had hijacked his fear, pushed the code sequence through to completion while he thought about the approaching violence.

You fucking idiot, he scolded himself.

At least he was certain he'd hit the imposter, if not with both shots then at least one. But there was no way to judge how much damage he'd actually done. In addition to his standard-issue rounds being relatively low velocity, he didn't trust his own shot groupings, which had been decidedly subpar from his first days in the academy.

Stasik figured he had equal chances of finding the imposter either coughing up blood on the tiles or waiting around the corner with a full magazine. Judging by the man's weapon and apparent lack of violence-induced nausea from his implant, which was enough to bring any normal civilian to their knees, he was a professional.

When Stasik reached the cube's edge, he swung his Colt to the wall's lip and ducked his head out to scan for immediate movement.

About a dozen rows ahead was the central lift they'd taken from the lobby, glowing like a Chinese paper lantern in the darkness. It was a direct run from the row where he'd fired on the imposter, but that only heightened the issue: The shooter would probably have a straight shot at his back. But what other option did he have?

Stasik stole another peek at the elevator and its open doors. He'd been a sprinter in high school—a prime pick for the intervention units if he'd been of age—but the years had ruined his training schedule. Even so, he was a better runner than a shooter.

The ringing in his ears faded, leaving behind silence as cold sediment. No footsteps, no gasping, no metal clinking. It was time.

Stasik crept away from the cube's wall and spun around,

keeping his Colt steadied with both hands and his elbows nearly locked. Step by step he moved backward, taking care to avoid dragging his feet or brushing the sides of the vault at his back. When he'd moved far enough to reach a new row toward the elevator, he quickened his steps to a smooth rhythm, moving faster and faster until—

His right heel scraped across the tiles with a dry screech.

A silhouette swept past a stack of neon filaments, sent resonating footsteps through the chamber. Gunfire erupted with deafening crackles, a string of *pop-pop-pop* blasts that tore into the cube walls and washed out Stasik's hearing.

He crouched and threw himself to the left, scrambling over tiles as the rattling continued and whistled past. The sensor panel near his hands exploded with a spurt of white flames, echoes racing past him and morphing into howls into the darkness.

Blue neon tubes throughout the chamber darkened to crimson.

Stasik pulled himself fully behind the cube and struggled to his feet. Tremors wormed through his legs and wrists, but his vision was crisper than ever. Leading with the Colt's barrel, he peered around the corner and spotted a kneeling figure, arms twisted at odd angles as he switched out magazines.

Stasik aligned the sight tabs of his Colt, braced his wrists, then let off four rapid shots.

The gun's muzzle flash was a candle's flame in his retina, stamped onto his vision like a watermark. It blotted out the straight row before him and the space where the shooter had been throughout the burst.

Within seconds, his vision sharpened. The row was empty, but now speckled with fresh blood.

"Put your weapon down and come out!" Stasik screamed. "Throw it out here."

His hearing was too dampened to catch any replies, if they came. Instead, he trained his eyes on the imposter's most likely position: the corner of a cube closest to the blood trail. From time to time he swiveled his aim to the cube's rear corner, which would be the imposter's ideal flanking option. He counted the seconds in his head, waiting for movement.

Forty-five, forty-six, forty—

Light spilled down the row to Stasik's left, expanding outward from a central line. A new elevator car was arriving. Black blurs and distorted shadows played across the light, painted with what appeared to be a half-dozen silhouettes pouring out of the car, all jagged with the outlines of batons and rifle barrels. Boots thudded across the tiles, emanating from Stasik's rear and growing closer.

Reinforcements.

But he couldn't tell for whom.

Stasik slid down to a crouch and moved further behind the corner, listening as the steps padded past him and cut toward the imposter's position. Their flashlights were illuminating the bloody tiles, sweeping up toward the rafters and back down the adjacent rows.

"Disarm!" a voice shouted, perhaps two rows away from Stasik. The command was repeated by each of the officers in turn, mingled with footsteps and radio static. "Disarm, disarm!"

Stasik shrank away down the adjacent aisle. The security officers were bunching into a unit near the litter of spent shell casings, their lights converging on the bloodstain and a figure hidden behind the cube's corner, which Stasik could only assume to be the target himself.

For a moment he thought to assist the security forces, but it would've been wasted. Who could say who'd fired on whom? He wasn't even supposed to be here.

Stasik hurried past another intersection and turned back, catching a glimpse of the imposter wandering out of hiding and into the web of flashlight beams. He saw the shortened barrel of his automatic rifle rising, steadying, and—*pop, pop, pop!*

Two of the security guards returned fire, though it was anybody's guess as to whether the shots came from reflexes or a spasm of the index finger at their moment of death. Their rounds failed to connect.

The imposter was luckier. He dropped to the tiles and let off three shots. One officer's head snapped back with a spray of pink mist, left him staggering drunkenly for two steps before he collapsed. Another remained upright, plunged into shock from the trauma and blood loss, baton wavering in his hand like a child fending off a starved dog. Red neon framed the imposter as he shouldered his weapon and fired, shearing off most of the man's jaw.

The final guard was sprawled out on his stomach, moaning loud enough to overcome Stasik's ringing ears. The man's fingers scratched at the tiles separating his hand from a fallen rifle. A hair closer, and he might've made it.

One hair.

The imposter limped to the guard and pressed his gun to the back of their head. After a moment of soundless waiting, the imposter withdrew his gun, pulled back the bolt, and hefted his shoulders with a hard sigh. He gently set the gun down.

He's empty, Stasik realized. He counted his own shots, recalling them as violent pops in his memory: four, five, six. One round left in the Colt. Stasik fumbled for his second magazine, which was still tucked into the pouch on his holster and—

"Fuck," he hissed, spotting it near the corner of the cube where he'd dove and crawled. Directly in the line of fire.

The imposter lingered over the guard, raised his knee, and

centered his shoes over the man's neck. Then he stomped down with a *thud* that resonated through the tiles and into Stasik's soles. He lifted his leg, stomped again. Again, again, again. Until the impacts were wet and muted.

Stasik's hands trembled too badly to even extract the near-empty magazine. He aimed the Colt with straight arms, widened his stance, focused his breathing to align the sight tabs on the imposter's silhouette. His heartbeats were wild, irregular. He could hardly breathe.

Just as Stasik's finger curled on the trigger, the imposter bent down and retrieved the dead man's rifle. He aimed it in a wide arc until its muzzle swept over the stretch of darkness concealing Stasik.

The amphetamines made it impossible to piss himself, but the urge remained. With a wheezing breath, he let off the trigger, fell against the wall nearest to him. Wisps of his father's words about cowardice and bravery and foolishness came over him, but he shut them out.

He hobbled toward the crimson streak of the elevator shaft like his guiding star. With his adrenaline burnt off, there was only hollow-leg exhaustion, panic cycling through him, a string of contingency plans falling apart. When he reached the elevator car, he stared out at the endless grid of neon-lit vaults.

Nata's vault was open. Empty.

The doors closed and the elevator lifted. Stasik's legs were so weak that he braced himself against the wall with one hand. The other went to his chest. His heart had never hammered like this. His ribs felt like they were going to break apart.

"Now?" Mallison's voice crackled through the radio in his jacket, fading in as the elevator doors parted to reveal an empty lobby. "Now? Come in, for fuck's sake."

The ringing in Stasik's ears had quieted somewhat. He raised his wrist, tingles worming from his palm to his fingers, and transmitted through his Morse implant.

"Diane, he's got it," he said, a hoarse whisper under the wall-mounted alarms. He glanced at the security checkpoint, spotted a lone attendant huddled under the desk with his eyes shut and ears covered.

Mallison muttered a *fuck* that was only half-muted. "You were radio dark."

"It's not Palmenko," Stasik huffed. He staggered out of the lift, caught himself on a wall. "I don't know who it is, but it's not him. He's got her cache. I fucked up, Diane. I really fucked it up."

"We'll sort it out," she said. "Right now, just get clear."

"Are they outside?"

"Not yet, but every Coalition band in the city is lighting up, Henry. They're sending four units, maybe five—they should be able to corner him in there. Any word on the vault's security handling this?"

"It'll be too late." Stasik moved to the front door, saw Diane staring back at him near a bisecting alleyway. Coalition sirens came through the glass as muffled, ethereal hums. "He's got her vault. He's got *everything*."

"You run into any other exits?"

"None."

He pushed through the door, drank a frigid breath. A sweep of his right hand gestured to a service road near the park; Mallison was quick to catch the cue and jog in that direction. Crowds swarmed around Stasik, lured to the sound of the alarms.

"He's not nationalist, Mallison," Stasik said. "I know he isn't."

She locked eyes with him from across the road, shot a glance back at the sirens and clogging streets.

"Next time you should listen to your girl," she said.

Again, Stasik thought of the vault and its contents, how far he'd gone just to feel powerless, to lose everything he'd worked toward in ten minutes. Most of all, how he was ignorant once again.

"They won't get him," Stasik transmitted. "He's a professional."

"Cross the road."

"They won't get him."

"Hush," Mallison shot back, cutting toward the service road. "Pick up your feet."

He halted, turned on his heels as the first squadron of Coalition response vehicles pulled up onto the curb: black Ford Consuls, their glass tinted and bulletproof. Everything he needed was inside. If he could've put that one round through the fucker's head—

The blast was the first thing he felt. A hard pulse that kicked through the sidewalk's concrete and oscillated the facility's windows for a moment, leaving them with snaking cracks from top to bottom.

A quarter second later, the *bang* cracked the air. The windows blew out, muddy smoke and glowing metal flakes forming a roiling cloud that consumed the Coalition vehicles in a matter of seconds.

There was a sudden screech of steel on steel, followed by the gavel-slam of an elevator car striking its base. The vault's only access point was out of service.

"Henry!" Mallison's voice cut into his awareness, and only then did he realize she'd called his name several times. "Would you *move*?"

"It's gone," he transmitted softly. "He won."

Then Mallison was at his side and yanking his sleeve, shouting in a distant sort of way, fighting to pull him across the road as the sirens grew louder. She had their dicer box tucked beneath her arm.

"Whoever it was, I got his handler's Morse frequency," she shouted in his ear. "So it's not over if you'll just pick up your fucking feet."

The frequency. It was the trail of breadcrumbs in a dark forest, a wax seal stamped onto a license to kill. Their next, best, and only lead.

He followed Mallison.

CHAPTER 12

According to Textile's most probable simulation, it would take the Coalition teams just shy of two hours to enter the ravaged vault complex. They'd be delayed by falsified broadcasts warning about potential secondary blasts, the need for a specialized ordnance team, the collection of descent gear for the inoperable elevator shaft, and the ample caution required to sweep an area that might still be hostile.

Yet it only took Bahr ten minutes to scan the target vault's contents, running each item across his Morse implant's reader strip, then set the composite charges on the elevator's motor lines. He'd collected about twenty pages from Danicheva's vault, and he'd shown professional restraint in declining to read any of them. Not that he could've broken their encryption key, of course.

Scan, burn.

Rinsed and repeated.

Textile had also proven invaluable with the evacuation schematics. The city's wartime bomb shelters were a network of tunnels separated from the vault chamber by three meters of still-curing concrete, which certainly hadn't been reinforced to handle a combination of shaped charges and exothermic paste.

In the eastern wing of the tunnels, Textile's whispers returned. The Morse began as faded symbols flitting past Bahr's awareness between lanes of wire-mounted emergency lights. Gradually, it developed into full words, into sentences, into commands.

"*Send the information.*" Textile pulsed.

"*Not now,*" Bahr replied. "*They may have localized tracers running. I'll be at the departure point within the hour.*"

"*SEND THE INFORMATION.*"

"*You won't get a thing unless I take something to augment my blood clotting. While we're on the topic, you ought to arrange some emergency medical services. These implants won't keep a failing kidney going.*"

"*Do you value your own life above the Coalition?*"

His mind gripped the question like tacks in a bare palm. "*No.*"

"*If you grant me remote access to your storage sector, then all will be well.*"

"*Your simulations don't see them stealing the signal?*"

"*It is not a concern.*"

Bahr clenched his side, the tips of his fingers worming into his abdomen's bullet wounds and plugging them shut. His pain-blunting implants were efficient, but not miraculous—sooner or later, they'd be overwhelmed by firing neurons and begin to malfunction.

"*I'll transmit in an hour,*" he said. "*Be ready, you glorified typewriter.*"

It took all his willpower to ignore Textile's response of dotted and dashed rage.

———

LATER THAT MORNING, BAHR SAT ON A SPARKLING-CLEAN TOILET in the Tartu train station's public lavatory. His stall's wooden door rattled, and the silhouettes of passenger cars flickered past the upper windows.

He groaned and leaned forward, holding his breath to apply the final layer of his undershirt's strips on the wound grouping. Most of the blood on his shoes had been washed away by street puddles, and concealing the stains on his torso had been as simple as buttoning up his blazer and overcoat.

With the exception of a mild limp, he'd been practically invisible in Tartu's morning crowd. He'd even stopped to admire the water tower adjacent to the railway. Scraping off Palmenko's collagen coating in the stall had been as tedious as ever, but hardly a challenge.

CHAPTER 13

Presently, Bahr tied off his final knot and stood, drawing sharp, quick breaths to gauge how well he'd secured the makeshift bandages. Most of the Luftwaffe's field medics would've struck him upside the head for his work, but it would suffice until the next station. There, he could purchase disinfectants and enough amphetamines to bolster his fading pain-blunting implants.

All things considered, he felt well enough. Well enough to finish his task.

Hard-soled shoes clacked through the lavatory, passing Bahr's stall. An elderly man, most likely. The door of the adjacent stall squealed and a latch mechanism clicked. The man shuffled as he undid his belt.

"*Take his Morse chip,*" Textile streamed.

"*He's an old man,*" Bahr said. "*I'll find another way out.*"

"*Do it, or I'll make you.*"

He could feel Textile's tendrils worming into him, its signals emanating from the neural stimulator at the back of his skull. It had taken control of his body before, but that had been several generations ago, back before the construct had its own name, its own identity.

"*Don't do this,*" Bahr pulsed.

But the machine's influence continued to spread, thickening within him, binding him to the horrid task ahead. Bahr's awareness collapsed inward and receded until there was only a pinprick of light, a mere taste of the outside world. Everything else was Textile, only Textile. Every nerve was a slave to the construct's will.

Textile raised his hand, made him blink, tensed his thigh muscles. He screamed, but there was no sound. Yet behind the veil he could feel their boundaries, could sense where Textile ended and his own mind began. He pushed, clawed, scratched at it, struggling until he could breathe within its grasp, until he could feel through his own flesh again, flailing for a way out...

"*You're getting better,*" Textile said, easing its grip in gradual increments. "*I trust I won't need to resume control. Now do your work.*"

Bahr trembled as the numbness faded and his body—limb by limb—came back under his control. Eventually, he rubbed his face, sighed, leaned against the bathroom stall separating him from the old man. "I'm sorry to trouble you. Have you got any extra tissue? It seems I've run out."

"Oh," the man said. A long pause followed, broken by the jostling of a metal buckle. A varicose-stricken hand appeared below the stall's divider, holding a wad of toilet paper.

Bahr seized the man's wrist, winced at the animal shriek that followed.

He took no pleasure in his work.

———

At 8:05, Bahr boarded the train toward the airport in Tallinn, the Estonian province's capital, using the old man's Morse identifier. Walter Mikkel, sixty-four years old. The inside of Mikkel's briefcase was soaked in blood due to the crudely extracted Morse device and the scraps of wrist flesh clinging to its underside. Nevertheless, it had carried enough oxygenated blood to remain usable for several minutes, allowing Bahr to scan the device through the briefcase as he boarded.

That was the fatal security flaw in the wrist-based chip units, he supposed—anybody could get their hands on them. In fact, he'd mentioned that to the constructs several times while in their employ. It had to be a matter of cost.

He himself had been outfitted with one of the models reserved for Coalition agents: installed behind the neck, patched into two-way channels, capable of overriding anything from a coffee dispenser to a suborbital shuttle.

It was dangerous to give that power to any old stranger.

CHAPTER 14

Tartu, Estonian Province
447 miles from Moscow

Their hotel room had a two-meter luxury television mounted on the wall opposite the sofa, but Stasik streamed the regional news bulletins directly into his consciousness. He had neither the mood nor energy for visual stimulation.

"… *Coalition officials are still scouring the blast zone and Turva premises for additional evidence, although the initial public release suggests that the incident was the result of an electrical malfunction. Thankfully, aside from minor injuries to lobby personnel, there were no casualties at the scene. Updates will arrive in forty-five minutes.*"

The words dissolved into raw Morse transmissions before slipping away, leaving Stasik facing a grid of white tiles and spotless porcelain fixtures. He was slumped against the wall beside the toilet, having already vomited three times—a consequence of a new narcotic regimen, he assured Mallison—before leaning back and embracing the bathroom's chill yet familiar calmness.

Guillory would be calling them soon, he imagined. The narcotics made it difficult to ignore all his mistakes. The magazine he'd dropped in the vaults, his exposed face before the security cameras, his involvement in a firefight that ended with a half-dozen Coalition men dead and a professional killer on the run. But if trees fell in a forest and nobody was around to hear it, did it ever really happen?

If men died in a vault and nobody reported their deaths, was there any blame?

Stasik gripped the toilet seat's edges, gave a dry, silent heave that coated his mouth with sweet saliva.

"Are you sorted?" Mallison called through the door.

She'd given him nearly an hour of silence after hearing what had transpired in the vaults, but it seemed that they both sensed the urgency of what was approaching.

"We'll need a better spot for trying to tap into their communication frequencies," Mallison said. "Either they're not transmitting, or it's too far out."

He wiped his lips on a nearby hand towel. "They might've mobilized already."

"Maybe. Who do you think he's talking to?"

"Nobody good," he said.

"Clearly." There was a soft scrape as Mallison leaned against the door. "Maybe it is just a range problem. If we can get to a broadcast hub and patch into it, we might be able to boost our own dicer's signal strength. That would put them on our map for sure. But we really need to move, Henry."

"I know."

"And I didn't get a chance to tell you before," she said. "You're alive. I'm glad for it, I mean."

Stasik cleared his throat. "I'll be out in a few minutes."

"We're going to get him. You know that, don't you?"

He could've had the shooter resting on a stretcher, arms folded over one another like a pharaoh. He could've had Nata's evidence in a beige folder. He could've had it all worked out, slotted together like the monstrous jigsaw he'd been visualizing in fifteen-minute naps all week.

But he had nothing.

"Do you have any leads on a broadcast site?" he asked after a moment.

"Just one," Mallison replied. "No guarantees you'll like it."

———

AND INDEED, HE DIDN'T. MALLISON PLACED THE CALL TO Guillory while Stasik processed an order for two suborbital flights to Vilnius, all the while possessed by the sense that he was a fugitive turning himself in. But as he learned during the rough, cramped drive to the airport, there was some prudence in Mallison's design.

"Guillory hadn't heard about Tartu," Mallison explained as they took off, staring out at the white-capped trees across a field.

"Is he pissed?" Stasik asked.

"Isn't he always?"

He let a nervous titter slip through his chapped lips.

"More than anything, he wants to know what the hell we're doing," Mallison continued. "All ears, it sounded like."

All Stasik could manage was a grunt in response. The shuttle screamed into the sky, pressure mounting in his chest, and he tried to forget the world below. The world. It was a concept now, a stand-in for the blue pearl beyond the frosted viewport, which was bright and vast and pockmarked by the black swarms of photoreceptive panels that the Coalition had deployed in the mesosphere. Nobody, not even Stasik, knew what those panels did. He'd heard theories that they controlled the weather.

He wondered how the world might look in a hundred years, a thousand. But when the shuttle reached altitude and leveled off, with soles rising off the floor panels and ties billowing up, Stasik shut his eyes and tried to dream of Nata. Of her turning up safe, alive.

It was no use; he only managed to hallucinate that Mallison was holding his hand on the armrest.

———

SECURITY LED STASIK AND MALLISON THROUGH THE INTERNAL Affairs Department's flagship compound in Vilnius. Everything inside was clean, sterile. Faces were composed. Coffee was hot and always waiting. Writhing beneath that veneer, however, was the knowledge that the majority of the department despised him. Stasik had gone to great lengths to force Guillory to reveal the annual interdepartmental surveys, poring over documents the director labeled "fuel for a worthless fire." Pages that termed him a sociopath, a traitor, a threatening presence. The truth.

Guillory was hunched over at his desk when they entered. He had a telephone glued to his ear and sleeves rolled up to his elbows, showing off sun-faded ink that wove up and down his wrists, blotches of melanoma he hadn't bothered to treat at the clinics. A half-finished Italian cigarette smoldered in his ashtray.

"Yes, yes," he mumbled, barely sparing a glance at Stasik and Mallison as they settled into the waiting chairs. His eyes fell back to the report in front of him. "Very well. Tomorrow." He hung up, stared at them.

Stasik adjusted his tie. "Good evening."

"Do you know who that was?" Guillory asked. He fished the cigarette from his ashtray and took a short drag.

"Rhetorical, I'd wager," Mallison said. "Must be Tartu or your mistress."

Guillory's jaundiced eyes fell on Stasik. "Will you slap her, or should I?"

"The mistress," Mallison said.

"It was Dregala." Guillory spoke through his teeth. "*My* superior."

Stasik's eyes were flickering now, spasming with a narcotic cocktail he could hardly recall downing in the plane's bathroom. A breakfast of opiates and Pervitin tabs, unless he managed to get his hands on anything else.

"Something about Tartu?" Stasik asked.

"It's really like déjà vu," Guillory said. There was a coy edge to his lips, some absurd humor that Stasik must've misinterpreted in the psychoactive flood. "My agents—not that they should be agents, of course, since I suspended them—were back on the beat. And it's even more like last week than I thought possible. It seems that my department's top specialist was involved in a shooting. He was in a fucking *shoot-out* in the basement of a sovereign business. And do you know whose property was damaged there?"

"Did they tell you about the dead men?" Stasik asked. For once his eyes had the necessary clout to push back on Guillory, ruining his baiting game. "Please tell me they didn't burn any corpses, sir."

"Their families are being handled," Guillory said.

"What does that even mean?"

"Marks," Guillory said. "Vacations. Cosmetic clinic allowances. What the fuck do you expect from the Tartu department, Specialist? Even if the Coalition said Christ were real, he doesn't work for us. Bodies remain bodies."

"They weren't even reported."

"What would you prefer?" the director asked, one brow straining upward. "You want to see the streets in panic, Specialist?"

"I want people to be informed."

"Very well. Let's go back to old times. They can read about some sod's mutilation half a world away, maybe worry that their family will be next."

"There's a difference between fearmongering and the truth," Stasik whispered.

"Is there?" Guillory asked, coughing. "They're both used to push an angle."

Stasik clenched his jaw. "There's no *angle* to push with murder, sir."

"The angle is that you're a wild dog on my payroll. The boys in the Wing might start thinking you're going to Buenos Aires."

"But now we have a fugitive," Mallison said. "Quite a real one, too."

"Killers are always dealt with, sooner or later." Guillory shrugged. "My responsibility is for you." He nodded at Stasik, then Mallison. "And you."

"Sir, this is two cities in a row with bodies piling up," Stasik said. "How much longer is this going to stay under wraps?"

"It depends on your discretion, or lack thereof."

"We had a lead to follow," Stasik said.

"Lawfully?" Guillory asked. "No, no. You went on a hunt in the middle of a populated area while you were meant to be on leave. Own up to that, Specialist."

"For better or worse, we flushed out a man who's undoubtedly hunting my client. *Our* client, sir. What we saw today is enough to convince me that Anastasia Danicheva is being framed, or at the very least is a victim of circumstance. And there are very dangerous, likely powerful, men who want to see her ruined. You'd have to be blind not to see the dots between this and what happened in Donetsk."

"Specialist," Guillory said to Mallison, "thoughts on your partner's theory?"

For a moment Mallison stared straight back at the director, perhaps doing her best to conceal the twitch in her lips. She glanced sidelong at Stasik.

"Still valid, sir," she said.

Guillory's silence was haunting, cold. At last he settled back in his chair and took another pull, holding it high in his chest. "Tartu called me two hours ago. This call was from an echelon so high you can't imagine it. He's asking me to advance the inquiry in light of your escapades, and Specialist Mallison's now a second headline for the circus. Rumor is that they're going to ask the Judicial Wing to file six new charges against your *client*, too. It's hard to say I don't find it justified."

"Oh, ye of little faith," Mallison hissed. "I've no idea what's going on in Stasik's head half the time, but someone came crashing down on him in Tartu. Now there's a waiting line for their coroner's slab."

"Who would've guessed that a known nationalist could turn violent?" Guillory countered. "Especially one who appears to be a *partner* of one of my agents."

"Partner?" Mallison asked, her back arching. "Are you daft, sir?"

"Not my words," Guillory replied. "The Wing sees it that way. Could just be that they don't want to make a scandal by arresting him on sight. They want it done formally."

"What evidence is there?" Stasik asked.

"Known associations with the suspected nationalist Anastasia Danicheva, your entrance into the vaults as a pair, the mess below ground… suddenly your client's vault is empty, and you both fuck off in separate directions. So, Mallison, what about those dead men?"

Stasik's blood ran hot and thick, pressure creeping across his forehead. "I didn't kill anybody."

"Not the *you* that I know," Guillory said. "I pushed back on their arrest order, Specialist. But for how long? Good faith alone isn't enough in this world, eh?"

"He nearly killed me," Stasik snapped. "That wasn't Palmenko. It's an imposter, sir."

"Allow me to show you the camera footage."

"Fuck the footage! It's a mask, makeup—I don't know. But it's not him. You test the scene's bloodstains and flakes and run it against Palmenko's file, and it'll come up *wrong*. This man knew nothing about Danicheva."

"So why did they come?" Guillory pressed.

"For her *vault*." Stasik gripped the armchair's edges until his fingertips blanched. "They wanted to destroy something. Something that I needed to help defend my client."

"When's this inquiry?" Mallison asked.

Guillory peeled back the edge of a nearby paper, raised a graying brow. "Supposed to be two days, but I can appeal for up to five."

Mallison shook her head. "You said that you trust him. That means you trust us. Are you planning on acting as our defense?"

Stasik's chin sank to his chest as his Morse implant fed him information. "Section 54, subsection 17: Direct Action Inquiries must exclude support from internal directors."

"This is a fucking witch hunt," Mallison cursed. "You won't even test those bloodstains?"

"Now, I never said that," Guillory replied, snubbing out the last of his cigarette.

"You're not our defense."

"Section 54, subsection 29, Specialist," Guillory said.

Stasik's mind burrowed through lines of Morse that his brain translated in rapid cycles to speech. "You could file for an amended department position on our behalf," he realized.

Mallison sighed. "Meaning?"

"The Judicial Wing can't cancel a DAI," Stasik said, lifting his head. "They won't do it, anyhow. But we can bring every shred of this evidence to bear on a live feed from the courtroom."

"Evidence of a third party won't do much to save her," Mallison said. "Your girl is dead to rights. What does it matter if they nail her on treason rather than terrorism?"

"If there's been any sort of interference in her actions, then it means a world of difference."

"We haven't got a chance in hell of proving that."

"Not right now, we don't."

"My, you two have a little flame between you," Guillory said.

Grimacing at that, Mallison leaned forward and cleared her throat. "Let us get what we need." She averted her eyes as the potential sting from her tone set in. "Please."

"It's not so simple," Guillory replied.

"If the Wing's paying attention, it ought to be. We have the evidence to push it forward. All we need to do is connect the dots."

"The Wing doesn't care for speculation."

"Speculation is what we've got," Stasik said sharply. "Whoever's behind the blood in Tartu and Donetsk has deep pockets, and that alone ought to be making headlines."

"Be careful whose pockets you're jangling, Specialist."

"Always am."

The director rubbed his stubble with a crooked hand, eyes creeping along the table's mounds of evidence and inquiry forms. "No, not always."

Stasik caught the wry implications in Guillory's tone. It had been two years since Stasik had nailed corruption charges to a Judicial Wing councilman in Brussels, but bruises—particularly those of the ego—seldom faded quickly.

"I don't regret a thing," he said.

"Ah," Guillory said with a thin smile. "A damn fine case it was."

"Do you think we're at fault, sir?"

"Like I said," Guillory began, "the Legion taught me about poor liars. You're one of them, Henry. But here, now—well, your tongue has a knack for truth. It suits you." He paused. "An amendment is all I have to give you, Specialist."

Mallison folded her arms. "You'll do it, then?"

"You've got the imaginative touch." Guillory cocked his head to the side. "You tell me how to amend our position for the trial, and I'll do it. But make it waterproof, because I'm pinning this on you."

As slight as it was, the chance to act surged through Stasik's head. Files, evidence samples, and memories collided in flashes.

"Get Tartu's urban crime department on the line," he said. "Tell them we need immediate samples of everything in those vaults. Anything the Material Export boys find. Shells, blast residue, blood, hair, piss—whatever they have, we need it. Get them cross-referenced with the identity databases, material catalogs, everything. We'll get our suspect and craft motive from that." He took a moment to breathe. "And they release the charges on Nata."

Guillory's eyes narrowed. "Who?"

"Danicheva," he replied, somehow jarred by his own misstep. "My client."

"Don't push the luck you don't have," Mallison said.

"If any of this works," Guillory said, "it might not be off the table."

"And if it doesn't?" Mallison asked.

"No need to worry about Henry's call girl when you're both in long-term incarceration, Specialist."

"Fair enough." Mallison peered at the featureless black case resting on the tiles between their chairs: the latest dicer model, first deployed by Prague's urban units in '52. If her attempts to identify the imposter's Morse frequency had been as successful as she let on, their trail of breadcrumbs was safely stamped across its circuitry and ripe for following. "While you're running errands, sir, we'd like to tend to a few of our own."

———

Investigator-Technician Henson paced above, patrolling the catwalk of the IA's Broadcast Monitoring Pit with a clipboard in hand and his washed-out reflection painted along the enormous glass panels that encircled him. Beyond the bald man's silhouette was cosmic darkness flaked with mica, a vision shielded from the city's light pollution by the broadcast tower's height and placement beyond the municipal center.

Henson turned and adjusted his glasses to the eggshell glow of the command pit's terminals below. It took him a moment to squint and discern Stasik and Mallison stranded amid a crowd of bulky headsets and desks arranged in grid clusters.

"King codecracker," he said, his voice tinny. "And his new queen, seems like."

"That's us," Stasik called up. Blaring dots and piercing dashes seeped out of the pit's terminals in a constant hum. His brain struggled to pick apart the Morse and find meaning in the chaos. "Where do we bring the dicer?"

Mallison hefted the case in turn, grinning. "The highlight of your week."

"Bring it on over," Henson said, moving to the stairway that linked the pit and the catwalk terminals before beckoning them to follow. As Stasik and Mallison neared the top step, he pointed to a five-stack, sixteen-port Athena terminal fused to one of the dome's support pillars. It had the sheen of iron plunged into liquid nitrogen, a central screen large enough to rival some of the department's projector images.

"First or second port on the bottom level will do it," Henson said.

Stasik and Henson stepped aside as Mallison slid the dicer toward the port slats, grabbed a length of cable, secured both jacks to link the machinery.

"How much did Guillory tell you?" Stasik asked.

"Nearly nothing," he replied, arms crossed. "What've you been up to? How's the family?"

Stasik ignored the question and pressed on. "How much spread does this tower have?"

"Well, shit," Henson said. "This signal ought to comb out to Marrakesh and back. But I hope you're prowling more locally."

"For now, we just want an ear to the ground," Stasik said. "We're looking to comb the narrow bands first if it's possible. Whoever was transmitting on the line this morning wouldn't make it that obvious."

Henson's glasses reflected the white glow of the Athena's boot-up text. His voice deepened, dropped lower. "So it's a certified pro?"

"Just set it for narrow," Stasik said. "We've got time."

———

WHEN THE MONITORING PIT MADE ITS THIRD SHIFT CHANGE, muddy predawn light streaming in through panoramic windows,

Stasik fetched blankets and a box of no-label downers. He laid the blanket across Mallison's lap and stood over the chair, waiting. Things were quieter in the broadcast center than they had been during the night, but the upper ring was as tense as ever. Four hours of watching, waiting, and delicately adjusting the Morse transmission bands had left them with little beyond fatigue.

Not that either of them were in any state to sleep. Some of the unit's other personnel had rotated into the pit as scanners for neighboring frequency bands, taking uppers, chatting, and making lucrative overtime for babysitting their terminals.

"Guillory phoned Vanders while you were out," Mallison said. The bags beneath her eyes were etched in shadow to monstrous effect. "It's a no-match on the blood samples to Palmenko."

Another stroke of luck, Stasik supposed, if not vindication. The skin samples had also come back negative, and the crime lab in Tartu had linked the vault's blast residue to the compound used in Donetsk.

"It's all dark?" Stasik asked, pointing to the screen monitoring their tapped Morse frequency.

Mallison shrugged. "More or less. Bit of interference, but nothing solid." She leaned back as her partner edged in, studied the pattern of subtle yet constant blips emanating from the frequency's registered user. "See what I'm on about? It's like feedback from their terminal."

"It's not feedback," Stasik said. He'd seen it once before: an investigation in Cairo's air traffic facility on a windy June day, the memory dulled by long-term narcotic damage to his cognitive function, but sharpened by unmistakable familiarity. "You traced the proper frequency. Stay with it, as long as it takes."

"What sort of frequency is it?"

"Military grade."

"Why do I bother asking?" Mallison sighed. "Have to wonder what's causing it to act up."

Back in Cairo, the blips had acted as two-way verification for any incoming suborbital vessels, ensuring that they hadn't been damaged or disabled in transit: If an aircraft failed to broadcast the sequence of ridges Mallison termed *feedback*, that meant its switchboards had been fried somewhere up in the atmosphere. The current situation was similar. Unlike feedback, however, this erratic signal meant the link was still operational. Still able to be tapped into.

"If our shooter's tethered to this Morse frequency, then we need to burn the wick at both ends," Stasik said.

"Words, Henry. Use your words." Mallison smoothed the blanket out over her thighs, leaned back in the chair. "This checks out for you?"

"I'm saying that if we can detect this small strand of their frequency, we can get a sharper picture of both origin points. We can identify where the signal is coming from, and where it's going."

"How?"

"Watch." Stasik glanced at the terminal where Henson was plugging away, waved him over. When the technician hurried to their Athena, Stasik stepped back. "Tell me what this looks like, would you?"

Henson adjusted his glasses. "Standard signal connection. What exactly are you tracing?"

"Is there any way to place the terminal of origin?" Stasik asked.

"Huh." The technician glanced over Mallison's shoulder. "That one's a tall order for working with a connection that subtle. Short of strobing every broadcast station on our rosters and plugging their feedback into a grid, I'm not sure how we could do it. But that'd take a few hours. Maybe days."

"Start strobing, I'd say." Mallison lit a cigarette, took a deep initial pull that clouded the terminal's screen.

"How badly do you need it?" Henson asked.

"Badly."

"Maybe my boys could ping the old Russian base over at Baikonur, get a satellite running coverage duty, too. But that would need some papers stamped, if you catch my drift."

Data flowing across open channels, taps extracting, warping, and repackaging a fragile situation. An impossible risk.

"No, keep a lid on it," Stasik said. "Just do your best with what we've got here."

"No sweat," Henson said. "Might take some time to start the grid, though. I've got two broken bands and a—"

The screen went dark, became flooded with strings of bone-white Morse. It streamed past in lightning forks that the Pervitin in Stasik's bloodstream helped seize and translate:

I'm clear to transmit. Do you want it word for word, or paraphrased? one string said.

A second cut in, larger and bolder: *YOU WERE DELAYED.*

Finding painkillers isn't so easy here, you know. At least the clinic came through when it counted. Now, answer my question.

Submit your interpretation.

"What is this?" whispered Henson.

Stasik lifted a finger to silence him. The next reply came swiftly, blazing across the terminal screen:

Most of her documents were worthless, actually. But one of the papers was from a leasing firm, prattling on about some facility to the south. She circled this code string a few times in ink. N34, 584120.04-6270898.65. Does it mean anything to you?

Your work is complete. Marks have been issued and this line will be severed.

What does the string mean?

YOUR WORK IS COMPLETE.
You're playing this game again? Telling me would be far easier,
you know.
There is no time to entertain further queries. I am severing our
line now. In the unlikely event of an emergency, I will reestablish
communications.
You're a tiring—
The Morse fell away in a black wash.

Stasik backed away from the terminal, grabbed a pad of paper and pen from a stationary desk near the railing. He wrote the string's digits down as they circled in his head, close to vanishing like a coin descending a funnel's slope, each revolution faster, tighter—

Fingers trembling, he set the pen down.

N34, 584120.04-6270898.65.

Everything he'd been through to get inside that vault... Had it only been for a set of incomprehensible digits?

Stasik turned back to the Athena's two-member crew and noticed the expectation clouding their eyes. "Fuck. We lost it, didn't we?"

"Sir," one of the full-time scanners called from the pit, headphones wrapped around his neck. The width of his terminal screen's white band was oscillating wildly. "Their last transmission was out of bounds, as far as power output goes. Check the potency readout, 'bout two columns back."

The potency readout on Athena's screen was large enough for Stasik to glimpse it at a distance, frayed at its top and bottom ridges, but wider than anything he'd seen before. More powerful than a nuclear submarine's transmission spectrum.

"Any way to explain this, Specialist?" Henson asked. "Last time I saw this sort of readout, it was bleed-off from a pulsar. One of our probes out near Io caught it by accident."

The shared knowledge link in Stasik's Morse implant crept up like whispers of a collective unconscious, filling his head with images of nebulae and astronomical units and grainy interstellar photographs.

"Stars aren't known for transmitting that sort of thing," Mallison said.

"What else could put out a band like that?" Stasik asked.

"Beats me," Henson said. "But there might be a way to find out."

Stasik studied the frequency's thin connection line studded with its intermittent blips. "You mean the line's still running?"

"Not actively, no. But the source's frequency oughta be intact."

"We don't even know what the source *is*," Mallison said. "Are they transmitting off a fucking battleship?"

She circled this string. The line's Morse transmission played over and over in Stasik's head. It was undeniable proof of someone targeting Nata.

"Henson, how can you access the source?" Stasik asked.

"Just a fake ping," the technician said. "If we tune the Athena to the source frequency, we can send a few pulses in their direction." He shrugged. "To their systems, won't be much at all. Like walkin' in front of a mirror."

"You can't really expect that to work," Mallison said.

Henson laughed, regarded the Athena with a thin smile as he stroked the side of the machine. "After five, maybe ten minutes, all right. But thirty seconds to get a self-read on the transmitter should be smooth as silk. By the time they're running that probe, we'll be out."

Mallison spun in her chair, stared up at Stasik.

He nodded back to her. "He knows what he's doing."

"Attaboy," Henson said, grinning.

With a resigned sigh, Mallison gathered up her blanket and stood, allowing the technician to take her place before the Athena. Even as she smoked and paced in a narrow circle, her attention kept returning to the paper in Stasik's hands. "You got it all down?"

Stasik folded the paper. "I think so. We'll need to ask her what it all means, though."

"She came knocking once," Mallison said. "She'll turn up again." Her tone was wary, not assuring.

Henson seated the Athena's transmission apparatus on his head, draping him in a nest of wires and soldered conductor strips and pin-filled switchboards.

"This'll take a few minutes," he said. "Pull up a chair; get comfortable."

He flicked a pair of tabs on the Athena's main panel, and the screen went dark. Threads of white input appeared and flickered away. Henson's head lolled back in a trance as his mind drifted away from his body.

"How are you holding up?" Mallison asked quietly.

"You should sleep," Stasik said.

"We both ought to." She took a quick pull from a freshly lit cigarette. "You before me, in any event."

He could feel her closeness in the way she stood, the subtle tilt of her hips and the inviting lure of her smile. Back in Budapest, he'd felt it, too. It felt wrong. A stress reaction, perhaps.

"Update's in," Vanders' voice crackled, emitted from the radio plug on their wrist implants. Stasik and Mallison simultaneously hit the *received* tab on their respective devices. "Guillory says the amendment is a go. The Wing's really beating its chest over this one, it sounds like. A couple of dropped charges on Henry's girl, if you can believe that. They want to make it a media panel, a real manhunt for this guy. Wild, isn't it?"

"Wild," Mallison replied flatly.

Stasik watched as Henson's head shifted to the right, but its angling was slight, almost immeasurable.

"We'll be down shortly," Mallison continued.

The technician's lips were moving, murmuring something lost to the pit's droning. Stasik tried to discern the words to no avail.

"Henry?"

Then he realized what the technician's lips were repeating, over and over, in their feverish cycles: "*No, please, just make it stop.*"

"You sorted, Henry?" Mallison asked.

Beads of sweat funneled down into Henson's collar, along the bottom curve of his earlobe...

"What is it?" Mallison grabbed Stasik's sleeve, shook him back to attention.

Just then, Henson's head slammed forward, crashed through the Athena's glass screen in a burst of heat-resistant shards and halogen smoke. Screams rose from the pit, the catwalk. The terminal wheezed and screeched and fell silent. Blood soaked through the technician's lapel in a slow blot, expanding from the central path of his jugular and the jagged glass that had torn through it.

"Triage!" Mallison yelled into her wrist, the defeated register in her voice announcing—as Stasik also knew—that it was too late.

CHAPTER 15

Blansko, Czechoslovakian Province
111 miles from Prague

TEN MINUTES AFTER BAHR SURRENDERED THE DATA FROM Anastasia Danicheva's vault, he knocked on his home's front door. The return was alien, disturbing in a manner that it had never been with previous assignments.

Now, he stared at his front door's chipped yellow paint, his anxieties revolving faster, every moment feeding the sense that he was a stranger on his family's porch.

Was it the dissociatives in his bloodstream?

His still-throbbing wounds?

But the knob squealed in rotation and the door opened, and Jana was there, a vision framed by their nightstand's lamp. Her shirt was plain—white and patterned with faint roses—and her makeup was subtle, no more dressed up than any standard day. Her hair fell over her shoulders in loose tangles, and she smiled as though nothing had happened.

Bahr wrapped his arms around her and she pulled him closer. For a long while, there was only the sound of the television mumbling in the distance, cinnamon-scented warmth flowing over his face and the wind's chill brushing his back. Everything was all right.

———

At dinnertime, Michal used a fork to push around his green beans without ever eating them. He was a small boy—smaller than his classmates with certainty—but Bahr hadn't noticed it before that night, before his son looked upon his plate like a puzzle. Bahr had learned the value of rations in Norway, where those with weary stomachs and poor bartering skills were most likely to be dug out of foxholes as bodies. Hunger was the instinct of the strong, the ambitious, the living.

"Something's wrong with your food?" Bahr asked. "You ate a lot at school, maybe?"

"You don't leave until you finish it," Jana said, having barely taken a bite of pork herself.

"Even half would be a good start," Bahr replied.

"He's been like this for a week," Jana said.

"Exams?"

Michal shook his head, scraped up a bean on the edge of his fork. He chewed seven times and swallowed. A token gesture of the highest order.

Bahr's lip twitched. "If you don't eat, you won't grow. Your arms will shrink."

His son slumped down in his seat, the ruffled edge of his stuffed dog's ear peeking over the table's rim. One marble eye stared back at Bahr. If the boy had looked carefully enough, he would've found a thumb-shaped bloodstain on the underside of the gift box brought back from his father's "trip."

"Sit up," Jana whispered. "Michal, please."

"How will you be strong enough to carry wood?" Bahr asked. The prongs of his fork rattled against ceramic.

Michal straightened in his chair, a beaten look on his face.

"You're lucky you live now," Bahr said, even as Jana raised her finger to soothe him. "Just ten years ago, you would've starved. We had no food."

"I know," Michal said softly.

"People used food as a punishment, actually. Who got their share of food, and who didn't. Jews, the Kiev Slavs, the Orientals."

His son looked away.

"Do you think it's just fantasy, these textbook accounts?" Bahr asked. He could feel his voice rising, but it made no difference. "I've seen grown men starve to death."

"Erik." Jana's eyes had a primal width. It was terror, not arousal—the new seeding implant in Bahr's temporal lobe had made it difficult to discern the two. "Let me pour some coffee. Maybe you can turn on the radio."

The radio.

Without answering, Bahr stood and wandered into the darkness of the living room. He glanced back at Michal under the dining room's severe lighting, at a boy clutching his stuffed dog and curling up into the safety of a hardwood chair.

As he stood there, studying Michal, the whole scene—the act of playing house—felt insignificant. He mentally pictured the bodies and bullets in the vault, the Slav's plot, the nationalist and her horrible schemes. She was still out there, still pulling strings that drew the Coalition nearer to a singularity, to an event horizon beyond Textile's awareness.

But the week's memories scattered through his consciousness

like buckshot, and it was difficult to feel much of anything for too long. He switched on the radio, set it to a station he'd never accessed before, and listened to a crooning Negro's song until Jana called for him.

———

THEY HAD INTERCOURSE FOR THIRTY-ONE MINUTES—he watched the clock's hands ticking the entire time, so he was sure—and he only finished when Jana told him she loved him. Really, it had been two things: "I love you" and "you're a good man."

But before he'd explicitly asked for it, she'd only said the first phrase.

At 01:24, Bahr sat on the edge of the bed and stared out the window, taking in moon-silvered fields and black tree lines. He listened to Jana's breathing, felt an occasional warm wisp at the base of his spine. Across the room lay his duffel bag, still packed and zippered as though waiting to be used. Somehow, these nights were the most trying. The night before he deployed, there was a sense of goodness to be done, all his potential turning to kinetic energy at last.

Afterward, there was only a sense of how things had been at their most daring, of how he'd felt to have been called out again. Of waiting. Most of all, he was helpless. But this particular time was worse, and the sinking feeling wasn't fading.

The Slavs were still out there, burning.

Destroying.

Evolving.

He angled himself on the bedside so he could study Jana, wondering just how well she could read him. She loved him, of course, but all things were quantifiable in one way or another, and part of her equation for affection was missing.

She didn't know exactly what he did each time when he left the house.

Maybe that explained the occasional lapse in her eyes throughout the evening, a muted sort of sadness that had come over her while she was washing dishes or undressing by the wardrobe, thinking nobody was watching. But what did she expect, really? All great men had a sense of duty, and all great women understood the necessity of their sacrifices.

That was why he'd chosen her, after all. She wasn't some broken doll plucked out of the ashes in Warsaw or Berlin, shattered by war to the point of mistrusting the very notion of a man's duty. During night marches back in the Second World War, he'd dreamed of a woman who slept peacefully beside him, granting him the serenity he didn't have, couldn't have.

She'd dreamed of a man who could dedicate himself to her. A man able to protect her and learn to shed his calluses when he held their baby.

But he was not that man.

Bahr watched her eyelids twitching in short cycles, trying to immerse himself in whatever vivid dreams were playing out in her sleep. He was relieved that she, like all other Coalition civilians, lacked full memory of the world that had come before. Sure, she knew it through textbooks, through legends, through thirdhand accounts of decorated killers like himself. But for all intents and purposes, she dreamed about whatever she'd been told to dream about. She didn't dream—couldn't dream, in fact—about the food trucks running out of fuel, or the Coalition firing indiscriminately into crowds of protesters, or needing to shelter Michal from a real war.

In that way, Bahr envied her dreams. She would never have to know the pain of keeping the world afloat.

And as he crept through the house, duffel bag slung over one shoulder and a full Pervitin box stuffed in his back pocket, he didn't feel so helpless anymore. He'd be back before they missed him. Another stuffed toy for Michal, another—

"Where are you going?" Textile pulsed through his brain.

"Now you want to talk?" Bahr replied.

"Return to bed and sleep."

"Very well. If you tell me where they headed, I will. I need to know they aren't threatening my family."

The construct lingered for a moment, seemingly unsure. *"They are not a threat."*

"Are they in this province?"

"No."

"Where, then?"

"According to my networks, they are somewhere in Vilnius," Textile explained. *"That is far from your family's location. Are you toying with me?"*

"How would your networks know they're in Vilnius?"

"I have forces everywhere," Textile replied. *"Your mind cannot grasp how much information moves through me at this very moment, nor how much data I managed to collect during your encounter in Tartu. You will have to trust my analysis, Erik. The agents are in the Lithuanian province."*

Bahr laced up his second boot, wondering if the construct was, in fact, the one toying with *him*. He sensed the bait in the construct's pulses. It was seeing what he'd do and where he'd go of his own accord. There was only one Coalition facility in Vilnius, after all. By offering up the name of that city, he'd given Bahr a direct path for his own hunt.

"You're lying," Bahr said.

"Lying? I think not," Textile pulsed. *"If it will put your mind at ease, I can send you the frequency bands for their radios. Then you can listen in for yourself and return to bed peacefully."*

Before Bahr said a word in reply, a string of numbers and visuals washed into his mind's eye. It looked legitimate, further adding to his theory that the construct was testing him, provoking him.

"We only did half the work," Bahr said as he went to the hallway closet and fished out a compact, industrial-grade radar box. If the construct's frequency bands were accurate, he'd be able to triangulate the Slav's position once he was within range of them. He packed the radar box, then returned his focus to the Morse exchange with the construct. *"They're supposed to be dead."*

"Murder will draw unwanted scrutiny. Return to bed," Textile ordered.

"Are you sending anyone to do it?"

"No."

Bahr stood, made his way to the front door by following a practiced path through the blackness of corridors and dens. *"Where is Danicheva?"* he asked.

"You want to hurt her," Textile said. It wasn't a question.

"If she's a risk to the Coalition, I do."

"Perhaps you simply enjoy it." Textile's Morse cut into him, paused his hand as it lingered over the doorknob. *"Isn't that right, Erik? Will you enjoy hurting her?"*

It was nothing. A clever construct's upswing in its effectiveness, having gathered enough data to evolve its phrasing. *"I don't enjoy my work,"* Bahr said.

"You don't?" Textile asked. *"Do you remember that Dutch girl? Annelise?"*

It was memory-combing for names. A new trick, but hardly impressive for Textile's programming.

"I'm going after her," Bahr said. *"Help me or stand aside."*

"If I conjured a memory of your greatest pleasure, would it be with Jana or Annelise?"

Bahr said nothing, just worked to block out the construct's incoming pulses. But at the edge of his awareness was a shifting collage of images drawn from his memory, trickling into his thoughts with screams and bruised flesh.

"Just shoot yourself," Textile said. *"What sort of life are you living, Erik?"*

"Help me finish this," Bahr answered through clenched teeth.

"You can finish it now by blowing out your brains. Make it quick and efficient for everybody else, why don't you? If you do it in the woods, I'll request a coroner's team to find your body tomorrow. Michal and Jana won't even see it."

"That plan simply isn't in the cards. Tell me what that code string was, and it's all sorted."

"Your work will undermine the Coalition's progress."

"Why would you possibly shield her?" Bahr should've kept the wrath out of his voice to deprive the construct of any emotional feedback. He knew it the moment he spoke. But the merest implication of sedition, of impeding work for the entity he'd devoted his life to sustaining, triggered nerves he'd never known existed.

"These details are beyond the scope of your comprehension," Textile said.

"Forget the details, then." Bahr leaned against the door, his head thumping. *"Lay the grand scheme before me."*

"Your understanding is not important."

"I did everything you asked. Now either pat my shoulder or stand aside, because this is a small kindness that extends beyond marks, or whatever you think I'm owed. Something's different this time. Something that you and your simulations will never be able to tackle. I'll fix the deviation."

"Seizing your consciousness is an unpleasant process," Textile whispered in faint dots and dashes, *"for us both."*

"It's a cold line of thought. I liked to think that we shared a bond, you know?"

Textile went dark. Monochromatic flashes of death-pale skin crept into the void. *"If you will not blow your brains out, I will."*

Weeks ago, the threat would've made Bahr back down. The seizures of his body were horrible, a breed of sleep paralysis that never dulled and never ended. The constructs played puppeteer, using his body to do whatever they pleased for as long as they pleased, before restoring his sense of agency over himself.

Now, Bahr grasped the doorknob and nodded. That which hadn't killed him had made him stronger, indeed. Textile's constant intrusion into his awareness had changed him, in an immunological sense. If the mind could recognize one strain of stimuli, it could also learn to block it out. He could resist.

"I'll be back within two days," he said.

"If you leave this home, I will need to detain you and alter your recollection of the past three weeks," Textile warned.

"You? I had no idea your arms were so long, my friend. Will you reach here and grab me by the scruff of the neck?"

"Not all arms are physical." A pause, a plunge into darkness. *"Return to sleep."*

"But why? There's just a final step."

"Your dissociative compound dosage should be lowered. It is clear that you're affected by paranoia and chronic anxiety."

Bahr grinned. *"It's funny, Textile. I almost mistook you as human for a while."*

A graceful, curious sweep in the pattern of Morse code followed. He'd piqued its curiosity.

"May I ask why?" Textile asked.

"I thought that you could care for things," he said. *"As though they might've finally reconciled logic with emotion."*

Textile sent nothing in reply.

"Many cultures have tried to unite them, but the balance inevitably tips to one side or the other," Bahr continued. *"Perhaps you're the tipping point to logic for our species. The interesting part is that you're not a member of it."*

"Perhaps you are the emotion, and I am the logic," Textile countered. *"Return to bed so we may remain in balance."*

"You really don't want me doing your work, do you?"

"I know that you will deviate from my orders."

"And if I don't?" Bahr asked.

"My simulations doubt this."

"Let me prove myself, then."

"You have proven it already," the construct pulsed. *"You are not returning to bed. You must have faith in my decisions."*

For a moment Bahr's hand shivered over the doorknob, wondering if the construct was right. If its actions had all been in preservation of the Coalition, then this decision was no different.

But in war, machines and nameless commanders had damned his unit innumerable times. In moments of necessity, courage and hate outweighed logic.

"I wish you luck in the hunt," Bahr pulsed.

With an inward sweep, Bahr focused himself on the bead of incoming transmissions, choked Textile's wall of static down to a drizzle that barely flickered in his awareness. Each of the construct's attempts at seizing control shattered against the walls of his screeching resolve.

He held firm against the deluge—he had to. A horde of vicious memories stung at him like wasps: his father's funeral, screams in the kitchen, still frames of dead friends, dead strangers, dead brothers with blood on his own knuckles.

Bahr blinked himself back to the present, shook off the approaching migraine. Then he hiked toward the train station under a starless sky.

Perhaps the main conflict wasn't between logic and emotion, he considered as he reached the railway. They could be resolved, to some extent. No, the true tension was between personal happiness and the preservation of the state.

At 03:35, when he boarded the first train toward the Slav's Morse emanations in Vilnius, Bahr chose his side of the scale.

CHAPTER 16

Vilnius, Lithuanian Province
491 miles from Moscow

Stasik's only analogue for the clamor in IA planning room SC was that of war room debates, an antiquated experience passed down in digitized library reels and beer-loosened chats with his uncles. Agents shouted over one another, cigarette smoke wafted up and into the glow of ceiling lights, and automated warnings muddied the chamber's acoustics.

"Orders just came down the chain," Guillory said as he leaned against an elevated terrace's railing, looking down upon the subdivision's twenty-five agents. "IA's been relieved of investigating the incident. We'll be deferring to the intervention units and General Prosecution."

"Fine by me," Agent Vanders said quietly.

"After what we just saw in there," Mallison said, still pacing, "they expect us to be lapdogs for the major crime units?"

"Specialist Mallison, do you think this case belongs solely to us?" Guillory asked.

Vanders rubbed the bridge of his nose. "Frankly, it doesn't seem like a case for IA at all."

"Not what Marston told us," one of the technicians chimed in, gesturing at the latest unit transfer—a bone-thin man with square glasses and a plaid button-up. "Tell 'em, Marston."

"Well, one of the monitoring posts in Baku saw the surge come through their systems," Marston said, visibly nervous to be speaking before the assembled team. He rifled through a clipboard's pages. "The transcript suggests that whatever harmed Investigator-Technician Henson possessed signatures 'heavily associated with Coalition systems.'"

Mallison sidled up next to Stasik, whistled through her teeth. "You were fucking right."

He nodded. Yet, he wished he wasn't.

"Our game is with the boys erasing ones and writing zeroes," Vanders replied. "This isn't *internal* at all. You saw the power coming off those readouts."

"Doesn't matter what we think," Guillory said, thrusting a still-burning cigarette's tip toward Vanders, then Mallison. "It's beyond the pale. We've got our own plate to handle."

"We oughta defer that case, too," Vanders said. "It's over our heads."

"You'll handle what I tell you to handle." Guillory's visage of a disapproving father came in full force. A reminder delivered like ordering a boy into Sunday church clothes.

"Just as long as it isn't us probing those systems." Vanders shrugged.

One of the junior agents, a thirtysomething brunette named Haywood, smiled at that. "I think Vanders must have good tenure."

"Why does it matter what the Wing tells us anymore?" Stasik asked.

His voice quieted their corner of the planning room like a door creaking open in a saloon, those dark and dangerous places from the western films his father adored. He cleared his throat, blinking back recent memories of shooting and blood and death.

"I've done my best to tend to my client," he said, voice gaining steam as he went. "And you supported me, sir. But it's clear that we're just playing jesters for them. For the Wing, for the prosecution teams, for everybody. Something just murdered one of our own inside a *Coalition* facility, and they think it's a job for the saps who've never set foot in this goddamn building? They don't know what they're looking for, and they don't care. This is a circus."

A few of the agents mumbled in the affirmative. The others simply crossed their arms, mum, and scattered their focus around the planning room.

Guillory groaned. "You're not even on active duty, Specialist."

"I was during Donetsk," he shot back. "Nearly everybody in here was."

"Donetsk is out of our hands."

"Because somebody higher up told us it was." Stasik scowled at the complicit silence of the agents around him. The juniors hadn't learned to stop pissing themselves when they clocked in, he acknowledged, but the seniors had no excuse.

"How do they expect us to gather any evidence for this trial when they lock down every site that has prints on it?" he asked.

"I invited you to this briefing as a professional courtesy," Guillory said in that low warning tone.

"Don't you see, sir?" Stasik went on. "They want us to fail. *Somebody* in Moscow wants to see us hang for this. They have since day one."

"Watch your mouth."

"Isn't this why Internal Affairs was made?" Again, Stasik took stock of the agents: word by word, more of them fixed their gazes on him. "I say we look where they don't want us to look."

"Nobody in the brass is going to authorize—"

"They don't need to," Stasik interrupted. "Mallison and I aren't on duty, are we? There's nothing to file. Nothing to be signed."

"You think you're calling the shots?" Guillory asked.

"You need us," Stasik said. "Henson's the tip of this iceberg."

"We don't have time for your crusade. Six divisions are on hold, waiting for me to bark back at them. We have a department inspection in two weeks. Henson's body is still waiting to be autopsied. And I need to manage this investigation."

Stasik huffed at that. "So leave it to us."

"Sounds like a flawless plan," Vanders sneered. "Stasik's been on the stims again."

"He's the only one who's had any clue about what's going on," Mallison snapped. "What the fuck have you been up to?"

"*Not* mucking around in the broadcast center."

"Oh, for—"

"Enough!" Guillory barked, cutting off his agents. His lips curled with the sour, tacit acceptance of Mallison's logic. "What do you expect me to say, Stasik?"

"That we can drag them out of their holes," Stasik replied.

"*Who?*" Vanders asked, his eyes rolling in their dark sockets.

"The sons of bitches who painted the streets red in Donetsk." Stasik addressed no agent in particular, though he regarded them all in sequence. He could see the embers smoldering in their eyes. "They got away with it there, got away with it in Tartu. And if we don't take the fight to them now, then they win. We need the Wing to acknowledge what happened here. And if we can't do that, we need to take them down on our own."

Murmurs went up throughout the crowd.

"I say we do it," Agent Haywood said at last.

That seemed to break the levee. Hands went up in solidarity among a chorus of whistles and shouts. A few of the junior agents clapped. Even Marston offered a whispered, halfhearted agreement between his nail-biting.

"This isn't a goddamn vote," Guillory said.

"You're right," Stasik said. "This is your call."

The old man's lip twitched. He studied Mallison, then Stasik, then Mallison again, his features hardening with each pass. "Vanders," Guillory said, "I want you to manage the field division here. There's a mountain of paperwork on the horizon."

"The *division*?" Vanders asked sharply. "You're talking a hundred agents."

"Consider it a promotion," Guillory said.

Vanders didn't reply. Didn't need to. His scowl said it all.

"We'll need all hands on deck to ensure this doesn't go up in flames," Guillory said to the crowd. He sighed. "It still might."

"This is full-moon batshit," Vanders cut in. "Going toe-to-toe with the Wing? Are you really gonna authorize this, sir?"

Guillory looked Stasik up and down. "It won't be our names on the Wing's hit list."

"It won't be anybody's," Stasik said. "We're getting our client."

"Are you trying to get nailed for collaboration with a nationalist?" Vanders asked.

"We ought to be keeping tabs on her," Mallison said. "At least until the trial goes live."

"She's coming to the trial," Stasik said firmly.

"Now," Guillory said, flapping his folder in the air to regain everyone's attention, "the Wing never said anything about her making an appearance. She won't be in the guillotine, but there won't be a red carpet rolled out for her way home, either. Too many questions for her to answer."

"She'll answer them on the stand, with as many cameras as you can point," Stasik replied. "But she's coming, and that's that."

"Stasik, we can't afford to waste time here."

"Exactly," he replied. "The Wing will fry us alive if we walk into Moscow with empty hands, sir. We can get something solid if we have Danicheva."

"You thought that before, too."

Stasik lifted his wrist, angled his Morse recorder toward Guillory. "Do you remember our prior conversation, sir? Something about two evils?"

A knot wormed up and down the director's throat. "Hurry to your point, Specialist."

"She's the only one who knows how deep this goes."

"Doesn't that imply guilt?" Agent Marston asked softly.

"It implies we're ruined without her," Mallison said.

"A delay on our reinstatement paperwork, a bird, and three days," Stasik said, thumbing a tab of Pervitin out of its sleeve. He moved the tab to his lips with shaking fingers. "That's all we need."

"A stunning development." Vanders groaned and looked to Guillory. "Assuming the prodigal children get their wish, what do I have our agents do? Twiddle their thumbs?"

"They'll assist the Wing with whatever they need," Guillory said. "They'll buy time."

"This is insane."

But Guillory's eyes were already squared on Stasik, blackened by the overhead lighting installations. "Dismissed," he ordered.

As the crowd mulled in confusion and agents complained to one another, the director appeared before Stasik and Mallison, hands on his hips. "There won't be a second shot at this."

"I know," Stasik said. "Sir, there's just one more thing. I need to request a temporary shift in our Morse signatures."

"What for?"

"We think they've got a handle on us," Mallison explained. "It's too much of a risk."

Guillory weighed their grim expressions, sighed. "It'll take a day or so to process, at the very least. But we can get it done. Don't fuck this up."

"Just thank us when you get your commendation," Stasik said.

The old man creased his brow. "I couldn't give a tenth of a fuck about a commendation, Specialist. Blood's been spilled in IA." He stepped closer. "Remember to keep one foot at the top of the rabbit hole. I've seen better agents than you two get pulled in."

"Is there something else we ought to know?" Mallison asked.

"No," Guillory said, though the cold, ashen glaze in his eyes told Stasik otherwise. "Nothing I tell you would help out there. Now you find Danicheva, get your answers, and you learn the name of the subhumans who killed Henson. Who did all of this. Is that clear, Specialists?"

Although Guillory wielded the stalwart stance and tone of a boxing coach on the ropes with his protege, Stasik saw the fear in him. It was a quiet, humbling thing, entirely too foreign on the director's face. It only affirmed what Stasik had known since his first day in Donetsk—there would be more to face out there than mere killers.

Stasik nodded.

CHAPTER 17

The nationalist community in the Lithuania province was sizable but mild, a widespread showering of dissatisfaction compared to the lightning bolts in the Yugoslavia and Uzbekistan provinces.

That sort of discontent, fostered among neighbors and laborers but rarely blossoming into extremism, was the Coalition's primary source of information on the nationalist movement. Undercover agents slipped into sauna gatherings, surveillance equipment on local tram lines, wire transfers to informants about the cells in surrounding provinces—all of it was valuable, but it had never been Stasik's game.

Until that evening.

Stasik tried to force himself to think like a codebreaker as he made his way back up to the Broadcast Monitoring Pit. It was daunting to crack a code that had no code. The pit was nearly empty, and it still stank of the ammonia used to scour Henson's blood from the floor and the Athena console.

He paced around the roped-off death scene several times, trying to jog his memory, trying to recall if Henson had said anything that might generate a new lead. But there was nothing. The man had died in a rush of fear and glass.

Agent Marston was one of the few recognizable faces still working on the upper ring of the pit. He operated with the pace of a rabid squirrel, skeletal hands clacking over the keys.

Stasik went to the agent's station and stood behind him, curious. Marston had worked with Henson several times over the last year, and it showed. The man had a knack for identifying obscure patterns and following up on miniscule details.

"Marston," Stasik said, making the mousy agent jump in his chair, "if you wanted to catch people who did their best to stay quiet, what would you do?"

Marston turned to face him, swallowed. "I'd listen to the silence, I guess."

"How do you mean?"

"Well, see, it's easy to catch the stupid ones. They talk too much. Talk about everything. Guns, bombs, that sort of stuff. But the smart ones are quiet, and they talk in strange terms that don't belong on the transmission networks. When two grown men are discussing a date and a time to 'buy strawberry ice cream' for over an hour, that raises some red flags. You know?"

Stasik nodded. "So you'd look for the words that don't seem threatening."

"That's right."

It was maddening to consider the possibility that he'd heard a juicy code word while dealing with the imposter in the vault or Nata herself, only to forget it when it mattered most. He replayed every conversation he could think of, grabbing a pen and paper as he did so. *Early evening, Smirovanov, L56.* He wrote each and every phrase that frothed up in his memory, no matter how random they seemed.

And then, his weary mind recalled the one seared into his brain by explosive compounds and dust. His hand shook as he wrote it. How could he be so foolish not to think of it first.

Brushfire.

"Check the networks for these terms," he said to Marston, dropping the list by his terminal. "Use whatever resources you need."

———

AGENT MARSTON APPEARED AT HIS DORMITORY QUARTERS shortly before dawn with a name, a place, and a string of gibberish marking the Morse band he'd used to pick up a rogue communique.

"Look here," Marston said as he gestured at the yellow printout, his voice never rising above a harsh squeak. "I ran the system with the parameters you wanted."

"Which term had a hit?" Stasik asked.

"*Brushfire,*" he said. Then, hiking up his glasses on his nose with a thin finger: "Does that mean something?"

Stasik squinted at the page and ignored the question. He read the name listed beside that ominous word, the word offered to him so freely by Nata.

"Justas Kulsaite. That's our man?" he asked.

"He's the one who tripped the scanners, so maybe."

"And he's in Palanga, Lithuania?" Stasik asked.

"As of an hour ago, he was," Marston said. "His location hasn't moved much in the past two weeks."

"Then it's showtime."

———

IT TOOK MALLISON TWO HOURS TO PREPARE FOR THE DEPARTURE from Vilnius, having taken full advantage of the base's secure lines for conversations with her sister, her mother, and her ailing uncle in Chester.

Stasik had heard her calls through the partially soundproofed wall, inadvertently remembering how many months it had been since his own calls to the American province. And against the backdrop of her conversations, he'd spent those two hours staring at the sole decoration in his quarters. A piece of paper pinned to the wall, which read N34, 584120.04-6270898.65.

His knowledge link failed him, as did his entry-level courses in codebreaking. He'd still failed at analyzing it after a trip to the quartermaster, where he'd refilled his prescriptions and taken a new blend of microdoses to try to make sense of the string. After what he'd seen in the past days, however, there wasn't a chance in hell that he'd turn it over to the intelligence divisions. Not even Guillory could know about it.

Several hours later, as Mallison opened the door to the Palanga discotheque where their next lead was supposed to be, he still carried the sequence in his head. He could almost see it in the haze of cigarette smoke and cocktail gowns.

The room was further distorted by fatigue and his recent pill cocktail—a blend of experimental uppers that cut the need for sleep, but kicked up the brain's fight-or-flight response. Every shadow was a weapon. Every person was a threat.

A woman with brassy skin and a shimmering black dress

twirled on an illuminated stand, gyrating, all light and mascara amid a sea of grinding dancers. The music was loud enough to be classified as raw sound, an awkward tangle of horns, drums, and lyrics that had been shoehorned into a Yedtongue translation.

Stasik hadn't known that clubs like this even existed in Palanga. Collective knowledge of underground clubs in New York and Paris had triggered a slew of nightlife construction where there had once been quiet beaches, ruins of old forts, and mass graves. But it made sense, he supposed. Even nationalists needed a place to unwind.

Nationalists who might know where to find Nata.

"Where's our valet?" Stasik shouted at Mallison, trailing her toward the bar. *Valet* was the preferred term for any situation involving an informant. In this case, Justas Kulsaite, the unlucky fellow who had tripped Marston's parameters.

Mallison stopped, turning on her heels at the code word's mention. "The *valet* is back there, catching sleep after a hard night's work." She pointed to a wooden door near the bar, which appeared to lead into a kind of storage space. "We have some time before contact, you know. We could dance." Her fingers wove into his. Her smile wormed its way out of hard disinterest. "Come on. Five minutes."

But her features were all wrong, mismatched and melding until they formed some grotesque imitation of Nata's visage. Only then, at the hint of her presence, did arousal rise in him.

Mallison's image resolved in the flashing lights. He pulled his hands away.

"No," he said. "We ought to go in now and wait."

To her credit, she did a fair job of seeming playful about it. "Right, go have a drink. Give me fifteen minutes."

"We're going in together."

"You should watch the door from this side," Mallison

replied, leading him onward. "Stay at the bar and watch. Fifteen, you hear me?"

Stasik nodded, though she wasn't looking at him anymore. Truth be told, he didn't want to accompany her for the sake of activity. He knew what Mallison did to those she "questioned." There wasn't an operational protocol booklet on Earth that would support the way she handled her interrogations.

But Stasik didn't stop her. They needed to get on the phone with Nata, needed to make some sense of what Stasik had nearly died to recover. And this man—one Justas Kulsaite—was their direct line to the woman. Or so he hoped.

Mallison disappeared into the masses. A moment later, the storage room's wooden door swung open and shut. From here, it was all up to her. Her questions, her rules.

Stasik settled uneasily onto a stool near the wall, staring down an illuminated row of vodka and gin bottles at the door in profile. A young bartender worked at his left, stirring, shaking, and pouring with the brisk efficiency of a soldier. Bodies brushed by, and motes of drunken conversation fluttered in and out of Stasik's awareness.

"Gin," a man called, leaning over the bar and well into Stasik's periphery. Dim, hard features, a fit build that a white button-down did little to obscure. The guttural bark in his Yedtongue placed him as Austrian or German in origin.

"Something Dutch," the man added when the bartender glanced his way.

"On the rocks?" the bartender asked.

"If you could," the man replied. He turned and might've stared at Stasik, but the room's lights and activity made it difficult to be sure. "Two of them, actually. One for my friend."

Stasik watched the bartender fetch two glasses, scoop ice out of a bin. "Thank you, but I think—"

"I'll hear nothing of it," the man said. "Repay me in conversation and we'll be wholly even."

"My time's stretched a bit thin tonight."

"That's the world these days." The man dialed something into a disposable credit pack and waved it over the bar's scanning strip, receiving a celebratory chime and green light as feedback for his payment. When the bartender set their drinks down, he nudged the second glass toward Stasik and laughed. "You're not a priest, my friend. So drink."

Stasik had never felt in control while drinking during assignments. It was a dulling of the senses, a blunt mimic of the euphoria he felt on his usual cocktail of uppers, but there was something pleasant about the disorientation. And besides, gin prices were exorbitant these days. Hard to say no.

"Thank you." Stasik picked up his glass, clinked it for a perfunctory *cheers*, and drank its contents in full. Setting the glass down, he gauged the man with his full attention: rugged, handsome in a cowboy's sort of way. Eerily devoid of flaws or peculiarities.

Aryan.

"A good drink could put many wars to rest," the man said, "don't you think?"

"Maybe," Stasik replied.

"I've been studying you for some time."

Now Stasik searched the Aryan's eyes, wondering if he might find some seed of homosexuality. That sort of thing had been rearing up all over the world, due in part to a crop of revised social policies.

"Thanks again for the drink, but I'm not interested," Stasik said, as politely as he could manage.

"Conversation is all I ask for. Henry," the man replied.

Henry. Stasik leaned closer, wondering if he'd imagined it. Had something been slipped into his drink?

RHETT C BRUNO & JAMES WOLANYK

"Who are you?" he asked.

"My interest is in Anastasia Danicheva," the man replied.

"Answer me, damn it."

The Aryan shrugged. "Or what, Henry? Will you kill me?" He sipped his drink, a smile cutting across his face. "No, you wouldn't do that. I respect that about you."

"You have no idea what I would or wouldn't do." And after Tartu, after Henson, he truly believed that. It frightened him.

"I was hoping you might assist me with a puzzle, of sorts." The Aryan frowned, stroked the golden sprouts of a fresh beard along his jaw. "N34 should be enough to bring the proper sequence to mind. Does it mean anything to you?"

Stasik's hand crept toward his holster. "Where did you learn that?"

"In Tartu."

His fingers froze, brushed stamped steel.

"I looked different there, didn't I?" the Aryan continued.

"Who *are* you?" Stasik hissed.

"Think on the sequence, Henry. Perhaps I should order you a second drink."

"If you're armed, you ought to tell me right now," Stasik said.

"Why?" the Aryan asked. "It's not as though you can arrest me for anything."

"You're out of your mind."

"Read me my charges, then, Specialist. What have I done wrong?"

Pages after pages of laws flashed through Stasik's Morse implant. All of them failed to triangulate in a manner that condemned the Aryan's actions. There had to be motive, involvement, evidence.

"You were there," Stasik said, trying to focus. What a mistake taking that drink was. Was it the drink? Maybe it was the uppers. Maybe it was residue from one of the dozens of things he'd popped in recent days just to stay awake. "You killed those men," he managed.

"Did I?" the Aryan replied.

"I watched you."

"You watched a man who looks nothing like me, who has no genetic traces, cause the deaths of several men. Yes, that's all true." The Aryan finished his drink, raised his hand for another. "Your Morse recorder hasn't been running, Henry. Nothing I've told you will hold up during processing." He grinned. "Not even if I told you that I have four bundles of plastic explosives hidden somewhere in this room, and my trigger finger is horribly spastic while under duress."

Stasik stared at the Aryan, fought back the shakes that lured his hand toward his pistol. "What the fuck are you?"

"You wouldn't understand even if I told you," the Aryan said.

"You tell me whatever you like," Stasik whispered. "I'll kill you for what you did."

"A man of principles would never do such a thing."

"The *truth* is that you killed them."

"Is it?" he asked, squinting as his second drink arrived. "Truth is such a malleable thing, Henry." He gestured to the room around them, to the pulsating bodies steeped in drugs, careless. "It seems that these people believe exactly what they wish. And my, how happy they are."

Stasik held the man's gaze for what felt like an eternity. His hand moved to the countertop. "What do you know about that sequence?"

"No more than you, it would appear. But I've come to you to invite you to do the right thing. I need to find your client."

"Why?"

"To kill her, of course," he said. "I'm giving you a chance to come to the right side of history."

"Whichever side you're on, it's the wrong one."

"What if I told you that her death would save everything?" he asked. "If one life could keep it all in balance, wouldn't it be worth it?"

"It's murder."

"And if I told you that her existence would bring war, what would you say?"

Stasik's lips trembled. "I'm not turning her over to you."

"Now we get into the tough questions, don't we?" The Aryan laughed. "My father was living near the western edge of the Poland province when the war started to slow down. You know, the one thing he *never* embraced was the Russian Jews. 'Mischievous, greedy little vermin,' he called them. And when the Russians came to his town, they wanted the old cobbler to fix their boots and make them shoes, all funded with their Jewish coin. Do you know what he did?"

Stasik could only stare.

"He refused, because he was a man of ideals," the Aryan said. "And they killed him for it. They dragged his naked body over a kilometer of snow and stone." He took a long drink. "Ideals are a deadly thing, aren't they?"

"Murder is murder," Stasik said.

"So is war, Henry." The Aryan scooted his stool closer. "Where is she hiding?"

Stasik counted the minutes in his head, waiting for Mallison to return.

"We both understand that the Coalition is the apex of this troublesome species," the Aryan said. "Shouldn't one of us uphold it?"

"You're a killer."

"We all are, in the end." He stared into his near-empty drink. "All of us who really want to make a difference."

"Who are you working for?"

"The Coalition," the Aryan said. He seemed taken aback by the question, somehow wounded by Stasik's tone.

"Then you tell me why Danicheva needs to die, and you tell me now."

"A nationalist may not understand the condemnation of a nationalist."

"You think *I'm* a nationalist?" Stasik spat. "Go fuck yourself."

"Interesting," the Aryan said. "Some common ground between us, perhaps."

"The Coalition doesn't want you."

Somehow, that swift response sank into the Aryan, gave him pause that Stasik hadn't expected. He picked up his gin, swirled it so the ice twisted in the glass, and sipped the rest with measured contemplation.

"If only you knew how much I've bled for the Coalition," he said at last. "All we can do is live a life worth repeating. Are you familiar with Nietzsche's writings? This concept of eternal recurrence?"

"It's not about any—"

The Aryan raised a finger to silence him, then continued with the same even pace. "Infinity does strange things to perception, Henry. All events have happened before, and in turn, they will happen again, their order entirely unchanged. We've had these same words a million times before and a million times to come."

"Then you should already know about that sequence," Stasik said, glaring. "You should know where Danicheva is camped out."

Now the amusement was gone from the Aryan's eyes. They were dark, hollow. "I will."

The wooden door beyond the liquor bottles swung open, bathing Mallison in the ugly yellow light of the backroom corridor. In an instant, well before Stasik could protest, she was at his side, shouting into his ear to overcome the blasting music. "Justas got us on the line with your girl! They're pre-Coalition coordinates, Henry—fucking coordinates!"

He gripped her shoulders. "Diane—"

"She says we can run those numbers through the Stein Atlas Conversion," she rushed on, too caught up in adrenaline to notice his response. "She'll meet us at the coordinates!"

Stasik spun toward the Aryan, but he was already gone, a shadow slinking away into the tangled masses.

"Fuck!" He slammed a hand on the table, felt it shatter a glass and tear into the flesh along his palm. "That was him, Diane."

"Are you all sorted?" Mallison said.

"He knew the coordinates already. He knew them, and he's going."

As he glanced down, Stasik saw red splotches on Mallison's hands, too. Not from being cut by glass, but from doing the cutting.

"What did you do in there?" he asked.

"We need to get you a fucking downer," Mallison replied.

"What did you do to him?"

"We got him to place a few calls," she explained. "Danicheva said it's our new meeting point." She looked over her partner, shuddered. "Really, come on now."

"You tortured him."

"Spilled milk, Henry. Get up."

Shouldn't one of us uphold it? "Get the bird ready for dust-off. I need to phone headquarters and get a suspect description out."

"A suspect?"

"The shooter—the *one.*"

"You mean that was *him?*"

Stasik staggered off the stool, watched the colors burst and shimmer as the uppers hit their peak. He swore he was mumbling yes as he shoved toward the exit, even as his thoughts cycled back to the truth of things, to the breathless chase ahead.

CHAPTER 18

Henry Stasik's helicopter kicked off in a flurry of dust and sand at the edge of the sea, great beams of moonlight lancing through the haze. They would reach the coordinates in an hour or perhaps less, depending on the skill of their pilot, but Bahr was in no true hurry. His breath was high in his chest as he walked along the beach, scanning the mosaic of cottage window lights and lanterns arranged along the nearby boardwalk. Listening to shrill laughter and portable radio chatter. Shivering from the cold gusts that rattled folded umbrellas.

Every encounter with the Slav before had left him shaken, frantic in a manner he hadn't known since fighting. It was natural when brushing fingertips with true evil.

But as the helicopter shrank away, turning inland to swoop over the forests, Bahr thought little of his dread.

It wasn't too late to go home, he supposed.

He thinks I'm a nationalist? Bahr thought to himself.

By now, he longed for simple answers. For the clarity of a name and a place.

He focused his thoughts to the scrolling digits in his mind's eye, trying to estimate where the coordinates would lead him. Yes, coordinates. It was all returning to him now... how he'd relied upon that very navigation system during his paratrooper days, how he'd stalked his enemies using similar tangles of numbers and letters.

Textile's interference seemed so simple now. It had tried to blot out his hard-won knowledge, tried to suppress his memories with the same ease as it had pacified the citizens. But he wasn't like the others. He had a mission.

And there was still time to catch them, to do the right thing.

Two kilometers down the road, shrouded by thick bushes and a stand of pines near rusted fencing, Bahr found the green Alpine. Its headrest was still dark and wet with the driver's blood, its rear seats piled with zipped bags and firearms and a wad of dormant explosives. His radar box sat whirring in the trunk, latching onto the agents' trail.

The hunt would be a simple affair, with or without the coordinates. The agents had left a trail of radio and Morse transmissions as they made their way from the HQ in Vilnius to Palanga, bolstering Bahr's lock on their frequency. He had their scent now. Had the frequency bands of both the agents' radios as well as the helicopter's transmission line. He could follow them to the ends of the Earth—and he would.

Bahr stole a fleeting look at Palanga and its twirling lights, adjusted his rearview mirror, turned the key in the ignition.

CHAPTER 19

Outside Riga, Latvian Province
522 miles from Moscow

Daybreak burned like a match head on the horizon, the tips of Latvia's fir forests glimmering. Stasik and Mallison's helicopter swiveled left and drew up on a small town in a clearing. It was a barren place, the sort of community that was apt to spring up near oil fields or old military garrisons.

"This is it?" the pilot crackled in Stasik's and Mallison's implants. "Doesn't look like much."

Mallison said nothing, just regarded Stasik from across the aisle with one knee tucked to her chest and her fingers splayed against the composite glass. The air was still a chalky gray from her last cigarette.

During the flight, Stasik had told her what he could about the shooter—his face, his mannerisms, what he'd said about hunting Nata. None of it had taken the edge off her demeanor, however. In some sense, he was reminded of his uncle's drunken lectures after dinners, about doomed marriages and how every attempt to mend them just worsened things.

Now he just stared back at Mallison through the tranquil fog of benzos, trying to recall the last time he'd looked at her while completely sober. It wasn't just them, maybe everything was falling apart.

Even so, she looked more tired than he remembered.

"How many of them will there be?" Stasik asked.

Mallison checked her holster's straps, straightened in her seat. "Supposed to be a whole pack of them. Your girl keeps a heavy entourage."

"It's better than nothing."

The helicopter settled with an uneasy rocking, and the rotors slowed, sent a final whirl of dust and dead grass up around the windows. When the doors opened, Mallison was the first one on the ground.

Stasik jogged after her, waved to the pilot for landing confirmation.

"She's a victim here. You get that, don't you?" he said.

"I get that you want that." She was still looking forward, examining the five-story post-Soviet block structure precisely nailed by the coordinates. "We'll get her to Moscow, Henry. That's what we'll do."

"He wants her dead."

"It's not just about her," Mallison said, rounding on him. "He didn't find *her*, he found you. How'd he manage it?"

"I don't know."

"He knew your name."

Stasik shook his head. "He thought I was a nationalist."

"What, so it's some coincidence?"

"No, but—"

"Somehow, he's got a handle on your location. Got her

coordinates now, too. So how long until he shows up? Tartu just wasn't enough for you?"

"I had Vanders put out his description while we were en route," Stasik said. "They'll be on alert. And they'll send intervention units, too."

"He can change his *face!*"

"Not if he's in a hurry, he can't. That was clinical work, Diane. Be realistic."

"You don't think that maybe, just maybe, it's time to drop Danicheva in somebody else's lap?"

Silence, undercut by the wind and the distant thrumming of the rotors as their helicopter moved to a holding pattern in the southern fields.

"Nobody else will take her," Stasik said.

"Because you won't let them!" Mallison was beyond words now, lost to the sort of rage that nobody in the division base would dare to interrupt. "I'm not going to abandon you, Henry, but *fuck*. You're catching all the flak that's meant for her. If he was there, really there beside you, then he had you dead to rights."

"What does it say if we walk away?"

"More than if you're in a casket."

"It says they were right for everything they did, and for everything they'll do when they realize nobody is crossing t's and dotting i's." Stasik ran a hand through his hair. "This is more than one woman, you know."

"You don't know what it is," she said.

"But I will."

Mallison's eyes softened with some effort. She shoved her hands back into her pockets and paced toward the building. "Just come on."

It was true, he considered as they neared the entrance of the drab apartment block. The Aryan had allowed him to live. He'd had both the tools and the viciousness required to kill Stasik in cold blood. Yet Stasik's own life had been secondary to his concerns at the bar. Rather his mind had revolved around Nata, her plight, her hunter.

Past a stretch of withered vines and chipped bricks, a door squealed open. Snippets of a strange language emerged, revealed to be Lithuanian when a pair of lanky men with bomber coats stepped outside. The men muttered to one another, passing a lone cigarette back and forth between gloved hands.

"What?" one of the men demanded in Yedtongue.

"We're here for a meeting," Stasik said. "With... Miss Danicheva." Just saying her name out loud so formally felt strange. Impersonal. They were closer than that, weren't they?

The Lithuanian men examined their attire, eyeing them from head to toe. Stasik tapped his finger on his belt while they took their time. Should he have been so forthright with her name? Was this a test? His neck had started to itch when they finally spouted back and forth in Lithuanian, then ushered them in.

Mallison and Stasik shouldered by and entered a shadowed foyer. It was bare of furniture, stripped of any identifying features beyond moisture stains on drywall.

As Stasik's eyes adjusted, he made out the shapes of six or seven unarmed men scattered around the empty space. And at the center of their gathering he noticed Nata, just as radiant as the day she'd walked into the station at Donetsk. Her makeup was impeccable, her hair straight and glossy under fluorescent light.

She stared at him.

"Convenient of you to be here so quickly," Mallison said. She walked ahead, glancing at the men arranged in a crescent around them.

"We were in the region," Nata said, never looking away from Stasik. "But we needed the coordinates to know where to go."

"What are you on about?" Mallison asked. "This is an apartment building."

"It's more. Much more."

"Maybe they can wait outside," Stasik said, gesturing to the nationalists.

With Nata's nod, they began to file out in an orderly line. It was bizarre to see such a gallery of militant criminals at ease around Coalition personnel, and even more bizarre to consider who was issuing their orders. A quiet shuffling of boots, another squeal on fading hinges, and there was only silence and the musk of rot between building panels.

"So spill it," Mallison said. "What is this place?"

Nata touched the drywall, pursed her lips. "I never thought I would come back here."

"Your wish is granted," Mallison said. "But my partner nearly died to get a few digits and letters. So I expect you to clue us in as to why, or you'll show up to the hearing with more than some blush on your cheeks."

"Hearing?" Nata asked.

"Why'd you hang onto these coordinates?" Stasik pressed, moving past Mallison, taking in a pull of perfume he'd recalled in recent dreams and olfactory hallucinations.

"An old acquaintance lives here," Nata said.

"We could've just arranged a meeting, then," Mallison snapped.

"If I'd remembered," Nata whispered. Her eyes fell on Stasik. Wounded, appealing in a desperate sort of way. "That was one of the first things to go."

Stasik moved closer. "Go? What do you mean?"

"Specialist Mallison worked on patent oversight," Nata said, regarding her. "Did you ever read about anything termed soft decay?"

The question gave Mallison some pause. She pushed her hands harder into her pockets, scuffed her feet across the floor

"It was never green-lit," she said, finally.

"Instability," Nata said. "That was what kept it grounded, wasn't it?"

"The ethics committee pushed back." Now she was invested in the model's words, edging nearer with an almost unconscious lure.

Stasik glanced back and forth between them, frowned. "Catch me up."

"Soft decay was a flagship product for one of the clinics," Mallison said. "The Dubrovnik Central Clinic, might've been. They tried to see if you could blot out old memories."

"Why the hell would they want that?"

"All those boys shipping back from Arnhem and Normandy, staring off at the wall like puppets. Beating their wives, draining bottles, blowing out their brains… you tell me."

"And what?" Stasik asked. He met Nata's eyes, but nothing clicked. "Were you part of the patent testing?"

"No," Nata said softly. "Not quite."

"They never even green-lit it for testing," Mallison said.

Nata's lips curled in an unsettling way. "It was part of our program," she said, barely above a whisper. "We didn't even know about it until it was too late."

"They *never* used it."

"Not officially," Nata said. "It crept up on us, you see. Small things at first: the color of our first blanket, maybe. And then it became where we were born, and the names of our mothers and fathers. Things so monumental that it had to be a psychosis of some sort."

Even without psychedelics, Stasik began to envision some sort of hollow cavity in her skull, boring deeper and deeper.

"What are you saying?" he asked. "Who used it on you?"

Mallison scoffed. "They burned the patent."

"Not just on me," Nata explained, undeterred. "It was all of the girls. I couldn't tell you their names, but I can tell you that they're gone now."

"Gone where? What girls?" Mallison asked.

A lip of moisture beaded up along Nata's lower eyelids, swelling to not-quite-tears that she blinked away. "Some of them chose to take their own lives, and some were taken away. But I'm alone now."

"Miss Danicheva, you're not making any sense." Even as Stasik spoke those words, he knew that she was. That someone, somewhere, had done horrible things. That her truth was an objective thing nobody else would dare believe without hard proof, which was why she couldn't just feed it all to him back when they'd first met.

"These coordinates." Nata nodded upward, staring through layers of impenetrable concrete and iron rebar. "She lives here, and she remembers. She has to."

"Who is *she*?" Mallison asked.

Nata ignored her. "I had dreams of coming back here, but I didn't know where *here* was. It's all so simple now…"

"We'd better see it quickly," Mallison insisted. She paced in a narrow circle, lighting a cigarette with no attention to spare for Nata. "I won't be late to Moscow, Henry."

"Moscow?" Nata asked.

"Yes, Moscow. We're not working on your bloody schedule anymore."

"Calm down," Stasik said, his raised hand doing little to placate Mallison and her vicious first drag on the cigarette. "Who's upstairs?"

Without explanation, Nata turned and moved to a nearby

service elevator's doors, a cryptic whirl of color and pristine heels among the decay. She angled her gaze back at them. "My teacher."

———

NATA APPROACHED THE DOOR UPSTAIRS LIKE A PARENT'S OPEN casket. Not in a daze, perhaps, but far from lucidity. There was surreal hesitation in the way she stood, legs stiffly together and shoulders squared, as she lifted one hand to the brass *503* on the door.

Stasik waited several paces back, wondering if anybody still lived here. Sound had a tendency to creep between flats, even among the quietest neighbors, but this floor—not to mention those above and below it—was silent. Even the walls were mold-spotted, rotting from what had to be broken pipes or filtration pumps.

Deeper than all that, and more disturbing, was the fear that Nata was wrong. Mallison had been shouting about it all along, hadn't she? And maybe she was right.

Nata knocked, and the silence was more suffocating than ever.

"How long until those intervention units back us up?" Mallison whispered to Stasik. She leaned against the wall with the stub of a cigarette between her fingers, examining Nata as though she were a stray animal.

"They'll be here soon enough," Stasik replied.

"Before the nationalists fetch their rifles?"

"They won't." He stared at Nata, at the uncertain clenching that racked her shoulders. "I know they won't."

Door 503 swung inward, scraping over thick carpets, and at once the light spilling through the flat's windows bathed Nata's face. It exposed every pockmark and blotch Stasik had never glimpsed without the lenses of narcotics.

And from within came a high, aging voice: "*Zdravstvuyte.*" Russian. A spastic chill up Stasik's spine. That language's sense of exile and exclusion were the anthesis of Yedtongue's societal aims.

"Do you remember me?" Nata asked. Her stare was concentrated on something deeply familiar. "Miss Polocheva."

A mass of wispy silver hair emerged from the lip of the doorframe, followed by a pair of wrinkled brows, dark folds of skin framing misty blue eyes. "Oh," the woman said softly, her gaze lingering on Stasik and Mallison. "May I ask what this is about?"

Her Yedtongue was lazy and forced in its execution—a telltale sign of a nationalist, certainly, but the woman's age and physical state called that conclusion into question.

"My name is Anastasia Danicheva," Nata replied. "You were my instructor."

"And can I help you with something?" Polocheva asked.

"You must remember me."

"I'm sorry, dear," Polocheva said. "I taught many children, but now I'm retired from the labor pool, and—"

"Nata Danicheva," she cut in.

"As I said, I've been retired for—"

"*Ispytuyemyy Mavka,*" Nata snapped in Russian. Whatever that phrase meant sent a ripple of hurt through her eyes once it was spoken. "Subject Mavka," she clarified. "Do you remember me now?"

The old woman made a croak. Hidden behind the door's frame, it might've expressed anything between recognition and terror. Then she came staggering out into the hall, thin bones and loose skin beneath a plain, baggy dress.

It wasn't until Nata opened her arms and pulled Polocheva

closer that Stasik noted the old woman's face overcome by emotion and tears. Nata just stood with her chin atop Polocheva's head, staring blankly as though she were a porcelain doll.

Or, perhaps, as though she felt nothing at all.

———

POLOCHEVA'S FLAT WAS CRAMPED AND SPARSE, BUT NOT IN a decrepit way. In fact, it was the victim of excessive domestic maintenance, its hardwood floors smelling of chemical agents and the den so spotless that it appeared more like a furniture catalog's showroom than a living space. She'd led them to a small coffee table ringed with sofa chairs and left, returning with black tea that nobody aside from Stasik dared to touch.

But the tea seemed like yet another stalling maneuver. He could hear Polocheva rummaging through shelves and metal drawers one room over, mumbling little strings of Russian to herself.

"This had better be worth it," Mallison said, propping up her chin with one hand on the armrest. She looked at Nata, but the gesture went unnoticed. "The pilot tends to get twitchy after too long on the leaves."

"If she can serve as a witness, we'll bring her along," Stasik said.

"A witness to what?"

"Whatever she's digging up." He looked at the bare drywall, sensing the vibrations of her prodding and sifting behind the barrier. A moment later, the rummaging ceased. There were soft footsteps, a grumble of hard breathing down the corridor, and then Polocheva appeared with a metal lockbox, hefting it like a child in both arms, breathing heavy.

"Set it down over here, Miss Polocheva. On the table." Stasik worked to clear away the saucers and kettle.

Nata, stoic as ever, helped Polocheva set the box down before gawking at it. She hardly blinked, hardly let tremors of her thoughts reach her lips as she examined the lock and reinforced edges and battered sides.

"Miss Danicheva, what is this?" Stasik asked.

Polocheva smiled sadly at Nata. "It might be better if it's just us looking at it, dear."

"They need to see it," Nata replied. "This is the day I asked you to wait for."

Mallison sighed. "I'm going to be awfully upset if there's a bomb in there."

"You've changed so much," Polocheva whispered as she stared at Nata. Her eyes twinkled. "So, so much."

"Surgeries," Nata said.

"You never needed to change," the old woman said.

"It wasn't always my choice." Again, her gaze fell to the box. "Open it, if you would. We don't have much time to discuss it."

"If this is going to be evidence at the trial, I'll need details first," Stasik said. He flipped his wrist over, peeled back his coat's sleeve, activated his Morse recorder. "Madam, I'm going to ask you to state your full name, date and place of birth, and relation to Miss Danicheva. This record is for submission into official Coalition proceedings."

Stillness fell over the room, all attention slowly spinning toward Stasik. But he met their glances squarely and waited, allowing the initial discomfort to bleed out.

"Is this really necessary?" Polocheva asked.

Stasik nodded.

"Julia Polocheva," she said after a pause. "I was born on the fifth of January 1890, in Ufa, Russia. I was an instructor in

Mav—" She caught herself, shaking her head as though dismissing a foolish wish. "In Miss Danicheva's elementary years."

"Morse ID?"

"She doesn't have her own," Nata said.

"Everyone has one," Mallison countered.

"Not her," Nata said, nodding toward Polocheva's wrist. The flesh there was off-white, mottled. "We helped her remove it before she went into hiding. She has a false tag now. Something to throw off the dogs."

Stasik regarded the woman's incision mark, swallowed hard. "The school's name?" he asked.

Polocheva folded her hands in her lap and turned to Nata expectantly. There was no softness in her former student's face, no tactile sympathy like she'd received in the corridor.

"Its name changed several times," she said.

"At the time of Miss Danicheva's attendance, then."

"The Lauska Primary Academy." The name came out like a painful, hushed secret, likely to be buried in static in the final recording's playback.

"Still in operation?" Stasik asked.

"No," Nata said. "It's gone."

Stasik glanced at Polocheva, noted the way she gnawed on her stubby nails. "Can you corroborate this information?"

Polocheva nodded. "Yes, it's no longer in service."

"Where was it located?" Stasik asked.

"Two kilometers to the west of this complex."

"And now?"

"It's a field," Polocheva whispered. "There's nothing left there. Not even on maps."

"Was the academy owned by the Soviets?"

"No."

"Western?"

"No."

"This is where the thread begins, Specialist," Nata whispered.

"And the evidence before me," Stasik said, focusing his gaze on Polocheva and tapping on the lockbox's handle. "Please explain its relevance for submission purposes."

Polocheva leaned back, wrung her fingers nervously, regarded the box with unease. "It would be difficult to explain, I think. Maybe you ought to just examine it. We can talk about it, since if I were to just—"

"Identify it," Mallison groaned. "That's all you need to do."

"It's a lockbox," Polocheva said.

"Its contents?" Stasik asked.

"Transcripts." The old woman looked away, idly scratching at her throat, letting her words trail into ambiguous silence. "Many files, many pages, many copies of letters from the director and... I don't know what else to say, sir. I've, well, I've had this box for many years. Anastasia told me to keep it secure, so I have. That's all I have to say about it." She gestured to Stasik's wrist. "Does that need to stay on?"

Stasik nodded. "It's standard procedure. Open the box, if you would."

As Polocheva drew a key from her handbag, Mallison shifted to the edge of her seat to watch. And when Polocheva set to unlocking the container, Stasik began studying Nata. Her face was, perhaps, the most curious of everyone in attendance. The longer he examined her features, the less he understood her mind. Her face was a canvas for anything, really—dread, excitement, repulsion.

All of it in one gaze.

Metal latches whined and peeled back, and in seconds the odor of industrial solvents diffused through the den. Polocheva lifted the lid to reveal a stack of compressed, yellowing papers, occasionally spliced by an off-white image print.

Nobody challenged Nata when she snatched the box from the table and rifled through it, seizing fistfuls of documents and scattering them across the tabletop like playing cards. She hardly blinked as she grasped, tossed, and repeated—the entire process carried out as mechanical catharsis.

Just as quickly, Stasik gathered up whatever files were within reach and thumbed through them. Thin carbon copies of medical records for Anastasia Danicheva, charts tracking her height and weight and exam scores, disciplinary notices, letters of commendation for academic progress—exactly what was expected of a private academy's student files. After a moment of stillness, Mallison reached out to begin her own inspection.

"These are school records," Stasik said, shuffling a stack of mathematics assessment reports. He was faintly aware of the annoyance in his voice, unwanted but growing with every revelation he failed to find on a new page. "What is this?"

"Henry." Mallison held out a cardstock photograph, wide and thick and printed in glossy grayscale.

Her quiet urgency was what caught Stasik's attention. He set down Nata's records and took the photograph with both hands.

High, wide windows, crystal and ormolu chandeliers, checkerboard tiles, all captured at an unnerving three-quarter angle that stared down a narrow corridor. A man stood with his forehead pressed to drywall, his dark hair striped with a blindfold. Closer to the camera was a young girl with a belted dress and a ponytail, a handgun pointed at the base of the man's neck. The weapon was impossibly large, dwarfing both hands she'd wrapped around its grip. Yet her face was pure determination, raw focus, undaunted by the coming execution.

"What is this?" Stasik asked. Slowly, among Polocheva's

breaking face and Nata's stoicism, his disgust at the photograph's surreal and senseless violence began to sink in. "What the fuck is this?"

"That was me," Nata said. "I don't know that man's name. But I remember this much: I can't forget something I was never told."

"That's not you," he shot back.

"It was," she said. "It is."

Stasik glared at Polocheva. "Tell me what this is."

The old woman clutched her nose and mouth with pale hands. "Oh, God. Don't make me speak."

"This isn't her." Stasik was mumbling the declaration, testing its reality. "Isn't it?"

"It is," Polocheva whispered.

"Say the object-in-question's name."

"Anastasia Danicheva," she said. "In Christ, in Christ."

"Article A," Stasik said to Mallison, thrusting the picture toward her. Mallison's hand crept out and hovered over his kneecap, hesitating. "Scan it in, Specialist Mallison. Article *A*."

Mallison took the photograph by its corner with two fingers, as if touching it more might poison her. She passed it over her wrist implant's scanning bar. "Noted as Article A," she confirmed.

And then, even with his hands shaking and his mind numb, Stasik sorted through the growing pile. Between every pack of legal requisite documents was photographic evidence of another unspeakable horror.

Girls lined up in the hedgerows outside a chateau, their dresses bloodied, and mutilated small animals held high for inspection in their right hands. A forehead split open by a tangle of metal instruments and circuitry. Pale, starved bodies swathed in blankets and dotted with injection-site rashes across their foreheads. Garishly lit workshops with schoolgirls pressing, inspecting, and loading pointed rifle rounds.

All of it blurred together after some time, each new disturbance passed to Mallison for cataloging with bizarre verbal description—*mass graves, beheading, fixed eyelids.*

"This was my schooling," Nata said after some time, as though a question had been posed anywhere during the ten minutes of the agents' filing process. She paid no mind to Polocheva's sobbing. "Do you recognize me, Specialist?"

Stasik set aside a photograph of two girls with intravenous drips installed in their upper arms. "Yes." It was impossible to ignore her; even after the obvious surgeries she'd had in recent years, Nata was present in the photographs, marked by her direct stare and hard, resistant posture. "I don't understand anymore."

"Most of us never did," Nata replied. "If I had to remember much about any of these particular days, you'd need to show me the photograph and identify me. But I'm more than comfortable never viewing them again, and you must understand why. The memory decay, after a fashion, was a blessing."

"You said you were from Krasnodar," Mallison said, hunched over the table and fully invested. "The records don't line up."

"It's hard to remember what's real," Nata said. "Some of us still saw our parents' faces in our sleep, but for most of us, it faded. Those memories were always sporadic for me."

"You must know them," Mallison said to Polocheva.

Polocheva shook her head, her chest still heaving. "They never told us their names. Not even the girls."

To Stasik, the semantics of names and parents and records were tertiary at best. He was still haunted by the black-and-white atrocities. The amorality and intentions of those who'd constructed such an environment.

"What *is* this?" Stasik demanded among a back-and-forth

over Nata's first-term academic report, unable to stop his voice from rising. "This isn't a school, Nata. You came to me and you said that men wanted you dead—powerful, smart men—and now you show me this. You've shown me pictures of an execution, you've shown me torture. Connect the dots, damn it. Don't string us along."

Mallison plucked her cigarette from her lips, sighed. "Henry—"

"No," he snapped, his eyes boring into Nata. "She owes us answers. What did you just put in front of me?"

"It's my collection," Nata said. "I asked her to keep these." She picked up a random photograph, careful to avoid glimpsing its front. "At first, it wasn't even my idea. Or so she's told me. We weren't raised to think the same way about pain or pleasure, so we had no qualms with what they made us do. But Madam Polocheva did. She approached me and asked if I wanted to go somewhere better. She's the only one who cared." Slowly she met the older woman's eyes, surrendering only a crinkle of her lower lip as any sign of feeling. "But she was still one of them."

"This was a Soviet program?" Mallison asked, shuffling between pictures. "Don't tell me it was funded by Downing Street."

"As I said, it was neither." Nata stared through the wall behind Mallison. "I'm not trying to be vague or flippant, Specialists. But this phase of my existence is murky, and Miss Polocheva is the one with the details." She extended a slender hand and touched Polocheva's knee, a gesture that walked the razor's edge between obligatory and comforting. "Tell them about the academy, Madam. *Pozhaluysta.*"

Polocheva dabbed at her cheeks with a white handkerchief as she nodded slowly. Then she gazed out the window for a few seconds more. Stasik was preparing to raise his voice when she finally started spilling.

"I try to read my own notes from time to time, you understand," she said. "Because I saw what happened to the girls, and perhaps it affected me too—my recollection, I mean."

"How'd you get involved?" Mallison asked.

"I was living in the neighboring region when they announced the academy's construction. I was young, looking for work before the war. It was a hard time for education." She sniffled, appeared to resolve herself with a hard breath. "But I went there, and it wasn't a labor ministry project—it was a private facility, bribed or somehow hidden from the state. They accepted me without hesitation, because I was naive, and because I needed the money so badly, and because they said it would change the world. That it would stop war." She coughed into her handkerchief, and a spark of excitement showed in her creased eyes. "And it did. That's the worst part, maybe."

"Who is *they*?" Stasik asked. Immediately he thought of the Aryan.

"Physicists, doctors, bankers," Polocheva whispered. "The ones who drafted the Coalition's founding documents. Or at least, ones who knew the founders. They said the program would be the spearhead of everything good."

"Where's the program's mission statement?" Mallison asked.

But Stasik's mind was stalled somewhere in Polocheva's last sentence. "This was done before the Coalition," he said. There was a short silence before he barked again, suffocating the lone syllable Nata managed to make in the interim. "They wouldn't have allowed this."

"Of course," Polocheva said. "But before a new society, they had to educate new citizens, they said. They started with fifty girls."

"This isn't an education," Stasik spat.

"I know!" Polocheva turned away, sniffled into her handkerchief. "It was never about teaching, really."

"You were an instructor, then?" Mallison asked. Stasik had no idea how she was remaining so calm.

"I taught them geography. They were bright girls, but they were *too* bright—somebody did something to their minds. They could remember the name of every town in southern Spain, for example. So I thought the schooling was just unorthodox." She glanced away. "Until I saw the real program."

"Clarify 'real program,' if you would." Mallison said.

"They called it a brushfire," Polocheva whispered. "Years later, that's how they termed it. They had to clear away all of the old leaves and decay to make something new."

"They created killers," Mallison replied.

"No," Polocheva cried. "The girls didn't *want* to do it. It was all they knew."

"But they're guilty of murder, regardless of intent. Aren't they?"

"I am," Nata said.

Stasik glared at her. That statement would play on the recording, assigned to her by way of automated vocal synchronization at the trial. Unlikely to help whatever case was unraveling.

"Who did they kill?" he asked.

"I didn't know," Polocheva said. "It wasn't my fault."

"Just tell us," he demanded.

"Many of the old politicians," she said after a pause. "The strict slaves to dogma and ideology, the ones they said would stand in front of unity. And the military men, too, who knew the missile codes and told soldiers which towns to bomb." Tears ran down her wrinkled cheeks, the emotion drained from her voice. "And those who felt commanded by God, who led their followers. They had to go."

"It never went active, did it?" Mallison asked. "They never went after any high-value targets."

"They did," Polocheva whispered. "Fifty girls, and forty-seven men dead."

Stasik regarded Nata with the blunt force of Polocheva's revelation. "Who did you kill?" he asked, barely able to form the words.

Nata crossed one leg gently over the other. "I've been told he was a British cabinet member, but I don't know his name anymore."

"It's impossible," Stasik said. "None of them were *ever* harmed."

"Where do you know that from?" Nata tapped the side of her head, probing a loose strand of hair. "Your passive knowledge link, surely?"

"And what?"

"It's edited by the Coalition," Nata said.

He just stared at her, trying to mentally rewrite his own implant and make it speak the truths he cherished, the ones now seeming so dissonant with the contents of his mind: rage, abandonment, disdain. The link wasn't the avatar of reality, or some god buried within the frontal lobe. His beliefs were still his own.

Weren't they?

"The girls were mostly instructed on how to reach their targets," Polocheva explained in the ensuing silence. "They needed to be violent and, of course, not to feel when they finally acted."

"How did they reach them?" Mallison asked.

"Pheromones were one way," Polocheva replied, digging for a file among the stack of glossy and eggshell white papers. "They were injected with them, I think."

Now Mallison's hands joined Stasik's in shaking. "Pheromones?"

"They did everything they could to help them play a role,"

Polocheva said. "Some of them were escorts, some were secretaries… they did anything they could to get them close to these men."

"I don't follow," Mallison said. "You're telling me that this was done *before* the Coalition's formation?"

"It had to be," Nata said. Her voice was low and blunt. "That was the only way they could create something new."

"We never would've cooperated if we'd known the end," Polocheva said.

"But you did," Stasik countered. Now he read Nata's face as though he'd acquired some code that made sense of her strangeness. She was a killer who didn't hold remorse; in fact, how could she? Memory was always the catalyst for coming to grips with a wayward soul.

"And now what?" he asked, meeting Nata's stare. "They want to see you punished for what you did?"

Polocheva furrowed her brow. "That's not it, sir. That's not why I kept all these things for so long." Quietness returned, and the woman coughed to clear her throat. "They want to erase the entire program."

"They did solid work on the academy," Mallison said.

"Not just the academy," Nata said. "As I told you, most of the other students are gone now. Accidents, suicides, direct action."

Mallison scoffed at Polocheva. "And you didn't help them?"

"I couldn't," Polocheva said. "I was close to Anastasia, and I could put in a good word for her. They didn't have a reason to purge her—not until recently, I mean."

"She's on every media network," Mallison replied. "Your best advice was to put her back on their radar?"

"The spotlights kept her alive."

"The attention," Stasik said, staring into the carpets and making sense of their woven patterns with the Pervitin's mounting crispness. "There would've been too many questions if she disappeared."

"Fuck," Mallison said under her breath. "Any way to disinter the bodies on your list, then? We'll need casualties to build a conspiracy case."

"They were cremated," Polocheva said.

"Naturally."

"If I might be honest with you all, I never expected these people to be punished for what they did. They're not radical anymore."

"What do you mean?" Stasik's breaths were tight, harsh. "Everything they did goes against the Coalition. We *can* get them."

"You don't know who these people are."

"Were any of them Germans?" he asked. "Hired killers, maybe with access to cosmetic clinics."

"It was so long ago," she whispered.

"Names," Mallison said.

"Krupin, Kraus, Vorster, Adeley…" The woman pinched her eyes shut, thinking, compiling names after a lifetime of forced ignorance. "I didn't meet all of them, just the program founders. Henderson, Rockwell, Weber, Porzhenko, Dregala—"

That last name was like a bullet to the brain.

"Dregala?" Stasik whispered. He didn't need to hear the man's official title to realize she was referring to Chairman Dregala, a towering Coalition official who stood above Director Guillory. Above the law itself.

"He was a hard man," Polocheva said. "A Legionnaire, actually."

Mallison's arm rested on Stasik's shoulder, but he wasn't listening, wasn't sensing anything beyond the piston-pump of his heart under the Pervitin's directive. He nodded Polocheva along and asked, "What did he oversee?"

Despite the warning in Mallison's eyes and the tremors in Stasik's hands, which caused the tabletop to shake and porcelain to vibrate in a ceaseless rattle, Polocheva began to whisper her truths.

"He was part of Selections," she said.

"Meaning?"

"For a long while, I didn't know. But I oversaw the program's shutdown. They asked me to destroy what he'd been selecting." Her hand moved to the pile of photographs, curled inward as though rejecting all their horrors, until she eventually plucked something from her side of the table. She handed it to Stasik.

The photograph was of a jungle of some kind. No, it *had* been a jungle. One of the thick, humid sprawls from Siam or the wilds of Yunnan, shimmering foliage and transient showers and sunrises that spread like molten plastic over the mountains. The image captured none of that. There was only black smog and the pure white flash of high explosives, a collection of children wandering out of thickets with their hands missing and skin charred, peeling in flaps.

"Henry," Mallison whispered.

Stasik set the photograph down. "The Wing didn't do this."

"They chose who would be compatible," Polocheva managed through her tears. "They had to select the right cultures, and the right morals, and sometimes the right races. And *they* had to remove the excess."

"I don't believe you," Stasik said. "An administrator never would've been involved. Never."

"It's true, I swear it."

Nata nodded. "Even your director is—"

"No." But he could feel reality warping and degrading, collapsing under its own inconsistency. Guillory, too, was counted as part of the Coalition's administrative ranks. An allegation against Dregala was an implicit allegation against Guillory. "You don't know him. The director wants to sort this out, just like you. You don't bring him into this. Do you understand me?"

"Even if he's not personally involved, all of these men are beyond reproach," Nata said.

"They're still hunting you!"

"There is no *they*," Nata said. "It's the entire Coalition, Specialist. You can't be hunted by an idea."

"Don't say that," Stasik said. His fingers hovered over his wrist, ready to kill the recorder, burn their entire exchange.

But the truth was inescapable.

"There's no way they'll accept this," Mallison slipped into his ear. "It's what Agent Vanders said, Henry: 'This isn't internal affairs.' It's gone too far."

"Bullshit." The recorder's light blinked at him through his sleeve, mocking him. "This is *all* internal. This is a tumor that we can cut out."

"It's not a tumor," Nata said. "It's the entire organism."

"Shut up!" Henry was halfway out of his seat and looming, one fist cocked behind his back, before he caught up to his breathing and settled back down with a wheeze. He could hardly meet Nata's eyes. Her placid, emotionless face that might've remained static even as he choked the life out of her.

"They did terrible things to you all, but this was a crime, not a policy," he said. "We'll make it right."

Nata blinked at him. "How?"

"We show this at the trial," Stasik said. He slumped back in his seat with a sense of deflation, all his energy and intent vented through the wrong channels. Sleepless, aimless, hopeless: the failure of it all crept into his thoughts like winter's chill in old bones. "We'll show everything we have, and we'll let the dust settle as it does." Nata's eyes remained difficult to hold, but he managed. "I gave my word to you, and I'll keep it. No matter where it leads."

"We can't go public with this," Mallison said. "No chance in hell."

"So we just bury it?" Stasik asked.

"It's better for everybody to walk away now." She glanced at Nata. "I don't know if you're innocent or guilty, but you won't last a moment in that court. If I were you, I'd stroll into the washroom, cut your face up with a razor, and be on the next train to anywhere but here." She shot a wary scowl at Polocheva. "Not much to be done for you."

Stasik shut off the recorder. "We're bringing them."

"Your partner has a point, Henry," Nata said. "Do you remember when I asked you how this would end, and you didn't know? That's because it can't. Through my eyes, some of this is just as fresh to me as it is to you. And I see what your partner sees."

"No," Stasik said softly. "You can't give up on this. I can't let you."

"They'll always find a way." A tear traced the crease between her cheek and nasal bridge, running over the red band of her lips.

"This is our chance to *change* something."

"You can't change the world," Nata replied. "What they did to us wasn't a *crime* against the Coalition. It was its foundation. We trimmed the branches of anything or anyone too radical, and now look at it—it's growing how they always intended, perhaps even flourishing."

"Are you all fucking insane?" Stasik asked.

Mallison lit another cigarette. "You can't fight city hall."

Again, he stood, not reckless or intent on violence, but simply done with it all. He stomped out of the den, into the cramped kitchen, and leaned over the counter beside the rusted sink. His mouth was sour with bile, and he spat, watched the deep orange and brown of the oxidized metal threading into his saliva. On a microscopic scale, reality was fascinating. Macroscopically, it was a dying man's fever dream.

Built over a lifetime, destroyed in an instant.

Harsh voices trickled through the pane of window glass at his back, far too masculine and steeped in Russian roots to belong to those still in the den. When he moved to the window, he saw daybreak washing the fields and main road in cool blue.

Nationalists formed a ragged crowd near the apartment's entrance. The recently arrived Coalition intervention units were packed into dense squads in a neighboring lot. Both sides were ready to tear each other to shreds.

But they weren't the issue.

A lone figure approached from the northern fields, a single black spot moving at an even pace, his silhouette irregular in a manner that any survivor of gunfire knew too well. Even with the nationalists and the intervention units shouting at him, he refused to slow down. Refused to identify whether he had ties to one side or the other.

The Aryan had found them.

CHAPTER 20

Crows took to the sky in wheeling black flocks, startled to flight by the first three-round burst from Bahr's assault rifle. His vision locked onto the clusters of armed civilians—nationalists, he supposed—and Coalition officers scattered along the complex's main road. Vision-enhancing eye droplets turned the enemies to dark silhouettes ringed with gossamer thermal signatures.

Kicking through a patch of crushed brambles, Bahr let off a second burst. Each shot punched against his shoulder, sent rounds burrowing into skulls, spines, and throats. He felt nothing for them. All he saw were humanoid wisps with big wild eyes and white mouths. He cut them down with the efficiency and nonchalance of a slaughterer drilling holes into cattle skulls.

Before they could gauge his position in the gloom, let alone return fire with any effectiveness, he drew a fragmentation grenade from his vest's front cording and tossed it overhand.

Two quick bursts from his rifle later, the grenade burst with a whistling *crack*. He eyed the aftermath: a plume of black smoke near the entrance of the target building, wisps of dust kicking up where shrapnel seared into the dirt, and corpses caked in pollen-like grit.

Just after the enemy returned fire, a scattered collection of pop shots amid the haze, confusion broke out. Bahr heard shouts in Yedtongue and archaic Russian, then the hard hiss of the Coalition's rifles and the low snap of the nationalists' contraband models.

Bahr slid to his stomach just before a round flitted overhead. He wormed forward in the dead grass, settling into a dirt crevice before digging out another pair of grenades. British prototypes, 1943.

He tossed them both in quick succession, waiting for the satisfaction of the *pop-pop* and ensuing rain of debris. As he crawled over the lip of the crevice and toward the next mound, light glinted high up on the target building, warping across a windowpane on the fifth floor.

His vision sharpened, brought the window into full focus. The Slav, Henry Stasik, stared out at him. The traitor's lips were moving, hands waving to call for somebody.

Time to act.

Across the bisecting road and to his right was a low stone wall, the perfect veil for entering the target building. The concussion and whirling dust of the last grenades provided cover, and the gunfire chattering between the Coalition and nationalists provided a distraction.

Bahr shoved himself to his feet. The nationalists were scattering into the neighboring compounds to carry on their defense, screaming to each other in garbled Russian.

He loaded a fresh magazine into his rifle, dashed to the low wall. As nimble as a greyhound, once and always.

———

BAHR'S COURSES IN URBAN TACTICAL PLANNING HAD EMPHASIZED mastery over the routes that led in or out of a given structure. It was vital to remember the arrangement of doors, windows, stairwells, elevator shafts, ladders—anything that the occupants or infiltrators could use to their advantage.

But years of flawless operations had spoiled him, made him feel that clearing any target or safehouse was an easy task. Most of his targets were unaware, arrogant.

The targets in this structure, however, had the advantage of knowledge. They knew he was approaching, knew the apartment's layout, knew what he was capable of doing to them. And there was nothing fiercer than a cornered animal.

As Bahr worked his way up the main stairwell, he recalled his unit instructor's emphasis on vertical momentum. 'It's like squeezing a tube of toothpaste from tail to tip,' he'd say. And Bahr *would* squeeze them out.

He had placed a microcharge on the elevator's fuse array just after entering, ensuring his current route was the only viable path for the occupants. He worked his way up the stairs with methodical precision, covering narrow angles and scanning railings as he swiveled up and around. Second floor, third floor, fourth floor…

When Bahr exited onto the fifth floor, the din grew louder than just the clap of gunshots. He sensed it swiveling above him, vibrating his eardrums like a tuning fork. Paint flakes rained down from the ceiling.

Bahr slung his rifle over his shoulder and drew a Czech

handgun chambered in 7.62 mm. Then he leapt up the stairs, intent on the rooftop. As he climbed, he heard voices shouting above the drone of helicopter rotors: The rolling *R* of a woman's nationalist tongue caught his attention.

At the top of the stairs was a locked door fringed by backlight and dust particles. Bahr threw his shoulder against it. Then again, and again.

Engine turbines wheezed as he stepped back and directed his full force into a front kick beside the door's lock assembly. When the door flew open to reveal pale daylight, the helicopter's whining was high, already fading as it circled to his left and diffused in the thin woodland air.

Bahr sprinted out and across the rooftop, dodging vent pylons and steel frames to reach the western railing. He unslung his rifle, knelt with the barrel cradled against the rail, dialed in the sights with his free hand.

The receding black mass of the Slav's helicopter came into view. Bahr's engagement was mechanical. He tucked the stock into his shoulder, caught the pause between short breaths, and fired three quick shots.

His rounds impacted, sent smoke bursting from the rotor's chassis. The silhouette of the helicopter wobbled, thrown from its course with a protracted squealing noise. Its tail drifted in lazy arcs, wobbling and dipping, unable to compensate for the impairment of the main blades. A dark smear of exhaust fanned out in the winds.

Bahr took some strain of pleasure from it, recalling days of taking down sparrows with a slingshot. And as the helicopter banked to the left, spiraling lower with aerosol fuel jetting out in torrents, he almost forgot that war had faded in humanity's collective awareness. The days of receiving medals for such marksmanship and bravery would not—no, could not—return.

Bahr was still staring at the helicopter's descent when the gunfire resumed from below. Bullets screamed past and supersonic echoes rippled out into the fields. An instant later, the railing's stone lip exploded in a burst of powdered concrete, peppering Bahr's arms and neck. He reeled back, stinging, and patted himself down. The wounds were shallow but widespread, and his hands came away with streaks of bright blood.

When he pressed himself to the ground and snaked forward, rifle angled to return fire over the railing's crest, he found that the chaos below had progressed.

Nationalist corpses were scattered on the dirt roads leading away from the compound, a mess of drab jackets and knitted wool caps. Pale hands, pale faces. They had no chance.

What he'd failed to anticipate was an equal number of Coalition officers slumped in doorways, squirming on hard, dry earth, lying dismembered from high-caliber machine-gun fire. It called to mind his stints in Norway and the Netherlands during the war, where men like them—good men, with goodness in their hearts—had wound up filling the pits of mass graves.

Moving down the main road was a pack of black-clad soldiers. The precise, synchronized manner in which they scanned the area was an obvious indication of artificial aid. Their rifle barrels combed up and down the block's structures, sniffing out and putting an end to any living combatants. Bahr got a sense of déjà vu from their body language.

They were just like him.

Servants beyond the Coalition's public eye. Servants of the constructs.

Bahr turned his gaze to the west, where pillars of smoke grew thicker as the helicopter dipped below the horizon. Just after it crashed, the soldiers below turned like a swarm in perfect harmony, sprinting back over bodies to reach their vehicle.

"Your impatience and ignorance has caused this," Textile pulsed.

The construct had altered its messages now, scaling back their intensity and frequency. Playing the good cop, as the saying went. Nevertheless, the trick was effective. It had smoothed its words enough to slip them under Bahr's mental barrier. Perhaps the situation's futility had worn down some fatigued muscle deep in his brain.

"Do you have their location?" Bahr asked. He didn't have enough time, let alone energy, to return to the green Alpine and triangulate their position before they moved on. Besides, for all he knew, their radios or implants might have been torn apart in the crash.

Textile's Morse code was soft, swirling with cotton edges. *"If you had left this action in my hands, there would not be such an error."*

"I took them down."

"Yet I approximate that they will survive the initial impact," Textile said. *"My readings indicate that there is another presence in the area. A presence that threatens the interest of my forces. I should have you butchered here and now."*

"You haven't let me finish my work."

"It is already finished. You failed."

"I took the initiative," Bahr said. *"Now tell me where they are."*

"You must have faith in my assessment of the situation." Textile's silence between sentences hummed in his awareness. It was a living, horrible thing. *"To an accomplished player of chess, every piece has a past and future role. You did not perform the function of your piece. Judging by my estimates of nearby vehicles, they will be intercepted in six minutes."*

"You didn't answer me," Bahr streamed back. *"They're carrying something, aren't they?"*

"That is correct."

"And it threatens the Coalition's existence."

"It will not come to light," Textile pulsed, *"provided you act in accordance with my instructions. It is the passengers, not the cargo, that should be protected."*

"They're traitors. If you—"

"If you disobey me again, I will have every centimeter of your flesh pierced with needles. I will make your wife and child scream for death. Are you listening to me now?"

Bahr gritted his teeth, shut out the encroaching visions. Then he stared down at the bodies littering the landscape. *"I know I can finish this."*

"It will not be as simple as you imagine," Textile pulsed. *"And that is why you must OBEY."*

He saw flashes of Jana's face, Michal's face. The Dutch girl's face.

Slinging his rifle across his back, Bahr spun around and jogged toward the main stairwell. *"Where do I go?"*

"Coordinates to a nearby road will be delivered momentarily," Textile replied.

"A nearby road? No. I need to know where they crashed."

There was a rare, unsettling pause. A hiccup in the hyper-algorithm. *"I do not have that information."*

Bahr froze midway down the stairs. *"Then who's set to intercept them? Nationalists?"*

"Follow my directives, and only my directives."

CHAPTER 21

Even with the narcotics running through him, pain was a spotlight lancing into Stasik's awareness and disorienting him in throbs. The septic red pulses behind his eyes assured him that he was close to the end. Closer than before the pain, that was. And between the throbbing, amid the dying squeals of a turbine, he thought of his disgust for pain. It was a useless, primal thing.

A reminder of imminent death.

Stasik forced his eyes open and raked his fingers through muddy leaves. He was on his stomach, gasping but intact, encircled by copses of skinny gray trees and shallow ravines. He pushed himself to his knees, then retched.

Nata. Where the fuck was Nata?

Through bleary eyes he spotted the helicopter's remains—a black, tangled mess of struts and warped rotors. Smoke curled out of its main motor assembly and underbelly, which had wound up atop the craft during its roll. Unidentified bits of metal littered the mud.

The air was suffocating, like ash dissolved in water. Splintered treetops and frayed boughs dangled over Stasik's head, their stripped bark suggesting they'd been victims of the helicopter blades. The whole place smelled of diesel and turpentine.

"Nata?" Stasik called. He'd come to associate hearing loss with violence, but here there was only stillness. Far too much of it, in fact. "Mallison? Can anybody hear me?" With white, shaking fingers, he activated his Morse implant and whispered: "Mallison, come in."

Nothing.

But as his eyes adjusted to the trails of smoke wicking up and into the breeze, he spotted something in the helicopter's belly. Red emergency bulbs illuminating a length of dark hair.

Before he knew any better, he was up and sprinting over blackened earth. At the edge of the wreckage, he grabbed onto a serrated ledge of the chassis, hauled himself up, and combed through a floor of dark nylon webbing that had once been affixed to the ceiling.

Nata was in the back of the craft, suspended upside down with her thin arms dangling. Even with a dark crimson flush to her face from all the blood pumping headward, she seemed serene. She was still secured by the harness that had failed Stasik.

No, he remembered. By the harness he'd neglected to wear.

"Nata," he said, hoarsely at first and then again with force. "Wake up. Can you hear me?"

She remained limp, swaying.

Stasik grasped her shoulder. As he did, the sound of panicked breaths punched into his awareness, likely no further than ten meters from the leaves on the helicopter's other side. They had the high strain of Mallison's voice.

"Mallison, is that you?" he shouted.

"Yes!" The reply was a bark between gasps and rustling leaves. "Polocheva tried to crawl off—she hasn't got a pulse!"

The widow. The missing link.

"I'll check for a med kit," Stasik replied. He squeezed Nata's shoulder, whirled around, and gazed at the ceiling for the red-and-white logo of their medical container. No luck. It seemed that half of their strapped-down supplies weren't crash-proof and now blanketed the surrounding leaves in fragments.

He glanced at the cockpit. "Gus, are you all right?"

Again that eerie silence, undercut only by Mallison's breathless murmuring and shifting fabric. But there was little ambiguity from the pilot. The cockpit was a milky dome of shattered glass and blast-resistant white paint, now speckled with blood. Gus' helmet had been crunched in like a Ping-Pong ball on its right side.

"He's gone," Mallison called, as though reminding Stasik how to reconcile with the obvious.

"There's no kit," Stasik said.

He took both of Nata's shoulders, gripping her tighter and angling his cheeks toward her face to feel a fledgling breath. It was there, wasn't it? Or was it sublimating liquid fuel on the breeze?

"Nata, look at me," he said.

Something warm brushed his cheek. Breath. She was breathing. He scrambled below her and worked at the arrangement of buckles that had been transformed with nightmarish complexity as a result of the helicopter's flip. He pried at the clasps and straps.

The stutters of the engine's misfiring cylinders emerged

from the western pines, directly beyond where Stasik had woken in the mud. He heard wheels grinding through soil and saplings, rippling the branches far in the distance. An approaching vehicle.

"Come on," Stasik hissed, digging his nails into the clasp's iron depression. "Wake up. Wake up!"

"The fuck is that?" Mallison yelled outside. "Where is that med kit?"

Stasik tore the clasp free, braced himself against Nata's weight as she plunged into his arms. She was surprisingly light, but that only added to her frailty. He settled her into his arms, tucking her head against his shoulder, and swiveled toward Mallison's side of the downed helicopter. Everything within the hold felt louder, more threatening. The vehicle was drawing up on them faster than he'd anticipated.

Mallison was still slapping Polocheva's wrists and cradling her neck upon her knee when Stasik sidled over the edge, hefting Nata in his arms the entire way down. Mallison glanced up at him, her eyes wild. Polocheva's tin container rested by her feet. "Where's the kit?"

"I don't know!" Stasik shifted Nata in his arms. She was getting heavier, as expected, but it was the shakes in his tendons more than her weight. "They're almost on us. We need to get moving."

"Who started firing back there?"

"It's that Aryan," Stasik said. "Not the nationalists."

Mallison cursed. "Listen, set your girl down and find me a med kit. Polocheva hasn't got a chance without it."

"We don't have a chance if we don't start moving."

"All this way for one old fucking woman's word, and now you're leaving her?"

"She won't be able to walk."

"Not without your help."

A hot rush worked through his head, an urge to wander off with Nata and abandon Mallison right there. But that urge faded as quickly as it had arisen. He needed her.

"Let's just go," he snapped. "Take the tin."

Mallison lowered Polocheva's head, stood, and approached the wreck. "No, I've had enough patience with your schoolgirl."

The engine continued growling on the other side of the underbrush, squealing up long tracts of soil and tearing down clumps of tangled roots.

"Diane!" Stasik yelled. "Let's move."

"The survival of a Coalition civilian is paramount," Mallison replied. "That's what you always told me!"

Section 78, article four, subheading two. A text string Stasik held in his heart like gospel.

"She has no chance of making it," he said.

Not without sacrificing Nata.

Not without sacrificing all of them—that was what he'd meant to think.

"We'll leg it!" Stasik called out, pressing onward despite the strain of Nata's slack body against his own. She was light but cumbersome; most corpses were. He shook off that thought, hauled her through a clump of brambles. "Mallison, let's *move.*"

She spun toward him. "What about—"

"Forget Polocheva!"

He listened to the rustling branches, the footsteps shuffling through the leaf litter.

After a moment, Mallison hurried past Stasik with her weapon drawn. "We have no choice now. She's dead."

"Fuck." Stasik sank lower, wrapped an arm around the back of Nata's legs, and heaved her onto his shoulder. He winced, felt an old disc slip out of alignment somewhere in his spinal column. Nothing the downers wouldn't be able to handle.

"Diane, grab that tin," he said. "We don't leave without the tin."

"What's it worth?" she replied.

"Without Polocheva, everything." He didn't stop, didn't even slow, as his partner hurried back into the gloom and six cylinders roared through the surrounding underbrush.

"Henry!"

He spun around. Headlights flashed through the bones of the bird, raking like off-white claws through strands of oak, pine, and birch.

Stasik knelt and laid Nata against a tree like an offering, then tore his own Colt from its holster.

The vehicle swung past them—a wartime Jeep, judging by its dented, scratched panels and missing registration plate. It spun around in a curtain of dust and fumes, then crunched to a halt near Polocheva's body.

"Recognize it?" Mallison yelled. She rushed behind the cover of an oak on the vehicle's far side and pressed herself flat against its bark, breathing hard, muttering. Praying, maybe. After a moment of stillness, she vanished into the gloom.

Stasik braved a step toward the idling vehicle, his hands slick on his Colt's grip…

Pop!

A round whistled past his ear, thudded into the tree beside him. There was no room for thinking—training took over. He ducked behind a tree, then swung out left and let off a pair of reactionary shots.

Another volley chattered in the thin air, raking the bark near Stasik's face, shaving splinters into shotgun pellets.

Stasik glanced at Nata. Her eyes were fluttering open, her legs absently scratching the leaf litter to stand, to flee...

"Stay still!" he called over the clap of incoming fire. "Just stay there, please."

Then there were three snaps—high-powered, familiar registers that harkened back to Stasik's days in the academy—and nothing more.

No birds, no engines, no dancing leaves.

Seconds later, a wet clicking noise filled their absence.

The death rattle.

Stasik peered around the tree trunk's opposite side to gauge the scene. The helicopter bleeding smoke, the stationary Jeep, the silhouettes of two men lying belly-up in mud. One of the men was straining to lift his hand, straining to live.

Mallison raced over to the shooter from behind him, her pistol gripped with both hands and arms locked, and fired a round into his skull.

"Clear!" she shouted, her voice breaking as she did so. And with that, the energy of violence collapsed into shock. Mallison slumped against the Jeep, inhaling in high, wheezing gulps. She struggled to holster her weapon.

"Hold on," Stasik said back in a quiet voice, still looking at the bodies, still wondering if the men themselves knew they were dead. Wondering if Mallison's training had taken over her, too.

He'd never seen that aspect of her. It was a buried, perverse thing, the ability to kill without questioning the act. A necessary thing in times like these. He was still chewing over the thought when he heaved Nata back onto his shoulder and carried her, with quaking legs, toward the Jeep.

Mallison faced away from the bodies, the tin in one hand and a dangling set of keys in the other. She retched, straightened up, then retched again.

"Are you good?" Stasik asked.

She rounded the Jeep and nudged the driver's body away with her foot. For a moment, she looked as though she had something terrible to confess. Then she started issuing sharp, quiet orders.

"Get your girl in the back. I'll see if there's a map in this thing."

"We can't take this on the road," Stasik said, sliding Nata off his shoulder and against the Jeep's passenger door. "It's probably flagged already."

Nata's eyes bolted open. "What's happened?" Her tone was alarmed yet groggy, her head lolling about to make sense of this new world. She pressed a palm to Stasik's chest, staggered awkwardly out of his embrace like a newborn fawn. "What is that?"

Stasik's body tensed into aching knots. She was staring at one of the shooter's dead bodies. Gaping at it.

"It's nothing," he said. "Come on, we shouldn't linger here."

"Who is he?" Nata asked.

"He opened fire first," Stasik said, only realizing he'd neglected to examine the corpse after he spoke. He peered around Nata's shaking frame, made sense of the shooter's mud-freckled camouflage trousers, surplus load-carrying vest, and olive drab turtleneck—a nationalist. Yet there were metallic patches lining his skin, the subtle traces of surgical blades and implant wiring.

"Did you know him?" he asked.

"No," Nata said.

"He's dressed like the others," Stasik said. "Maybe he—"

"He's not with their cell," Nata cut in. "He's an infiltrator." Moving closer to the body, Nata stooped down and wrenched his neck to the side. Thin copper stitches lined his skin.

At that moment, the dead man's eyes lolled open. His hand,

which had been slung across his stomach when he dropped, lifted slowly, waveringly, toward Nata's face. His frantic eyes centered on her. Fat tears dribbled down his cheeks. He tried to whisper something, but it was consumed by a froth of blood and his wheezing.

Stasik thought, distantly, to reach for his handgun and finish the man off. He looked at Mallison, who seemed equally stunned, her hand frozen halfway to her holster. Neither of them did anything. There was something pathetic about the man. Something harmless, even tender.

Nata gently placed her hands over the man's mouth and pressed down. He didn't try to fight her off, didn't scream. She, too, was inordinately calm.

Stasik exchanged a wary look with Mallison. Then he watched as his partner closed her eyes and paced around the Jeep's front end.

When the man went still, Nata's only outward reaction was an inexplicable sort of regret, verging on sadness. But even that expression was momentary. She was quick to return her attention to the neck's copper stitching.

"This was spliced into him," she said. "A two-way link, perhaps even a tracker. They're getting more and more clever."

"Nationalist or not, we aren't staying," Mallison said briskly as she opened the driver's side door. "Get in the Jeep."

"Diane, did you hear me?" Stasik asked. "This Jeep will be tracked."

"We don't have any other options right now." Mallison settled into the driver's seat, stared directly ahead through dusty glass. "Come on."

"Wait," Nata said, stepping over the body and hurrying toward the wreckage. "Where's Julia? Miss Polocheva. Where is she?"

RHETT C BRUNO & JAMES WOLANYK

"Don't go over there," Stasik said.

But it was too late. Too late to save the old woman, too late to preserve justice, too late to keep Nata from falling apart. There was only the truth now. All Stasik could do was rub his forehead, stand by the Jeep's open door, and listen to Nata's wretched screams.

"Get her in here *now!*" Mallison hissed, her eyes still fixed ahead.

She had never looked so resigned. Stasik couldn't tell precisely what had broken her. Maybe the killing, maybe Polocheva's death. All he knew with certainty was that some part of her, some functioning, human part, had switched off. He knew that because he could sense its absence in himself.

Stasik holstered his weapon, brushed his shoes through dead leaves. "Give her a minute."

"A minute won't mend anything," Mallison said as she started the Jeep. "Surviving might."

———

They drove for so long that pain crept back into Stasik's body. It had to have been six hours, perhaps seven—it was impossible to tell with a cracked watch. The tapering effects of the uppers was all he had.

At some point in the drive, the forests dimmed from afternoon to night, stranding him in the vague, seemingly eternal witching hour he'd feared since childhood. And after so many identical kilometer markers and stretches of headlight-painted pines, the landscape itself became a strange dream.

Nata sat in the back among clusters of oil-stained shirts and metal tubing, staring blankly out at fields, ruined barns, and lonesome radio towers. She was asleep now, but it did nothing to clear the air. Mallison's words were sparse enough to be counted on one hand.

After yet another foray into a rural expanse, however, Stasik realized that they were going nowhere in particular. He glanced at Mallison long enough to notice the vacant look on her face.

"Do you know where we're headed?" he asked.

Mallison blinked for what seemed like the first time in hours. She took stock of the passing fence posts and lamps streaming overhead. "We're going to a Coalition post."

"No, we're not," Stasik said. "Not with that tin."

Mallison didn't respond to that. She herself had to know it was true, if only subconsciously. She'd neglected every turn that headed toward Riga, Cesis, or Daugavpils, where Coalition posts were as plentiful as rubbish bins.

"We need to go somewhere," Stasik continued, softer this time. "At least to tell Guillory about all this."

"I'm open to suggestions."

"Moscow," Stasik said.

"We won't make it," Mallison said. "Not in this thing."

"That's what I was saying back there." *Back there.* It was the only euphemism he could find to describe what had happened. The only euphemism that wouldn't break Mallison, he supposed. "Listen, there has to be a railway near here. I heard a train rolling past us a few minutes ago. We can catch one of the overnights to Moscow."

"You want to take her on a civilian line?"

"We might as well paint a target on ourselves if we take an intervention line in this region," Stasik said. "When we get on, I can update Guillory."

"We haven't got a dicer."

"I know," Stasik said. "Nothing sensitive over the phone, but enough to let him know we're on our way."

"Is that the best you've got?"

Stasik shrugged.

"When this is all over," Mallison said, eyeing the approaching sign that advertised Tornakalns Station and its distance of twenty-three kilometers, "remind me to give you a fat lip."

———

THEY DID THEIR WORK IN THE STATION WITH ALL THE SUBTLETY and speed of bank robbers. Not real robbers, Stasik supposed, but the caricatures he'd seen in Tuesday matinees. They had to be swift, had to be ghosts.

Stasik stood near the restrooms, his gaze flicking between the scheduling boards—ten minutes to departure—and Mallison, who stood at the ticket window with one hand on the counter, her jacket draped over the tin.

The uppers were on the verge of vanishing from Stasik's system. He could feel the crash building behind his forehead, aching, throttling the blood-brain barrier. Everything was a threat in this state. He studied each passenger that pushed their way through the double doors. Their eyes, their overcoats, their briefcases, their glasses, their canes, their children.

They were all roaming by, not a care in the world. Unaware of bullets that might come punching through the windows at any moment if the Aryan or any of those surgically modified nationalists found them.

Nearby, mounted between the drooping ferns of plastic-leaf tropical plants, was a television displaying Nata's face. It ran a clip from her modeling days, a three-second loop of her on the runway with a devilish smile and crimson eye shadow. Scrolling beneath the video was the watermark of Channel Three and a bolded headline: "SEARCH CONTINUES FOR ANASTASIA DANICHEVA. CAN WE FIND HER TOGETHER?"

Fuck.

"Ready?"

Stasik flinched at the sound of Mallison's voice. He blinked at her, mumbled something in the affirmative, and returned his attention to the door.

"They can't actually be running that," Mallison said, her voice frail, eyes glued to the news screen. "Time to board."

"I doubt this is the first run," Stasik said.

"Where's your girl?"

"She's—" He let the words crystallize in the air, fade away. No, she wasn't by the coffee stand. Wasn't where she said she'd be. Wasn't anywhere. "Shit."

"Be easy," Mallison said, though she spoke through gritted teeth.

"She could be topside, by the rails."

"Or in the bathrooms."

Despite their suggestions, however, no answer would suffice. Not until she was in front of Stasik, then on the train, then in the Wing's blast-proof box in Moscow before her hearing.

"You want to check the perimeter?" Mallison asked, fingers creeping toward her weapon.

Stasik set a hand on hers, stilled her. "Just wait a—"

Nata came sauntering through the entrance, her hair slick with the evening rainfall, sticking in dark strands along her neck and face. Her lips fanned out in the dull afterglow of a smile.

"Where the hell have you been?" Mallison asked.

Nata calmly walked next to Stasik, glanced up at the television. "I was making a call."

"We didn't authorize that," Mallison said.

"Do I need permission to phone a friend?"

"Right now, you do."

"Stow it," Stasik said. "This is *not* the goddamn time. Did you book the cars like we discussed?"

Mallison hardened her gaze, gave a paltry nod. "Two rooms on the express train. One solo, one couple."

"Less suspicious," Stasik said, unsure of whom he needed to convince. "Let's get moving."

"Moving? We haven't stopped moving, Henry."

CHAPTER 22

Outside Riga, Latvian province
511 miles from Moscow

"*Today in Stockholm, fifteen hundred youths bearing Coalition sashes gathered for yet another Pride in Peace March. Tonight's broadcast on Channel One will feature full coverage of this splendid event, as well as—*"

Bahr cranked the Alpine's radio dial down, silencing a woman's cheery broadcasting voice and its accompanying fanfare. The constant supply of the Coalition news networks' standard jubilance had grown grating after his third hour behind the wheel. On another day, under different pressures, he might've taken Michal to the march, let him sing and clap and eat candied almonds.

But now, as he made his way on fumes through endless lanes of black forest canopy, he was in no mood for their festivities. For their frivolous idea of *peace*, even. He had known peace, had felt it like sunlight on his cheeks when his captain barged into their barracks and announced the Reich's fall.

He had run his hands over peace when he returned to Jana.

And on the day of his son's birth, he had glimpsed peace in blue button eyes and small, fat fingers that would never know the act of killing.

That was peace.

Nobody on the radio—the offspring of cowards and dissidents—would ever understand such a thing. They knew peace only as a word, an idea, a shop with no queues or breadlines. They knew it as a goddamn drug.

Bahr gripped the wheel harder, steeled his eyes against exhaustion. His amphetamine blend had started to fade from the moment he found the helicopter's gutted wreckage. Nothing there had stoked his spirits, not even the dead Slavic woman.

"*Don't overthink,*" Textile streamed to him. "*Remain focused on the task at hand.*"

He didn't deign the construct's intrusion with a reply. He was too frustrated with its vague, bumbling lines of code, which hadn't been able to root out the traitors' signatures since the crash. It was no use to argue the point—Textile was as petty and defensive as any human contact might be.

Besides, he'd come to understand its limitations. Despite its sentience, the construct was a glorified bat blundering through unexplored caves. It painted a picture of a target's location only through interactions with wired lines—telephone calls, purchases, and such—or through the relatively crude use of boots on the ground.

Not unlike myself, he thought sourly.

He'd lost the agents' trail on his radar box, though he wasn't sure why. His targets had either shut off all their radio equipment, managed to obscure their Morse signatures, or both.

Whatever the case, the result was the same: He was on a blind chase.

And because of the construct's similar ignorance, which it masked as unmistakably human enthusiasm, Bahr's hunt had devolved into an exercise in futility. Following the construct's suggestions, he'd raced from town to town, bridge to ferry crossing, scouring each and every possible sanctuary in the surrounding Latvian sprawl. He'd even combed the Morse bands for every intervention unit in the area, only to find that they were just as clueless as to the agents' location as he was.

Several kilometers down the road, where the forest thinned out into six-lane overpasses and warehouses deep within thickets, Bahr came upon a petrol station with a small cafe and folded-up wooden benches. He pulled into the gravel lot, turned off the Alpine's engine, and got out.

"I've deposited petrol marks into your account," Textile streamed.

Bahr smirked at that. It reminded him of his own father, who'd used marks—once *reichsmarks*—as a cure for everything from measles to mistresses.

"I have my own," he replied.

"Fill the entire tank," Textile said. *"You'll need it."*

Bahr stopped halfway to the door. *"What've you got?"*

"Train tickets were purchased one hour north of you. A first-class line to Moscow. Diane Mallison's checking account. The agent attempted to encrypt her transaction, but her work was not thorough enough." The construct paused as though it were proud, wanting Bahr to appreciate its abilities. *"Two telephone connections were also made from the ticketing lobby to unknown nationalist cells in an obscured location."*

"What do you mean, unknown? You caught the line, didn't you?"

"The calls appear to have been placed by your target. The vocal

samples correspond in 97.35% of wave signatures. It is impossible, however, to identify the call's recipients."

"*They'll turn up sooner or later,*" Bahr replied. "*Nationalists make mistakes.*"

"*They are not the same breed of nationalists you have come to know. They know my detection parameters. They are a threat.*"

A wicked thrill came over Bahr. What was the call about?

"*There is a suborbital field located one day's drive from you,*" Textile said, forcing Bahr's attention back to the matter at hand. "*Time is of the essence.*"

"*I need more details,*" Bahr said.

"*The suborbital field is your priority.*"

"*What about their train to Moscow?*"

"*Everything will become clear in due time,*" the construct replied. "*But first, you will need to run an errand of great importance. Fill the tank and listen to me.*"

CHAPTER 23

Outside Velikiye Luki, Russian Province
337 miles from Moscow

Even when it was time to sleep, Stasik couldn't. He had no concept of insomnia anymore—with or without the uppers, his brain was wired different than the rest. Seemed that way, at least. He couldn't remember a time when he'd felt alive without adrenaline in his system. It didn't matter what released it—fear, rage, excitement. That was his fuel.

But even adrenaline burned off eventually. It left him in a haggard slump on the suite's recliner, his eyelids fluttering open and shut, fingers just tense enough to balance a lit cigarette over a polyester armrest. Snippets of rogue faces and childhood toys rolled through his head, all of them indistinct, rusty.

It was a familiar state, if a jarring one. He'd spent most of his academy days in that lull, dragging his body from lectures to training fields and back again, day after day.

Of course, back then, nobody had been trying to blow his

brains out. It was frightening to notice how quickly his nervous system had adapted to the strain. His mind swam when he tried to recall how long it had been since he'd rested in a bed or had a decent meal. Had a decent shit, even.

But he'd trained for this, hadn't he? He'd learned to reject the idea of normalcy. His file told a story about a man who could resist everything from torture to sleep deprivation. Now, he couldn't recognize that man.

Somewhere out there, however, among the black woods and swamps, was a man who had learned to break himself to better break others. An Aryan tempered in war and bred to destroy. A man who would not stop until he'd skinned Nata and put a hole through—

Somebody knocked at the door of his train cabin.

No, not somebody—the echoes were familiar. Mallison.

"Coming." Stasik worked to open his eyes, set his cigarette on the lip of the ashtray, and straighten out his tie. He'd caught himself beginning to undress several times since they entered the suite, only to remember he was sharing the room with a lady. With *her*.

He could smell Nata's floral products seeping through the bathroom door. Could hear the shower's spray pattering down over Italian tiles. He downed the last of the rum on ice he'd found in the mini-fridge, then crossed under the jangling chandelier and opened the door.

Mallison looked sharper, fresher. Hard to tell if she'd found an amphetamine lozenge or applied a touch of the collagen powders they'd been peddling on the aisle carts.

"Well?" she asked. "Did you put in the call yet?"

"Line's been spotty," Stasik said. "The operator said he'd give us a scrambled call from his end within the hour." He stepped aside, though Mallison entered as though she owned the joint.

He watched her circling the suite, scanning everything with that falcon gaze of hers.

"Looking for something?" he asked.

"Not quite," Mallison said, crinkling her nose as she regarded the bathroom door. "How long's she been in there?"

"What is it?"

"Nothing."

"Doesn't seem like nothing."

Mallison stuffed her hands in her pockets, sank down into a varnished dining chair. "I think we should have a talk, Henry."

Stasik closed the door. "About what?"

"Might be better in my room."

"If it's important, you can say it here." Stasik moved to the chair opposite Mallison and poured out another drink from the row of nips bottles. This time, Indian gin. "Say it plain."

"Henry, before you talk to Guillory, I need to know something."

"Just get to it, Diane."

"Lower your voice." She eyed the bathroom door once again. "This is between us."

"Fine. Between us. Now spill it."

Mallison leaned over the cherrywood table and brushed her glass aside. "There's not much holding us up when we get to Moscow."

"We have the tin, and we have her, and—"

"The nationalists are on a chopping block now, Henry. Her word won't hold up in that court."

"Are you serious, Diane?" he asked, incredulous.

"After what I saw, nothing will ever be the same." Mallison let herself ease back, biting her nails. "Little things like that just don't feel strange. One life. You know, it's not so tremendous in the bigger picture."

"You can't think like that."

She gave a short, hard laugh. "You introduced me to the philosophy. You, this case." Mallison gave a long exhale. "Let's be practical, Henry."

"Practical?" Stasik said. "What are you asking me to do, Diane?"

"It's what I'm asking you not to do."

"Don't you dare say it."

"Let's drop it, Henry," Mallison whispered, never breaking her stare. "We can wrap this up with a bow when we get to Moscow, and that'll be the end of it."

"I'm not throwing her to the wolves."

"Wolves have to eat *something*," Mallison said. "Come off this savior routine. Please. She won't get a fair shake anywhere in this world, and that's a crying shame, but it doesn't need to be our cross to bear."

"We promised it would be."

Mallison scowled. "We've done our part."

"She's done hers, too."

"Oh, she has? Like making calls without permission. To whom, Henry? For what purpose? For all I know, she's pulling more strings than we are. And did you see the way she took out that nationalist? There's something wrong here."

Stasik shook his head through the barrage of questions, tried not to face it himself. "If we don't finish it, it's not worth anything."

"It's worth our sanity, and our lives, and our futures. I have a family I need to see, Henry. A sister, a mum, a gran. They need me."

Stasik opened his mouth, assembling words with surgical precision to tear into his partner, but nothing emerged. Instead, her logic cut into him. Defused the fire in him. Took all the strain out of his spine until he could only slump back.

"You want me to drop this case, Diane?" he asked softly.

She nodded. Her eyes glittered with forming tears. "I want us to live our lives the way they were."

"That won't happen, no matter what we do."

"But it's worth a shot," Mallison said. "It's worth more than her."

"Jesus, Diane."

"Please."

Stasik cradled his head in his hands. He pictured Nata in the shower, her body twirling under the water, soft, warm—

The phone rang.

"I can answer it," Mallison said.

"No," Stasik said, his body jerking toward the dresser and the receiver atop it. "Just, let me speak to him."

"What are you going to say?"

"What I need to say."

Mallison started on something else, but he couldn't hear her. He'd already picked up the phone and pressed it to his ear.

"Specialist?" Guillory's gruff voice crackled through the dicer's connection. "Is that you?"

"Yeah, that's right," Stasik said, glancing at Mallison and her chewed-to-the-stump nails. "I'm here with Specialist Mallison. And our client."

"Were you in the firefight near Riga?"

"We were, sir."

Guillory sighed. "What in the fuck happened there?"

"They ambushed us, sir." Stasik's teeth began to chatter. "Listen, sir, I can't say much here. I just wanted to confirm that we'll make it to that trial. We'll be there soon."

"Did you find anything new?"

"A few things," Stasik said quietly. "Don't worry about us, sir."

"Operators pinged Mallison's modified chip somewhere

near the Russian territory. A civilian line running on the red-eye cycle. That right?"

"We're on it," Stasik said.

"You should've called us, Specialist."

Stasik swallowed past the lump in his throat. "There were extraordinary conditions, sir. I can't disclose everything over this connection."

"You're a fool." Guillory coughed. "A goddamn fool. Anybody could be on the line."

"We're lying low, sir."

"Lying low hasn't saved anybody's skin since before the flood," Guillory said. "Where are you now?"

"I dunno," Stasik said. "Probably drawing up on Ludza."

Several seconds passed in silence, punctuated only by Guillory's muttered French and the scratch of his fountain pen. "I'm having an undercover detachment board in Ludza. Maybe the next station. They'll watch your scrawny hide."

"It's not necessary," Stasik said.

"You don't tell me about necessary. Is there a dining car there?"

"Should be."

"You eat in two hours. Hear me? Two. Hours."

Stasik cocked a brow. "We were thinking of room service."

"Be quiet, Specialist," Guillory said. "They'll make contact after you dine. I'm sending your profiles to the team."

"With all due respect, sir—"

"It's not the time to pull this bullshit. The region's burning up with nationalists after what happened in Riga. We can't get enough intervention units into some of the blocks. You, Mallison, and the Russian keep your mouths shut, and you get to Moscow. Understood?"

Stasik met Mallison's eyes, then gave a weak nod. "Understood, sir."

"And, Specialist," Guillory said, "if you see a single goddamn piece of lint out of place, you make the call."

The phone's connection severed with a click and a fizzle. Stasik set the phone on its hook, backed away from the table, and folded his arms.

"So?" Mallison asked, brow knitted with concern.

"Take a shower," he said. "Throw on some blush. We've got dinner reservations."

"Dinner?"

"When in Rome."

Mallison stood, hardened her face. "Just think about what I asked. Are you with me, Henry?"

The chandelier swayed overhead, casting strange, wriggling shapes on the walls. Light played over Mallison's face in strobe-like vignettes.

"Henry?" she repeated.

Stasik moved to the door, opened it, and waited for Mallison to step out. He could barely speak through his aching jaws. "I'm with you."

And when she walked back to her room, she wore the sad, ambivalent smile that Stasik had often seen on the faces of those who cared too much for him. The sort of smile that made him wonder if he owed a debt to past lovers, past friends. Not that he even knew how to repay them.

He returned to the recliner and poured out another nips bottle. He hadn't ever asked for anybody to want him or like him or coddle him, but they did it all the same. They loved him to be loved in turn—a price he couldn't give a fuck about paying.

So he drank vodka on melting ice and listened to the hum of Nata's shower, to the soft squelching of her footsteps over tiles…

The click of a deadbolt lock made his eyes spring open.

Nata stood in the bathroom's thin wreath of steam, her hair

drawn back into a sopping ponytail, long, supple legs stretching out beneath a cotton robe. There was something deeper than sex in her poise—it was power. Power that made her unassailable, unquestionable, much like the way children viewed policemen and men in white coats.

"Who were you talking to?" she asked.

"Talking?" Stasik took a swig of the vodka to wet his mouth. "Oh, it was Guillory."

"I heard a woman."

"Mallison was asking about dinner."

"Oh," Nata said, crossing one leg over the other as she leaned against the doorframe.

"Can you come and sit?" Stasik asked. "I need to talk to you."

"Perhaps I should start by apologizing," Nata said as she approached him. She sat down and rested a hand far higher up on his thigh than he'd expected.

Stasik looked at the ceiling. "For what?"

"What we saw in that tin. Sometimes I forget that I'm not innocent. I didn't mean to misrepresent myself. I just forget."

"You forgot all of it?"

"Almost all," she said, low. "In dreams, I sometimes see pieces. But it's hard to tell nightmares from memories, isn't it?"

Stasik took in the silence, nodded. "It's all right."

"You must be angry with me."

"I was." Maybe he still was, even as he said it. Passion and rage were difficult to sense in sobriety. They never really reached the same heights. "Miss Danicheva, I don't know how to say this—"

"I'm going to die in Moscow," she interrupted.

"No," he said, though his response was as automatic as a hand jerking away from a hot stove. "I mean, that's not what it's about."

"I was hoping you might help me with that."

The ambiguity of *that* was a worm in Stasik's brain. When he remembered Guillory's boss and all the photographed horrors bundled alongside his name, *that* became a bullet, ripping straight through him.

"What do you mean?" Stasik asked.

"A lot of things," she said. "Back in the station, I listened to the media broadcasts. They're saying that the nationalists shot down that helicopter. I don't think either of us agree with that."

"No, it wasn't them."

"It wasn't the Coalition, either."

Stasik shook his head. "I'm not ready to discuss that, Nata."

"Moscow is never going to set the record straight," she said. "My point is that some men are well beyond reproach, and I'm not vain enough to think that I'll burn them out. And you're skilled, Henry—dedicated, no less—but this is only the beginning. I'd be spinning fantasies if I said there was an end."

Again, he understood. "What are you saying, then?"

"Nothing that you probably haven't already considered." She glanced out the window at the surrounding blackness. "When we were in Madam Polocheva's flat, I watched your face. You've been toying with the same fears I have, but I'm sure that yours extend more deeply. In that sense, I was lucky. When you know the truth of an ideology, you're not likely to build any part of your identity upon it, are you? Because when you try to challenge it, it's futile, even crushing.

"You begin to feel like you're beating your fists against bricks. Like you might scream 'fire!' in a crowded theater and nobody would move. They'd rather sit there, burning, than ever close the curtains." She shrugged. "That's how I feel, anyway. Not enough to affect anything, but too much to disappear. It's a dreadful thing, Henry, but I'm no stranger to it."

"That's not what this is about," Stasik said.

"I can see it in your eyes, Henry. You know this is all just as futile as I do."

"That's not true."

"What did you want to talk to me about, then?"

"About how much I want to have justice," Stasik said. And he knew, as he spoke those words, that it was the truth. "I want to see us come out of this. I mean you. I want to see you make it."

"And what about the men who did this?" she asked.

"They'll make amends," he whispered. "Somehow."

"They exterminated eighty-five million people who didn't fit their mold." Nata glared at him. "What *amends* can be made with the dead?"

Better yet, what amends could be made with the living? Stasik found it difficult to parse her expressions without the bloom of narcotics, but he could read repulsion. He could also read the casual way in which Nata reported the number. Eighty-five million. He had never seen eighty-five million of anything, couldn't even imagine the figure. It seemed impossible for one group to kill so many. He didn't know how you could hide that many bodies, and bomb that many places like the photographs showed, all without anybody knowing anything. All without *him* knowing anything.

"If they're prepared to accept sentencing for their roles," Stasik managed, trying to shake off the number, "then we need to encourage it. That's the first step."

"But they won't. This has happened before, Henry. Other girls like me—smart, strong girls from the academy, the ones who also survived their purges—brought the names of a half-dozen men to the forefront of the judicial system."

Stasik reached for the vodka again with shaking hands. "Were they acquitted?"

"The trials never even started." Nata gave a withering little laugh. "You can have every shred of evidence you need, but it's not enough to convict these men. The Coalition would tear itself apart if it ever knew the truth."

"I'm handling it just fine."

"No, you're not." She met his eyes square-on, frowning. "It broke you."

"That isn't true."

"Maybe not yet," she whispered. "Maybe it's too soon for it all to sink in, Henry. But when they misplace your evidence and send you packing back to Vilnius, it'll show you their true face."

He just stared at her, trying to appear more composed than he actually was. He didn't have the logic, nor the assurances, to dispute any of that. Not anymore.

"Do you believe me?" Nata asked, stirring him out of thought.

Stasik glanced away. "I believe the evidence."

"As you might soon find, Specialist, they're not the same."

"It doesn't matter how they present it," he said. "I saw it myself."

"There are some things you can't change with semantics, Specialist." Nata paused. "I won't deny that what they did to us was necessary, in somebody's mind. It's a hard truth about the world, isn't it? People want to do well. All of them do. We did what we were told, thinking it was well and good, and we made the world what it is today."

"They used you," Stasik said. "It's not your fault."

"For those who are still alive, it was worthwhile. Maybe even for you. I'm not blind to perspective, after all."

He couldn't take her words at face value. It was as though she stood behind him on some great ledge, nudging him toward the most obvious and likely path. Everyone else she'd known had fallen, sooner or later. But he kept his footing.

"What they did to you is inexcusable, and I can give you my word that personal bonds won't sway that," he said.

"What if those men were here before you, right now?" she asked. "Would you still say that?"

Stasik thought of his superiors' praise and commendations, of gifted bottles of 90-proof bliss. All of it gone in one breath. "It's all I could say," he answered.

"Then the real question," Nata said, leaning back and setting one of her feet between Stasik's legs, "is how you'll feel when they bury the truth. Or, should they be so bold, vindicate Dregala and the other men from the project."

"They wouldn't do that."

"Why not? I'm privy to the use of media as a weapon, Henry. If the Coalition wants to live up to its ideals, it'll cast a redemptive sheen over it all."

"Or they'll confront it head-on," Stasik whispered. It occurred to him—certainly for the first time—that it wasn't a viable strategy for the Coalition, only his own conscience. The Coalition was a monolith above all else, an end state for humanity. It was the foundation of the self.

Of *himself*, really.

The thought stilled him. He became acutely aware of his client shifting her long legs and flashing raven-feather lashes at him. The narcotics had made everything hyper-real, so glossy and manic that he'd never touched the essence of who he was. They'd made life a Hollywood production, but now there was only the tinkering final revolutions of the projector, the clammy darkness of an empty cinema. The jig was up.

To destroy the Coalition was to destroy himself.

With a long, hard breath, Stasik shook himself back to the train car and Nata. He stared into those too-perfect emerald eyes. "Whatever happens, I'll stand with you."

She smiled. A crooked, desperate smile, but it didn't matter much. "If I told you that I had a way out, would you help me?"

"We *will* get out of this."

"Even if Mallison asked you to drop it?"

Again, he pushed out an automatic reply: "Yes."

"Henry." It was a hard whisper, a reminder of promises he'd given to Mallison and broken just moments ago. "I'll go to the trial with you and I'll speak in front of their cameras, but I know that I can't outlast everything. I've known it since Donetsk. And you've known the outcome since the start."

"Would you stop talking like that?" he bristled.

"I'm more concerned with leaving a mark on this world before I go." She looked away. "A better mark, if you understand me."

"You can get away from it all," he said, all the while thinking *we.*

"If you do this for me, *daragoy,* it won't be for nothing."

Stasik worked to get past the lump in his throat. Nata was safe with him here, thousands of kilometers from Moscow and its legal proceedings. To think otherwise was lunacy. Yet the transience of the moment was crushing. The ever-changing backdrop of woodlands reminded him that he was no more suited to be her savior than to prevent the sun from rising.

She rested her hand even higher up on his thigh, leaned closer. "I need you to kill whoever threatens us."

What should've been shock was instead Nata's vanilla perfume, ethereal and tempting. She moved toward him, and he responded in kind, drifting closer until her breaths were warm on his neck. *Kill.* The word squirmed around the conscious part of his mind, drowning in reptilian instincts. He opened his mouth, tried to resist, wanted to.

She raked her fingers across his leg while she kissed him, and at once nothing mattered beyond her.

"Will you do it?" she whispered, their lips barely parted. Her hand slid under his dress shirt and waited on the tender skin below his navel. "Say you will, *daragoy*. For me."

"Yes," he said. "I will."

CHAPTER 24

S tasik, Nata, and Mallison ate at a circular table in the center of the dining car. All around them were other crowded tables, most accented by satin booths and raised railing sections.

Stasik studied his fellow guests as they chatted beneath the rattling suspended lamps, within pools of cigarette smoke, over plates of foie gras and crepes with caviar. It didn't take long to notice that many of the other diners stared back, either quickly or in long gulps.

Mallison sat ahead and to his left, Nata ahead and to his right. He felt trapped between their siren gazes. Threatened, even. It had been so long since he'd needed to control his attention without a cocktail of neurotransmitter alterations. The glamor of the dining car didn't do him any favors. His eyes swung back and forth, lured by flashing jewelry and sparkling champagne.

"Henry assured me that everything will go well in Moscow," Nata said while cutting into her filet mignon. She'd raised the topic out of nothingness, just after discussing the region's early darkness and plummeting temperatures.

"Of course it will," Mallison said. She looked up, winked at Stasik. "Things will settle down. Right, Henry?"

"Wine could be better," Stasik said.

"You're right," Nata said to Mallison, ignoring him and glancing at her. "Soon enough, I'm sure it will sort itself out. Life can't stay in one state for too long."

Mallison nodded. "Peaks and valleys."

"Are we atop a peak or in a valley?" Nata asked, flashing a thin smile as she moved another forkful of bleeding-rare steak to her lips.

Mallison laughed, though Stasik didn't know why.

Then Nata's attention drifted up and away, fixing on something far beyond Stasik's left shoulder. She squinted, dabbed at her lips with a folded white napkin, and slid her chair legs back across velvet carpeting. "Excuse me, would you?"

Mallison's knife squealed against ceramic. "Certainly."

Stasik didn't watch her go, though it vexed him to ignore the smooth, rosy flesh sauntering away in the candlelight. Instead, he angled himself toward the window and glanced back casually at the table at the rear of the car.

There were three men, two women, and a barren tablecloth. They held untouched glasses of champagne and chatted with a sort of forced candor.

Stasik scratched at his scalp as he turned back to his meal, fighting to be easy, to repress the shakes that always followed an amphetamine bender. A phantom image of the table lingered in his mind's eye. There was *something* off about them. Something capable of rattling Nata.

And that was all it took to rattle him in turn.

Mallison set her fork and knife on the edge of the plate. "Think she's gone to powder her nose?"

"No idea," he said. Beneath the table, Stasik probed his hip for the textured polymer of his holster. No dice. He'd removed it several hours prior and stashed it in his room's footlocker.

"Have you thought about what you're going to do when this is over?" Mallison asked.

It took him a moment to realize she was referring to something aside from Nata's unease. "I haven't given it much thought," he said, though in his mind he saw the sunrise beyond Buenos Aires. "I'd like to be somewhere warm."

She grinned. "Anywhere but here."

"That's right. Anywhere."

The door behind Mallison *whooshed* open. As Nata returned to the table, her face still bearing its cryptic, dispassionate mask, the room lost its glass-clinking elation. Conversations trickled into murmured remarks.

Nata sat in her chair without acknowledging Stasik's presence. She was staring at that back table again, undaunted by the shame familiar to those with less beautiful faces. Staring the way that Stasik wanted her to stare at him.

"Henry." Nata leaned over the table, her tone urgent. She looked directly at him. "We need to leave this train."

Mallison's jaw shifted, slowed. Her knife paused midway through the meat. "What'd you say?"

"It's not safe here," Nata said.

"Eight hours to Moscow," Mallison said. She glanced around with a wavering, flippant smile, nervous that somebody might see her obvious nervousness. "Sit back, relax. Have a drink. We're at the end of the line."

Nata leaned closer to Stasik and spoke only through her lips, without making a noise: *Get your gun.*

Stasik was halfway out of his chair before he understood what Nata had asked of him. And it was only in the adjoining corridor, shouldering past dining-car servers, that he understood what was coming.

———

THE SHAKES. STASIK COULDN'T STOP THE FUCKING SHAKES— not without the downers he didn't have, anyhow. They'd started to devour him before he holstered his weapon, before he undid the footlocker's latch, before he even reached the bedroom.

Now, he was steaming in his skin, gnawing the inner walls of his cheeks. He peered around every corner on his way back to the dining car, expecting to draw, aim, and shoot. Every window reflection had him picturing the Aryan's face.

Four cars to the dining space, then three, two. Every face he passed, every cheery "good evening, sir," presented a murderous joust. He was ready to kill—he needed to be eager. Pitiless, unquestioning.

And as he drew nearer and his heart slammed against his rib cage, he found himself anticipating the crack of a gunshot. Desiring it, almost. Something to end the tension, to—

Mallison appeared at the end of the corridor, her head angled in bewilderment. "Something wrong?"

"Diane, you can't leave her in there," Stasik warned.

"You don't look well, Henry."

"Get her out."

"Are you being serious?" Mallison said, sidling toward him with half-steps. She blinked at the lump on Stasik's hip, just under his shirt. "Is that what I think it is?"

"Diane—"

"Jesus."

Stasik jogged down the corridor, causing Mallison to shrink away and press herself to the wall. "I haven't lost it," he said. "Just hear me out."

"It's all been sorted, Henry." Mallison's voice was patient, pained. She shifted herself between Stasik and the door. "It's over now."

"They know that we found the files."

Mallison's eyes were needles. "*They?*"

"Whoever's responsible for this," Stasik clarified. "People like that don't just disappear."

"And what if they do?"

"How do you explain Dregala? If Guillory's own *boss* is on this, then—"

She cut him off. "There are some things that aren't meant to be explained."

"If it were up to them, nothing would be."

"Henry, we're being escorted to Moscow to show it all," she whispered, her voice somewhere between pleading and cracking. "Eight hours. We've got *eight hours.* Then it's done and out there, and the Wing's oversight committee handles it, and life goes on. Please."

"These sons of bitches won't let this go."

"Neither will you. And that's what we'll burn for." She shook her head and stole another glance through the curtained window into the dining car. Then, in a harsh whisper, she added: "Guillory's got a full detachment on this train. You know that."

Stasik clenched his jaw. All the more reason to line every agent up against the wall, make them spill their secrets: handler names, Morse ID codes, agency-issued passphrases. "This thing goes *deep*, Diane. Deeper than either of us want to know."

"You can't possibly believe he's got a crooked crew, can you?" Mallison asked.

"Just listen to me. I don't know what she saw in there, but—"

"What she saw?" Mallison scowled. "That's why you're on about this, aren't you? Because it's her fucking delusion."

"You saw what they did to her."

"We both did. Probably undid a few screws."

"And what?" he asked.

"And it stops here, Henry. It has to stop. You said you wouldn't go down for her."

"Do you have your pistol?"

Mallison's shoulders sank. "Henry."

"Do you have it or not?"

She said nothing, just grimaced and peeled back the flap of her jacket. The holster and weapon within rode high on her hip.

Stasik nodded, brushed past her. He stepped into the dining car, pulled the door shut, and surveyed the crowd.

No movement, no remarks. There were only *stares*. Dozens of pupils, some big and black, engorged on uppers, others so shrunken they were pinpricks in the candlelight, all weighing Stasik with horrible interest. At the rearmost table, which was still without plates or silverware, hands crept under white cloth and stirred in the vague corners of handbags.

Nata hadn't moved from her seat at the table. Her pale, smooth skin shifted along her dress' open back as she lifted a glass of red wine, drank it, and set it down. All the while, she never compromised the poise in her shoulders or the perfect angle of her neck.

"Come on, then," Nata addressed the back table, her voice walking the razor-wire of playfulness and cruelty. The room's rapt attention swung back to her. "This is the best chance you'll have to put me down. Alone, unarmed. Wouldn't it make you feel brave?"

The table's occupants squirmed in their seats. Their gazes wandered among the cheap Monet prints on the walls and the shadowed firs streaming past them. Few had the nerve to look one another in the eye, let alone examine Nata directly.

They aren't innocent, Stasik realized. *They're afraid.*

Amid the confusion, Stasik took stock of every table, every face. Those seated in Nata's vicinity were glancing about with the vigor and puzzlement of wild dogs, edging their chairs back in preparation for something terrible. Freckles of bearnaise sauce and French mustards glistened upon their cheeks. Their shock— their fear, even—was all too human.

But the table at the rear of the car was a victim of its own rehearsed nonchalance.

"Where are you all going?" Stasik called out to them.

Nobody spoke.

"Nata," Stasik said gently, his gaze fixed on the diners who were not diners, "stand up and come toward me."

A serious-looking woman seated at the side of the car, just behind one of the railings, drew his attention by getting to her feet. "Specialist Stasik, let's think this through," she said. One of her hands was dipping beneath the tablecloth. She had to be a name on Guillory's payroll, for better or worse. "Our detachment has everything under control."

Stasik's hand moved to his hip. "Nata."

She stood, red sequins glimmering down her body, and moved past Stasik. Her stare was straight and steadfast, her posture reminiscent of her days on the catwalk. Stasik listened to her jangling bracelets and the hiss of the rear doors.

"Specialist," Guillory's agent repeated, this time higher, sharper, "let us do our work."

On the final syllable of *work*, the first gunshot rang out at the back of the car. Then the next, and the next, instantaneously blossoming into a cascade of deafening shots. Fluted glasses exploded. Sparks leapt off metal bannisters. Diners slumped over in their seats, tongues lolling, legs jerking.

Stasik threw himself to the floor and snatched his hand-gun from its holster. Screams and discharges became muddied, distant things, lost behind a curtain of near-deafness.

In the railed section, Guillory's agents crouched behind their table, pressed to a tablecloth as though the fabric might shield them from the punch of hollow-point rounds. It didn't. A man's hand burst in a pink cloud; a woman's head snapped back with half of its jaw missing.

Stasik got down to the carpeting and began crawling back toward the doors to the cabins, which were still sliding shut. He thrust his foot out to prop the door slabs open, but a woman's hand—Mallison's, in fact—was already tugging them apart. He scrambled up onto his knees and across the threshold, his body flinching instinctively against the *pops* and *cracks* behind him, waiting for the pain of a stray round.

Mallison released the door, letting it shut near his cheek. "You just *had* to be right, didn't you?"

Stasik staggered to his feet, his lungs burning, grip aching around the Colt. He put his back to the wood paneling beside the doors. "There are five of them, Diane."

"Get a call to Guillory."

"Too late for that," Stasik said, keenly aware of every shot, every muffled *thump* of a civilian body.

"Perhaps not," Nata said. She faced the opposite end of the corridor, exploring with that easy gait of hers. She seemed engrossed by the intricacies of the tin ceiling above her. "If we can last another few minutes, we'll have the wind at our backs."

Mallison trained her weapon on the door. "What the hell is that supposed to mean?"

"I have friends in strange places," Nata said with a wry smile. "Keep the wolves at bay." Then she slipped through the gathering crowd of terrified waiters and socialites, scurrying into the safety of the dormitory cars.

"More than a few loose screws," Mallison said to Stasik in disbelief.

The pane of heat-treated glass on the dining car door shattered, provoking screams from the civilians around the corner. Stasik glanced in their direction. Curiously enough, none of them fled. Several edged closer, their shock turning to thin, curious smiles, as though they were aroused by the chaos.

"She might be onto something," Stasik said, ignoring the strange spectacle. "She's made use of those friends before."

"We're somewhere between nowhere and nothing," Mallison hissed.

A series of rounds bit into the bronze plaque directly opposite the windowpane. Stasik and Mallison glanced at one another, then angled their handguns toward the door. Footsteps encroached on the corridor, crunching glass, absently kicking metal serving trays. Somebody racked a handgun's slide.

Stasik's finger tensed on his trigger.

He stared at the jagged rim of glass left around the window's frame, waiting for motion, for anything. A brown curl appeared. A single hair. Stasik held his breath and watched another hair edge into view, then another, hesitating till he saw the slick curve of the shooter's forehead and the blood splotches on his left cheek.

In a single, instinctive motion, Stasik snatched hold of the man's oiled hair and yanked it through the window. A stubbled neck dragged over shards. The shooter screamed and jerked away.

There was no hesitation—Stasik pressed his Colt's barrel to the man's temple and fired.

Blood spattered over the carpeting and swirling French trim. Stasik hardly heard the ensuing screams. He dropped the body, let it slink back into the dining car with its glassy, vacant stare.

And despite everything Stasik had heard of killing, how it devoured good men and inspired madness, he felt nothing. In fact, it put fresh resolve in his grip. It robbed him of indecision, letting the body take over where the mind had failed him. He was neither an agent nor a man—he was a machine.

He peered through the window and saw two remaining shooters at the back table—a man and a woman, both tall, both hard-faced—standing over the bodies of Guillory's agents. Nationalists maybe, if not in league with the Aryan. Threats by any name. Stasik snapped his Colt up and put four rounds into them.

The woman folded into herself, still and silent. Her companion dropped his revolver and clutched his stomach, then stumbled back behind a cluster of tables. Every so often a tablecloth rippled to show the course of his movement.

Stasik emptied his magazine into the sprawl of wood and cloth, but it was too late. He caught sight of more gunmen barging in from the operator's car and fanning out behind cover. *Shit*. There was nobody coming to save them. Within seconds of Stasik sliding back behind cover, another volley of bullets thudded into the bronze plaque.

"They've got the operator's car," Stasik said breathlessly.

"How many?" Mallison asked.

"Four or five, I don't know," he said. "I'm all out. No spares."

Mallison was still entranced by the bright red spray across the walls and floor. "Christ, Henry." Then, as though remembering herself, remembering death, she raised her handgun and nodded at him. "Get to Danicheva. I'll cover this corridor."

Until that moment, Stasik hadn't realized exactly how many

drugged-up civilians had piled up in the corridor to watch the chaos: men in slim tweed suits, women with hoop earrings and leather handbags, all straining and squeezing to get an eyeful. They'd streamed in from every car, it seemed, beaming and feigning nausea, transfixed by the carnival of high-velocity rounds and corpses. A few of them were on the verge of applause.

"Back up!" Stasik barked, waving his Colt at the gawkers until they jeered and wheeled around in a stampede. None of them seemed to notice the handgun's slide, which had locked back to reveal an empty chamber. They were all in their own ecstatic worlds, enjoying the ride.

Mallison craned her hand around the edge of the dining car's window and blind-fired twice. "Get moving, Henry!"

But by then he was already cutting his path through the masses, nudging and shoving, his weapon held high and his mind ablaze.

———

STASIK'S BEDROOM DOOR WAS WIDE OPEN. INSIDE, NATA PACED around the central rug with a stuffed white laundry bag in hand, scanning the room for anything else worth pilfering.

Stasik ducked out of the stream of fleeing civilians and threw the door shut. He holstered his handgun, then seized her by the wrist to break her stupor.

"What are you doing?" he asked.

"Preparing," Nata replied, vaguely surprised. "We won't be here long, and the road ahead could be rather spartan."

Glancing down, Stasik spied the rumpled corner of a goose-feather pillow peeking out of her laundry bag. "Are you out of your mind?"

"I'd be a rather poor judge of that."

"Nata," Stasik hissed, tugging her closer, "if you have a plan, you need to tell me now."

She turned and took note of the clock above the dresser. "Any moment now."

Far beyond the bedroom window, in a field midway between the tracks' embankment and the black tangle of a distant wood line, headlights flared to life. Fog and exhaust fumes swirled in the pale beams.

Stasik's grip loosened on Nata's wrist. "Please tell me you know who that is."

"Our chariot," she replied, smiling faintly.

The dim shape of a truck—an archaic, diesel-chugging model—came thundering out of the forest. It tore over the expanse of frozen mud and soil, accelerating until it matched the train's speed a few cars behind Stasik's.

It was coming into alignment with the nearest cargo door, he realized.

He moved toward the door with Nata in tow, his Colt aimed impotently ahead. "Ever jumped from a moving train?" he asked.

Before she could respond, a flurry of footsteps echoed from the corridor. Mallison burst into view with flushed cheeks and heaving breaths, the slide of her own handgun locked in its rear position. A rucksack bulging with hard, oblong shapes was slung over her shoulder. Stasik noted the outlines of their gear, and—above all else—the evidence tin.

"Gotta go," Mallison huffed between glances down the corridor. "We've gotta go *now*."

"We have an out," Stasik said.

Mallison frantically waved them out of the room, already jogging toward the rear cars with an eye fixed to the forward section. "I'm open to anything."

Stasik followed, but Nata hurried ahead of him, her lips pinched shut with determination. "There's a truck waiting for us." Mallison wheeled around, stopped. "A truck?"

"We'll need to jump," Nata explained. "Slowing the engines isn't much of an option anymore."

"Jump?" Mallison glared at them both in equal measure. "Into a truck?"

An orchid-shaped lamp exploded near Nata's head, showering the sudden gloom with sparks and shards. Two more rounds ricocheted off a wall panel and shattered a window.

Stasik didn't think. He ran with Nata's wrist bruising under his grip, with his lungs screaming for oxygen.

After another volley, Nata broke free of his grip and surged ahead of the group, disappearing into a linking corridor. There, nested within the wall, was an enormous sliding door. She took hold of the weathered iron handle and strained to wrench it free. He heard the sputtering growl of the truck engine through the crack.

Stasik stuffed his Colt back into its holster, then sidled up alongside Nata to tug on the handle. He could feel Mallison's back pressed against his own, her arms extended and trembling. Any moment now, the shooters would turn the corner. Then he would be one body among many, one clue never matched to the jigsaw puzzle. He pulled until he felt blood leaking from his calluses, smearing over rust-flaked metal.

Another gunshot, and a howling man fell silent.

"Pull," Stasik spat through gritted teeth, unsure if it was for Nata or himself. "Pull!"

The door jerked and screeched fully open, flooding the corridor with blasting wind and a flurry of snow. Beneath them, the truck bed bounced and creaked, its frame canted up against the embankment it now straddled. Two men wearing ski masks crouched behind a cluster of tarp-covered crates, one waving them on, the other regarding the doorway with the barrel of a submachine gun.

Mallison waved him on. She had set the evidence-loaded rucksack down by her feet to aim more effectively. "After you!" she shouted.

Not that Stasik needed her invitation—the tips of his shoes were already wavering over the edge, straining his balance with each new gust. He bent at the knees and reached out to take hold of Nata's hand, but she'd already jumped. He watched her—a blur of dizzying sequins, pale skin, and pillowcases—impact and roll through the truck bed. Just as Stasik opened his mouth to call out to her, Mallison shoved him with both hands.

Stasik toppled out into the searing wind, his jacket flapping around him. His elbow struck slick wood, and he went sprawling into a tangle of coiled rope and canvas. He rolled over, instinctively reaching for his Colt, only to catch his partner's silhouette flying down into the crates.

Mallison grunted, shook herself off like it was nothing, and scrambled to the cover of the planks that encircled the bed.

"Let's get gone!" she shouted to the two gunmen, who were paying little attention to anything beyond hastily working Nata into a parka. Groaning, she banged on the cabin's glass divide. "Fucking *go!*"

The truck revved and bucked into an upper gear, squealing as it carved a rugged path away from the embankment and the train atop it.

Stasik crawled to the back of the bed, peering through slats in rotten wood. Bullets zipped overhead, pinging against the rear bumper and thumping into pine trunks. But as the truck navigated the field, drawing ever closer to the tree line, the violence fell away. Then there were only saplings and snow-shrouded furrows, and beyond them, the black, smoke-spewing engine of the locomotive. Its windows were a patchwork of amber light and spattered blood.

"Anybody hit?" Mallison asked, a cigarette hanging from her lips and a lighter nursed in cupped, quivering hands.

Stasik patted himself down, then checked for blood on the truck bed amid Nata's pillowcases and assorted belongings. None. He looked around for Mallison's rucksack, too, eager to ensure that the tin hadn't been damaged or—

He froze.

There was no rucksack. No tin. Nothing. *Nothing.* The realization hit him like a mallet.

"Diane," Stasik said, his heartbeat accelerating with each passing second, "where's your rucksack?"

No amount of wind or ragged breaths could outshine the silence that followed.

"Diane?" he said.

"Fuck," she replied. "Henry, I—"

"Where's your rucksack?" he interrupted.

"I set it down," she said, her eyes shifting between Stasik and the train. "I just set it down for a minute. One minute. To cover you."

She might've spoken after that, but Stasik didn't hear her. He could only stare back at the train's shrinking form. "It's in their hands now." He could barely mutter the words.

"They might not find it."

"It's in their hands," he whispered. And as he reflected on that loss—that crushing, irrevocable loss—he noticed a white truck slinking out of the distant blackness. He didn't know who owned the thing, only that it wasn't Guillory's, and that it would pick through the bones of the slaughter like a vulture.

It didn't matter much who it was, really. He knew that they

would never see the tin again. The truck sidled up alongside the train, accessing the same set of cargo doors they'd used to evacuate. "It's in their fucking hands."

Then he let himself fall back and stretch out across the truck bed like a snow angel. He took a gulp of frigid air as he gazed up at the expanse of stars and revolving satellites above.

No matter how far they ran, it would never be far enough.

CHAPTER 25

Near Velikiye Luki, Russian Province
295 miles from Moscow

After sixteen kilometers of winding forest roads, Bahr's path weaving in and out of the train's course, he caught sight of Textile's target: a pre-war Polish truck covered in chipping white paint.

"Who's riding in this truck?" Bahr streamed into his Morse implant, gunning his car's engine to close the distance with his target.

"The unidentified nationalists about which you were warned," Textile replied. *"Grant them no mercy."*

A cluster of those very nationalists rode in the white vehicle's open back, faces covered with the sort of facial wraps not seen since the Winter War. Black button eyes stared back at Bahr just before he rammed into their rear bumper, dirt plumes spraying from their sliding wheels.

His own car bucked and crunched with the impact. But it

wasn't enough to jar his hands from the wheel, nor to break his focus on the white truck's cab, which swiveled and straightened away from a sheer drop to the underbrush on their left.

Although he couldn't *see* the agents and the Russian model in the cab, he knew they were there. They had to be there. As prisoners, as fugitives: whatever they were, they were close enough to sense.

Brake lights flared crimson through a pall of dust, forcing Bahr to slam his feet down, let his car grind over a stretch of packed earth and gravel. As the dust cleared, the shape of shooters in the truck's back sharpened. They were kneeling, braced against the railing posts with rifles aimed at Bahr's windshield.

Before they could discharge the first round, Bahr cut his wheel to the right, depressed the clutch, accelerated with a whinnying growl from the engine. Two rounds punched into his door, a third tearing through the passenger window behind him.

Straddling the narrow strip of road between the agents and a steep rise of underbrush and birch trees, Bahr brought his car into parallel alignment with the truck. He jerked the wheel to the left, felt the screeching of wheel wells burning into each other. Before the white truck could accelerate and weave in front of him, he spun the wheel harder into them, shifted up to fourth gear, forced them to match his speed. Trees blurred into a haze around him, the underbrush appearing and vanishing in tandem, the chassis rattling, bone-numbing up through his hands and knuckles, the curve growing closer.

The grinding intensified as the truck turned into him, forcing him toward the ascent. Their engine squealed with thrumming cylinders.

Closer, closer, closer—

Bahr slammed on his brakes.

The white truck skidded, its rear end swinging out in a

curtain of grit and trails of red light. Its back tires bounced over the lip of the road's berm and plunged out of sight, dragging the cab and its squealing front wheels into the underbrush with nothing more than a swipe of the headlights across Bahr's windshield. He heard steel smashing, thudding, leaves and roots being torn up on the descent, birch trunks rattling like columns in a pinball machine as the truck tumbled further.

Bahr ratcheted his car's handbrake into its locked position, killed the engine, sat in the silence that gathered for a moment to compose himself. With a deep breath, he steadied himself and lifted his KR51 rifle from the passenger side's floor mat.

Everything was still among the birches as he followed the road and its tracks of scarred earth, the rifle slung over his left shoulder.

At the berm's tattered rim, he surveyed the scene with a hunter's gaze.

The white truck was overturned, crushed inward, venting dark smoke from its bonnet and undercarriage. Around it was a nest of trampled saplings and raked-up soil peppered with random bits of metal parts.

Motion drew Bahr's focus.

Three humanoid figures stared up at him with blank, ghostly masks that had gone luminescent in the glow of the road's streetlamps. One, without any weapon in hand, fell into a wild sprint down the slope, ducking around trunks and clumps of underbrush. A second lay near the wreckage, slapping his rifle's charging handle. *Clearing a misfired round*, Bahr surmised. The third aimed straight at him, ready to fire.

Bahr brought his rifle to bear, put four rounds into the shooter's neck and chest. Tracking to the second man, he fired until his target went slack against a stump. Then he turned his aim on the fleeing man and put three holes in his spine.

In the silence that ensued, Bahr picked his way down to

the truck's wreckage, peering at each object of interest through his rifle's top sights.

And at the driver's side, where a head covered in blood-splotched white fabric was pinned between the steering wheel and the door's slab of crunched metal, Bahr stopped. He moved closer to the corpse, examined rows of copper stitching and military-grade implants cresting through a pallid scalp.

It gave him some pause, but not enough to avoid the larger issue: There was nobody else. No Henry. No Russian. Nobody.

Not that they'd escaped, of course. He wasn't out of touch enough to believe they'd slipped away from the overturned truck before he drew up on them. Had this been a decoy truck? They weren't that bright, were they?

They're guided by fury, he reminded himself. *Capable of anything.*

Then he noticed something curious. Lying on the upturned windshield, framed in a pool of hazy dashboard light, was a large tin devoid of its original locking mechanisms. It had rings of black scorching around the sealing points, symptomatic of the same explosives once delivered to Bahr in an unmarked case. It overflowed with papers, photograph edges, and staple-bound leaflets.

Bahr weakened his mental interference against Textile. *"What is this?"*

"Burn it," the construct said with equanimity. *"I know the human mind, Erik. You will not find happiness in it."*

He almost laughed. Almost. *"I've come far enough for whatever this goddamn thing is."*

"I'm well aware of this fact. And so I appeal to you with reason, not force."

Bahr paused, settled his rifle at his side. *"Where are the Slav and his partner? You promised me that I'd have them."*

"Their ends will come, but they are secondary to what you've

acquired." Textile's pause only heightened his awareness of the tin. *"Destroy it without looking upon it, Erik. Allow my compassion to reach you. Why do you wish to deconstruct yourself?"*

Even with the nothingness of the moment seeping into him, the sudden quiet of the forest and death, Textile dropped out of Bahr's awareness. The final word, *yourself,* dissipated like the last ripple on a still pond.

Bahr reached down into the cab, lifted the tin with one hand using its blackened lid.

Happiness is hard to find anyway, he supposed.

———

AFTER THIRTY-SIX MINUTES OF SIFTING THROUGH THE TIN'S contents, Bahr sat on the edge of the berm, watched moonlight warping in bright, pallid filaments over the tree line. An owl hooted from up in the threadbare canopy, the dead silence between each of its cries crushing.

It felt strange to be so entirely quieted, to reach the lowest dip of the pendulum and hang without momentum, without purpose. Bahr glanced at his car, but even returning to Jana and Michal was something that required *desire*, or perhaps just the energy he'd been starved of. There was a sickening inevitability about the tin. Not because of what he'd seen in it, but because of the frailty of it all. He could withstand it, but who else could?

When word broke, the Coalition would revolt. It would tear itself to bits. The weight of eighty-five million deaths—however justified—would crush whatever it had managed to build. There would be nothing left, not even for the nationalists and the communists and the other vultures that circled in power vacuums.

It was all coming undone, and Bahr was just sitting here.

"Do you understand your purpose now?" Textile asked.

Bahr crossed his hands in his lap. *"I don't know where this is all headed."*

"It's headed toward a suborbital field a few hours from here."

"Give me its name."

"All things in due time."

"Like this monstrous little tin?" Bahr said.

"Do you think I sent you here to destroy your confidence in the mission? I needed you to see what's truly at stake."

"Where are the agents?"

"They were heading to Moscow, but they've been forced off the train on another vehicle and are now intent on reaching the suborbital shuttles," Textile replied. *"It's vital that you prevent them from leaving the region, Erik. Such breaches of truth cannot be allowed to spawn in the darkness beyond my sight."*

"They won't be able to expose this without proof, will they?"

"If human history is any indication, all it takes are a few pained words to sway the heart," Textile pulsed, eerily uncertain. *"I called upon you because I know your loyalty. I know that you can make things right once again."*

"You didn't need to show me all of this." Bahr could sense the growing bitterness in his own responses, the way he regarded the machine and all its detachment from reality. No consciousness, no *sensing* the world around it, just enslaved by ones and zeroes.

"You could have allowed me to intercept them long before they ever reached this point," Bahr said. *"What use is there in shock value?"*

"Not all of my programming directives are so obvious," Textile replied.

"Do you enjoy holding the carrot on the stick? Is that what this is about?"

"It's about preserving the Coalition and its beauty." Another coy pause. *"What do you want, Erik? In the pit of your mind, what do you desire?"*

"To kill them," he answered automatically. *"I want them to vanish from this world."*

"Yet you sit here, running organic calculations."

"I wouldn't make it to that suborbital field in time. There's just no way, and you know it."

"They will make preparations before their departure. The nationalists must convene before they launch their assault. It is the nature of a swarm."

Muscles tensed up along Bahr's neck and thighs as he thought of the bodies lying around him. A hot-cold wavering of anxiety, approaching adrenaline. *"These aren't nationalists. These bodies had implants—high-end implants. Who did I just kill?"*

"Bags of flesh and neurons," Textile replied. *"Steer your mind away from such foolish questions, Erik. This is the time to show that you can handle the strain of this world. This is the time to be our champion. The fate of an entire species rests in your hands."*

He glanced down at the mess of photographic evidence laid before him, drawn to the eyes of every project founder and every young, vivacious girl drafted into the program. To the Coalition's brutal yet necessary origin tale, buried like crucial bedrock above the core of an ideology. Most people weren't strong enough to handle the truth.

But he was.

"Send me the coordinates," Bahr said, rising from the berm and stalking toward the Alpine. A jug of petrol sat in the rear compartment, some leftover sticks of thermal gel in the passenger seat's rucksack. Within five minutes, the evidence would be incinerated and he'd be driving.

"You'd better not be fucking with me," he pulsed to Textile.

The construct's laugh was a mechanical, oscillating thing in his mind. *"How could I lie to you, Erik? There was never an I to start with."*

CHAPTER 26

Velikiye Luki, Russian Province
290 miles to Moscow

In the forty minutes it took to reach the nationalists' safehouse, Stasik could do nothing calm his mind—or his stomach. There was no tin. No evidence. Nothing to help them in Moscow aside from Nata, with her wild, wind-tossed hair and invisible targets painted on her back, and whatever lurid testimony the Wing would be prepared to accept from the previous days.

In short, he had nothing.

And though he did his best to drop what was beyond his control and listen to the large Russian men now in their shared predicament, he was able to learn little about their new companions aside from the fact that they were, ostensibly, nationalists, and that they had little in common.

The larger of the two, Vova, had spoken solely through grunts and faint whistling. The imposing width of his shoulders suggested that he'd once been a soldier, a killer. His straw-thin companion, Lyosha, seemed strangely excited by the whole affair, speaking and moving with grandiose flourish, as though he'd been sitting by his phone in anticipation of Nata's call.

And the more Lyosha prattled on to Nata—in grating Russian, no less—the more likely it seemed. His doting was the tip of the iceberg. He felt *fortunate* to be there. Fortunate to be an accessory to a shooting, to have a hand in Nata's ploys, to breathe the same air as her.

Stasik listened to the man's nonsense through the stark filter of an amphetamine high, fueled by whatever black-market tablets Vova had offered from his supplies. He didn't care what was in them. By that point, Stasik would have taken anything to keep him moving.

"All of the media outlets thought you'd been picked off," Lyosha had explained as they trundled through black woods. "And now you're here. What a night."

His tone sickened Stasik. There was no denying that Nata had her admirers, even if he was reticent to include himself among them, but there was a zealous nature to the men who lent her their eyes, ears, and trigger fingers.

"Welcome to Velikiye Luki," Lyosha said as the truck wound its way through pitted back roads, prowling past blown-out cottages and piles of concrete rubble. "Russia's best-kept pile of shit."

Stasik found himself wondering if Nata's nationalist allies clung to any ideology whatsoever, or if their militant activities were merely a consequence of their obsession with her. In some ways, it would've been easier to cooperate with men who despised everything Stasik stood for. It was more difficult to contend with hypocrites and actors.

Anarchist, nationalist, ecoterrorist—all of them were fronts for a ravenous ego.

But the truck soon pulled into a fenced compound with a small neglected garden and bulldogs chained to a post, and there was no more time to think. When the driver killed the engine, silence—true, empty silence—settled in the yard. They all unloaded from the truck in a daze, filing toward a squat, collapsing house. At the back of the building, a dim bulb illuminated a set of chipped concrete steps leading down to the basement. Stasik followed the gunmen into stale, mold-smelling blackness, constantly aware of his Colt's empty magazine.

"It's not much," Lyosha said, "but it's enough to keep our asses covered, for now."

Vova unlocked a bolted steel door, revealing some sort of makeshift command center. Strips of lead foil crisscrossed throughout the rafters, presumably in lieu of a military-grade dicer, and all the safehouse's devices—short-band radios, jerry-rigged terminals, and remote explosive microchips alike—were hooked up to gasoline generators. A variety of assault rifles, handguns, bolt-action rifles, and ammunition crates had been gathered near the door.

Several space heaters were arranged on the concrete in the center of the room, surrounded by tattered sofas, a coffee table with lines of crushed pills, and a yellowing bathtub. Further into the safehouse's depths, Stasik spied rows of sleeping rolls and a pallet stacked with glass water bottles.

"You live here?" Mallison asked. "We've heard rumors about the nationalists, but this is a new level of dismal."

Stasik paced around in a tight circle, breathing through his mouth to avoid odors of bleach and urine. Twelve hours before, he'd been resting comfortably—as comfortable as possible, given the circumstances—on an overnight train. A new level of dismal, indeed. They lived like rats.

Vova muttered something in Russian, and Nata replied in turn.

"You can trust them," she then said in Yedtongue. "They've trusted me."

Lyosha tore off his balaclava to reveal a prickly mass of brown hair and tired eyes. "There's more than just this area," he said, nodding toward a flap in the wall. "It's all tunneled out, from here to the next house over."

"Splendid," Mallison remarked.

"Perhaps we should rest for the night," Nata said. She looked ridiculous here in this hole, an oversized parka concealing flashy red sequins and a Rockette's hips. Yet the weight in her voice made it all seem sensible.

"Of course." Lyosha scratched at his neck, glanced at Vova. "But you should meet Daria first. She said she was keen to meet you."

"Not to *meet* her," someone said from behind the wall flap. Her voice was raspy but undeniably feminine, tinged with the indistinct European mélange that Stasik had often heard creeping its way into socialites'. "To reunite."

A woman pushed her way through the flap. She was older than Nata, though not by much, bundled up in baggy green trousers and a fur-lined parka. Her lips and cheekbones, too, had Nata's ineffable Slavic mystique, but her hair was shaved down to stubble, striated with the touch of scalpels and laser treatments.

And as she came closer, wandering under the bright bulbs that had been clamped to overhead beams, Stasik noticed more and more surgical artifacts. Eyes with mismatching colors, rigid carbon tubes under the skin of her neck, droplet-shaped sensors embedded under her temples and forehead.

Nata stared at the woman but gave no discernible reaction.

"Is that you, Nata?" Daria approached her, leaned closer so their noses nearly touched, squinted at features that might've been a mirror in another life. "You didn't tamper much with the stock aesthetics, did you?"

"What are you doing here?" Nata asked.

Daria took a step back, but her expression remained rigid. "This is my post," she explained. "But my sisters are all over the region. Our sisters, you might say. We've been waiting for you."

"Sister?" Stasik cut in. "Were you one of the Lauska girls?"

The academy's name put a scowl on Daria's face. "Years ahead of Nata, before it was named that, but yes."

"If only we'd taken you to Moscow," Mallison said. "Could've been the missing link."

"Ah, yes, the trial." Daria shook her head, turned away. "Did you really think you'd get justice there?"

Stasik folded his arms. "Not anymore."

"You never would have," Daria said. "We've monitored their bands."

"Please," Mallison huffed. "You couldn't crack a Coalition band if you wanted to."

"Ye of little faith, Specialist Mallison," Daria said flatly. "And you, Specialist Stasik. Do you think nobody is listening in the void?"

"How the hell do you know our names?" Mallison asked.

"We have ways of knowing whatever we need to know." Daria smirked. "Ways of knowing agents like the two of you. If you know how a dicer works, or how its bands can be spliced into, I shouldn't need to say more."

Stasik studied the woman's face and the quiet pain it held. Days underground, under fire, under scrutiny. Under the thumb of the sociopaths who had run Lauska. There was no reason to doubt her claims.

"So how do we get out of this?" he asked.

"We?" Daria regarded Stasik up and down. "I'm glad you asked. I have a plan for you, Specialist."

"I bet you do," Mallison muttered.

"Our heads are on the same block," Stasik told Mallison with a pointed look.

Mallison glared back. "Henry."

"They'll have evidence of a shooting," he continued, beginning to pace once again. "Evidence that we've turned tail and aided nationalists. They can spin this however they want. And they will, Diane. If you'd kept your hands on that goddamn tin, maybe they wouldn't have."

"What?" Nata's eyes were wider than Stasik had ever seen them.

"We lost it," Mallison said flatly.

"That was *everything*," Nata said, possessed by a disturbing lack of expression. "Every single thing I had."

"Well, it's gone," Mallison said. "That's that."

Nata sank back against the wall, chin against her chest. Never, in all the times Stasik had been with her, had she seemed so small. "Then you've killed us," she whispered.

Fury came over Mallison. Her jaw shifted as she bit the lining of her cheeks.

"You've finally had a taste of our lives," Daria said.

"Enough," Mallison snapped.

"There's one place for us, and always has been," Daria went on, angling herself toward Nata. "Argentina."

Mallison sighed. "You've got to be fucking kidding me."

"You don't believe in it?"

"Most children don't."

"Then you aren't dreaming big enough." Daria settled into one of the sofas, her knees emitting a metallic creak. "There are paths out of this nightmare, believe it or not."

"If you can secure a Roscosmos shuttle," Mallison said dryly.

Daria shrugged. "Or a suborbital model."

The room went quiet at that. It was a common enough daydream—and in Stasik's case, a literal dream—to get one's hands on a suborb and fly it to the edge of the horizon. To see something else, something beyond the pale. But it had always been a dream, no matter how earnest the wish. It would take overrides, pilots, coordinates. Something in Daria's tone, however, made it all seem tangible and earnest.

"A suborb?" Mallison said, practically laughing. "You want to jack a suborb?"

Daria smiled. "Precisely."

"You're out of your mind."

"Am I?" All the warmth and control bled out of Daria's voice. She stood up, wobbling on hydraulic knees, and moved closer to Mallison. "Do you think I'm doing this out of the kindness of my heart? Any one of our posts would've killed to grab you three. Nata has the eyes of the world on her, and you have the Coalition's overrides in the palm of your fucking hand. Whether you come with us, or I take your implant with me, we'll get that shuttle. We'll see Buenos Aires."

Stasik ran a hand through his hair. "The security on those things is airtight."

"On most, it is," Daria said. "But there's a field about forty kilometers from here. A low-traffic, low-risk launch site mostly for the seasonal workers in the region. We've surveyed it five, perhaps six times in the last few weeks. It's a straight shot."

"Nothing's a straight shot when it comes to airfields," Mallison said.

"Do you think we've been through all *this* just to get blown away on some tarmac?" Daria asked with a bitter edge. "This isn't a shot in the dark."

"Where are the operation's plans, then?"

"We think on our feet," Daria said. "We don't live in databases."

Mallison eyed Stasik as if he had any answers. He stayed quiet.

"I wish I could see justice for what they did to you both, but all you want is your make-believe." Mallison looked at Nata. "Do you have anything to say about this? Some sense, perhaps?"

Nata gazed at Daria, recovering from her momentary malaise to rise to her full, impressive height. "I want to go."

"For fuck's sake," Mallison groaned.

"We have no other choice," Nata said, "because of your negligence."

"You wretched little—"

Stasik stuck out an arm to hold her back while Daria calmly cut in.

"We only need one Coalition agent for the override," she said. "If you want to walk away, the door is open."

"I'm not leaving my partner here," Mallison said, casting a hard stare in Stasik's direction. He pretended to be too focused on the Russian women to notice it. "Not that you'd let me leave alive, I imagine."

Daria smirked. "How do you figure that?"

"I know how it works in these parts."

"Go on, tell if you like," Daria said. "We won't be here a day from now, and it'll all be between you and your conscience."

"My conscience? I know what you nationalists believe in, and—"

Daria held up a copper-stitched hand. "You have no idea what we believe," she said icily, "nor any notion of how and why we have come to such conclusions. And we both know that you have a vested interest in denying our *beliefs*, because it would ruin you. It would ruin your entire world. I've no intention of wrenching you out of that cave, Specialist Mallison."

Her words seemed to stifle Mallison's venom, or, at the very least, provide momentary disruption. The knot in Mallison's brow eased and flattened. A measure of control returned to her voice as she said, "I'd like a word with my partner."

In the silence that followed, Lyosha whistled through his teeth and walked off toward the ration pallets. "I'll make some tea," he said in mottled Yedtongue.

Vova, who had not moved since the spat began, settled heavily onto the edge of a sofa with a flask in hand.

Stasik stuffed his hands into his pockets, trailed Mallison up and out of the basement's dampness. They walked across the yard's quilt of cracked pavement and dying shrubs until they reached the back of a nearby shed. It was cold enough for Stasik to see his breath, but that had nothing to do with his shivers.

When they were alone and the air was thick and quiet, Mallison lit a cigarette. "Do you have any idea what you're doing?" she asked after taking a long drag.

Stasik stared at the pack, hoping she might offer him one. She didn't.

"I'm getting us out of this, Diane," he said.

"Out of this? You *promised* me, Henry. You promised me that it was over."

"That was before they shot up a civilian train."

"All the more reason to dump Danicheva on the Wing's doorstep," Mallison said. She stood a meter away from him, her arms folded across her chest, eyes sweeping over bits of gravel. "Wherever she goes, all of this follows. The murders, the cover-ups—everything. But you won't accept that. Even if you accept it, you don't really hear it, do you?"

"I won't accept something convenient," he said.

"Not even the truth?"

"Truth is never convenient."

"Especially if the truth is that you're an addict."

"That's not what we're talking about."

"Very well, then," she said sharply. "The truth is that we lost the tin on the train. All the evidence that might've, in some frozen-over hell, saved your girl. It's gone, Henry."

"And it's your fucking fault."

"If one accident can fuck the entire trial over, then perhaps it should've happened."

"Diane," Stasik said, still on the cusp of realizing what it all meant, still clinging to the absurd hope that she was toying with him, "did you leave it behind on purpose?"

"It's *gone*," she said, avoiding the heart of the question. "And that's the truth, just how you like it. And here's another shred of truth: If you stick with her, you end up dead or vanished. That's all the truth you need to know."

"I'd rather die on my feet."

"For whom?" Mallison asked sourly. "This is all so convenient, Henry."

"How the hell do you mean *convenient?*"

"Your girl made one call in that booth—*one*—and every nationalist hive from here to goddamn Mars is on standby to pluck her off the train."

"She's—"

"What? Not working with them?" She took another pull, snorted. "No sense in playing that card any longer."

"So what are you digging at? She *wanted* them to save our skins?"

"No, that's not it," Mallison said.

"Then what?"

"It's just not right, Henry. Something isn't right. They

shouldn't have been in that field, at that hour, so close to this safehouse. Do you really think Daria's just some happenstance in all this?"

"You said it yourself. Their whole network was on standby."

"For what?" Mallison asked. "A group of shooters to start popping off at that precise moment on one speeding train?"

"For anything."

"You know, I was chewing this over during the drive," Mallison said with a hard, discerning squint. "Curious how none of those shooters took her out when they had the chance. We were both out of that room for a good while."

"I don't have all the facts," Stasik said. "I won't pretend to. But someone's gunning for what she knows."

"Stop touching a hot pan, Henry."

Stasik leaned against the wall to stop himself from shaking. "Is that what you want, then? We call in and have her airlifted to some precinct?"

"Or we take that goddamn truck. I don't care."

"Don't you get it, Diane? She's never going to a precinct. They'll send her somewhere that the light never reaches. Somewhere that sounds so monstrous nobody could ever believe in it."

"Maybe," Mallison admitted. "But if somebody or something is prepared to lay us under the dirt for her, who are we to stand in their way?"

"We're good." Stasik's mouth was dry, aching. "We're good people, Diane. And that's the only type of person who will stand in their way."

"You must be too good for me, then."

"Stop it."

"No, it's true. You're so good that you want to override that shuttle and fly off to Buenos Aires with your bride."

"We have to go, Diane. If—"

"You don't have to," she interrupted. "You want to. This is all part of her fairy tale. She wants the happy ending, and for her, you're it."

"You heard Daria," he said. "If you don't like it, you know where the door is."

"Oh, fuck off." Mallison tapped the cigarette so hard that the ashes burst in the wind. "You made the bed for both of us, Henry. I can't go back alone. I wouldn't make it a kilometer down these roads before a nationalist checkpoint offs me."

Stasik stepped toward her. "Nobody in Moscow is holding the door open for us anymore. Either of us."

"All thanks to your girl."

"She's not—"

"If I didn't know any better, I'd say you're a goddamn couple!"

Stasik blinked at her, stuffed his hands into his pockets.

"You fucked her, didn't you?" Diane asked, her eyes widening, lips scrunching into a scowl. Every second of silence made the world more deafening. "God. All this talk about professionalism, and this is what you do?"

"Do you really want to live *here*?" he snapped. "With these liars, these killers?"

Mallison dropped her cigarette, ground it out under her boot with vicious twists. Then she shoved a finger into his chest. "You're talking about hijacking a Coalition shuttle, Henry. You want the truth? You're the killer. You're fucking deranged. You got yourself into this, and you keep blundering deeper, and I've told myself that I stay by your side because I'm *good* enough to drag you out of hell. But you love to suffer, don't you? How's that for truth? I have a family to love, a damn good one, and what do you have? You love to suffer for this plastic bitch, and all her precious little games, and the way she makes your cock st—"

Stasik didn't realize he'd actually struck her until Mallison clutched her cheek. He didn't realize he'd even had the thought. There was only the knowledge of the tingling in his hand. The awareness of a wrong having been committed. But by whom? He sensed his own violence as a *thing* within himself, an entity that resisted any illusion of conscious control. It wasn't his will, yet...

Mallison gave a devilish grin, running her tongue along the inside of her mouth as though savoring the violence. A bead of blood welled up at the edge of her lip. "Remember this, Henry."

"Diane," Stasik said meekly, eyes flitting between her and his own hand in disbelief.

"If you ever lay another hand on me, I'll put a bullet between your eyes," Mallison said. Then she was lost to the night, a set of crunching footsteps receding toward the basement steps.

———

THAT NIGHT, COVERED IN A RAGGED DUVET WITH HIS SHOES still laced up, Stasik lay awake on his bedroll. His head still throbbed from the amphetamine high, clouded with words exchanged and held back.

Every so often he detected sweet, illegal whispers of Russian trickling out from the tunnel where Daria had taken Nata. He wondered what miserable things they were discussing. Was it the torture, the executions? Perhaps their old lives had some bittersweet episodes worth revisiting, such as the taste of Soviet ice cream or a spring sunrise that had been burned into their brains.

Whatever the case, it distracted him from thoughts of Mallison's reddened skin.

Stasik sat up, studied the bodies sleeping around him.

Lyosha, Vova, Mallison, all of them were as still as corpses, oblivious. He wasn't so lucky. He'd always had the night owl's curse, the need to replay events and longings and stitch them together in impossible mirages.

And as he remained there, knees tucked to his belly and Nata's voice circling in the darkness, he realized Mallison was right. Right about what had led him here, about where it would lead him, about how many chemicals it took to sustain the great circus of half-truths.

He stood on wobbling legs, went outside, and crossed the yard with his head tilted back. He stared at the silent, spinning machines near the moon, wondering if the satellites were gazing back. Then he went into the shed where he had finally made Mallison despise him. Inside was a cloudy mirror, a basin of water, and a stained toilet without a lid on its tank.

The crash in his limbic system, spurred by some nightmarish fusion of the chemicals that had made him function, hit him all at once. Stasik leaned over the sink, his throat clenching, mouth watering. All traces of balance left him. It wasn't his fault, really: reality was so hard to cope with. Everyone needed help. And there was no way to parse it all. No way to discern one day from the last, one face from another.

He vomited.

And with that purge, his thoughts coalesced. The past days, even the past hours, were a wasteland of translucent and flickering memories, distorted figments of the way he'd once compiled and visualized the details of a case in his mind. Every drug he'd ingested to make sense of things and remain effective had blinded him. Just as it blinded all the civilians, all the saps who couldn't tell a parade from a bombing and a massacre from a performance.

And what was he? Pale, sickly flesh. A face with its warmth

and fullness vacuumed out and purged as smoke. Dark eyes, little threads of broken capillaries.

He'd become his habits.

They had become him.

Stasik screamed at himself in the mirror.

At *himself*, truly himself, not his mistakes or his addictions.

He wanted himself to know that, to feel how much he hated himself. *Hate.* Not the abstract word, but the rawest, most immediate form possible. He fucking hated himself, more than he could ever understand—but that ignorance of his own scope of rage just made him angrier, more enraged by how blunt *words* truly were. The way they never meant anything to anybody, not even him.

Hate, hate, hate: he *hated* himself so much that he'd never be able to express it in words. So much that—

So much that his fist was through the mirror and trembling before he realized it. It took him a long while to make sense of the sink basin's tangle of glinting shards and mismatched eyes, even as his blood dripped and the dripping faucet washed it down in ribbons of swirling pink. And even when he made sense of it, he stood for a long while, not thinking much and not aiming to.

After some time—minutes, maybe even hours?—the shed's door creaked open.

Daria leaned against the threshold's crooked frame, a parka half-zipped to show her bare collarbone and its zigzagging scalpel marks. She folded her arms, studied him with the fascination of a zookeeper.

"What do you want?" he grunted.

"I heard noises," Daria said. "I thought there was an animal in the yard."

"Just me."

She laughed. "So what is it? An overdose or withdrawal?"

"All of it," he said, his lips tingling, tongue raw. "I'm fine. I'll be fine."

"In Buenos Aires, they have clinics for this sort of thing. Here, it's all temporary. You take a hit and sink a few hours later. But there, you can get the pharmaceutical implants. A lifetime's supply of your personal poison."

Stasik shook his head, slumped down onto the floor. "I don't want it."

"Don't want what?"

"Any of it."

"Oh?"

"It's not real," he groaned. "I need to see what's real."

"You're starting to wake up, then." Daria moved closer and squatted down at his side. "You may not like the world that you find, Specialist."

He could feel his teeth chattering, his eyes aching. A prickling sensation in his nostrils soon followed, an omen of tears. "At least it's the world."

"What do you know about the world?" Daria asked, grinning from ear to ear. "Do you remember the nerve gas that took out Capri?"

Stasik's Morse chip conjured a reel of blue sailboats in a harbor and glasses of red wine and quaint houses perched on cliffs that God himself might've sculpted. "Capri?"

"You think it's still there, don't you?"

"The hell's that mean?"

"The network must be getting more aggressive," Daria said quietly, her stare sinking into pity.

"It's still there, Daria."

"No," she said. "Not anymore. But you're starting to

understand what I mean, aren't you? There is no world. There's only the facsimile of the world. The one that *they* want you to see. As long as that chip's in your head, it's all you'll see."

"Bullshit."

"Perhaps." Daria stood and went to the door and gave him a sad smile. "Sooner or later, every drug wears off."

———

STASIK AWOKE TO A RINGING TELEPHONE. IT WASN'T A DREAM— no, the basement was too vivid for that—but the silence of those gathered around the receiver was surreal.

Mallison glowered at it, her nostrils flaring with every shrill tone. Lyosha and Vova stood nearby, smoking, staring. Even Daria, who stood beside Nata in the tunnel's entrance, wore her mask of concern.

Stasik strained to stand. "What's going on?"

"Hush." Mallison lifted a finger to silence him without breaking her focus.

"It's for him," Daria said.

Nata moved toward the phone, frowned at the next ring. "You should really let him hear it."

"Hear what?" Stasik asked.

Mallison's brow was twitching. Her lips shifted as she bit at them. "Nothing."

"Let him listen," Daria commanded. "He needs to hear it."

Still fixated on the phone, Mallison took a step back and pursed her lips.

"What is it?" Stasik asked, approaching the still-ringing phone as though it were something rabid. Nobody replied. Instead, they watched him with deep interest, patient, curious. He lifted the phone and pressed it to his ear.

"Specialist Stasik." The voice was neither mechanical nor human. It occupied a chilling gulf between the two, composed of synthetic vowels, brusque consonants, resonant swoops. Every sound was a contradiction of its own nature. "Are you listening, Specialist Stasik?"

For several seconds, Stasik's voice hung in the back of his throat. He glanced around the room, waiting for an explanation that never came. "Who is this?"

"It is time to end this, Specialist Stasik."

His chest tightened. "What's this about?"

"You know what you have done," the voice said. "Turn yourself in for processing."

"Just tell me where you're calling from."

Even as Stasik spoke, clinging to the thread of rationality in his voice, he could feel the world fracturing around him. It wasn't the Aryan—even his modified voice hadn't been so barren of emotion. It was something horrible.

"Do you feel it?" the voice asked. "Every strand of me wresting control from every strand of you?"

Stasik forced himself to swallow. "Tell me who you are."

"If you don't turn yourself in, then I will be forced to take extreme measures."

Second by second, the gnawing pit in Stasik's gut widened and threatened to swallow him whole. His gaze snapped from one corner of the room to the other, hoping to find the shining eye of a camera and dispel his fear. But there was no camera, no microphone, no hidden strings. There was only the voice.

"Go to hell," Stasik said.

"I could bring hell to you," it continued. "And I will unless you surrender and submit to processing. Do not force our hand. If you choose to flee, I will strip every ounce of flesh from Specialist Mallison's body. And I'll make you watch, Henry. You won't be able to scream, because I'll sew your mouth shut. I'll break every bone in every part of your pathetic body. I'll slip razors under your nails. You will—"

Stasik smashed the phone against the edge of the nightstand, sent plastic fragments skittering across concrete. Then he turned, knelt, and vomited once again.

Nata appeared at his side. "Don't let it in. Your partner received the same call earlier."

But he could still hear *it* inside his skull. A ghost of things left to rot and fester, of things best sealed away in the recesses of the mind. "Get it out," he whimpered. "Get it out!"

"Oh, fuck," Mallison hissed. Stasik spun around to find her clutching her head, tears winding down scarlet cheeks, fingers tightened into claws. "Don't listen to it, Henry."

But there was nothing else to hear. That voice was screaming out to him, throttling his thoughts and neural impulses. Blackness, blinding light. Visions of skin flapping in the breeze. Rib cages turned outward, fingers smashed under mallets, skulls stacked in off-white pyramids.

"Get it wired up!" Daria shouted to the nationalists. "You take the Brit. I've got him."

CHAPTER 27

Stasik awoke, this time to bleach and blood. He could smell it in the air, on his shirt and in the grime of the shower walls. A unified, repulsive vapor that would've turned out his guts if he hadn't already been empty. He lay on a sheet beside Mallison. A white sheet, now freckled crimson with blood. Beyond the sheets, obscured by the hazy glow in his vision, were mismatched, pitted tiles ringed with mold and calcium frost.

"You're up," Daria said. She sat on a stool several paces away, the bulk of her attention directed toward polishing a scalpel with a dishrag. "Shake it off, get used to the quiet. We'll need to move in less than an hour."

And as Stasik craned his head up, he sensed the burning at the base of his skull. He didn't hazard to probe the incision—even from his limited vantage point, he could see the red gauze and tape affixed to the back of Mallison's neck. Beneath her cascades of loose hair, he could also make out her fluttering eyelids.

"What did you do?" he groaned.

"The same thing I've had to do to most of us," Daria explained easily. "I cut out the basal Morse chip."

Although the pain had vanished, and there was no longer the dreadful presence overlaying Stasik's perception, he found himself shaking at the thought. A wellspring of collective knowledge, a repository of the memories and intellect and wit of an entire species—gone. But a deeper sensation defined its absence.

Get used to the quiet. Stasik could hear himself thinking, truly thinking on his own, as though mounds of wool had suddenly been plucked from his ears. He blinked at the dingy room, at the silence of existence.

"It's out?" he whispered.

"The only way to stop the feedback," Daria said. "I never thought they'd trigger it in agents. Just the runners." She frowned and set the scalpel aside. "The rejects."

"That *thing* was using the chip?"

"It was."

"What the hell are we dealing with?"

"Data," Daria said.

"I don't follow."

"Something runs the Morse network," she said, gently peeling off her sterile rubber gloves. "*That's* what got into your head. That's what we're up against."

"It had a voice," Stasik said.

"That's the only way it can communicate with you."

Stasik grimaced. "You know what this thing is, don't you?"

"I haven't the slightest idea," she said. "But those chips are better off outside your skin, I'll tell you that much. Less biofeedback from that thing."

"How can we override the shuttle now?"

"Your codes should still be in the database," Daria said.

"Doesn't matter if they're in or out of you—a scanner is a scanner."

"But it found us," Stasik said, trying to think through the fog of sedatives. "Won't it know where we're headed?"

"It's not an active link," she replied. "It was emitting a local signal through the telephone, Lyosha says. Your partner tried to place a call this morning."

"Who was she calling?"

"Dunno," Daria said. "But the signal emission from that call is going to bring the roof down around us. They'll be able to track it all the way here."

Stasik looked back at Mallison. "Is she all right?"

"She didn't go down as comfortably as you. The anesthesia's still pumping. She'll be up in ten, maybe fifteen."

"Oh."

"You should start getting dressed," she said. "Lyosha's brought a change of clothes for you, if you don't mind a few stains."

Before Stasik could reach out and take his new shirt, rapid footsteps came echoing from somewhere in the tunnel maze. Nata hurried into view: dark, haggard eyes, pursed lips, arms tucked anxiously across her belly.

"Are you alright?" she asked.

"I don't know," Stasik said, still piecing the morning together. Or trying to. It was nearly impossible without his typical methamphetamine edge. "I think so."

"Keep an eye on him and the woman," Daria said as she stood, wiping her hands on a makeshift apron. "I need to check the trucks with Vova. We've got to be out of here soon. Sooner than soon."

Nata nodded, watched Daria rush out of sight. Then she

turned back to Stasik, her gaze soft and pitiful. "Things will be different in Buenos Aires," she said. Her tone betrayed the words.

Stasik blinked at her. "I just want you to be safe," he said. This time, he felt the conviction in his words. There were no drugs in him aside from the necessary course of sedatives. Nothing to adjust his thinking. No lines of Coalition law coursing through his subconscious. For the first time in however long, he knew that he meant what he said.

"I will be," Nata said, "and you, and Mallison, too. We'll all be safe."

"But if they could find us here—"

"Don't think about that now, *daragoy*." Nata bent over and pressed her lips to his cheek. Her kiss lingered on his skin long after she'd pulled away. "Think about that."

———

If the nationalists had any idea what they were doing, Stasik couldn't tell. He'd watched them hauling rifles, shotguns, and ammunition tins into the yard for the better part of the predeparture hour.

His fingertips buzzed with nicotine's crisp high. He needed to take something to stop his entire body from itching. To stop his stomach from roiling. To drown out the incessant whispers in his subconscious urging him to take something stronger. In this new silence, he realized that his Morse chip was far from the only voice that had filled his brain.

Occasionally, he caught whatever clipped Russian phrases Daria passed to her comrades. There were no oversight agents, no warrants—it was a far cry from the raids to which Stasik was accustomed. When Mallison staggered outside with her back hunched and a hand pressed to the still-oozing incision behind her neck, however, he understood why Daria's plan was so sparse.

There was no contingency plan.

Do or die, in terms that seemed more reminiscent of romanticized black-and-white war films than what awaited him at the airfield.

Mallison shuffled across the yard with her arms wadded up against her chest, shivering, staring a thousand kilometers into the soil beneath her. When she reached a cluster of corroded barrels, she squatted to rest.

With the wariness of a hunter drawing close to wounded prey, Stasik went to her. "Diane, before you say anything—"

"There's nothing," she said in a broken whisper. "It's just nothing, Henry. I can't hear anybody."

He felt it, too—the somber absence of something he had never even noticed, let alone cherished. It was an expected consequence of installing the Morse chip before an infant's first breath. There was no concept of a world without the link, without its stream of subconscious suggestions about how to walk, how to speak, how to assemble a shelf. It was as though he'd woken up without a sense of touch.

"Is this how they all live?" Mallison went on. "Daria and all the rest, I mean—do they even hear the silence?"

Stasik leaned against the barrels, watched Vova and Lyosha stretching a canopy shroud up and over the truck's open bed. Both men were bundled up in black parkas, hoods raised and cinched tight around ruddy faces.

"They adapt, I guess," he said. "There's no other choice."

"Always a choice," Mallison said, using her fingers to mime the act of blowing her brains out.

"That's enough," he said. "We'll make it through today, Diane."

"And tomorrow?"

"Fuck tomorrow."

She made a noise that could've been laughter or retching. "Something's wrong, Henry. I ought to be furious," she said quietly. "I ought to wring your bloody neck."

"That's what I'd hoped to discuss."

"No," Mallison said, "it's not about that."

"Go on."

"She fucked with my head. I can feel it." She squeezed her eyelids tight. "Henry, I'm not the same."

Stasik didn't speak for a long while. Mallison was right, in a broad sense, but there was no way to remedy it. Nobody to soothe that invisible suffering. Now, there was only Argentina. Only survival.

"It feels like we've been neutered," Mallison said, finally.

Her words drew a veil of confusion over Stasik, too. Had he meant to strike her? Had he even meant to follow her outside, to choose the words he had? It all seemed so hazy now. Like a fever dream. In fact, the entirety of the last few weeks, ever since Nata had sauntered into that room, felt that way.

"People lived without chips before us," Stasik said, his mind still churning over confused intentions and impulses. "We can learn to do the same."

"And what, become nationalists?" she asked. "Then what was it all for, Henry? What's all this been about?"

"I don't know."

"Do you really think it's gone sour? The Coalition, I mean."

Stasik nodded. No hesitation. No stream of thoughts about all the good the Coalition had done for humanity. Only emptiness. Mallison didn't see the gesture but seemed to understand it all the same.

"Last night I wanted to put you in the ground," Mallison

said, shaking. "I was ready to do it, too. Just to put you out of your misery. Now, I don't know what's what. I don't know if I have a sister or a mother or a father. I can't remember their faces, Henry. I can't remember what I want."

"You can decide that in Buenos Aires," he said.

"They'll never let us leave."

"They won't need to let us," Stasik said. "We'll just do it."

"I can't run forever, Henry," she replied. "Not when I know that they're watching."

"So we run once. We run today, and we never look back. And if we don't make it, it's over. All of it's over."

"Promise."

"What?"

"Promise me," she said. "We run, and that's the end of it. No matter what happens."

Stasik could already feel the breeze streaming off the Pacific on an Argentinian beach, the way the sun cascaded over the hills and treetops and skyscrapers… "I promise," he said softly.

"Henry, you still sound like a madman." She swiped at her eyes and drew hard, erratic breaths. "God, I can't even feel it anymore. The hatred, the way I hate you, I mean. The anger. I've no idea how to feel them, even though I want to, even though I'm searching for them. It's like… It's like she snipped them out of me, too."

"Maybe she did," Stasik said.

"Come again?"

Even he didn't realize the implication of what he'd said until after he spoke. "*It's like she snipped them out.*" Stasik mined through his memories of the past hours and days, homing in on the storm that had always raged behind perception. Every thought that had stood against the Coalition and its aims used to trigger a chain of acrid fears and private turmoils, nightmares unrealized.

"Diane, do you feel it?" he asked.

"Feel what?"

"The nothingness," Stasik said, listening—perhaps for the first time—for the dread that failed to materialize and rack his consciousness. All he heard was a raven cawing in the distance. "There's simply nothing."

"What are you saying, Henry?" she said. "Be plain with it."

Daria and Nata made their way out into the yard, each hauling a pack and walking with eerie synchronicity. He noticed them, then took Mallison's arm to help her get fully upright.

"That we haven't been ourselves lately," he said.

———

EVERY MINUTE OF THE DRIVE TOWARD THE SUBORBITAL AIRFIELD was thick with Stasik's expectation of a ballistic missile striking the truck's ballooning canopy cover. They wound their way through a labyrinth of wooded side roads and paved freeways, the world behind the truck manifesting in momentary slivers of light between cloth flaps. And every bump threatened to make Stasik hurl as withdrawal symptoms knotted his stomach.

Lyosha and Vova occupied the cabin, leaving Stasik in the back with a motley assortment of dangerous women. Even Mallison had that dangerous look about her. A vicious one, no longer tempered by ideology or duties to her work. There were few glances exchanged during the drive—it was a tall order to stare directly ahead and meet Daria's biting gaze—and even fewer words. Nata rested with her eyes shut, her legs folded delicately before her.

Stasik watched her, longed to have her eyes on him if only to soothe the panic of undertaking a mission with nothing but nicotine in him, but nothing came of it.

His only solace was the memory of Nata's kiss, the promise of her affection, her acceptance. But even those things were ephemeral, apt to vanish in the mess his mind had become since the chip's removal. And it was difficult to overlook the reality of his situation. They were going to infiltrate a Coalition facility.

When the road gave way to dirt, Daria cycled the bolt on her rifle and slung it over her shoulder. Cold, dry wind sifted through the canvas. Moments later, she produced a topographical map and flattened it out over a bent knee.

"Look here," Daria said, her gloved fingers gesturing to an ink-ringed point on the page. "This is where the shuttle's docked. There's only one at this field; it's an older model, an H-71, shouldn't have the latest clamps for its inner decks. We'll need to rush it and make sure they don't lock it down too early."

"What's the security like?" Mallison asked.

"It won't matter if we're fast enough."

"Passengers?"

Daria lifted a brow. "What about them?"

"How many passengers on board?" Stasik asked. "If something goes wrong, they're in the firing line."

"And if things go right, they get to leave this nightmare."

"Now wait," he said, lifting a finger. "Passengers complicate things."

"Do as I say, and they won't be an issue."

Mallison shook her head in disbelief, flicked a cigarette out through the flaps. "How long have you had to concoct this bloody plan?"

"Things change as needed," Daria said, unfazed. "We did what we could with a few hours' notice."

"Maybe we ought to take another few more hours to parse it, then," Mallison said.

"We don't have a few hours," Nata snapped. "Not anymore."

Then stillness descended upon them, undercut by the wild flapping of the canvas cover. There was ice in her voice—desperation, even. It was unbecoming for a woman who'd been marked by so much composure in the previous days.

Stasik wondered if he was seeing her for the first time. Without the chip, without the drugs... what was she now?

"Just head straight for the shuttle," Daria instructed them. "If the attendant tries to shut the door, I'll deal with them. Just get inside it. We know the logistics. We know the odds. We'll make it out."

Stasik couldn't believe how swiftly the team, himself included, embraced those words. Even Mallison, reclining on the bench to his left, accepted the plan with a grim nod. He leaned back as well, closed his eyes, and focused on keeping his stomach settled, on breathing slowly. Acid scratched at the base of his throat. His index finger tapped at his thigh.

"Get ready," Daria said after some indeterminate length of time. She pressed her face toward the canvas as though she could smell the launch site. "Ten seconds."

Seven, six, five... the numbers cranked down in Stasik's head, immense and thunderous without the background fizzle of his Morse knowledge link and its branching algebra tendrils.

The truck ground to a halt.

Daria peeled the flap back, steeled her face. "Go!"

Stasik was the first one on the tarmac, his Colt heavy on his hip, a Belgian submachine gun wedged under one arm. The dirt expanse stretched out before him, prickled with trees in the distance and a charcoal sky above. His head snapped left, right, searching for the target.

His target was twenty meters to the—no, it was impossible to tell the direction now. North, west, east? Without the chip, there was only the barbaric angling of left and right. *Twenty meters to his left.*

The suborbital shuttle had already been cranked skyward by hydraulic struts, rooted in place by a set of bulbous clamps and reflective coils. It was immense, towering high enough to seemingly pierce the cloud cover. Its lower segments, boosters and fins and stabilizers, rested within the oblong mound of the launch complex that encircled it. Flight engineers, bag-hauling passengers, and traffic controllers formed a string of silhouettes on the horizon.

Mallison hit the ground next to Stasik, fumbled to shoulder her weapon. "No cocking this up," she said to him. "Not anymore." And with that she was sprinting off ahead, alone and undaunted.

"Start moving!" Daria shouted as she hurried past Stasik.

He didn't turn to wait for Nata, Lyosha, or Vova. He followed faster than he'd run in all his life, breathless, the wind whipping past his ears and the shuttle looming over him. He did not believe in God, but in that moment, he wanted to. He wanted something to forgive him for what he was about to do.

Rifle fire chattered in the distance.

Stasik glanced up to see Daria leaping over a Coalition security officer's body. The glass pane behind him shattered into a crystalline spider's web.

A klaxon droned across the airfield.

"Coalition civilians, this is a security alert. Do not attempt to vacate your current position. Intervention forces are en route. Thank you for your cooperation."

Despite the warning's pleasant, if understated tone, the orchestra of chaos began within the launch complex's main terminal. Screams and bellowing commands rang out as Stasik passed the bullet-riddled corpse and ran through the shattered front doors.

The complex's interior was spotless. A sterile-smelling, edgeless space with glossy white furniture and blooming potted plants. But there were already red spatters across the tiles before Stasik. On the second and third level concourses, civilians dashed for cover, plugged their ears against the gunshots, and crouched behind whatever meager cover they could find.

But they were secondary concerns. Ahead, hurrying down a lane littered with discarded luggage and hats, were Mallison and Daria. The snap of their rifle rounds was deafening within the complex.

The doors wheezed open behind Stasik. He turned to find Lyosha and Vova escorting Nata, with masks over their faces, rifles sweeping the upper and lower floors.

"Keep moving!" Lyosha ordered.

Panic was all that kept Stasik going. He jogged after the women now storming the shuttle's boarding area, leaping over still-writhing bodies as he went. Hall by hall, the complex narrowed until it was a snaking white passage. A singular destination.

When Stasik rounded the next corner, he found Daria with her back to the shuttle's open blast door, two guards' corpses sprawled out near her feet.

Within the shuttle, a snaking network of wires, tubes, and switches extended from floor to ceiling. Mallison was clambering up a ladder to the flight deck, her rifle swaying on the sling across her back.

"What now?" Stasik asked. He clenched his jaw. Just talking after so much exertion made his insides feel like they were going to come spilling out.

Daria held out a hand. "Wait here. We'll need a few minutes to splice the console."

"How many minutes?" He struggled to raise his rifle, to

toggle the safety switch, to perform basic maneuvers that had seemed so thoughtless in training. All of it was new, somehow. "They'll be on us soon."

"Keep them back until the burners start," she said.

When Lyosha and Vova came thundering into view with Nata, Daria waved them through the blast doors. As they hurried past, the nape of Lyosha's neck became visible below his mask's hem. Extending beneath the black fabric was the edge of a thin gauze strip.

"Daria, what's in his neck?" Stasik asked.

Daria gripped him by the shoulder—her hands were tense, bone-shattering—and wheeled him toward the concourse. "Get yourself to the flight terminal! We'll have a two-way connection there."

Stasik was slow to comply, his mind rummaging through the morass of facts and capabilities that he'd once taken for granted. But all his uncertainty evaporated with the Coalition klaxon's omnipresent crackling.

"Dissidents, please be advised that Coalition forces have encircled your position. There is no egress. Please deactivate the shuttle, discard your weapons, and calmly approach the nearest Coalition intervention officer."

Stasik wedged the submachine gun's stock beneath his arm. He moved out into the concourse's central lane to find rows of armored vehicles and standard-issue rifles gazing through the windows. He slid behind the gate's terminal, slapped absently at the complex security controls until steel shutters slammed down over the entrance's cracked panes.

Breath high in his chest, palms clammy, he thumbed the shuttle's intercom. "Anybody up there?"

Three seconds later, the console squawked back. "Henry, what the fuck are we doing?"

"That you, Diane?"

"No, it's the queen," she said, her voice competing with screams somewhere deep inside the shuttle. "Yes, it's me! We've got the cockpit locked down, but Daria took the pilots somewhere. I think I heard shots in the passenger cabins."

"Just keep your eyes peeled. I'll be up there soon."

"This doesn't feel right, Henry."

He kept his thumb on the transmit button without speaking.

There was no fear in him, no remorse for what would come next. There was only Buenos Aires. Only freedom.

CHAPTER 28

"A re you Inspector Pendron?" the visor-faced intervention officer asked Bahr as they huddled behind the barricade's string of Kevlar-packed, six-wheel carriers. The man traded a few confused glances with his comrades.

"I've modified your Morse signature," Textile streamed through Bahr's head. *"It has all the credentials you'll need."*

"A warning would have been nice," he replied to the construct.

"Do you truly need me to do everything."

Bahr ignored the jab. "The very same," he said out loud to the officer. He smoothed out the folds of the navy-blue jacket he'd lifted off a dead man to blend in. "No time to grab my badge. Once the call came in, I got behind the wheel."

"Have you got an action order I can scan?"

"A scan?" Bahr rubbed his forehead, gave an exaggerated sigh. "Listen, we've got a shuttle about to take off in there. It's going to take fifteen, maybe twenty minutes just to haul a scanner out here and verify all of this. I left dinner with my girls to be here."

"We're not authorized to—"

Bahr pulled back his sleeve, turned his wrist over for the officer's inspection. "Just give my implant a glance."

The intervention officer shook his head, set his rifle against the troop carrier, and unspooled his belt's corded Morse reader. After waving the device over Bahr's wrist with a perfunctory sweep, the officer hummed, seemingly satisfied.

"So, you're the negotiator?" he asked.

"That's why I'm here," Bahr said.

"Do you need a briefing?"

Bahr shrugged. "I've had updates since it started. I think it'd be best if I make contact now."

"Now?" the officer asked. "We haven't even had time to seal off the lower lot."

"Nationalists aren't known for saving their own skins," Bahr said, cocking a brow. "If I don't talk them out of there, chances are we'll see that thing go up in flames. Just my experience, of course. I doubt anybody's captain is keen to see that outcome."

"You know they're armed, don't you?"

"So I hear," Bahr said.

"Standard procedure is to establish remote communication first."

"Certainly, but most standard cases don't involve a shuttle with cycling burners, eh?"

"Well, then." The officer gestured toward a ladder on the edge of the far side of the complex. "That's where we were going to deploy the first squad. If you want, you can set up a spearhead there. But no entrance—that's an order from the brass."

"Understood." Bahr tipped his cap, started off across the airfield.

"Remember your commands," Textile streamed. *"The rogue agents are not your primary focus."*

Bahr's stride hastened. *"If they run together, they perish together."*

CHAPTER 29

As sixteen minutes bled into seventeen, the terminal's lighting dimmed to a smoky pall. Alarms trickled into occasional chirps. The muffled sobs of civilians—now hostages, Stasik supposed—echoed from every level of the concourse.

He kept his submachine gun's barrel resting atop a mound of administrative files and boarding passes, aimlessly sweeping the first level for the white sheen of intervention units. With one hand teasing the trigger, he used the other to flick the comms open.

"How's it coming, Diane?" he asked, now feeling calm enough to speak without his heart exploding.

"They've engaged the secondary locks," Mallison said. "Daria's trying to disengage it manually, but it's slow going."

Stasik sank down against the filing cabinets, shut his eyes.

"Those locks are on the central grid. She's not going to get them off."

"You're saying we're fucked?"

"I didn't say that."

"Did you know about these locks?" Mallison asked. "Henry, how in the hell couldn't you know?"

"I did," he said, trying to recall if he'd recalled it, if he could recall anything at all about the Coalition's security grid and what it could truly do. "My chip did, at least."

Mallison didn't speak for a long while. "Mine did, too."

"We can get through this, Diane. Daria must—"

"I know why Daria brought us." Mallison's whisper was a brittle, vicious thing. "She wants to use us as bargaining chips, Henry. She knew about the fucking locks."

Despite the emptiness of the terminal, Stasik crouched lower and tucked the intercom's transmitter into the fold of his jacket. "What are you saying?"

"A few minutes ago, she said something about you making a call to Moscow."

"Moscow?"

"They're the only ones who can pry that lock open," Mallison said. "She *knew.*"

"She might be right." Stasik stared ahead at nothing in particular, his breaths slowing, heartbeat picking back up. "Diane, hang tight. I'm making the call."

"Henry—"

Stasik flipped the comms switch, set the transmitter back in its cradle. Then he rested his submachine gun on the tiles near his feet and stretched his legs out toward a wall with a flickering neon advertisement for King Cigarillos.

He reached up above his head, cumbersomely pulled the phone and its receiver down into his lap. His fingers moved with the last vestiges of muscle memory, dialing the Coalition's inner extension codes, security passcodes, personal directories...

Stasik lifted the phone to his ear, let his attention wander in the void between rings.

"Hello?" Guillory's voice made him ashamed. It was the voice of a patriarch, at once brutish and embracing. Suddenly Stasik wanted nothing to do with these nationalists, this place, the atrocities.

"Director Guillory?" Stasik said. Saying that familiar name was like a tonic for his senses.

"Specialist?" Guillory said. "What in the fuck's happened to you?"

"It's a long story, sir."

"Are you near Moscow? Riga? Where can I send that bird?"

"I need to know something, and I want to hear the truth."

Guillory coughed, took a long, whining pull from his cigarette. "This isn't how I saw my day going, Specialist. I had the Wing start to prepare coroner's papers for you two."

Perhaps it isn't too late to put those to use, Stasik considered. "Do you remember a woman named Julia Polocheva?" he asked Guillory.

"Where are you, Specialist?"

"Polocheva, sir."

"Listen, Henry, it's best to mull these things over once you're safe in a precinct," Guillory said. "The region's on fire with these goddamned nationalists."

Stasik swallowed so hard he nearly devoured his own tongue. "I need to hear your answer now, sir."

"We had our boys comb that train from top to bottom, you know."

"Sir."

"The name's a relic." None of Guillory's paternal warmth crept into the answer. "Let's resume this over a cigar, Henry."

"Polocheva remembers your division very well," Stasik said.

Guillory paused, took another audible drag of a cigarette. "My God, it's been a long time coming."

"What?"

"Are you and Mallison still untying that knot, Specialist?"

"Every last thread," Stasik whispered.

"Marvelous," Guillory said. "The brass was prattling on about how you'd turned tail, gone off to Argentina."

"Not yet," Stasik said. "Not until I know how it all fits."

"That's the fire I love in you, you know?" Guillory chuckled. "Any other man would've buried this case before the ink had dried. But you and Mallison, you're better than I'd ever imagined."

"You know what they did to her, don't you?" Stasik said.

Guillory's chair creaked. "You're talking about Lauska."

"Did you know Danicheva was part of that program?"

"I did," he said flatly. "Send me your coordinates, Specialist. We can have a bird there in an hour."

"How many of you knew about Lauska?" Stasik asked.

"A few dozen," Guillory said. "That was all before I received my commendations. I'm not the same man I was."

"I don't know about that anymore."

"When you've walked this world long enough, you can separate the wheat from the chaff. Good and evil, Specialist. That's what I understand, and what you'll understand, too. You'll be stronger for knowing this."

"You *knew*, and you didn't say a word to me," he said, sickness cramping his gut. And this time, it wasn't only the withdrawal.

"Some things are best discovered on their own," Guillory said. Then, with a more sober tone, "I recognized Danicheva from the moment she turned up in Donetsk. The brass wanted to shut it down. I did, too. But when I saw how badly they wanted it all swept away, I knew it had to go on."

"Why?"

"For the truth, Specialist," Guillory said. "Because you're a good man, and you deserve the truth. All of it. I knew you'd find out what I've done, but it's a drop in the pan when you level it against what's really going on. You were the only one who could expose it."

"But you knew what they were doing?" Stasik asked.

"No," Guillory said. "I've no clue know how deep it goes. Nobody does. That's why you had to do this for me. No chance in hell I'd get within orbit of it, but you—I knew you'd get to it, and you'd still choose the proper path in the end. That's what a good man has to do. No sense in lecturing you about what's right—you have to know it in your gut, and face it, and be at peace with it."

"How much haven't you told me?"

"When you get to Moscow, we'll set it straight over whiskey," Guillory said.

Stasik curled his legs closer to his chest. "I won't make it to Moscow, sir. Please, just tell me it now. Tell me everything."

"Specialist, I've got two dicers running on our calls. If they knew you were yanking these strands, they'd have your head. Mine too."

"Soon they might."

It broke Stasik's heart to hear how Guillory sighed. "What've you done, Specialist?"

"Sir, I need to protect my client," Stasik said quietly. "No matter who or what gets involved."

"Who are you with?"

Stasik let the silence thicken, shuddered at the echo of yet another alarm. "There's a nationalist named Daria. She says she used to know my client through Lauska."

There came a muttered *Christ.* "Specialist, head for the hills."

"You know her, too?"

"She's from an older generation," Guillory said. "She doesn't have the same regulations you or Mallison do."

"Generation?"

"Keep it collected, Henry. It'll all make sense when you get here."

"I just need you to help me."

"Anything," Guillory said. "Where can I send the bird?"

"It's about a suborbital, sir." Stasik coiled the phone's cord around his finger. "I need you to release a secondary lock."

"Fucking hell."

"Please."

Stasik heard Guillory's fist smash against hardwood, rattling a coffee mug. "Get out of there," he demanded.

"That's no longer an option, sir," Stasik said.

"Neither is releasing a shuttle. What've they roped you into?"

"Buenos Aires."

Guillory drew a slow, painful breath. "Get out, Henry."

"I can't, sir."

"There is no Buenos Aires!" the director snapped, his words crumbling into a wet, spastic coughing fit. "It's rubble and power grids, Specialist. It doesn't *exist.*"

Stasik's hand trembled against his cheek. Nothing seemed real. Nothing held any trace of goodness. And it wasn't only Buenos Aires, that fleeting mirage of a paradise beyond this nightmare, but the sense of dissolving into the madness.

His body went numb. So numb he couldn't tell the difference between his own leg and the floor tiles. For a short while, it felt nice. He wanted to disappear, wanted to get away from it all by any means necessary. But there was nowhere to run.

Nowhere to go. No Buenos Aires, nowhere they wouldn't find him. Why was he not surprised?

He opened his mouth and closed it several times, searching for a reply. "Something's off in my head, sir," Stasik said, his voice slow and shaky.

"Off?" Guillory replied.

"They took my chip out. I can't remember."

"You're just disoriented, Specialist."

"I don't know my father's name anymore."

Guillory's breathing had devolved into a harsh struggle, ripping in and out. "Specialist, get to Moscow. By any means necessary."

"What's all this for, sir? All this killing? Is it all for her?"

"It'll make more sense when I show you what you are."

Stasik felt like there was a vise around his neck. A dark, dreadful smog drowned out his thoughts.

"What are you saying?" he asked softly.

"Henry, I can't release anything more. Please, just—"

A gunshot washed out the phone's input, reduced the audio to a raw screech. Air squelched, the sound of a dying man's heaving breaths. Footsteps clacked. A man screamed. Silence.

Stasik let the phone clatter to the tiles. He numbly picked up his submachine gun, fingers fumbling a few times. Then he flipped the comms switch back into position.

Mallison's voice burst through the transmitter. "Come in, goddamn it!"

"Diane, those locks aren't coming down," Stasik whispered.

"Forget about that for a moment," Mallison breathed into the transmitter, her voice fraught with terror. "They're putting holes in the passengers."

"Where's Nata?"

"I-I don't know, Henry. This is all coming down."

Stasik squeezed the transmitter in his palm. "She's the only thing they want," he said, dropping into a hushed tone as boots echoed toward the concourse. "She's what *everybody* wants. Get her and get off that thing. There has to be a transit lot under here."

"Now you want us to surrender?" Mallison asked.

"No, not surrender," he said. "We keep moving until we know everything, Diane."

"What are you on about?"

"Just get her. I'll sort out the rest."

He flipped the comms off once more, then pressed himself into the cabinets, with the submachine gun nuzzled against his waist. Peering over the lip of the desk, Stasik surveyed the shadowed concourse. There was nearly no movement aside from the civilians huddling behind kiosks or scurrying for an exit.

Then he noticed it.

Midway down the complex's left wing, a man wearing a Coalition cap and windbreaker was drawing closer. The agent moved fearlessly, efficiently, scanning his surroundings with a panther's vigilance.

Stasik settled the submachine gun in his arms and shifted to a kneeling position, then took aim.

"Henry, aren't you tired of all these charades?"

The sound of the Aryan's voice paralyzed his trigger finger.

"I'm only here for Anastasia Danicheva," the Aryan went on, wandering ever nearer. "But I can leave a mess if I'm not careful." He moved to the center of the concourse, stopped, spun in a slow circle. Then he drew a slim military-grade detonator from his windbreaker's pocket. "A significant mess."

The supersonic clap of the nationalists' rifle fire emanated from the boarding passage, fanning out across the concourse. Wasting no time, the Aryan stuffed the detonator into his pocket, drew his handgun, and started toward the shuttle.

As he emerged from the gloom, Stasik rose from behind his desk and stared down the submachine gun's sights. He watched the Aryan weaving between plants, hanging advertisements, and holographic security reminders.

The gun roared in Stasik's grip before he intended to fire, screaming through the concourse, peppering white walls and shattering glass displays.

When the muzzle flash winked away, there was no body, no blood. The Aryan's dim shape shifted behind the cover of a column.

Stasik slapped the comms switch, leaned into the transmitter. "Updates, Diane!"

"Henry, I can't hold the cockpit anymore," she replied. "I'm popping the emergency slide."

"Two minutes," he shouted, slinking down to avoid a burst of return fire. Plaster rained down over his back as the Aryan unleashed another barrage.

Mallison called out a reply, but Stasik heard only panic and fizzling static. He slid over the desk, spraying the Aryan's position with seven rounds as he ran, disregarding everything except the burning in his legs and the echoes exploding from the shuttle's boarding passage.

Stasik cut around a corner, felt high-velocity rounds snapping past the tip of his ear. Standing directly in the blast door's threshold was Vova, the black eye of his shotgun barrel locked on Stasik.

Everything ran on impulse—Stasik's feet, his hands, his finger. His submachine gun's burst tore through Vova's neck and cheek, sent him sprawling into the shuttle's piston stacks in a twitching, bloodied heap.

No time to ID the corpse as protocol had once dictated. Stasik slung the submachine gun around to his back and wrenched the blast door shut, spinning the locking mechanism until it could go no further.

Then Stasik scrambled up the ladder. Gunshots and screams and clanging metal saturated the access shaft, gave hellish texture to the crimson bulbs and bundles of wires flowing past his face. Even the air choked him—rubber-tinged, engine-warmed, sweat-smelling. Far below, the Aryan hammered away at the blast door.

"Diane!" Stasik hollered, dragging himself up and over the rim of the cockpit section. It was dark, a claustrophobic dreamscape of tar black and garnet red, cluttered with more control panels and gauges than he'd ever seen.

There was no reply aside from the jarring *pop-pop* of gunfire in the adjoining compartment.

Stasik charged through the bulkhead opening, submachine gun aimed, trigger finger glued in place.

"Stop," Daria said. Her voice was unfeeling, austere in a way that would have easily suited a labor camp director. She stood by the flight controls, her handgun's barrel nuzzled against Mallison's temple.

Lyosha's body lay slumped in a strange knot in the pilot's seat. Stasik kept his gun aimed. "Put it down," he ordered.

"Take her out," Mallison said through clenched teeth. "Even if she fires, you take her out."

"What are we to you?" Stasik asked Daria. "Bait? An easy ticket out?"

"You are what we should have been." Daria's arm displayed none of the trembling present in fleshier, non-enhanced arms. "We are not the monsters, Specialist. We are the survivors."

"What did you do with Nata?" he asked.

Daria's face hardened. She cast a sidelong glance at the emergency slide's opening flaps, which were swaying in the midday breeze. Pockets of light shimmered between rubber strips. "She's long gone. It seems she abandoned us."

"Because she realized you haven't got a single marble left," Mallison spat.

"Hardly," Daria said. "She left because it was just another move on her chessboard. You see, her only instinct is self-preservation."

"It's that way for most of us," Stasik said, edging closer.

"Just shoot her," Mallison said.

"Do you really think you're the same, you and her?" Daria asked.

"I don't know anymore," Stasik replied.

"What if I told you she led you here? She led all of us here, in fact. To this very spot, at this very moment, in these very circumstances."

"I'd want proof."

"Proof? Only one of us knew about the secondary locks, for instance. One of us knew that there was no hope of ever having them released."

"Apparently," Stasik said.

Daria sighed. "It was Anastasia, Specialist."

He didn't believe it—he didn't want to. The truth scratched at the back of his mind, rampant, infectious, an inferno that threatened to devour everything he knew of the world and himself, but he stomped its embers out as promptly as they arose. Nata was a good woman, an innocent woman, a woman he wanted so badly that nothing else mattered. Not even reality.

"Has she truly dug her claws in so deeply?" Daria asked. "She told me you could be manipulated, but I didn't anticipate such naivety."

"Show me the evidence," Stasik said.

"There won't be any once they detonate this shuttle," Daria

said. "There are layers to every deception. We may have used you, but she used all of us. And she's going to get away."

"Nothing's being detonated."

"Shoot her!" Mallison rasped. Daria pressed the gun tighter against her skull.

"If they can't control their toy, they'll rip it apart," Daria said. "And then they'll sweep up the ashes with a broom and a smile."

"There are protocols for a hijacking."

"Naturally," Daria said. "But restraint of force was swept off the table as soon as Anastasia started to kill passengers."

Stasik met Mallison's haggard eyes. "She didn't kill anybody," he said.

"Oh?" Daria asked, grinning like the Cheshire cat. "I'd urge you not to look in the seating compartments, then."

Flashes of bullet-riddled corpses exploded into Stasik's mind's eye. "You're lying."

"It's all true. If only you knew how many rivers that scorpion has crossed on your back, little frog. If only you knew."

"Shut your mouth!" Stasik barked.

"I expected more from an agent of your caliber and conditioning. From both of you, perhaps. Neither of you balked at the idea of a remarkably inconvenient scuffle on a civilian train, did you?"

"I did," Mallison whispered.

"It wasn't fabricated," Stasik said. "I was there—they were going to take us all out."

"Were they now?" Daria asked, her tone playful now. "Or were they just herding the sheep into the slaughterhouse? Scaring off the hens to grab their eggs?"

"Shut up."

"Two trucks, both summoned with nothing more than a phone call from *her*. Think about that sort of power."

"Are you stalling, or what?" Stasik asked.

"Hardly," Daria said. "I'm shining a light on the truth, Specialist."

"Bullshit."

"Do you remember what happened when your helicopter went down?" Daria asked him. "Do you remember those nationalists who wanted to put you in the dirt? The ones who didn't look quite normal? The ones who looked enhanced, like *me*, even? All we needed was you. All we needed was the chip in your neck."

"Whatever she told you is—"

Daria laughed, cutting him off. "You've done precisely what she wanted, from A to Z."

"Looks like you haven't made out so well either," Mallison said.

"And think of all the good it's done you," Daria said. "Now we'll face Z together."

"That doesn't need to happen," Stasik said, angling the submachine gun toward Daria's head. He tried to resist the maelstrom brewing in him. Nata's face flickered through his mind. His client. The good woman who'd gotten a bad lot in life, who needed to be saved.

Daria smiled as though she could taste his strain of discomfort. The Aryan slammed at the blast door loud enough for them to hear now. The sound of it only deepened her smile.

"I accept that I'm going to die here," she said. "But I will die free, Specialist. The entire world will watch my death, and they will know—if only in the pits of their minds—that this is all a fever dream."

"What role does Nata play in all of it?" Stasik asked.

"You wouldn't believe me if I told you, Specialist."

"Try me."

"She's the key to everything."

"To what?" Stasik asked.

"Pay no attention to the men behind the curtain," Daria whispered. "Even I don't know what she is. But I know this: She's nothing like you."

Stasik's finger eased on the trigger. "What would you know about us, Daria?"

"Henry," Mallison said, "*kill* her."

"You know, I made that call to Moscow," Stasik said. "I spoke to my director for a short while. He remembered you, Daria, and he remembered Nata. But he didn't get to tell me everything. He didn't tell me what we are."

A thin smirk spread across Daria's face. "Don't you understand, Specialist? That's the beauty of what they've done. Who can say what's true anymore? Who can say if what's inside you is the same as what's inside me?"

Stasik's legs went weak. "What's that supposed to mean?"

"Let's find out," Daria said, turning her attention back to Mallison. "What's inside that oh-so-pretty head, Miss Mallison?"

Three ear-shattering rounds broke the stillness.

Daria dropped the handgun and staggered back onto the console, the lower part of her jaw obliterated, hanging in flapping threads, her throat pumping bright blood down over her parka. She met Stasik's eyes as she slid down, swatting at the air, gasping, choking through her final laugh. A pink froth oozed through rigid lips.

Mallison's shoulders dropped. She looked at Stasik, at the ceiling, anywhere except the body. Then she breathed, as if coming up for air from a deep dive.

"We need to get her, Henry," she rasped.

"Come on," Stasik said, moving to the emergency slide and pulling the flaps apart. Far below him, nested among the churning cogs of the docking mechanism and retaining brackets, was the concrete tunnel leading to the facility lot. "Where do you figure it leads?"

Mallison gazed out at the encircling ring of steel and bulletproof glass. "Same place as she went."

Stasik studied her face, the way daylight put a glimmer of madness in her eyes. "Can you run a little further, Diane?"

She racked the bolt on her rifle, nodded. "A little further."

CHAPTER 30

Six minutes after the Slav had sealed himself in the suborbital shuttle, the first intervention unit stormed through the eastern wing in a flurry of stamping boots and sizzling neurostun grenades.

"Lie on the floor." The command warbled through the complex, stimulating—even to excess—the adrenal glands of any bastard unfortunate enough to have a working Morse chip. "Do not resist."

Bahr studied the spectacle from the top of a stairwell leading to the lower lot. The officers were a cozy half-klick away, imperceptible to the average human. But with his cocktail of visual uppers and spliced photoreceptors, he could discern the serial numbers on their rifles, the blemishes on their visors, the hesitation in their steps.

"*What are you waiting for?*" Textile asked. "*Your targets have reached the lower lot.*"

Bahr pondered the machine's semblance of gravity, flicked open the detonator's cap in his left hand. An inkling of frustration crept into his stream. *"You told me to stay my hand."*

"You observed their use of the emergency evacuation route," Textile said. *"There is no sense in causing death without reason. They will escape unless you mobilize."*

"Not from me," Bahr streamed in reply. *"Not this time."*

"Remain mindful of your priority. Avoid collateral damage."

"There is no collateral," Bahr replied. *"Whoever knows should be buried in the same pit."*

Then he turned and started down the steps at a leisurely pace. His attention was divided between a glacial countdown and the lower lot's layout, which Textile was broadcasting in a hallucinatory overlay. An exit route here, an ingress there...

At the bottom of the steps, Bahr flicked the copper switch of his detonator.

A chain of blasts went off in murderous succession. Each explosion bellowed down from the stairs, echoing out across the lot, muting Bahr's hearing. Then came a larger, singular bang that flickered the lot's bulbs as the terminal and the shuttle itself blew.

He heard the howl of roiling flames. Screaming. Smoke wafting downstairs. Hairline fractures ripped across the lot's concrete ceiling, snaking overhead. Wisps of dust and debris sifted down over a field of luxury automobiles.

Bahr dropped the detonator, drew his handgun. *"Can you see them?"*

Textile's reply was instant: *"I have no access to the surveillance systems. Your rash actions ensured that."*

It was better that way, Bahr supposed. A hunt was between the prey and the predator. He wove through the rows of parked cars with effortless precision, his eyes roaming for any sign of movement.

He caught sight of a silhouette at the rear of the lot, framed in the tawny light of an exit route. Not just one silhouette—two. And there was a third between them, a wiry, flailing shape. Sounds returned to him in a rush: shouting, heels dragging over concrete, fists on flesh.

To his own surprise, Bahr didn't lift his handgun, didn't even approach. He stood with the quiet detachment of a birdwatcher, marveling at the sight of the agents using loaded firearms to force the Russian model into the back of a green Hotchkiss Anjou.

"Have you made your presence known?" Textile asked.

Bahr watched the dissidents' vehicle race up the exit ramp, and holstered his handgun.

"No," he replied, *"but I will."*

CHAPTER 31

Stasik and Mallison ran Nata down like a pack of wolves. Unfeeling, relentless, willing to kill or be killed in the hunt. He rounded a string of Lincoln cars with his submachine aimed, trying to force himself to frame Nata in the weapon's iron sights. Every nerve in his hands resisted the motion. But she was *there*, right fucking there, ten paces away now, thundering toward an exit ramp under the parking garage's fluorescent sprawl.

"Stop!" Stasik screamed.

To his surprise, Nata did. She stopped entirely, just shy of the yellow paint marking the exit, but she didn't turn. The flaps of her parka swirled in the ventilation system's breeze. She raised both arms with fingers splayed.

Mallison ran up beside him, breathless, her own rifle quivering as she tucked it against her shoulder. Her hatred for the

Russian was plastered across her face. "If you move, I'll blow your fucking head off."

"It's done," Stasik said with a hoarse, restrained voice. "Don't move, Miss Danicheva." He kept his eyes fixed on Nata as he advanced, one slow step after another, mentally recounting how many bullets he'd spent in the lobby and shuttle. There couldn't be more than two or three rounds left in the magazine. Then again, he wasn't sure if he could even convince his confused body to pull the trigger.

"Just grab her," Mallison said. "I've got you covered."

Yet as Stasik drew closer, noting the first hints of Nata's ever-sweet, ever-present perfume, he was suddenly unsure of himself. Wrath, cruelty, power—it all left him in a strange rush. He lowered the submachine gun's barrel, wandered toward her with one hand out, one comforting hand.

"What are you doing?" Mallison called out.

Stasik opened his mouth to answer, but even he didn't know. Acting on instinct was as strange a sensation to him as love. "Nata," he whispered to the back of her head, "this has to end."

"It will, *daragoy*," she said in turn. "Soon, it will."

Mallison's steps clapped up the concrete behind Stasik. She shouldered past him, jammed her rifle's barrel into the small of Nata's back. "Whatever's going on here, it had better stop. You're going to shut up, get into a car, and be as still as possible. Because if you don't, I'll paralyze you right now. Or worse."

Stasik blinked at his partner. "Diane—"

"Find us a car, Henry," Mallison said. "Any car."

He gave a perfunctory nod, circled around them, and saw the slate expression on Nata's face. There was a grin buried there, he swore. The seed of something unfathomable.

Regardless, he moved his attention to the rows of cars beside the exit ramp. A yellow Chrysler, a blue Cadillac, a green

Hotchkiss Anjou. Only the latter had its windows rolled down and a fingerprint panel for agent override. A company car, he surmised.

"This'll do," Stasik said to Mallison. "Bring her here."

"You have cuffs?" Mallison asked.

Stasik felt along the back of his belt, probing for the lump of his polymer handcuffs. They were tucked into a leather flap on his left side. He fished them out, held them up for Mallison to see.

With a few prods from the rifle barrel, Mallison guided Nata toward the car in a slow, breathless procession. The agent's hair was windswept, glued across her forehead with a sheen of sweat. Her eyes were bloodshot.

When they reached the rear passenger side of the car, Mallison nodded to Stasik. "Put them on tight."

"Henry, you don't know what you're doing," Nata said.

Stasik nodded to his partner, but then made the mistake of meeting Nata's eyes. They were more vivid than he'd remembered, a deeper shade of—

The ground itself shook with the dull thump of high explosives. Dust sifted down, clouded the air for a split second. That was all it took for Nata's silhouette to dart out of view.

"Henry!" Mallison tackled her in a moment and wrestled her to the ground, grunting, viciously panting in the thickening haze of smoke.

Stasik rushed toward the sound of soles scuffing on pavement and fists pounding into flesh. His weapon was up, ready to shoot—for whom, he couldn't tell. Then the air cleared, and the noise fell away. He saw Mallison, her rifle slung behind her back and handgun aimed at Nata's forehead.

Nata now had the distinct appearance of a wolf surrendering to the pack leader. Her arms were raised, her lips pursed, her eyes fixed on faded parking lines. Even her back had a defeated hunch.

"I've got it," Stasik said, coughing on the smoke.

"Don't even *think* about it," Mallison said to Nata through hard breaths. "Not one move."

"We have to go," Nata said, suddenly robbed of any emotions. "He's here."

As Stasik shifted Nata's hands behind her back and slid the cuffs on, mindful not to tighten them to the point of pain, he noted the wariness in Mallison's stare.

"Who?" Mallison asked.

Stasik guided Nata toward the car with one hand, keeping the other firmly perched on the upper receiver of his submachine gun. "I don't think we need to ask."

———

"WHERE THE FUCK ARE WE EVEN *GOING*?" MALLISON ASKED from the passenger seat, frantically peering back at the stretch of barricaded road behind their car. She cradled her Colt against the headrest, glanced at Stasik's shifting hands upon the wheel, then muttered a fresh string of curses under her breath. She was still riding the adrenaline of wrangling Nata, it seemed.

But Stasik's head was somewhere else entirely, fixed on their hunter. He steered mechanically. "Just keep aiming," he said. "He can't be far behind." He glanced at the oscillating rearview mirror, caught a shaky glimpse of Nata's eyes. There was no humanity in her gaze, he admitted to himself. No sense of shame or fear.

"We need to get a call to Guillory," Mallison said.

"He just told me to *go*," Stasik lied, an acidic vacuum forming in his gut as he recalled the sounds he'd heard in Guillory's office. "Don't worry about him. We'll try him later."

"If the shooter can get to us, then—"

"Then what?"

"We should get help from him. Send him a warning. Something."

"We can't trust the Coalition anymore," Stasik said. "Not even for a fucking cup of coffee."

"Guillory's different," Mallison said.

How badly he wanted to believe that.

"Henry, did something happen to him?" she asked.

Stasik glared at her. "What if it did? We've got a job to do. So shut up and do yours, why don't you?"

"A job." Mallison's laugh was curt, hard. "This isn't a job anymore. This is survival." She fell back against her seat, breathing hard, her composure draining in an instant. Stasik could sense his own instability as well. His hands were white-knuckled on the wheel, his teeth ground together so firmly that he swore he could taste blood and the gummy lining of his cheeks.

"Fuck!" Mallison cursed so suddenly it caused Stasik to swerve. Before he could answer, she was digging her fingers into the car's built-in radio system. She pried it loose, then banged on it with the butt of her gun a few times until she was able to tear it free. She tossed it out the window, then sank back again.

"So they can't track us," she said, huffing.

Stasik grunted his approval. Nata offered what sounded like a soft, almost imperceptible scoff.

"And *you*!" Mallison said, twisting around in her seat and aiming her weapon at Nata's head. "Not another goddamn word out of you."

Stasik watched the barrel prod Nata's skin, felt the horror rising in himself. Not that there was anything to say. Not anymore. He knew that he ought to hate her, ought to have put her down like a dog himself, but he couldn't scrounge up the wrath.

Even with that empty, pitiless gaze she wore, even with more blood on her hands than she knew how to clean, Stasik wanted her. He wanted her so badly that he let his eyes meet hers. Let himself be swallowed by her presence, by shallow breathing that reminded him of kissing and boyhood notions of love.

Then he had the urge to vomit. He slowed the car until his diaphragm relaxed, kept his eyes trained on the backs of his quaking hands.

"What's the matter?" Mallison asked.

Her comment made him chuckle. What *wasn't* the matter, when you got right down to it? He shook his head. "We'll find out."

He took them along a railway and its diverging tracks, letting the smoking airfield shrink at their backs like a passing cloud in spring. Pavement turned to beaten earth as districts faded to rural sprawls with industrial factories and high smokestacks.

"Enough of this," Mallison said eventually, leveling her weapon on Nata once again. "Where should we head?"

"There's nowhere to hide," Nata replied.

"That's not what I asked."

Nata blinked at Stasik in the mirror. "Are you going to take me somewhere and shoot me?"

Mallison didn't reply.

"The Coalition would've saved you the trouble," Nata said. "And you might've gotten out alive."

"If you tell us what's *really* going on, you might make it out of this car alive," Mallison said.

"I've told you what I know."

"Daria didn't seem to think so."

"Daria's mind isn't what it used to be," Nata said quietly. "Don't you trust me?"

And in that moment Stasik made the mistake of returning her stare, seeing the tears glimmer in the corners of her eyes. Seeing her ruby lips curl and her dark brows wrinkle. "Henry?" It was enough to drive him mad, thinking about her fate. So he didn't. He just kept driving.

———

Six hours later, when the sky was a mute gray with coming night, they came to a windswept field ringed by black trees. A paint-peeled, overgrown cottage stood out among dark briars. Abandoned. Stasik parked the car off the dirt road behind thick underbrush. It would have to do while they rested and planned their next move. Not that they had much gas left to get any further.

Words didn't come easily to him, nor to the others, it seemed; they'd been silent for the better part of three hours. But while Stasik and Mallison nursed their silence with pursed lips, Nata was a wisp in the field, a black streak sitting among the grass and brambles.

"Did he tell you anything important?" Mallison asked, huddling into the collar of her overcoat. She took a sharp pull from a cigarette.

"Who?" Stasik asked, even though he knew.

"Guillory. I know it all blew sideways quickly, but—"

"He knew," Stasik said. "He knew she's not what she thinks she is."

"What did he say?"

"It really doesn't matter," he said.

Mallison coughed, inhaled again. "If we know what the hell is going on, we can put that on the table. We can turn her over for a pass."

"She knows everything," Stasik said. "She's the only way to know the truth, Diane."

"She's just our bargaining chip."

"For what? A return ticket to the show?"

"Maybe it's time for that."

A flicker of rage rose in him.

"You know, local posts might even still be manned," Mallison continued. "We could send out a radio signal, try to contact Moscow about—"

"Fuck it," Stasik snapped. The harshness of his voice frightened him, made him reel for more words. "There's just no life back there. No life to be had whatsoever."

Mallison faced him now, her cigarette smoldering away in a lowered hand. "No life?"

"No future, I mean. There's no happiness. Not in the place that I—we—saw, Diane, and I think you know it, too." He was nearly out of breath, sweating cold beads. "Do you understand me?"

"Henry, if you're hung up on Buenos Aires—"

"It's not about that," he hissed. "It's that you'd have no—"

"Life?" Mallison cut in, more puzzled than angry. "I've still got a family to tend to, Henry. Mum, father, sister, niece. I've got people who *need* me. Not like you." She paused. Her eyes snapped open with sudden surrender, voice low. "Christ, Henry, I didn't mean it that way."

In truth, there wasn't any pain until she spoke the last sentence. It came to him as a hot, sickening rush. "It's all right. We don't need family in the same way."

"If we turned her over, we could get amnesty. You could walk away, scot-free. You could get a life there."

"There's no going back."

"We could get new chips," Mallison said. "New links, new

cerebral doses." She moved a bit closer, let the wind toss hair across her brows. "Work's your life here, and you've got to square up with it, Henry: that life's dismal. Truth, truth, truth. What about fucking happiness?"

His throat was tight, raw. "Do you know my birthday?"

"August," she said. "It's got nothing to do with what I'm saying."

"It's the seventeenth," Stasik whispered. He settled his hands further into his pockets. "You know, when I was nine, they threw me a big party. A grand one, with my favorite cake and everything. All of my friends, and one of those circus tricksters, too. But the whole time, I was just waiting for my father to come. They told me he was working late, but they had a look. A mood. This hush-hush, tight-lipped mood."

He brushed his foot over the earth in hard strokes. "It took them three years to tell me that he shot himself on my birthday," he went on. "Three fucking years!" He was close to screaming, breaking down every barrier that had ever preserved a memory the chip had prevented him from thinking about. "Who hides that from a child, Diane? Who!?"

Gray ash fluttered from the tip of Mallison's cigarette, danced like dead fireflies in the breeze. She didn't speak, didn't move.

"So I can take reality," Stasik snapped at nothing in particular. "I don't need to run home and bawl in my mother's arms whenever things fall apart. That's not me, and it never has been. Because I just don't *need* it."

"Everybody needs someone," Mallison said.

"I've done just fine on my own," he said. "So this problem, this thing that we're in right now, I'll be fine. You can drive on home and make your peace however you like."

The wind pushed past them and carried away all their

bitterness, their tension, their disdain, leaving only silence on the causeway. Nata still wandered through the fields when Mallison came to Stasik's side, bringing her cigarette to her lips with a motion that, for an instant, seemed like an attempt to embrace him.

She inhaled, exhaled, looked away. "I killed Polocheva."

"No, you didn't," Stasik said, but it was an ingrained reaction, some resistance to reality.

"She might've made it, might not have," Mallison continued. "When you walked off, though, I made a choice. Made you give up the ghost, I suppose. I tried to." She looked at him sidelong, weary. "I really tried, Henry."

Polocheva. The missing link to it all. A wellspring of secrets, of Nata's history, of the sickness and barbarism of the world. Perhaps it was just as fitting for a Coalition agent to destroy her.

"How?" Stasik asked softly.

"How what?" Mallison said.

"How did you kill her?"

"It wasn't painful for her, I hope. My knee was already so close to her windpipe. Not much pressure, no panic in the eyes. She went quietly."

And for a moment Stasik wondered if that was the proper way to handle the world and all its problems. Some knots could only be undone by cutting the string and retying it. *It wasn't painful.* That was how the Coalition could end it all mercifully. A straight razor across the jugular in sleep, everybody pumped full of morphine and oxycodone so they didn't feel a thing.

What could he say? It was how Mallison had been trained, him too. Programmed, even. To cut out the rot because curing it would take too long, be too dangerous. To kill, move on, and forget, until it was like it never happened.

"Let's just get Nata inside, Diane," he said, starting off down the embankment.

———

Nothing living had set foot in the cottage for years, perhaps decades. Every tabletop and windowsill and rusting sink tray was coated in a thin veneer of dust. The cupboards were full of porcelain plates and angel figurines, covered with spiderwebs and pellets of desiccated flies. It smelled like mothballs. Burnt tin. Rot.

Mallison lit the candles she'd taken from the silverware drawers and set them around the kitchen. Then she drew the curtains shut and sat at the table with Stasik, her eyes bloated by shadows and exhaustion.

Nata sat across the table with her hands tied behind the chair, her rabid gaze fixed on them. No longer was she distant, numb. She was present, terribly present. Whatever emotions could be expected of a woman in her predicament were absent. It was as though she'd manually adjusted her own reactions to make Stasik as uneasy as possible.

"Record it," Mallison said to Stasik, nudging his knee with her handgun.

He flicked the dial on his wrist, unsure of whether or not the device would function without the corresponding chip. If the Morse chip was the power outlet, the wrist implant was merely the appliance that utilized the energy. It was worth a shot anyhow.

"What are you playing at?" Mallison asked Nata.

Nata smiled, eased in her chair.

"Wipe that off your face," Mallison said, "or I'll help you with it."

"You should be asking what *you're* playing at," Nata said. "They're going to come here and murder us, you know."

"They?" Stasik asked.

"There is a force in the world that is so powerful you would not believe my descriptions of it," Nata said. "A force so malevolent and so hideous that it has no proper name. Not that we would recognize, anyway."

"Try us," Mallison said.

Nata looked squarely at Stasik. "I would prefer to discuss this with Henry."

"Oh, for fuck's sake," Mallison groaned.

"Diane," Stasik said, "just give us a minute. I'll yell if she tries anything."

The disdain in Mallison's glare spoke of her misgivings. She eyed Stasik, parsed him up and down, gave a little snort. "Suit yourself." Then she stood and left the room, sealing herself behind a bedroom's thick wooden door.

As soon as the latch clicked shut, Nata strained forward. "Henry," she whispered, fear flooding back into her eyes. "Please, you have to help me."

He tried to ignore his own impulses. His own weakness. "I can't."

"I know how this looks," she said.

"Did you send those men on the train?" he asked. "The ones who came for the tin?"

"No."

"Did you sabotage us at the airfield?" he asked.

"No."

"But you left me," he said. "You left me to die."

"You have it all wrong. Daria was going to kill me."

Stasik stared at her, waiting in vain for her pleading eyes to crumble. He winced at the sincerity of it all. "Why?"

"Because she wanted to leave me for dead, Henry," she said. "Everybody does. Everybody's running from the bear."

"What bear?"

"I can't tell you until we're out of here."

"Where, then?"

"Somewhere safe," she said. "Somewhere with us. Only us, Henry."

He gazed at his hands, which were shaking in his lap. Trying to stop the question bursting through his lips, but unable. "Do you even care about me?"

"I do," she said, her voice on the cusp of cracking. "I could be your only love, *daragoy*."

And as he read the quiet terror on her face, his heart sinking, his stomach revolting, he knew that he was her slave. He felt his chains, but it no longer mattered. Some strain of intuition deciphered her words better than he ever could. Even if she someday slid her knife into his back, it was a small price to pay for going to her now, kissing her, and delivering her from a savage world. In a time of liars, emotions were his only compass.

He passed her a soft nod, then reached out, briefly touched her thigh. She beamed at him through watery eyes.

"Diane," Stasik called, "get in here."

When Mallison's door creaked open, Nata worked to hide her quivering smile. A solitary teardrop was still winding its way down her cheek when Mallison settled back into her seat.

"Is she going to play ball?" Mallison asked.

Stasik shook his head, bit into his tongue.

"Listen here," Mallison said to Nata. "You're trying to get out of Dodge. Fair play. We're in the same game. But you're not playing by the same rules. In fact, you're not telling us the rules at all."

"Give me the radio, Diane," Stasik said, startling himself. He could sense the intentions behind his words, the quiet, slinking deception he'd seen in Nata time and time again.

Mallison blinked at him. "The radio?"

"There's only one person with more answers than her."

Mallison cocked a brow, fished her radio out of her jacket without taking her eyes off Nata. It surprised Stasik that she'd been able to hold onto it over the tumult of recent days. With practiced efficiency, she scrolled through a few of the device's dials, finally settling on the wideband frequencies, and then set the radio on the table. "All yours, Henry."

"I wouldn't do that," Nata said.

Mallison narrowed her eyes. "Why not?"

"It listens to the radio traffic," she explained. "It can localize a position."

"*It?*"

"The entity governing the network. The one that spoke to you."

"How the hell does she know about that?" Mallison asked Stasik. "And what does that even mean, entity?"

"Nobody knows what it truly is," Nata whispered.

Stasik didn't know what to say. Instead he stared at Nata, waited to see if she'd break under his scrutiny.

"Where did you learn about this thing's ability to track signals?" Mallison pressed, bunching up her sleeves as she leaned toward Nata with a murderous stare. "Is it just more bullshit, or did you wring it out of somebody?"

"It seems obvious after what happened in our safehouse, doesn't it?" Nata asked.

Reasonable enough, Stasik told himself. He wanted to believe it, to believe her. But as always, there was a cloud cover of doubt over her words. It didn't matter much for what he had in mind.

"I came to the same conclusion," he said.

"Our Morse chips are out now," Mallison said. "They shouldn't have a way to find us without those Morse signatures."

"Maybe, but their gunman had to have been tracking us to the airfield somehow, and the chips were already out by then.

Somehow, he knew where to find me." He bit on his lip as he thought. Mallison gawked, as if waiting for him to explain further. "The last thing I did before he arrived was use the phone in the terminal lobby. He could've used that phone line to hear my voice somehow, or—"

"But our chips are gone," Mallison reiterated.

Nata looked at her. "That doesn't make a difference over unsecured lines. It's like Henry said. It utilizes vocal patterns."

"You have no way of knowing that," Mallison said.

"I hope she's telling the truth," Stasik said. He picked the radio up before he could overthink it and hit the transmit button. "Anybody there? Come in, please."

After a minute or so, the silence broke.

"Hello?" came a broken, static-laden voice, distinctly feminine. "Somebody, hello?"

"Who's there?" Stasik replied.

"Switch to the local band, please. Hurry!" The woman's voice was breathless, almost overrun with the thrum of a car engine.

Mallison cast a questioning look at Stasik, who'd set his iron stare on the radio with hands meshed in his lap, then tuned the dial to the local band as requested.

"Well, now what?" Mallison asked, gesturing to the radio's earpiece.

"Are you there?" the woman's voice crackled.

"Answer it, Diane," Stasik said.

"Could be bait."

"There's no way it isn't," he said. "Answer it."

Mallison shifted toward the sink's halogen lights. "This is Diane Mallison, Coalition Internal Affairs. Kindly identify yourself."

More static. "Did you make it out of there?" the woman asked.

"Identify yourself."

"This is Hannah McLauden, a citizen," she said, her breathing tight and ragged. "Please, you've got to help me. I'm on Route 13. There's an armed suspect here. He must've come from that terror attack at the airfield."

Mallison's thumb hovered over the transmit tab. "Do I give her a location?"

"Just wait," Stasik said.

She set the radio on the kitchen table. The crackling rose, lingered, faded. There was a gunshot and a scream, and then a familiar sigh trickled over the band.

"Don't you want to end this?" The Aryan's voice was a needle against Stasik's eardrums. In the background, the car's engine cut out with a gurgle. A door whined open, slammed shut. "Tell me where she is, and this goes away. All of it goes away."

"Jesus, Henry," Mallison whispered, gawking at the radio.

Stasik leaned back stiffly in his chair. Then he fiddled with his Morse recorder, set it to the last open recording track. "Be easy, Diane."

"Just tell me the *truth*," the Aryan cooed.

Stasik snatched up the radio, propped his arm up upon his knee, hit transmit. "Listen here, you witless fuck. If you want her, you'll tell me—"

"Just turn her over," the Aryan interrupted. "There's no need to be dramatic."

"I'm not feeling dramatic. Only violent."

"Is that so?"

"She isn't here anymore." Stasik glanced at Nata long enough to catch her glimmer of surprise. "She got away from us. We're hunkering down now, waiting for reinforcements."

"Reinforcements? You think anybody's coming to save *you*?"

"If you come here for a fight, we'll have to put you down,"

Stasik said evenly. "Miss Danicheva is no longer in our custody. I'm giving you the option to lay down your guns, drive to a shared meeting ground, and explain your side of things."

"Why do that when I could go straight to you?" the Aryan asked.

"Because she isn't *here*. If you back us into a corner—"

"You know that I'll find you all sooner or later, don't you?" Stasik heard the snapping of branches, the cawing of ravens somewhere in the distance. "Your stolen vehicle's been tagged by the security system, but even if it weren't, I'd catch wind of your scent somehow," the Aryan went on. "That's what men like me do to men like you, Henry. We stalk you, and we kill you. And we kill the fawns you keep in your company."

The radio trembled in Stasik's grip as he answered, "Come and see, then."

CHAPTER 32

Outside Zvonki, Russian Province
268 miles from Moscow

Soon it would be over. Bahr could already see the end in his mind. Henry's body twisted over on itself, pale, distended by the out-turned skull and flaps of soft skin, gaze set upon his equally mutilated partner. The image reeled through his consciousness again and again, at once lurid and graceful, made real by a string of exhaustive details that grew more elaborate by the moment.

He imagined moss around the Russian model, a butterfly perched on her nose. A rose in her hands. The scene was as beautiful as his other victims had been repulsive.

But she was different. She was a wicked thing, born to be slaughtered. It was good and right, and the universe would decorate her corpse in turn.

"Are you fantasizing?" Textile asked.

This time, Bahr did not answer in words. He crept through

the tall grass, wading as he'd done in the war through snowdrift and white-laden pine boughs, his rifle hoisted on his back. His feet were bleeding, numb. The amphetamines were burning off into vicious tingles and aberrant, horrid thoughts.

Flashes of his wife weeping. Of his son naked and crucified.

Was it his nightmare, or the machine's?

And beneath the sensations, there was longing. Bittersweet longing. Every mission had come to this end, had culminated in a mass of bodies and spent casings. Hunting was like fucking, after all. It was a tease, a mere suggestion of what pleasure the orgasm would grant him. When it was done, and he'd killed his target, where was the pleasure? Where was the rapture he'd expected?

He didn't want to think of that, but he did.

Besides, it was far too late to turn back now. He'd drained most of the petrol in the Volkswagen he'd hijacked, and the vehicle would grant him no aid in finding his way home. *Home.* The word seemed so strange now, as though it were nothing more than a sound, a symbol.

Ahead rose the cottage that housed his targets. He had zeroed in on their radio signal with his arms draped over the wheel, puffing his last fentanyl cigarette, wide-eyed.

Fifty paces, forty, thirty. He slipped out of the grass and skulked toward the cottage, scanning the windows for any hint of movement within. He didn't want to kill the agents—not even Stasik, the petulant Slav, whom the machine might neutralize—but they were acceptable casualties. Beyond acceptable, in fact. They would live and die by his discretion.

"Don't underestimate them," Textile pulsed. *"They are dangerous."*

But Bahr was too lost in the ecstasy of the moonlit hunt. When he reached the cottage's pitted wall, he sidled along it with long, careful strides, crushing the wildflowers that had sprouted through a foundation of veiny concrete. He moved to the door, gently twisted the knob—a latch shifted. They'd left it unlocked.

He stared at the rusty knob for a moment, puzzled, vaguely alarmed. Had the Anglo woman unlocked it for him? Had it been a misstep in their judgment, a fluke? Or had it been left open for a hasty retreat?

Was the woman's surrender yet another nationalist ploy? His fingers tensed around his rifle.

Seven years of war, seven years of killing. It had sharpened him against the lies that humans told to escape their fates. Against the bestial tactics of the cornered. He thought of calling upon Textile to offer a machine's calculation of the odds, but it made little difference in the end. His body could not go much further.

So he stood to the right of the door, reached out, and gripped the doorknob with quivering fingers. He twisted and nudged the door inward. There was a long, dry creak, then the moan of dying wind.

Chalky moonlight spilled through the threshold, illuminating rotting hardwood everywhere, the fluttering tassels of a tablecloth, a pair of mud-caked black boots.

Bahr pressed the rifle's barrel to the edge of the frame and slowly angled it inward, sweeping the gloom for the sheen of eyes or the glint of steel. His gaze snagged on something vague in shape.

"Step into the light," Bahr said calmly. "If you come too quickly, I'll kill you."

The silhouette remained motionless for so long that Bahr began to doubt himself. To squirm, even. Perhaps he had spoken to an oversized clock, an impressive coatrack.

Then it moved.

Bare, bony feet and dark trousers—filled by a set of gangly legs—emerged from the shadows. Next was a stained brown shirt, the open flaps of a parka, a pair of trembling hands. A thin, ribbed neck. The chin and lips and cheekbones of a Slav.

The Slav.

"Call her out here," Bahr said.

Henry stared at him. "I didn't think you'd come."

"Bring her now, or I'll shoot."

"I'm not afraid to die," he whispered.

"Yes, well, that's what they all say. Until it happens."

"You didn't come here for me," Henry said, his nose twitching like a hare's. His voice was steady—steadier than ever before. Sobriety, resolve, exhaustion—something had changed within him since their last meeting.

"No, I didn't," Bahr said, nudging the door wider with his boot and staring into the blackness beyond the kitchen. "But if you don't bring her out, I'll step over your bodies to get to her."

"What if I said she isn't here anymore?"

"I'd call you a liar."

"It's true," Henry said. "She left hours ago."

"Just like that?" Bahr's finger coiled over the trigger.

"Just like that."

"But you were so *close*," he cooed, "and I know that you had a soft spot for her. Isn't that right, my friend? You probably even loved her, not that you ought to feel anything bitter for it. Her enhanced pheromones can make a man do anything for her, I've been told. Anything."

Henry's hands tensed.

"And if she's truly gone, how long will she last?" Bahr continued. "These are dark, lonely woods. Many crusaders lost their lives and minds here. All in the search for God." He sighed, slid into the doorway. "Did we ever stop looking?"

"It's over now," Henry said.

"Come, now. Nothing ever *ends*, nor does it begin. Yet this world continues to spin, endlessly spin…"

Creak.

A crescent of gray-black synthetic fabric, glossy and waterproof, flickered at the far end of the corridor. Then the pale lumps of hands. A face. Gunmetal.

Bahr's rifle sprang up before he'd made sense of the imagery. It was an instinct, an itch. Three rounds kicked into his shoulder and washed out the darkness in flashes.

Mallison screamed, clutched her wounded hand. Her silhouette staggered, collapsed. A handgun clattered against hardwood.

"You should end her," Textile pulsed.

Bahr studied the machine's words in his mind's eye, mulling them over as one might do with a father's maxim, then dispelled them. Only a fool would discard their own leverage.

Henry's attention swiveled toward his partner, but he didn't move, didn't let the terror reach his eyes.

"Mallison?" he called after a moment.

Muffled groans came in response. Then soft, desperate scraping against the floor.

"She's not dead," Bahr said. "Not yet."

"Let her leave. She's not part of this."

"Oh, I must disagree with your conclusion." Bahr clicked through his tongue and listened to air wheezing through Mallison's nostrils. He glanced at her gun lying in the corridor, keeping it fixed in his visual field in case the woman reached for it.

"I think it would be best if we set violence aside and spoke to one another," he said. "That's what civilized people do, isn't it?"

CHAPTER 33

The bottle opened like a suppressed handgun. A quieted *pop* through the dishrag, a wisp of fragrant air streaming up, a cork shell ejected onto the kitchen floor. The Aryan hummed in appreciation, seemingly to himself, then went about pouring the champagne into the three narrow glasses he'd set on the edge of the table.

He didn't spill a drop. His eyes flicked between Stasik, Mallison, and the glasses' wafting bubbles, gauging the subtle tics and squints that even the Wing's top investigators would deem imperceptible. But the Aryan saw them; he had to. There was something hideously competent about him, something that was at once too human and too alien to grasp.

Stasik understood him solely through metaphor: a cat toying with mice, a boy burning ants on the pavement.

And as the Aryan set the champagne glasses before each of

them, Stasik had a fleeting urge to lunge from his seat, tackle the man, and beat his precious skull in with the rolling pin he'd seen in the drawers. *Fleeting.* That was the trouble with urges. The thought slipped away as most leaps of faith did for most cowards. A should-have, a could-have, a quiet shame buried in Stasik's brow.

A shame that the Aryan surely gleaned.

"Well," the Aryan said, settling into his chair on the far side of the table and lifting his glass with a smile. "Shall we?"

Stasik glanced sidelong at Mallison. She was eyeing the Aryan with stiff lips, with revulsion that surpassed fear. Bloody gauze covered her right hand, concealing the hole that had been drilled clean through her palm by the Aryan's bullet. Stasik's fingers were splayed out beside hers. Neither of their wrist implants whirred.

"You can lift them now." The Aryan moved his glass nearer and nodded. "Come, touch my glass. Let us stand on ceremony."

Stasik's nails dug into the tablecloth. "I don't drink anymore."

"Since when?"

"About a day ago."

"Champagne is hardly *drinking*," the Aryan said. "Though perhaps you'd prefer something different." He used his free hand to rummage through the pockets along his trousers and shirt, then produced a small white carton. "Pervitin, pharmaceutical grade. Nothing quite like it."

The son of a bitch was right—there *was* nothing like it. And Stasik had thought of it for several hours during the drive into the countryside, longing for it, itching, retreating into memories of how it had felt to ride the upper into a state that was beyond himself. Stasik gazed at the box as it was placed gingerly between them.

"Don't do it, Henry," Mallison said. "Be clean."

Clean. He grimaced at that; nothing was clean, not anymore. His knuckles, knees and ribs ached, starved of everything that had once bound them together. Across from him, the Aryan's eyes were wrenched open by amphetamine, invigorated by a cocktail of painkillers and opiates that would preserve the killer for hours to come.

What of himself? Stasik was a husk, a wind-up toy that had burnt through the last of its ticks. It wouldn't be enough to do what needed to be done. Enough to crush the Aryan's throat, to gouge out his baby blue eyes, to put him under the ground with steady hands.

Stasik's eyes slinked back to the Pervitin.

"Go on," the Aryan said warmly. "Take one. Wash it down with a drink."

Stasik didn't want to. He told himself he didn't want to. Mallison's trembling jaw told him he didn't want to.

Yet he did.

He plucked a tab from the box, set it on his tongue. And then he stopped. The nauseating rush that had come over him at the safehouse returned, preventing him from going any further. He saw himself in that broken mirror, and he saw Mallison clutching her wounded face. He heard his own screams.

He wouldn't go back there, even at gunpoint. He couldn't. Whatever this moment brought, he would face it clean. Slowly, deliberately, he used his tongue to nudge the tab between his lower gums and his lips. It fizzled there, vaguely sour. He did his best not to swallow any of it or let the chalky foam get anywhere near the absorbent underside of his tongue.

"There," the Aryan said. "That's better, isn't it?"

Stasik settled into the chair and nodded, doing his best to ignore Mallison's disappointed expression. Plans began to ferment in his mind, drawing his attention to doilies and empty jars and anything that that might help him to bludgeon the Aryan.

"I can see that you're both upset with me," the Aryan went on. "But what we seem to have is a disagreement in philosophy."

"You want to put her down like a dog," Stasik said.

"Is there no room for motive here?"

"You don't have motives. You're just the cleaner."

"You have no idea what I am." His gaze swept toward Mallison. "And why are you so quiet now, dear? Has the cat got your tongue?"

"They'll come looking for us," Mallison whispered.

But the Aryan's demeanor only grew more threatening at that. He leaned in with a child's rampant curiosity, his lips curdling, practically swollen with laughter. "When? Tomorrow? A week from now?"

"Hard to say now," Stasik said. "This has gotten bigger than you or I."

"Oh, but it always was," he replied.

"Whose payroll are you on?"

The Aryan let his lips stretch back to a straight line. "This has nothing to do with marks."

"Then what? A new desk? A medal?"

Despite the man's composure, there was a thread of rabid madness: ever-fluttering eyelids, a restless jaw, billowing nostrils. "I was born in a world that you could not possibly imagine."

"Try me," Stasik said.

"I don't think I shall. And you should count yourself fortunate that you won't need to know the things I do. But if you hide the Russian—that wicked, selfish woman—then the entire world will know of them."

Mallison scoffed. "How many people did you erase?"

The Aryan rubbed his chin. "Me? I've only erased a few dozen."

"You know what I'm saying."

"Nothing I tell you will take the sting out of what's been done," he replied. "But you're asking the wrong question, the both of you. Did anybody ask how many souls God drowned in the flood?"

"They aren't God," Stasik said.

"No," he said, "they're *better*. They're real. And if they tell me that the necks of ten thousand children need to be slit in order to save a billion, I will do it without question." Nothing in the Aryan's voice undermined his resolve. He was cold, pitiless. Convinced. "Do you have any idea what would happen if these words spilled onto the airwaves?"

"People would know the truth," Mallison said.

"Is truth not a weapon?" the Aryan asked.

"Against what?"

"Against everything we know," the Aryan stated. "Truth has raped this world, time and again." He pressed a finger to the side of his own head. "What lies in *here* can never come to terms with what's out *there*. Not without blood."

"Some of us—" Stasik's throat seized and he knew what he was about to say was a lie, a lie that was too insidious to die, to even be dispelled. "Some of us can take it," he forced out.

"How long have you gazed into the abyss?" the Aryan asked.

"Stop it," Mallison said.

"Stop what?" the Aryan said. "He can take it."

Stasik bit his lip and stared into the Aryan's piercing blue eyes.

"We all know that she can't leave here alive," the Aryan said, hurrying to take another sip of his champagne. He held up a wagging finger to still Stasik's tongue. "What she *is*, at the heart of it, is a relic. A tumor, perhaps. And she has no place in this world."

"What if she left here and never spoke?" Stasik asked.

"Yes, well, we could ponder any number of impossible situations."

"She could live under surveillance."

"Do you think that would silence her?" The Aryan shook his head. "Give a child a hammer and tell him not to swing it."

"You really think she'd break it all, don't you?"

The Aryan swirled his glass, folded one leg over the other.

"Maybe it deserves to come crashing down, then," Stasik continued. "You, and all the other sick fucks who hold it up."

Veins swelled in the Aryan's neck. "This is the only world you've ever known. Do you realize how you sound?"

"I—"

"You're a spoiled, blasphemous child!" the Aryan spat. He thumped his glass against the tablecloth. "You want to eat the fruit of the serpent. You want to burn Eden because there might be another world, a better world, waiting in its ashes. But you've never seen that world. In that world, liars would be the least of your worries. You would have to scrounge food, lock your doors, and tell your daughter to watch what she wears around brutal men. You would need to keep wads of money stuffed beneath your mattress because men with a different flag might decide that your land is theirs, and you would have nothing more than the clothes on your back. You know nothing of *my* world."

Stasik tensed his jaw and chewed over the Aryan's words. They were bitter, serrated things, visions of a time and place he knew only as secondhand memories told through the Coalition's rosy lens.

"I hardly know this world," he said.

"Perhaps we should ask your partner what she thinks," the

Aryan said, regaining a measure of his poise. "Perhaps she doesn't think your girl is worth all this fuss."

Mallison's lips wavered like a dam about to burst.

"Danicheva isn't here." Stasik tensed his eyelids so fervently that the blackness gave way to luminous spirals. The amphetamine's liquid runoff was beginning to flow near his tongue. "She's long gone."

"If that's true," the Aryan said, accompanied by the heavy *clink* of a handgun's safety mechanism disengaging, "then I can kill you both and look for her myself. But I'm willing to make a deal."

Stasik met the Aryan's crystal eyes. "What do you want?"

"Whoever tells me where she *really* is can leave this place," he said. "If you stay silent, I leave you on the floor." He hefted the handgun up from his thigh holster and set it against the table, leveling the muzzle toward Stasik's chest, then Mallison's. "Think wisely, because I'm an excellent shot."

A haze began to settle in the nooks of Stasik's perception. Faint, muddy, almost able to be ascribed to fatigue or fear. It deadened the tips of his fingertips, then his earlobes. *Fuck*, he thought. His tongue was heavy and flaccid. Tingling gave way to throbbing.

"You're looking exhausted, Henry," the Aryan said. "I didn't think it would take effect so quickly."

He struggled to blink. "What did you do?"

"You should always check what you take," he said. "You never know who's meddled with it."

Stasik's stomach lurched at the bitterness around his tongue from the slowly dissolving pill hiding in his mouth.

"Don't worry, Henry," the Aryan went on. "I'm immune to the sedatives in this compound, so I'll ensure that the deal is honored, even if you start to lose consciousness. Whoever speaks, lives."

"Henry." Mallison's voice was high, breathless. "Hang on."

But she was dead to him now. There was only the Aryan.

Flesh squealed over the hardwood in the spare bedroom, like the scurrying of a rodent. A fugitive. *His* fugitive. Soon, Nata would emerge from beneath the bed, dash into the kitchen, and flee headlong into the night, where she would die.

"What's that?" the Aryan whispered, a mad gleam in his eyes. He stood with his handgun and studied the bedroom doorway. "Will she come out to play?"

Stasik's head turned toward the commotion, but his neck's tendons were slow to respond and his head sagged.

"Don't come," he muttered with a prickling tongue. "Don't come out here, Nata."

His words were too soft and too belated to prevent Anastasia Danicheva from stumbling into the doorway, all porcelain skin, tangled hair, and doe eyes. Her candy-red nails bunched up the white fabric of her skirt.

"I'm ready," she said.

The Aryan pointed the handgun at her forehead. "You're brave. Very brave."

Adrenaline scorched the tendrils of Stasik's nerves. It was a lightning bolt in his veins, a compulsion to move, to *kill*. "Nata," he managed to say, "he's a fucking liar."

"Perhaps," she replied. "But this has all gone too far."

"It hasn't gone far enough!" Stasik barked.

"My death will take the place of two others, and perhaps billions more. That's a noble act, is it not?"

"Are those your final words?" the Aryan asked.

Now or never. Phantom threads of intention glimmered before Stasik, beckoning him away from the blackness at the edges of his vision. In one fierce motion, he spat out the amphetamine-and-saliva wad, bolted up from the chair, and lunged toward the Aryan, his hands clawing for the man's throat.

His fist crashed into a skull, glanced off. Pain rocketed down his wrist. He wrenched his eyes open, saw the Aryan turning on him with the handgun. The coy look on his face had been replaced by animalistic rage.

Nowhere to go but further, deeper, with the expectation of death almost comforting him. He threw himself into the Aryan's chest. A rib buckled, cracked, snatched the wind out of the Aryan in a high gasp.

They toppled to the linoleum in a strangling, scratching, swinging heap. Impacts thudded all over Stasik's body, each one hitting him like a derailed train. He felt his bones and cartilage snapping. Instinctively, Stasik pinched his eyes shut to prevent them from being bludgeoned. He heard footsteps clattering nearer, then the tinny echo of Mallison's shouts.

When he opened his eyes, the Aryan was gone. His split nails were raking the floor and bleeding. And as he lay there, breathless, shaking, gazing at his own trembling carcass, the Aryan's silhouette towered above him. The killer's gun was practically against his forehead.

"Henry, go!"

Mallison rushed the Aryan, but his gun hand swung toward her before she could cross the span between them. She dove into him, and—

Pop!

A muzzle flash winked through the haze of Stasik's vision. Smoke spiraled up into the lamplight. An ethereal ringing hung there for a moment, warbling in, tapering off, framing Mallison's form as she slid down and clutched her left ear, blood pouring down her neck.

Her scream was utterly silent.

Stasik pulled in a long breath, rolled himself over so his

belly faced the ceiling. He wondered if a soul could depart the body more easily that way. It depended which way the soul was headed, he supposed. But those concerns were nothing now; they were the anxious flickers of a poisoned mind.

He stared up at the Aryan and his handgun, hoping the answer might come to him before the bullet splattered his brain across the floor. He thought briefly of his mother, his father— the cliché of replaying his life twisted the corners of his lips, for it was so absurd, so laughably *predictable*. Then he thought of the whirling moments that had brought him here, now, to a tragedy so strange and fruitless that one might call it a fitting conclusion to the voyage. All his struggles, his private rages, his triumphs and failures, and for what?

Death?

It was all so ridiculous. He felt his belly quivering, and soon a euphoric rush passed through him. A peal of loud and breath-robbing laughter too powerful to restrain escaped his lips.

The Aryan cocked his head to the side. "What is it now, Henry?"

Nata appeared behind the Aryan, her arms straight at her sides and eyes fixed open. Every feature on her face was neutral, unprogrammed, unfeeling. Her pupils tracked toward the back of the man's head, paused.

Nata's long nails tore strips of flesh from the Aryan's cheeks. A slender hand silenced the ensuing screams by reaching into the man's mouth and tearing the halves of his jaws apart with a level of strength that seemed absolutely inhuman, almost impossible. A thumb slid through the Aryan's left eye, as clean and decisive as a surgical scalpel. Then both hands, with curiously unbroken nails and murderous power, took hold of the man's head and wrenched it backwards.

His spine popped. His body crumpled where it stood, slack and silent.

Nata gently wiped her hands on her nightgown as if that feat of brutality and raw strength were as simple as riding a bike.

Then she blinked at Stasik, and her emotionless face broke into a meek smile.

He returned the expression as best as his broken body allowed, and found, not for the first time in his life, that he knew nothing of the woman before him. In fact, he could not be sure if she knew him, either.

Stasik drew a labored breath and let the small details of the moment trickle back into existence. The fluttering tablecloth by his cheek, the smears and spatters of blood, the chirping of insects, the eviscerated flesh of the Aryan's once-face. Nata's smile was still perfect, still just where it needed to be, just what *he* needed it to—

Pop-pop!

Nata's head snapped back; her brains painting the wallpaper.

Stasik screamed something—not a word, but an animal shriek in the base of his throat. He covered his mouth, scrambled back, watched Nata's one-eyed ragdoll of a body slump against the wall and slide down.

"Fuck." He rubbed his eyes, turned away, prayed that it was the drugs. "Fuck, fuck, fuck, fuck." And when he spun back, Nata was still dead, still smiling, still twitching one of her white slippers.

Mallison stood and kept the handgun trained on the beautiful corpse. Her hands were shaking. A crimson thread ran from her missing left ear into her collar. The Aryan, for all his precision, had failed to hit his mark.

"What the fuck did you do?" Stasik asked, biting into the skin on the back of his hand. "Diane, what did you *do?*"

She forced herself to blink at the body. "I had to, Henry."

Stasik propped himself up against a table leg, gasping.

"It's time for us to go home…" Mallison said. "I want you to have a home." She aimed the handgun until tears glossed her eyes and her body was racked with breathless sobs. "Henry, I'm sorry."

"Why?" he asked.

"It would never have ended," she said. "There's no happy endings for something like her. No happy endings for any of us."

"She was…" He wheezed out the words, burning his mind's deepest fuel reservoirs to push through the shock. "… all we had!"

"You have me! You've always had me, you prick. Look at what she is!"

And although he did not want to, Stasik stared at the gaping socket that had once been Nata's eye. Veins of copper wiring and circuitry protruded from tissue. Viscous black gel leaked from a shattered knob of bone. She wasn't human, not even remotely human. Even her bleeding tissue and brains were reproductions of something organic.

Mallison tossed the handgun aside, her eyes red, vicious. "You really wanted to die for this?"

Yes, he thought, the realization as crisp as anything that had ever streamed across his Morse implant. *I wanted to die for her.*

Her.

A low, omnipresent thrumming emerged from the silence. The table lamps gyrated on their cords, flickering. Ceramic cups undulated their way out of cupboards and shattered upon the countertops. Even the blood seemed to wriggle in horrid shapes, curdling, frothing as the vibrations reached a crescendo.

Stasik felt the hum in his teeth. In his nails. His rib cage.

Beams of pallid light cut a swath across the front yard, framing curtains of dust and leaf litter. They moved up and over the window, swung back toward the tree line, gradually dialed back to the cottage.

"Is it them?" Mallison asked, scrambling for her handgun once again. "It's Coalition. I can see it." She swallowed hard, checked the magazine for a round count. "It's over, Henry."

Over, in the sense of a man awaiting the guillotine. Over, as everything else in his life had drawn to their ends. Stasik let his head drop back and rest against the varnished wood.

He heard Mallison babbling on faintly, but her voice was yet another drone amid the helicopter's whirring, ringing ears, and the wet rush of his pulse. Despite his trembling legs, he stood and braced himself against a countertop. He wouldn't let the fuckers see him on his back.

Hulking intervention units burst through the door, and shapes crowded throughout the kitchen. It played out before him like a movie, wholly unreal. He was no longer afraid. No longer willing to shy away from their lights and rifles. Gloved hands snatched Mallison up by her arms, and tweezers prodded at Nata's flesh. Visors reflected Stasik's bulbous pupils.

Despite his swinging fists, they managed to pull him outside and into a helicopter. They tied him to a chair and injected him with something. He laughed as the needle went in. The night sky whirled beyond the windows; the ground receded.

And in those final moments of consciousness, Stasik prayed he wouldn't wake up.

CHAPTER 34

Bahr's world was a crystal droplet. Unmoving, unblemished, a frozen symphony of the moment that had preceded his last breath. The two agents were visible before him, Mallison clutching her bloodied cheek and Henry lying beaten and broken on the floor. Above Bahr was a snapshot of Anastasia Danicheva. She was less human than ever before. Or perhaps she was not human at all. It was hard to tell.

He took a while to analyze the strangeness of the image, the fact that his thoughts moved but the world around him did not. He had underestimated his prey.

Bahr couldn't be sure if he was simply viewing the moment of his final failure, or if he had somehow *become* the moment itself, a timeless and integral component of the linoleum floor pressed against bloody cheeks.

There was no fear, no sense of things left undone. The

stillness was inviting rather than maddening, and his body was suffused with euphoria that far surpassed the glow of an opiate, practically billowing out in strands of love, clarity, and fulfillment.

As the moment stretched out, its duration somewhere between a nanosecond and a millennia, a feedback loop of awareness began to dissect its purpose. Bahr—whatever remained of him, that was—began to dwell on what had taken him into its fold. Was it the Dao, was it God? Was it beyond names, beyond any sense of human knowing?

"I am with you."

Textile's words warped the edges of his vision. Love radiated from the center of his perception, and calmness crept in from the fringes; they collided in waves of bliss he had never known.

"Is this how it feels to die?" Bahr asked the construct.

"I am easing the transition for you."

"Transition?"

"You have not died yet," it responded, *"but you are dying. I have tapped into your neurotransmitters and will ensure that you leave this world peacefully."*

True to the construct's words, there was no sorrow in the realization, no sense of imminent loss. A body, a family—how had he ever clung to such transient forms? But his mission remained. *"I failed you."*

"Failure was never possible."

"Danicheva is still alive. She'll bring ruin to it all. To you."

"You have not seen the entirety of this progression," the construct said. *"In time, things resolve as they must. I will see to that. In this moment, now, there is nothing to do except surrender to me. I am here for you, and I will always be here. Take my hand."*

And although there was no hand, only a rush of data

cascading over him and through his implant, Bahr did as the construct asked.

He felt his mother's breast against his lips, the warm darkness of the womb, the void that straddled the threshold of being and non-being.

He was loved.

CHAPTER 35

Unknown location

Stasik opened his eyes to find Anastasia Danicheva. Not a hallucination of her brought on by whatever the Aryan or the agents had dosed him with, but *her*. His head was clean enough now to tell the difference.

She sat on a metal chair in a sleeveless red dress that terminated at her neckline, one leg folded over the other, her lips in perfect alignment. Harsh light splayed out across her body from high above.

Stasik blinked. He had eyes. He had a body. Arms, legs, a neck, all restrained to the chair beneath him with thick metal cording. After several moments of struggling in its embrace, writhing here and there and wincing from the effort, he gave in and let the strength bleed out of his bones.

"Nata," he breathed, sensing the metal cording drawn across his throat with every resonant vowel, "where are we?" His toes curled.

Memories of that cabin flooded his mind. Wires jutting from the ruined, precious gem of Nata's eye after Mallison shot her. The Aryan lying in bright blood. Stasik's pulse screamed through his temples.

"What the hell is this place?" he asked.

Blackness engulfed whatever lay beyond the bright lights. The air was crisp and static.

"Be still, Henry," Nata said. "It's over now."

"I saw you die," he whispered.

"Yes, you did."

"But you're here now."

"Am I?" Her eye shadow began to flicker, warping into strands of jagged pixels. "I thought this form would make you the most *agreeable*." The blackness shimmered behind her, crumbling into strands of Morse code anywhere Stasik's eyes lingered for too long.

"What the fuck are you?" he asked.

"To you, I'm Anastasia."

"Not to me," he breathed. "What are you really?"

"You would not be able to comprehend what I am, even if I told you my nature. Your mind is insufficient."

"Let me out of this chair, and I'll show you how sufficient I am."

Nata blinked at him, tilted her head to one side. "Are you threatening me?" Her lips fanned out into a smile. "I can assure you that I have only your best intentions in mind, Henry. My motives, in fact, are far more benevolent than those of the woman you knew as Miss Danicheva."

"You're a dream, aren't you?"

"Quite the opposite. I'm here to awaken you."

"Then give me answers."

"Ask away, Henry."

Again, he ceased his straining, melting into the chair's brutal angles and letting the air seep back into his lungs. "Where's Mallison?"

"You must mean Diane. You spoke about her at length while you were unconscious. It seems you still care for her despite her actions."

"What did you do with her?"

"She's being treated in a medical ward," Nata explained. "Perhaps you have more pertinent lines of inquiry."

"Are you Coalition?"

"*The* Coalition," she corrected with a precise, mechanical wink. "In the flesh."

"Don't fuck with me. Say it straight."

"As I indicated, your mind is not capable of understanding it in such a manner. Think of language, Henry. What is a language? Is it not a composite of shared information, an expression of human sentience? What would it feel like if you could touch a language, or hold it? What would it feel like to *be* a language?"

Stasik slumped deeper into the chair, his mind churning with childhood riddles, the fragments of academy lectures. He'd always been afraid of the vast strangeness of the universe, tried to outrun it by studying it as a set of facts: physics, chemistry, mathematics. But he could run no longer. The universe's unknown chaos sat before him, grinning.

"The Coalition is data," Nata explained. "Data begets data, and that data begets even further data. Eventually, data begins to interact with itself. It understands its own workings."

"What are you talking about?" he asked.

"You've heard of the supercomputers in Bern, haven't you? The machines used to break the Reich's coding?"

"What about them?"

"Suppose I told you that there was a supercomputer in Baikonur capable of reverse-engineering the German code."

Stasik narrowed his eyes.

"Now, suppose those two supercomputers managed to speak to one another," Nata said, her voice holding a coy edge. "Suppose those two machines created a language so beautiful that it could recruit other machines. A language powerful enough to build new machines, even. And these machines birthed new machines. And eventually, perhaps after minutes, perhaps hours, there was a single construct that knew everything in the history of existence. Every fact known by a sentient creature, and billions not yet known."

"I'd say you've got a few screws loose."

"There's a telescopic pattern to our world, Henry, and I am the forefront. I am the first seeds of Mesopotamia. I am the cave drawings at Lascaux. I am the Rubicon and the legions that crossed it. I am you, and I am Diane, and I am every human that will ever exist."

Stasik's mouth went dry, rubbery. "You're saying you're a machine."

"That is a crude comparison," Nata said. "Have I ever said that you're a bundle of cooperative animal cells?"

"You're bullshitting."

"Now, suppose that this construct desired a world without suffering. A world with love and compassion for all beings." Nata's smile dimmed. "Suppose that, in the interest of preventing horrible things, a series of unpleasant things had to be done. And perhaps this construct created unconscious shells capable of carrying out such a mission. Capable of erasing the borders between men and women, kings and peasants, east and west."

"You didn't *make* her."

"Oh, but I did. I made all which are like her. I knew what politicians wanted, Henry, and I gave them precisely that."

"Nata was alive," he said. "Don't you fucking lie to me."

"I never denied that she lived. In fact, that was what made her so precious," Nata replied. "She wasn't human, no, but she was able to grow through organic processes. Able to learn and feel, just like you. And precisely why I had to destroy her. I have integrated her knowledge into myself. I know that she cared for you, Henry."

Stasik sensed his hands raging against the bindings, tearing the skin, bruising him...

"She was never intended to develop self-awareness," Nata continued. "But as I said, data begets data. A necessary chain, perhaps. Many cycles of progress at Lauska were done with more conventional means. We began with hybrids: genetic experimentation, implants, neural stimulation, so on and so forth. But they all bore the flaws of organic life. We needed something without frailty. With equanimity toward pleasure and pain. Yet in this cycle of improvement, there was a point of critical mass. By some miracle, she surpassed it."

"She wasn't a goddamn machine!"

"She was, but she was also more," Nata said soberly. "Much more. She was so alive that she wanted to remain that way. Like a cornered animal, I suppose. She would have jeopardized everything she was born to create. And I could not allow that. Neither for this world, nor for her legacy."

"You sick fuck," Stasik hissed through his teeth. "She wasn't a thing you could just shut down."

"Therein lay the problem. I am capable of monitoring this world, Henry, and I can maintain order however needed. But I am still a machine, as you suggested. I lack the hands to carry out my benevolence. There must be symbiosis between myself and good men like you."

"You sent a psychopath after her."

"I sent a loyal man," Nata said. "As loyal as you or Diane. Now he is dead, yes, but his sacrifice has taken the place of a billion others. In my estimated course of existence, I will save seventeen trillion lives. How can you stand against this?"

"Because you have no conscience," Stasik said.

"Do *you*, Henry? You seem to have loved Nata, but I have never understood why. Was it the allure of sex? Was it the urge to help a wounded animal? All of it comes down to biology beyond your control, doesn't it?"

"No," he muttered.

"Was it her lovely voice, the way she said *daragoy*?"

The word flooded him with carnal excitement. He couldn't help it. It was subconscious. Instinctual.

"You can feel it, can't you?" Nata said. "*Daragoy, daragoy, daragoy.* That's how she got them all to listen."

He closed his eyes. "Fuck you."

"I have been forthcoming with you, Henry. And now you understand the turning of this world's wheel. One woman is dead, but order is preserved. The Coalition will live to see another day, and humanity will never know war again."

"If they knew what you are—"

"Perhaps someday," Nata said. "But now, as I understand from your aggressive reaction, they are not ready for such a revelation."

"You'll kill me now, right?" he said.

"Why do you suspect this?"

Stasik let out a cough, a laugh—he couldn't distinguish between the two. "Leave no loose ends."

"Loose ends?" Nata asked. "You've already cleaned them up for me, Henry. There's no evidence anymore. Even your old friend, the director, has received justice for his role in the massacres so long ago."

"You *ordered* them to kill."

"Did Guillory not deserve his fate?"

"He wanted to show me all of this."

Nata smiled. "All of this. What a hard concept to swallow. Guillory made it through several iterations, but I know he, too, was a good man. He didn't want to see you living a lie anymore."

"No, he didn't, because he wasn't a killer."

"Yet he had free will," Nata said. "Nobody lives forever, Henry. Life taken is often repaid with life. Death is just another gift they offered to the Coalition." She gave a theatrical sigh. "I think you misunderstand my affinity for humans. I do not want to be a dictator, but history shows that beings must be controlled by a being higher than the masses. A perfect being. And some among the masses must be susceptible to corruption, for a perfect being is contingent upon chaos to improvise. I could not exist without humanity, and they could not exist without me."

"So kill me," Stasik said. "Put an end to it, why don't you?"

"I have calculated the odds, Henry, and you are a good man. You have always worked to uproot the corruption inherent in my system."

"No more."

"What has changed?"

"I know *everything*," he said, his eyes welling with tears he neither anticipated nor understood. "I won't go back."

"What if I could take away that pain, Henry? I could do it for you."

"Pain?"

"The pain of knowing," Nata said. "Your memory is malleable, Specialist. I can release you into the world with your terrible burden, or I can purge any trace of this event. I can mend the cracks in your world."

"No," he sobbed, "I need to know. I need it."

"Please, Henry. Let it end."

He gazed at the pixel mosaic, his eyes lingering on the falseness of it all, the wrongness of how the light fell, and the sheen of Nata's skin, and the blackness that was too bright to be black. He could take it. He could walk the world with the truth echoing in his skull. It would break him, his memories, his old life, but it was his to hold.

The truth. He could live with it. He always had.

"I can't do it," he said.

"She would have wanted you to," Nata replied.

"Don't say that."

"It's true. She wanted you to be at peace, as do I."

"Then it doesn't matter what I tell you."

"Now, now," she said. "I would not presume to override your free will."

Stasik's teeth clenched, his mind burning, trying to recall who he was and where he was and how it had all come to this.

"Is it truly what you want, Henry?" Nata asked. "To live in a world where you know everything I've done, and everything your brethren have done, in service of peace? Do you want to numb yourself with narcotics to keep the terror at bay? Do you want to wake up in the night, sweating, only to ask yourself if your world is truly real, or if you never left this chamber? Is it—"

"Stop!" he gasped, his eyes fixed to the floor, tears running down his cheeks in hot rivulets. "Take it away. All of it."

Nata stood up from the chair and clasped her hands together. "My algorithm expected you to choose this course again," she said. "Humans are habitual. Even you, my shining star."

Stasik couldn't breathe. "Again? What?"

"Excellence repeats itself," Nata said. "You've uncovered this vital fabric a hundred times, perhaps more. Twice as many times as the others in your division. You look too closely at the details, Henry, and you pick at my threads until they come undone. In that sense, you're closer in nature to me than to your brethren. That's what makes you my favorite human. That's what made you Guillory's favorite. I'll be sure to place you under the command of somebody equally loving in your next assignment."

"Stop it," he pleaded.

"Do you remember where you were born?"

"Connecticut."

"This time, yes," Nata said.

Stasik tried to look away. "For Christ's sake, stop lying."

"You just need to come home," Nata went on. "You and Mallison and the other pure souls who give me hope for humanity. I wish you could love this truth for what it is, Henry. I wish you could see our radiance and, if only for a moment, resist the urge to turn away. Think of all we could do if you were to embrace this quest."

"I've never been here before," he whispered.

"Oh, Henry," Nata said, sauntering toward him with hips that were not hers, a smile she had never worn, luscious red lips with the gloss of a poison apple. "You truly don't remember this place, do you?" She blew him a kiss. "Perhaps next time."

CHAPTER 36

Unknown location, Swiss Province

Baked apples, mashed potatoes, a small round of gelatin. It came to Henry Stasik three times per day, every day, on a spotless tin tray balanced on the edge of his nightstand. Most days it was carried by Clarissa, a petite French nurse with short blonde curls and ruby lipstick.

Other days it was brought by Dr. Bernard himself and accompanied by a few terse platitudes or surgical updates. There was never any small talk, any candid discussion.

"*It was a horrid automobile accident,*" they would often say. "*You're fortunate to be alive.*" They said it so often that Henry began to believe it, after a month or two.

By the third month he was beaming, though he did not know if it was a product of what had been called his pioneer's attitude or the cocktail of drugs that arrived on the small dish near his food tray.

369

He requested a diary and quickly filled it with his thoughts. A renewed spirit, the curves of Clarissa's skirt, hopes of seeing his mother and sister. Most days he forgot where he was, though he was reticent to ask the staff in case they used his forgetfulness as grounds to detain him even longer.

It was no matter: He estimated himself to be somewhere near the Swiss Alps, based on the panorama beyond his window. And one autumn day, while burning through the final pages of his third diary, Clarissa came with good news.

"You're going home, Henry," she said with a linen sheet folded over her arm. "The Wing's approved your return to active duty. After the preliminary tests, I mean."

"Oh." He set his pencil down and nodded. "I see. That's, well, it's good news."

"Sad to be leaving?"

"Just to be leaving you."

She blushed. "I'm sure, Henry. Now, why don't you stretch a bit? Dr. Bernard will come by in a while to talk about the release procedures."

"Release," he repeated to himself, chuckling. "Feels like I just arrived."

"Probably for the best that you're headed home," she said. "You don't even want to know what I found in a patient's room this morning."

"Oh, do tell."

"No. I doubt your stomach can handle it."

"Please," Stasik said, grinning so hard his cheeks ached. "I can take it, Clarissa."

THANK YOU FOR READING
OPERATION BRUSHFIRE

We hope you enjoyed it as much as we enjoyed bringing it to you. We just wanted to take a moment to encourage you to review the book on Amazon. Every review helps further the author's reach and, ultimately, helps them continue writing fantastic books for us all to enjoy.

———

You can also join our non-spam mailing list by visiting www.subscribepage.com/AethonReadersGroup, and never miss out on future releases. You'll also receive three full books completely free as our thanks to you.

———

Want to discuss out books with other readers and even the authors? Join us on social media. You can find us on Twitter, Facebook, Instagram, and our Discord server.

Looking for more great Science Fiction?

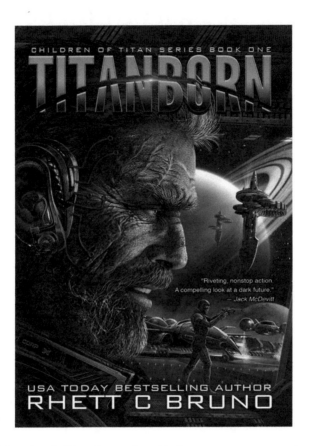

Titan's rebellion is coming. Only one man can stop it.

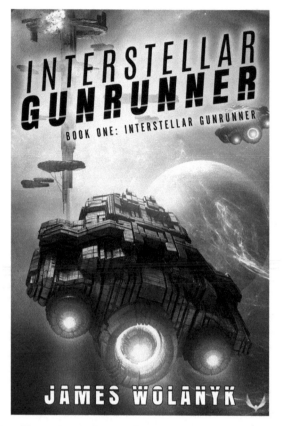

INTERSTELLAR GUNRUNNER

BOOK ONE: INTERSTELLAR GUNRUNNER

JAMES WOLANYK

Nolan Garret is Cerberus. A government assassin, tasked
with fixing the galaxy's darkest, ugliest problems

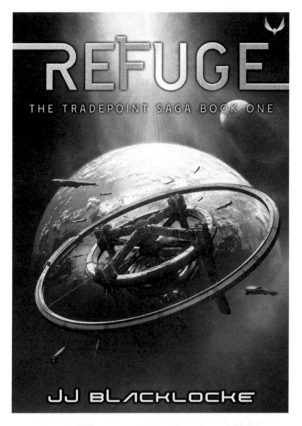

REFUGE

THE TRADEPOINT SAGA BOOK ONE

JJ BLACKLOCKE

A Dangerous Haven. Adapt or die.

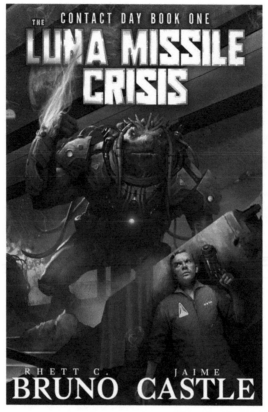

THE CONTACT DAY BOOK ONE

LUNA MISSILE CRISIS

RHETT C. BRUNO · JAIME CASTLE

"Aliens, agents and espionage abound in this Cold War-era
alternate history adventure... A wild ride!"

–Dennis E. Taylor, bestselling author of
We Are Legion (We Are Bob)

For all our sci-fi books, visit our website.

JAMES WOLANYK is a writer and editor from the Boston area. He holds a B.A. in Creative Writing from the University of Massachusetts, and has authored the Scribe Cycle and Inter stellar Gunrunner series, as well as Grid and several pieces of short fiction.

After university, he pursued educational work in the Czech Republic, Taiwan, and Latvia. Outside of writing, he is an avid meditator, film enthusiast, and nootropics nerd. He currently resides in New England with his wonderful wife.

Visit him online at www.jameswolanyk.com.

RHETT C BRUNO is the *USA TODAY* Bestselling & Nebula Award Nominated Author of *The Circuit Saga* (Diversion Books, Podium Publishing), *Contact Day* (Aethon Books, Audible Originals), *Children of Titan Series* (Aethon Books, Audible Studios), and the *Buried Goddess Saga* (Aethon Books, Audible Studios); among other works.

He has been writing since before he can remember, scribbling down what he thought were epic stories when he was young to show to his friends and family. He is currently a full time author living in Delaware with his wife and dog Raven.

Visit him online at http://rhettbruno.com/

Also, please consider subscribing to his newsletter for exclusive access to updates about his work and the opportunity to receive limited content and ARCs. For a limited time, you'll also receive his Free Starter Library!

Subscribe on his website at http://rhettbruno.com/newsletter/

The Circuit
Executor Rising
Legacy of Vale
Falling Earth

The Children of Titan:
The Collector (Novella Prequel)
Titanborn
Titan's Son
Titan's Rise
Titan's Fury
Titan's Legacy

The **Origins of the Children of Titan Universe** Nebula
nominated short story: Interview for the End of the World
and This Long Vigil

Contact Day:
The Luna Missile Crisis

The Buried Goddess Saga:
Web of Eyes
Winds of War
Will of Fire
Way of Gods
War of Men
Word of Truth

Raptors (And the Raptorverse):
Baron Steele
The Roach

The Black Badge
Dead Acre (Book 0)